CHILDREN OF ENOCHIA

BOOK THREE OF THE ENOCHIAN WAR

LUKE MITCHELL

For anyone who's ever felt caught in the storm.

For the storm, too.

1

REPUTATION

Clinking glasses, creaking stools, and rowdy voices. That was about all I could make out as I sat in the corner of the greasy tavern. Greasy, I decided, much more by merit of its denizens rather than by any fault of its sturdy, well-aged oak tables, or its rustic decorum. The place was bustling, which was some combination of surprising and sad given that it was midday of a fresh new cycle, when all the respectable people of Divinity should've been hard at work out there, bringing peace and prosperity to our fine world.

But these weren't the respectable people of Divinity. And, honestly, I guess we weren't either. Hence the corner seats I'd chosen, as far from the light fixtures as possible. The dark, hooded cloak and the shaders I wore to obscure my face from sight might've been overkill. They were definitely conspicuous. But few people in this particular tavern *weren't* conspicuous for one reason or another. So far, aside from when I'd walked in, no one had paid me any undue attention. Not nearly as much as I'd been paying to the dark booth carved into the wall a few tables away, at least.

I couldn't see Elise and Four in the booth where they were seated with our mysterious contact, but I knew they were there. I could feel them in my extended senses as plainly as I could smell the utter lack of recent showers from a trio of rough-looking neighbors to our right. What I couldn't do was hear what they were saying, and it was driving me mad.

Hearing what was being said from across a noisy tavern, of course, wasn't something that anyone—save for maybe a raknoth—could reasonably expect to do. But I knew from practice that it was possible for someone with my gifts to perceive sound—or vibrations, at least—with much more range and specificity than what a human ear could accomplish.

That said, I wasn't well practiced with the technique. Making auditory sense out of vibrations in the air without the intermediary aid of one's actual ears took some getting used to. More importantly, the tavern was significantly louder and more hectic than anywhere I'd tried this before. Even focusing in on the right voices was proving difficult. I was just starting to manage when Johnny's voice broke into my thoughts from right beside me.

"How are we looking over there, flyboy?"

I glanced over at my friend, who was dressed to match my slightly suspicious but hopefully unidentifiable appearance.

"Not really sure. I'm trying to focus."

"Right." There was a pregnant pause. "So what are they saying?"

I turned a dark frown on him only to remember that my eyes and face were largely obscured by the shaders and the hood. Johnny got the gist anyway.

"Right." He cleared his throat, brandishing his polymer cup. "I'll just go back to drowning my sorrows, then."

"You're drinking sweetfizz."

Instead of arguing, he took a long, noisy sip, then lowered his cup with a satisfied sigh. "I feel better already."

Shaking my head, I settled back into my extended senses. Now wasn't the time to be joking around with Johnny. Not when my girlfriend was sitting at a table with a colleague of Alton Parker's. And not when I'd risked my head—and maybe Glenbark's as well—even stepping foot out of Haven to be here at all.

Finally, I found the sweet spot with my experimental focus.

"—been quiet since the scud all hit the turbines last season," came the slippery voice of Alton Parker's contact, his words slightly rounded with the accent common to the slums of Divinity. "Honestly, it's been a relief since finding out... well, you know. Can't let people think I'd willingly do business with a bunch of red-eyed bloodsuckers."

"Sure," Elise said. "Wouldn't want anyone to go thinking you were the disreputable sort, right?"

"I resent that, pretty lady."

"And you never set our red-eyed friends up with a hideout?" Four's voice broke in before Elise could tell the sleaze ball what he could do with his resentment. "Somewhere they could lay low if something like this ever happened?"

"My sincere thanks for reminding me of what a hideout is for," came that slippery voice, but for all his derision, I felt him shifting his weasley frame uncomfortably on the wood bench. He knew something. Of course he did. This goodfellow, Dex as he was apparently called, was what unsavory sorts referred to as a fix-it man. The kind who made bodies and other inconvenient problems go away with little more than a palmlight message and a generous handful of coin.

Dex, as we'd had it from the mouth of Alton Parker himself, had made more than a few bodies disappear for the raknoth back when he'd simply thought they were conniving murderers in high places—before it had all spilled out into the open war that'd nearly torn Enochia apart on the claws and fangs of the hybrid hoards. According to Parker, the fix-it man was our quickest and easiest shot at finding where the last two renegade raknoth might be hunkered down, waiting for their freshly-commandeered Seeker host bodies to grow strong enough to wreak Alpha only knew what manner of havoc on Enochia.

It was about the only thing Parker had actually coughed up in the few days since he'd turned up at Haven declaring his surrender—which is why I'd refused to sit this mission out, Sanctum death threats or no. Because in my mind, there were only two real possibilities here. Either Alton Parker truly wanted his last two brethren caught and killed for reasons unknown... or this was some kind of trap.

"So you're telling us there's nothing?" Four was asking Dex.

"It's not really the kind of business I do."

"We understand," Elise said. "Listening to secondhand murderers spout bullscud lies isn't really the kind of business we do, either."

I resisted the urge to telepathically urge her to keep it civil. When it came to getting information, she knew what she was doing far better than I did. She was Franco Fields' daughter, after all.

"Where'd you find this girl?" Dex asked, his head swiveling back and forth between Elise and Four.

"Let's all play nice now," Four said, but only half-heartedly.

"He doesn't care," Elise said. "He works for coin, not compliments."

Dex chuckled. "I do. I totally do. I like this one."

"Impress me, then," Elise said, pointedly jingling a hefty purse of Legion-allocated coin.

I might've imagined Dex sleazily leering at her more than I actually felt it, but I found myself just as willing to wipe the look off his face with my fist all the same.

"There might've been something, now that you mention it," he said. "Hard to keep track sometimes."

"I'm sure," Elise said, setting the coin purse down on the table between them.

"Best as I can recall," Dex said, "there were a few places in the city. Few places outside the city, too."

"Any of these places happen to have names?" Four asked.

"Or coordinates?" Elise added.

Dex reached for the coin purse. Neither Elise nor Four stopped him as he rolled it around in his palm, inspecting the weight.

"Not here," he finally said.

"Scud," I whispered.

Johnny turned from surveying the tavern with a questioning tilt of his head.

"He wants to change locale."

"—happen to have an office at this fine establishment?" Elise was asking, at the table ahead.

"Something like that," Dex said, standing from their booth. "Let's take a walk."

I reached to Elise with my mind. *"Lise, don't—"*

"Do you feel any raknoth hiding out back?" she sent before I could finish. *"We're fine. Four and I can handle one creepy civie, and we've got the Hounds on standby, anyway. Stay put."*

"Ah, scorched," Johnny said beside me with a knowing grin, even though he had no way of knowing what had passed between us. I turned my frown on my non-telepathic friend. He just spread his hands. "What? Did she or did she not just burn you a new one?"

I opened my mouth, closed it, and settled for scowling down at my unwanted cup of sweetfizz.

"Caaalled it," Johnny declared in sing-song.

"You're a ginger beardsplitter," I muttered at the table.

"But I'm *your* ginger beardsplitter."

We traded a glance and half a grin, then both sobered at the sight of Dex the weasel stepping out of the booth ahead and into plain sight. He was followed a moment later by Four's brooding, dark-clad form and Elise's equally tall but decidedly more pleasing one.

I watched my beautiful warrior of a girlfriend and the ex-Seeker follow Dex the weasel through the busy crowd, resisting the urge to open my palmlight and tell Ordo Dillard to keep his eyes open out there. They'd be watching. After everything I'd been through with the Legion's 51st Hound Company in the past season, I trusted that much.

So I forced myself to try to look relaxed as we sat there nursing our sweetfizz and biding our time long enough that our departure might not arouse suspicion if Dex happened to have any friendly eyes around. I doubt my act was all that convincing, but at least I managed to refrain from tapping my feet and drumming on the table.

At some point, a rising tide of voices drew my attention to a fresh wave of tavern-goers who were pushing into the busy space, making their ambling way to the bar as they looked around in vain for an empty table. One of them, a broad-chested man who looked like he was no stranger to tavern brawls, lingered on me and Johnny a few seconds too long for my liking before he continued scanning the rest of the room.

Johnny gave a noncommittal grunt beside me, apparently noticing as well.

If I'd needed a cue, that was it.

"Let's move," I said, starting to stand.

"Orrr," Johnny said, catching my arm, "we could stick to the contingency plan and let Dillard do his job out there. Finish our drinks and leave like we're just another pair of creepy no-good-in-the-hood guys."

I hovered a few inches off my seat. He was right. It was just that guy's standard territorial man-glance that'd set me a touch on the jumpy side. There was no reason to be hasty. Elise was covered out there, and the big guy was currently giving the same look to every third or fourth person in the tavern—aside from the ladies, whom he favored with a hungry smile.

I was turning back to my room-temperature drink when Johnny spoke again.

"Orrr we leave now..."

Confused, I looked over and saw that he was staring at one of the displays behind the bar. The display that was currently plastered with a big image of my face, right above the red banner that read in big, white letters: *Haldin Raish reported at large, Westside, Divinity.*

"What the scud," Johnny breathed, already busy with his palmlight under the table, either checking for more news or calling for evac.

"It's fine," I said softly, doing my best to appear casual as I tipped the remainder of my sweetfizz back, stood, and clapped a hand to Johnny's shoulder. "We're just two brotos getting back to work."

"Back to work," I heard Johnny mumble as I lost the battle with my apprehensive eyes and glanced back to the crowd by the bar.

The big guy was glaring straight at me, and some of his friends were turning from the display to join him.

"It's him!" one of them called, jabbing a finger out and turning half the heads in the tavern our way. "It's Raish."

"I knew it!" cried someone else from the other side of the bar.

"What, this guy?" Johnny called back, pointing at me and pulling off his shaders to show his admirably sincere surprise. "This guy, the Demon of Divinity? Are you kidding me? This guy cried one time when a bird hit our skimmer. Does that sound like the Demon of Divinity to you?"

"What's his name, then?" someone called from the now fully attentive crowd.

"Uh…" Johnny hesitated a moment too long. "Beard… face?"

"His name is Beardface?"

"Hey," Johnny shot back, "you tell me how many of you nosy scudspouts are looking to share your real names in a place like this."

"Hey, that's that Wingard kid!" someone else called.

"Ah, scud," Johnny groaned.

It hardly mattered anyway. Captain Man Glare was already stalking toward us, his belligerent-looking friends close behind. We weren't making it to the door without getting past them. Behind them, I was vaguely aware of the WAN caster reading off the now standard reminder that I was to be considered extremely dangerous and that anyone spotting me should contact the authorities immediately.

Apparently Captain Man Glare didn't give a scud about that.

"Just for the record," Johnny called, "we've got a whole company of legionnaires ready to rush in here at the snap of my fingers."

Captain Man Glare and his Manly Brawlers didn't seem to care about that much either.

I pulled off my shaders and drew my hood back. That, at least, gave the brawler crew pause. Or maybe it was just that they were nearly at striking distance.

"We're leaving," I said. "We don't want any trouble, just let us pass."

But more people were filing in behind him now, emboldened by his fearless approach and the fact that he hadn't been struck down by demon fire on his way to me.

"He don't want any trouble, people," Man Glare called, his hard eyes never leaving mine, his slum accent so thick that it almost sounded fake. "You know who else never wanted no trouble, Shiny Shoes?"

I was actually supremely impressed that Johnny refrained from chirping in with a, *"Your mom?"* or something along those lines. He probably sensed the same thing I did in my gut. For whatever reason, this guy was deeply pissed at my existence, and he was either angry enough or stupid enough to think he could take me down. That, or he was counting on the sheer weight of numbers behind—which was admittedly a much less stupid bet.

Briefly, I considered making a quick and brutal example of him with telekinesis and the nearest oak table, but I was hesitant to give these people reason to believe all the Demon of Divinity bullscud. There were at least twenty people between us and the door now, and several more around the tavern frantically speaking into their palmlights—the room a hissing choir of, *"Yes, yes he's right here!"* and, *"Yes, Haldin Raish!"* and, *"Yes, for the love of Alpha, you can ping my location, just help us!"*

Not good.

I stepped forward, hoping Captain Man Glare might just stand down but mostly expecting more posturing from the burly man. He didn't posture. He just swung.

It was a hard punch, I'd give him that, but even without my extended senses, I saw it coming with plenty of time to step outside the blow. As he planted through and fixed to pivot after me, Johnny caught him side-on with a solid punch, straight to the temple. The guy staggered. I was surprised he didn't drop cold. The crowd had gone completely silent, every pair of street-tough eyes and eager fists waiting to see what their neighbors would do.

Then Captain Man Glare let out a wordless bellow, and half the damn tavern charged.

2

REFLEX

One of the first things they tell you in basic combat training is that most fights are over almost before you know it. Hence all the drills. Motor memory and all that. The less you have to think—the more things happen automatically—typically, the better your chances of survival.

But even knowing all that, and having been through as many fights as I'd survived since my parents had been taken from me, I still wasn't quite ready for what happened when I let go and gave myself over to my extended senses. It was something I'd been getting better at, letting my senses take the wheel. Fighting raknoth and hybrids, it had probably been the only thing that kept me alive. Fighting day-drunk tavern brawlers, though? That was a first.

I actually felt bad for them. Not that they gave me much of a choice.

I watched with a kind of morbid fascination, an outsider to my own body, as I dipped and twisted clear of innumerable grabbing hands and wild punches—my fists, elbows, knees, and boots all lashing out so fast I almost had trouble believing they all belonged to me alone. I felt the impacts of blows falling, felt the jarring in my own fists and feet, saw the same look of surprise in each face that stepped forward, sure they'd caught me only to find themselves crashing to the floor or into an oak table the next instant.

I'd never fought so smoothly in my life. Not that I wasn't still taking my fair share of hits too. But they all felt oddly distant—like my senses were too busy with the dance of weaving fists to properly register the pain right then.

I was vaguely aware of Johnny yelling something nearby, but I couldn't spare much more focus than a glance. He was on a bench behind our over-turned table, shouting into his palmlight while kicking to fend off a pair of burly men trying to grab him. Apparently done with his palmlight business, Johnny curled his fingers closed, shouted, "You spilled my sweetfizz, you goat-groppers!" and scored a firm groin kick on one.

My senses spun me clear of an incoming strike, and I almost staggered when I realized it was a knife I'd narrowly avoided. I kept rotating, caught the would-be killer with an elbow to the temple, drove a hosa kick back into his neighbor who thought to catch me distracted, then found the knife and buried it deep into the plastwall ceiling with telekinesis.

I spun to meet the next enemy only to find there was no next enemy, or none that felt like taking a shot, at least. More weapons had appeared—knives, hardsteel knuckles, and even a few wooden stools held as unwieldy clubs—but for the moment, their owners all just watched warily. I looked around for Captain Man Glare, wondering if he would rouse them to a second push, and realized he lay unmoving in an overturned mess of tables and chairs I didn't even remember having slammed him into.

Noticing that the rest of the action had paused, Johnny and the guy he was wrestling with pushed apart to return to their respective sides in truce —at least until the guy took an impromptu swipe.

Johnny ducked it and shoved him back into his camp. "Beardsplitter move, broto."

That action alone seemed to rekindle reckless thoughts in some of the onlookers. Luckily, before anyone could work up the courage to lead the next charge, backup arrived.

"Party's over people," rumbled a low voice from the direction of the tavern entrance.

I followed the sound and was relieved to see my favorite mountain of a legionnaire, Edwards, marching our way. He had two tavern-goers pinned by the necks, one under each arm, and was dragging the burly men along like they were nothing but unruly children. Behind him, more of the 51st Hounds were pushing into the tavern, brandishing stun rods and weapons grade *back the grop off* stares.

For a few tense moments, the crowd hesitated. Then they parted without a word, some of them drifting off toward the back exit like they thought the legionnaires might not notice at all if they simply moved slowly enough.

"You two okay?" Edwards asked as he drew up to us, still dragging along his two head-locked passengers.

Johnny tilted his head at a burly bald man picking himself up from beside our table, clutching at his groin. "Well, that guy owes me a drink, but other than that…"

Edwards grinned and only then seemed to remember the men tucked under his arms. He released the pair, who straightened and rubbed at their necks with indignant expressions. Edwards just hooked a thumb in silent invitation for them to beat it—which, after a traded glance, they did. Rapidly. Edwards watched them go, shaking his head, then turned back and surveyed the trail of brawlers we'd laid out across the tavern floor—some apparently unconscious, others just stewing in the pain or slowly trying to pick themselves up.

"We can't leave you two alone for five minutes, can we?"

"To be fair," Johnny said, "this place kinda sucks."

Still grinning, Edwards gestured for us to follow him, but I was still stuck in place, staring at the men I'd reduced to groaning heaps and the crowd of onlookers who were watching me like I was an alien entity that might explode at any moment. Behind the bar, the WAN caster was just finishing her update on Haldin Raish, Demon of Divinity.

"How did they know?" I asked quietly, more to myself than to Johnny or Edwards.

"We should probably figure that out back in the safety of our own fortress," Johnny said, eyeing the sea of unsettled spectators. "And maybe find you a publicist while we're at it."

"Come on, kid," Edwards added, waving for me to join them. "Let's get back to Haven."

I forced my feet to move.

Johnny fell in beside me. "So when we tell this story," he said quietly, "I think it's only fair we say ol' Johnny did half the work here, agreed?"

He was just trying to pull me out of my head and lighten the mood after what had just happened, I knew. I tried to smile, but I couldn't seem to move past all those shocked, distrustful stares, and all the hatred flowing from them. No more than I could stop thinking about how good it had felt in the moment to let myself go and wipe the walls with their ignorant asses.

The very people I'd been fighting to protect all this time, and all they wanted was to see me hang. Had they not been paying attention when I'd equipped the Legion to retake Oasis from the raknoth and turn the tide of the hybrid war? Did they not understand what I'd sacrificed?

I halted just short of the exit and turned back to face them before I could stop myself.

"You people… You have no idea what I've been through."

They watched me, and I could see the fear in their eyes. They didn't care what I'd been through. Didn't care that I'd lost my parents, lost Carlisle. Didn't care that I'd lost my freedom and any semblance of a normal life just so I could bleed in the fight to stop the raknoth from turning the entire population of Enochia into livestock. They didn't understand. Never would. Not even if I spelled it out for them. To them, I was a demon, and they just wanted me gone.

So I turned for the exit and didn't look back.

Outside, any notion of finding a moment's peace was quickly washed away by the buzzing sirens of incoming enforcers.

"Alpha's wrinklies," Johnny groaned as the first of the tan and black skimmers rounded into view a few blocks down the dull gray line of permacrete buildings, red lights flashing.

"Not for five minutes," Edwards reaffirmed, shaking his head.

I watched the enforcers approaching, thinking that I should feel angry. But I just felt tired. Plain tired. How else was I supposed to feel? The persecution was relentless. Never ending. To think I'd actually believed it might get better when we'd exposed High General Kublich and the raknoth, and then again when I'd helped the Legion win their war…

It had been a dream. A dream based in a world where people used their eyes and their brains to see and understand what was actually happening in front of them rather than blindly following the dogmatic word of a holy man who wouldn't deign to even leave his White Tower to see with his own two eyes who and what he condemned to damnation.

The first three enforcer skimmers set down nearby and promptly began disgorging armed pairs of grim-faced men and women who looked ready to see that that holy man's will was done—although none of them seemed in any rush to hop to it before the rest of their considerable reinforcements began touching down.

"Get to the transport, kid," Edwards said beside me.

I was about to ask him *what* transport when it crested the permacrete highrise above the tavern and began a hasty descent toward us.

"Dillard's orders," Edwards added unnecessarily as the transport touched down and Ordo Dillard himself came striding down the rear ramp at a brisk pace.

Elise was right on his heels, wearing one of those worried looks that I seemed to put on her face a little too often. When they reached us, I gratefully accepted Elise's hug, but kept my eyes on Dillard over her shoulder. The ordo scanned the scene, weighing his options. He didn't look happy, but I was also pretty sure the displeasure wasn't particularly directed at me.

"Ordo Dillard," one of the enforcers called from the cover of their skimmers, "we have orders to apprehend the apostate Haldin Raish. We ask that you step away and allow us to proceed."

Edwards gave an amused huff, like he would've enjoyed seeing the enforcers try to take me away. Dillard hushed him with a look before turning to me. I waited patiently for his order. Rough as our working relationship had been at the start—admittedly thanks to my own stubbornness more than to any fault of his—I'd come to trust Dillard after everything we'd been through. He was a good man and a good ordo, and I was pretty sure he had my back.

Either way, I was done making messes of these things myself.

"Get on the transport, Citizen Raish," Dillard said, tilting his head that way.

I didn't hesitate. I turned with Elise and Johnny and started walking, not stopping when I felt the lead enforcers tensing behind us.

"Ordo Dillard," their speaker called, "if you disregard our orders—"

"Do you mind explaining where those orders came from, Enforcer?" Dillard called back.

I glanced back only long enough to see the enforcer's wary look as he glanced from Dillard to me, and back. "Our orders come from the Central Justice, sir, as I'm sure you already know."

"Hmm," Dillard said. "The Central Justice. Well, last I checked, you serve the Legion in times of war, which is exactly what this is, according to the Central Justice. And I have a Legion order right here that says Haldin Raish is to be returned to Haven, alive and unharmed."

"With all due respect, I believe settling the proper jurisdiction may be above our pay grade here, sir. If you'd prefer to help us escort Citizen Raish to the Central Justice, I'm sure we could…"

I couldn't hear what Dillard said, but I could feel that he'd closed ground with the enforcer, and I could only imagine it wasn't to trade his favorite goja berry pie recipe. I suppose I could've looked back or reached out to better hear what passed between them, but I wasn't sure I even wanted to know. Right then—plodding up the ramp with Elise's hand in mine, the aching aftermath of my first tavern brawl beginning to well and truly burn across my knuckles and forearms and torso and pretty much everywhere else—all I really wanted was to get back to Haven and crawl peacefully back into my sad little prison.

At least until I finished scanning the line of seated legionnaires and saw Dex sitting beside Four in the rear corner of the cabin with his hands bound behind his back, and my surprise pawed aside my somber fatigue.

I looked confusedly from him to Elise. "You kidnapped Dex?"

She directed a hard look at the weasley fix-it man. "Only after he tried to kidnap us."

I stiffened. "What?! Are you okay?"

"We're fine," she said, guiding me down to one of the seats across from Four and Dex. "Like I said, we can handle one weasel. Especially one who thinks a couple locks are enough to keep me and Four stuck in a back alley hidey hole."

"Rookie move, broto," Johnny said, shaking his head at Dex.

The fix-it man gave a series of indignant grunts through his gag, and his shoulders and head heaved animatedly, as if he were trying to talk with his bound hands but the effort was simply migrating up the kinetic chain.

"Did you learn anything from him?" I asked.

"Not really," Elise said. "We're still trying to figure out if he actually knows anything or if we should just turn him over to the enforcers."

I hooked a thumb in the direction of Dillard and his new pals. "I bet those fine peacekeepers out there would be happy to take *someone* back to the Central Justice right now."

I doubted anyone was actually thinking about simply handing him over to the enforcers without asking more questions first, but Dex didn't need to know that.

Elise shrugged. "Ehhh, he must at least have *some* way to get in contact with our two raknoth if he thought it was worth trying to kidnap us." She shot him a look. "He wouldn't be stupid enough to do something like that on a whim."

Dex favored her with an unwieldy sneer from behind his gag, but I was pretty sure there was a hint of murderous glare in his eyes. He knew something. Maybe. Or maybe he was just angry at having run up against an opponent he clearly didn't understand. Alpha knew I had the aches and bruises to prove that people tended to fear—and sometimes frantically pummel—what they didn't understand.

"Well," I said slowly, "I'm sure he'll be willing to point us the right way once he's had a chance to think about what would happen to a man willing to sell his planet out to bloodsucking aliens for a few measly coins."

Dex mumbled something past his gag that sounded suspiciously like, *"Go grop yourself."* Elise let me know with a look and a gentle pressure on my arm that she wanted to speak with me in the more private upper cabin.

As soon as we were more or less alone, she wrapped me in a much warmer hug, kissing my cheek and stroking my hair with one hand.

"Are you okay?" she asked softly, still holding me close.

"Just a few cuts and bruises. I'll be fine once—"

"That's not what I meant, Hal. I'm talking about having an angry mob turn on you. I'm no expert, but I can't imagine that's a pleasant feeling."

I shrugged, pulling back to show her I could smile about this. "Not really so bad after you've experienced the thrill of a hoard of feral hybrids roaring for your blood by name."

She searched my face, and I felt my smile cracking under the weight of her scrutiny. "Okay," she said finally. "But you know you don't have to put on a brave face for me."

I pulled her close again. "I know."

"And next time," she said against my chest, "maybe you find a way to avoid punching out half of Divinity and confirming all those nasty stories about you."

"I tried to get out, Lise. Those assholes rushed us before we had a chance."

This time, she was the one to pull back and fix me with those knowing blue eyes of hers. "They tried to rush you *because…?*"

"Probably because the wrong punch-happy scudhead saw the most unfortunately timed WAN feed in history."

She tilted her head. "Annnd because you were there at all. There at the tavern."

"Where I could keep an eye out for the all-too-likely trap you were walking into."

"But where you *actually* ended up punching out half the tavern while Dex was trying to kidnap us—which, by the way, we handled ourselves without breaking a sweat."

I stared down at her, wanting to say that wasn't exactly fair, feeling like I should be angry at her implication, or at least apologetic that I'd ended up not being there when I could have actually helped. I definitely shouldn't have felt like laughing. Yet, as we held each other's eyes, I couldn't help it. I let out a soft chuckle.

Maybe I'd taken more blows to the head than I'd realized. Only I wasn't alone. Elise's cheeks twitched in a losing war to hold down her growing smile.

"Lesson learned," I promised, cupping her quivering cheeks and pulling her in for a kiss. "I love you."

Her smile won the war. "And I you, my brave brawler." She stroked my cheek, her expression sobering. "But we can't let something like this happen again. The Sanctum's already looking for a reason to demand Glenbark deliver your head. When they find out you slipped out of Haven for a field trip…"

I grimaced, knowing she was right. Sure, I'd refrained from blatantly throwing my powers at them. I'd done my best to keep it as subtle as I could. But even if half the tavern wasn't currently flocking to the White Tower crying demon, it seemed naive to think the High Cleric wouldn't eventually hear about this little incident.

Glenbark wasn't going to be happy.

"Let's just focus on finding these last two raknoth," I said, turning to look down the stairs to the main cabin when I heard Dillard's voice, along with a distinct lack of shouts or gunshots. Had he talked the enforcers down, then?

"Once we're sure Enochia's safe from them," I added, "then we can worry about properly pulling my ass out of the Sanctum's holy fire."

She gave me that look. The one that told me I was being shortsighted, or naive. Or both. "And if those flames spread faster than we expect?"

Dillard appeared at the bottom of the stairs, looking tired and—once he'd cleared the sight of his Hounds—more than a little troubled. The look didn't wane when he met my eyes.

I looked back to Elise. "Then I guess I'd better find some fireproof pants."

3

DETAILS

"Interesting turn of events today."

On the other side of the four-inch thick nearly indestructible polymer window, somehow looking pristine and unruffled even after several days of imprisonment, Alton Parker watched me with a bored expression. Even in his dull brig grays, he managed to look like the suave businessman he'd once pretended to be.

"Forgive me," he said in that smooth tone of his, "if I'm not stirred by what you might consider interesting."

It was pretty much what I'd come to expect as Standard Parker from the few conversations we'd had since he'd arrived at Haven six days ago and freely turned himself over to the Legion. Or, more accurately, to the Solemn Nation of Haldin Raish. Even now, he was apparently refusing to speak so much as a word to anyone but me—though, of course, he wouldn't say why.

All he'd told me was that we had business together, he and I. I almost didn't want to know what the scud he meant by that, but it wasn't like I was in any danger of finding out anytime soon, by the looks of things.

While I wanted to assume that even raknoth had to eat and drink at some point, Parker had yet to show any sign he was suffering—had in fact declined when I'd offered him water for information on Day Two. When they'd instructed me on Day Three to insist he drink water for fear that our raknoth prize might simply die of dehydration, he'd sipped at the water casually, all placid predator, as if three days without drink had meant nothing.

On Day Five, when Glenbark had finally authorized the use of pain to make him talk, our interrogators had quickly come to the conclusion that, in addition to their ridiculously resilient hides, the raknoth had an almost sickening tolerance—bordering on ignorance—for pain.

The only other thing left to hope on had been his inevitable need to feed on human blood. I'd seen it in Al'Kundesha's memories just as clearly as Therese Brown had demonstrated to us in her Haven lab: without fresh infusions of human blood, even a raknoth would eventually die. And yet here Parker stood, unshaken, displaying not even the faintest trace of the dark spider web lines I'd seen on the flesh of hybrids and raknoth who'd gone too long without feeding.

And so it was that somehow, even trapped in the heart of a Legion fortress, sealed in an unbreakable cell that I'd thoroughly cloaked against telepathy, Alton Parker was still somehow succeeding in making us play this game of his.

He'd tell me what he wanted to, *when* he wanted to. So for now, all I could do was walk away, or play. It wasn't much of a choice.

"Your friend tried to kidnap my people," I said.

His brow furrowed in a way that somehow made him look genuinely thoughtful and yet supremely all-knowing at the same time. It was a look I was getting used to seeing on him. "You're going to have to be more precise. To the best of my knowledge, friends are not a commodity in which I've much invested."

No kidding.

"Your contact, Dex," I said, not wanting to get sidetracked into some pointless discussion on the value of friendship—or lack thereof in the eyes of the raknoth. "He tried to grab two of our people."

"Did he?" Parker considered that. "Well, I can't imagine that turned out well for him. Tell me, was Elise Fields one of his intended targets?"

I searched his calm face, looking in vain for some indicator as to what he was playing at. "Why do you wanna know?"

He just studied me for a short while longer then waved the thought aside. "It matters little. I assume that slippery coward failed to provide any valuable information?"

"Then why the grop did you send us after him in the first place?"

A faint smirk touched his lips. "I hadn't realized I possessed the power to send you anywhere, Haldin. Forgive me. If you'll recall, I never suggested that I believed the cretin would be of particular use to your hunt. I merely said that, seeing as my extensive list of potential hideouts had proved fruitless, Dex was the most likely of my contacts to have the information you were looking for."

"So you're telling me you really don't know how to find them."

"No. I'm telling you that any other leads I provide will be less likely than Dex to know where my brethren are hiding."

"Well thank you for that clarification," I said through gritted teeth.

It was like arguing directions with an autoskimmer.

"You're welcome, Haldin," Parker said with a sincerity that raised my blood temperature a few degrees. "Though I feel compelled to remind you this hunt of yours is hardly the most pressing of our troubles."

Alpha, it made my skin crawl when he used words like *we* and *our*. Like he actually believed there was any world in which I would ever willingly work with the creature who'd helped turn thousands of Enochians into feral beasts and drained even more innocents to keep those pet beasts well-stocked in blood.

"Great," I said. "We're back to The Big Bad Threat again? The one you've so conveniently refused to tell me a single thing about since you decided to step this game of yours up and 'surrender' yourself to us?

He hauled back and slammed a fist into the thick window with all his considerable raknoth strength, and without a moment's warning. I couldn't help it. I jumped. The sound was like a full speed skimmer collision a foot away from my face. I shuffled backward to catch my balance, my heart thundering at the unexpected violence.

"Does this look like a game to you?" Parker asked, watching my shaky recovery with a calm that was all the more disturbing in the wake of his bestial outburst. "I did not surrender myself to this pathetic imprisonment for the petty amusement of watching your Legion trip over its own clumsy feet to stop two of my brethren."

"Then why are you here, Parker? Why won't you tell me?"

"I already have," he said, the first hints of frustration creeping into his eyes. "Nine times now. I am here for my own safekeeping until it is time for us to confront the greater threat facing your planet."

"Which you won't tell me the first gropping thing about."

"It is not yet time."

I barely managed to restrain myself from taking my own turn pounding on the thick window. What I wouldn't have given to reach in there and give him a good, strong telekinetic uppercut. But there was a damn good reason

I'd laid down the cloaking runes to seal the room in its own little bubble. The inability to reach in and smack the raknoth around with my powers was a small price to pay to assure he couldn't reach *out* and start mind-jacking any passing legionnaires to come let him loose.

Still, it would've been nice.

"Most of the generals are calling for your execution, you know," I said, deciding to try another angle.

"I find that perfectly unsurprising."

I'll bet he did.

"Well good for you," I growled. "But that doesn't change the fact that you might find yourself staring down one scudstorm of a firing squad soon if you'd rather keep stringing us along instead of actually telling me something useful."

"It is not for personal satisfaction that I delay. It is because you are simply not yet ready to do what must be done when the time comes."

I chewed on that, opening my mouth multiple times to tell him he was full of scud, that he didn't know the first thing about what I was or wasn't ready to do for my planet. But it wasn't worth the breath. Not when anything I said could—and probably would—just further reaffirm his smug assurance that he saw and understood far more of the whole picture here than my sad little human brain could ever hope to comprehend.

"You wanna know what I *am* ready to do?" I asked. "I'm pretty damn sure I'm ready to tell Command that they're right: that I'm never gonna learn anything useful from you and that they might as well pull the plug on this whole bullscud exercise and see just how many pulse cannon bolts it takes to put an end to you. Scud, some of the generals might even start liking me after that. You have any good reason I shouldn't tell them to simplify my life, here?"

For a few moments, I actually thought he might crack. Then he showed me a cold smile instead.

I turned to leave, having handily reached my bullscud threshold for the day—or for the entire damn season, for that matter—and thinking maybe I *should* tell the generals to do their worst and have at Parker. Not that many of them actually gave a scud about what I thought—least of all General Auckus, who had a hold on Legion Command nearly as strong as High General Glenbark's and probably would've paid his own personal coin to see me dead if he'd thought he could get away with it. But even Auckus would be happy to play along this one time if it meant the end of seeing me in a place of leverage with the alien asset who would talk to me, and to me only.

If I declared defeat here, if I refused to meet with Alton Parker again…

"Haldin."

I paused at the door, wanting little more than to walk the rest of the way out—maybe to go sign the raknoth's death warrant, or maybe just to make it clear that I wouldn't be so easily yanked back and forth. But I'd already hesitated. There wasn't any pretending like I hadn't. Parker was a predator, and I'd just shown him that, on some level, he still had his hooks in me.

Because I couldn't deny it: I *wanted* to know what he was hiding. Badly. It was probably stupid. It was definitely pathetic. I hated myself for it a little more with each passing second I failed to step through the doorway. But I needed to know. So I turned and watched, waiting.

For the first time this visit, his eyes were not on me, but fixed on some thought or distant memory. It took him a little while to finally speak. "I've given thought to the problem we previously discussed."

I opened my mouth to give him a dose of his own bullscud and tell him he might have to be more precise, but he roused and pushed on before I could.

"The degrading hybrids," he said. "It's possible I could design a solution that might reverse the transition process."

I tried to hide the flicker of excitement I felt in my chest, not only because I didn't want him to see it but also because this was Alton Parker I was talking to. If not an outright liar, he was at least a bender of words even at the best of times. But if there was even a shot he could help undo what had been done to the hybrids…

Devastating as their hit-and-run campaign across Enochia had been—especially as the oldest of the hybrids had begun maturing and adopting more of their progenitors' strength, resilience, and telepathic prowess—the hybrid army had never been all that large. The Legion analysts estimated they'd peaked around 5,000 active members leading up to the battle for Oasis. After Oasis, the army had been broken and scattered.

I didn't love that there were still a few hundred hybrids out there, roaming freely in the aftermath of Oasis, but the Legion trackers were dealing with them, and it was hardly as troubling as the other half of the hybrid problem: the roughly 1,000 innocent people still stuck in hybrid breeding chambers, irreversibly transitioning into the wild beasts who would thirst for human blood day by day until the demand eventually outgrew even *their* ability to violently procure it.

I thought of Johnny's sister, Annabelle, lying in stasis in one of the cells they'd constructed outside of Therese Brown's lab as Therese and her team labored to find some way to help her, and all the others like her. The familiar tinge of nausea swept in, thinking about the way the sweet red-haired girl had looked the last time I'd seen her, caught somewhere between her meek human self and the beastly raknoth influence taking hold of her. Even removed from the breeding chamber, her too-pale skin seemed to grow rougher every day, the sickly green hue of raknoth hide slowly but surely creeping in.

Johnny could keep pretending like it wasn't happening. I could keep telling him that Therese and her people would figure it out in time. But if Parker had the answers...

"What's the catch?" I asked. "What do you want in return?"

"If it should work, consider it a gesture of good faith."

Good faith? Seriously?

"Why now, then?" I asked instead. "Why not make this gesture of good faith days ago, when I first asked?"

He frowned at me. "Believe it or not, reversing a complete species trans-mutation is not particularly easy. I told you I'd think about it because I needed time... to think about it." He said the last words slowly, as if he were worried about my ability to keep up with such a challenging thought.

"And that's it?" I asked, ignoring his jibe. "You're telling me this sudden good faith has nothing to do with whether or not I might walk out of this room and let the generals have their way with you?"

His lips twitched in a faint smirk. "Perhaps I feel some remorse for the lives my actions have effectively ended."

"I buy that about as much as I buy all this, 'You're not ready yet,' bullscud."

"Then perhaps you'd be willing to think of this as nothing more than a dastardly bribe. I am not your enemy on this planet, Haldin. Not anymore."

It was my turn to frown. Not anymore? Did he mean since Oasis, or even before then? It was true that Parker had started his apparent rebellion against his own kin well before the assault on Oasis—right after we'd destroyed his hybrid breeding facility at the decommissioned Vantage labs, in fact. But that was hardly proof he was a sincere ally. Had something else changed since then?

"What would you need to implement this solution?" I asked. "You're not getting out of here to visit the lab."

He shook his head. "That won't be necessary. I'm already developing the counter treatment as we speak. My only requirement will be a courier to carry the treatment to the afflicted."

I didn't like the way he said the word, afflicted. It was subtle, but there was derision there, or something like it. Like he was mocking me for suggesting that what had been done to those poor people was actually a tragedy at all. It hardly inspired confidence in this magical treatment he was suddenly touting. And what the scud did he mean, he was already developing this miracle cure as we spoke?

The heavy clacks of the antechamber door unlocking broke my wary train of thought.

I turned in confusion to find Johnny and Elise both standing there—which didn't bode well, seeing as I knew neither of them would've interrupted a potentially useful talk with our raknoth captive for any trivial matter. Taking in their expressions, I was pretty sure they hadn't.

They looked like they'd just watched someone die.

"What is it?"

They traded a glance before warily eyeing the raknoth over my shoulder. I couldn't help but notice they both looked a few shades paler than normal.

"What happened?" I asked again, the first jitters of panic rippling through me.

Johnny tilted his head back toward the waiting room, a gesture that indicated I should join them. Something he didn't want Alton Parker to know about, then? That didn't make me feel any better.

I followed them out into the second chamber where they'd been waiting, not pausing to explain myself to Parker. Johnny keyed the security door shut behind me and looked at Elise again. She tapped her ear and pointed in Parker's direction, suggesting the raknoth might still be able to hear us.

"Guys…"

Johnny waved for us to follow him and started across the chamber for the door that opened into the high security wing of the Haven brig. I caught up and grabbed Elise's hand to stop her.

"Guys, you're scaring me. What's going on?"

Elise glanced from Parker's cell chamber back to Johnny, and they seemed to come to some agreement.

"The High Cleric just released a statement…" Elise started.

My stomach fell. "What, over the tavern brawl?"

"It's not just that," Johnny said.

"What? I've been marked Enemy of Enochia for almost a cycle now. What more can he do? As long as Glenbark—"

"This is different Hal."

I froze at the gravity in Elise's voice. Beside her Johnny was nodding slowly, not a single trace of humor on his face.

"It's not just you," she continued. "And I don't think they're posturing this time, either."

I stared at them with unseeing eyes, my head floating with a memory of my recent meeting with the High Cleric. Had it only been a cycle ago? It felt like half a lifetime since our discussion, sitting high in the White Tower, as he'd so casually dismissed the entire subset of gifted Enochians as *abominations*—unholy accidents in need of correcting. As casual and scholarly as his demeanor had been, though, I'd never forget the look in his eyes in the one moment his mask had slipped. The righteous fury. The utter disgust at the mere fact of my existence.

I saw those keenly piercing eyes now, flashing with a deep, long-buried malice, staring me down right there over the background of Elise's and Johnny's pale faces. I felt dizzy.

"What did they do?" I asked, my voice barely a whisper.

Elise's hand was gripping mine too tightly, her lips parted but seemingly unable to find the words she sought. Johnny filled the silence for her.

"The High Cleric just declared open war on every Shaper on Enochia."

4

———

THE CALL

Elise, Johnny, and I huddled over Johnny's tablet, watching with mouths agape. The vid was a replay from not even an hour earlier, taken from the expansive courtyard outside the White Tower, where the High Cleric had reportedly taken to delivering his sermons while the Great Hall was being rebuilt atop the Tower, high above.

"It is with great humility and grave tidings I come before you today," His Holiness started, "not only as High Cleric, but also as a concerned Enochian. Most of you have heard the rumors these past cycles, reports of true demons walking the streets, every bit as real as you or me. Even a cursory glance at the reels will reveal multiple mentions of the Demon of Divinity, who was formerly known as Haldin Raish."

He looked around at the thousands upon thousands of loyal Sanctum devotees gathered below his dais, assessing their reactions.

"Perhaps you have heard more troubling rumors. Perhaps you have heard that he is not an anomaly—that there are, in fact, many more like him, hiding in the shadows, preying on the unsuspecting people of Enochia…"

Another look around. A big, fat dramatic pause.

"It is true."

I shot a worried look with Elise and Johnny, who were both watching this for the second time now, looking sick.

"What's he doing?" I asked, but Elise only nodded her head toward the tablet, silently urging me to pay attention. Not that I needed much goading.

Even from the camera up on the High Cleric's dais, we could hear the murmurs of the sprawling crowd. The cleric himself raised his hands in a peaceful request for silence.

What the scud was he thinking?

"It is true," the High Cleric continued, "that for centuries, such demons have walked among us. I would like nothing more than to tell you that I was ignorant of these unholy abominations until now, that it was only brought to my attention after my elevation to High Cleric of the Sanctum. But that would not be the truth. For nearly two decades, now, I have been on the forefront of the clandestine fight to banish this evil from our world. It has not been an easy fight. The demons are devious, their roots as persistent as they are pernicious. But we have fought on, nonetheless. Then came the raknoth, the beings some misguided spirits would have you believe are aliens from another galaxy, come to visit their fury on us for reasons unknown."

He paused to look around at those gathered before him. "Aliens." He shook his head—a slow, mournful gesture. "I have a better explanation. One which does not spit in the face of Alpha's teachings." A troubled look settled over his features. "One which I have lacked the courage to share from the beginning, for fear it would tear our beloved world apart. But Alpha has come to me in our time of need. He has shone his light that we might all find our way. And I know now what I must do."

He licked his lips, gathering the courage to press on. My heart was thundering, not caring that this was a replay and that I already knew how it was going to end. It was almost worse, knowing the man on the screen was going to declare war by the end of this—like I already had the casualty list but was simply watching the footage for a more explicit look at the gory details of this slow motion tram wreck.

"The raknoth are not aliens. They are but the next stage of demonic evil, the harrowing test each and every one of us must now face for our collective transgressions in these troubled times." The High Cleric dropped his gaze, bowing his head. "They are the punishment awoken by our failure to protect this world from evil. Because we *have* failed to protect you, my beloved Enochians. And for that, I am immeasurably sorry. Innocent blood has been spilled. Faithful lives ruined. This burden lies squarely on myself and the rest of the Sanctum, I do not deny it. But now we stand at a crossroads, hanging to the light by bare threads even as darkness threatens to swallow us whole."

The High Cleric surveyed his flock, raising a solitary fist in a quiet show of power.

"I do not intend to let it be so, Enochia."

I could practically feel his audience responding, shifting on their feet, leaning desperately in for the answers to the frightening world of problems he'd just splattered down at their feet.

"For too long has the Sanctum attempted to contain this darkness on its own. For too long have we let our own pride and honor convince us that it was the only way." He looked back and forth, reeling the crowd in with his magnetic drama. "For far too long has evil roamed our streets, twisting and corrupting the minds of Alpha's children to suit their unholy needs. Call them demons, call them raknoth, it matters little. By the Will of Alpha, they must be stopped."

He paused—at first, I thought, simply to allow the surge of reverent cries and applause to settle, but then he gestured to someone off screen, and the vid cut to a feed featuring a dramatically spliced together montage of raknoth horrors. Monstrous hybrids flooding the streets of a dozen different cities, grabbing up helpless civilians, killing those who put up a fight. Black smoke rising from Oasis as scaly green forms swarmed its ramparts.

And through it all were flashes of Shaper mysticism—always visually startling, never in context. There was me inexplicably floating in midair at the Sanctum gallows, the noose hanging limp and useless around my neck. Me sailing through the air in an impossible leap from the great worship hall in Humility. There was Four conjuring a swirling firestorm around himself —I wasn't sure where, but that hardly mattered.

My heart panged when a vid snippet of blood-crazed hybrids gave way to footage of Carlisle dropping into the Great Hall on a rain of shattered duraglass. Coming to save me. Coming to his death.

The High Cleric's voice returned, speaking over the shocking footage as the montage continued.

"I will not tell you to belay your fear, my children, for these are fearful times, even for the most faithful of Alpha's servants. What I plead is that you do not forsake hope in these dark times. Yes, we have strayed. But it is only when the night is dark and our feet have lost the path that we are offered the chance to find our way back. To find redemption."

If I'd been breathing at all, I stopped when the vid montage cut to footage from earlier that very day at the tavern. I watched in horrid fascination as, through the chaotic sea of limbs, the shaky videographer caught snippets of me blurring from attacker to attacker faster than seemed possible, always in motion, sending a steady stream of civilians crashing into furniture or walls or floors all around me.

I didn't look human.

Which was exactly what the High Cleric intended to communicate, I realized, as the vid finally cut back to him in the Great Hall. His expression was that of a parent who'd just had the sad but necessary task of revealing to his children that the family pet had died in the night.

"Our world lies in the clutches of darkness," he continued, "and for too long has the Sanctum stubbornly ignored our only true hope at resolving this conflict. But Alpha has shown me. Which is why I've come here today to ask for your help, Enochia. Today, I ask you to take up the call. Together, let us finish this war we have too long kept hidden, too few in number to properly see through. Together, let us bring an end to these fearful times, that we might find our way back to Alpha's Grace."

The crowd was tensed. On the hook, but not quite ready to burst. They sensed what was coming. Sensed it, and welcomed it. A fresh world, free from the evils that'd had the collective planet ducking for cover these past seasons, rightfully worried that each and every day could be the last for them and their families.

I felt sick.

The High Cleric spread his hands wide, reaching as if to envelop his flock across all the world.

"Together," he called, "let us banish from our world the demons, and the raknoth, and all else that would seek to turn us from the light."

Cheers spilled forth in a tidal wave that built and built until the High Cleric finally fanned it down.

"Your commitment to Alpha humbles me, my children. Indeed, it makes me marvel that, for so long, my predecessors have continued clinging to the failing ideal that we alone can win this fight. Which is why today, in the name of Alpha, as the High Cleric of the Sanctum, I hereby declare open war on the evil that plagues Enochia. You know what is at stake. You know who threatens it. Go forth, my children, and help us clear the way, that Alpha's light may shine on us all, free of taint or burden. Go forth in the name of Alpha."

"In the name of Alpha!" someone screamed in the moment before the thunderous roar burst forth, putting everything before it to shame. I watched until the vid reached its end, unable to move.

Open war.

Open war with no clear target. None except me, at least, and Four and the few others who'd been featured in the propaganda reel, provided anyone actually recognized them. They must've been Seekers like Four and Eight—ones I hadn't yet met. Wouldn't meet at all, I guess, if the High Cleric had his way.

Convenient, that he'd forgotten to mention those demons of his had been on Sanctum payroll up till about a cycle ago.

I looked at Johnny and Elise. They were watching me, neither of them sure what to say. I wasn't sure either. Mostly, I just wanted to disappear. I would've even taken a good, healthy surge of rage. But I couldn't seem to do anything at all except sit there in shock.

Then something thumped against the hallway door, and my faculties returned in a startled jump. I'd pulled a telekinetic barrier around us almost before I knew it, half-expecting the door to fly out of its housing on the back end of breach charges. My thinking brain caught up and reminded me that, aside from the fact that anyone looking to kill me would probably just open the door and toss a bomb in, I had more productive ways of establishing our immediate safety.

I reached out to take stock with my extended senses and breathed a sigh of relief. "It's Dillard."

That discovery was followed by another blip of panic. Because what if the ordo had heard the High Cleric's call and decided the herald of Alpha might just outrank his Legion orders? But as quick as it came, I pushed the thought aside as ridiculous. The look of understanding on Johnny's face confirmed my gut feeling.

"Yeah, that…" he let out his own deep breath, relaxing his shoulders and standing to go to the door. "I knew that. Totally."

Elise and I stood to follow. I didn't remember having grabbed her hand, but the mutual deathgrip we shared suggested one of us had made the move somewhere along the way.

What little relief I'd felt at Dillard's presence soured somewhat when Johnny got the door open and I took in the ordo's expression, shortly followed by Edwards' hulking form over his shoulder, and what looked like all of First Squad lined up behind them in the max security hallway.

The brig attendants had probably loved that.

"We need to get you both to Central Command, immediately," Dillard said, looking between me and Elise. "Glenbark's orders."

"We're with you," Elise said.

I just nodded dumbly. I still couldn't seem to find words.

Had Dillard seen the High Cleric's broadcast? Did his Hounds understand what was happening?

Did I?

We fell in and hurried silently down the hallways at the center of their formation, Dillard keeping close enough that I heard the steady stream of orders he delivered to Carter and Second Squad, who sounded to be prepping the area outside the brig for our expedient exit. The tense silence of the Hounds rattled me. Not that any of Dillard's men normally shirked their duties during an escort, but this felt different. This felt like we were already in an active combat zone.

I wanted to step aside with Dillard and ask him for an honest rundown of what we were about to step into, but I also wasn't sure I'd manage to find the words, and it felt like we didn't have the time to spare besides. So I just held Elise's hand and did my best to match her gentle telepathic reassurances. We didn't exchange words exactly, more just a general sentiment that we were okay and that whatever was happening, we'd get through it.

I almost had myself convinced this wasn't even all that different than my time being declared Enemy of Enochia when Dillard pulled us aside and halted First Squad right at the brig exit.

"If anything happens out there," he said quietly, "let us handle it. Protect yourselves if it becomes absolutely necessary, but you cannot—I repeat *cannot*—make it look like you've attacked Legion personnel. Do you understand me?"

I traded an uneasy look with Elise.

"Do you expect something to happen out there?" Elise asked Dillard quietly.

He chewed his lip, something I'd only seen him do maybe twice before. "We've got you covered, no matter what."

It wasn't exactly an answer. But he was already giving the signal to move before we could argue. The Hounds plunged forward, sweeping out of the brig ahead. I was starting to fall in with them beside Elise when Dillard laid a hand on my shoulder, holding me up with a meaningful look.

"Eyes open and shields up, Raish."

It wasn't a comforting last command.

5

———

SAFE HAVEN

Outside, there was no surprise ambush. No bombs or sudden hails of gunfire. In fact, nothing really seemed awry at all, except for the few curious glances we drew as the 51st Hounds shuffled us across base in a march that was a little too hurried—not to mention a little too cover-oriented—to appear as casual as we all tried to make it seem. There were looks at me and Elise, of course. There were always looks. I was the Demon of Divinity, and even those who didn't know who Elise was—which seemed to be a dwindling number among the Haven population—were usually tempted to take a second look at her anyway. But most of the looks didn't strike me as particularly murderous. I tried to pay them no mind.

Word of the High Cleric's bold declaration of war would no doubt be spreading across base already, but maybe it hadn't reached all that many ears just yet. Still, it was going to take more than a lack of death glares to get me to relax and let go of the energy I'd been holding in reserve ever since we'd stepped out in the open. Especially once the big amps kicked on and delivered an oddly ambiguous reminder.

"Hear the call, Haven, and heed this warning. Any legionnaire raising arms within base premises and without explicit orders from Legion command will face the full available repercussions for their insubordination. Such actions will be regarded as treason where possible. For anyone questioning the matter, the highest chain of command we know, as stated in the Legionnaire's Oath, ends with the High General of the Legion. That is all."

It was impossible to miss the ripple that caused across Haven. We pushed on, trying to hurry without hurrying. It wasn't far now. Less than half a mile.

At first, I was encouraged by the number of legionnaires I saw shooting genuinely confused looks up at the amps. It *had* been a strange announcement, after all. They *should* look confused, unless they happened to know exactly who and what it was intended to warn them off of.

Which is why it put a lump of cold softsteel in my gut when I noticed one legionnaire glaring at a nearby amp, his brow working overtime, his rifle gripped too tight. And he wasn't alone. He stood with at least one full fireteam, all of them pointedly not looking at us.

Before I could tell Elise, I felt her mental alarm and realized she'd spotted another suspicious cluster. We both looked around for Dillard—right as he broke off from his side of the detail, charging straight for us.

It was a testament to my growing trust for the man that my jittery nerves didn't demand I stop him with a telekinetic sucker punch, just to be safe. It was good I didn't. He caught us both in a two-armed tackle even as he cried, "Take cover!"

We hit permacrete, and the gunfire began.

It was over almost as fast as it started. A few slugs pelted off the telekinetic barrier I pulled over the three of us. One of our Hounds, a woman they called Jinn, dropped to one knee, spitting curses and holding a wounded shoulder. Edwards, Johnny, and the rest of First Squad snapped weapons to the ready, but no one fired. No one needed to.

A Legion base, it turned out, is not a good place to try to assassinate someone, even if you *are* a legionnaire.

The shooters, as far as I could see, had been tackled down by their fellow soldiers nearly as soon as they'd opened fire. Most of our impromptu allies didn't seem to know precisely what was happening, aside from that I was involved—which seemed to surprise no one—but Demon of Divinity or no, when slugs started flying, the ones doing the shooting were the ones who got incapacitated until the proper questions could be asked.

Thank Alpha—or the doceres and their drills, rather—for that.

Still, the ill-advised ambush hadn't been without effect. Jinn was definitely hit, though she appeared to be handling it okay. The surrounding area was quickly becoming a mad house of activity as our rescuers restrained our would-be attackers and others flooded in to see what the fuss had been all about.

Except judging by the furtive looks I was noticing from the crowd here and there, I got the distinct impression there were still at least a few gun hands who were thinking about trying their luck now that their brothers had drawn the attention.

"Come on," Dillard said, pulling Elise to her feet and turning to me. "We need to move."

I didn't argue, nor did anyone else as Dillard ordered Fireteam C to get Jinn to the medica and got the rest of the Hounds marching for Central Command again. Even if anyone had wanted to, I think we were all too shocked to form the words right then.

Legionnaires didn't shoot other legionnaires. It simply didn't happen. Once the training was survived, once the oaths were sworn...

There were your blood relatives—your mother and father, your brothers and sisters. And then there were your fellow legionnaires. Like them or hate them, it didn't really matter. They were yours in more than blood.

That wasn't to say friendly fire couldn't happen by accident in the field. And then there was the catastrophic scudstorm the raknoth and their hybrids had wrought when they'd had the sinister idea to telepathically compel our people to turn their weapons on one another. No one here would ever forget that horror. But to see presumably mentally intact legionnaires willingly turning their rifles on their own brothers and sisters just to chance a questionable shot at me...

I felt sick that anyone could be that desperate to see me dead. But not surprised, I realized, as the initial shock began to subside. Because the High Cleric had finally given the word loud and clear. And when the mouth of Alpha spoke, Enochia listened.

He'd taken the entire raknoth invasion, and pretty much every other bit of evil that ailed this world, and thrown it all straight on my head. Well, my head, and the heads of every other gifted individual on Enochia. Maybe gifted wasn't the right word anymore.

For the first time, it truly hit me how serious the situation was. Open war. It was easy to say that, but it didn't really mean much. Not until we saw how far either side was willing to go—and, more importantly, whose side was whose. By the letter, the Legion and the Sanctum had been parted into two discrete entities for a couple hundred years now, but even as tyros, we'd all known the real truth. The Sanctum got what it wanted. They held the hearts of the people. They held the sanctity of our spirits, for the love of Alpha.

The Legion, on the other hand, just made sure no one got rowdy and shot the good people. And clearly, there were plenty of legionnaires who cared about the former more than the latter.

Maybe that's why it was only a small comfort when we arrived at Central Command without further incident. Safe for the moment. But what would happen when the High Cleric's message had spread to the entirety of the Legion? How many would honor their oaths over the purported Word of Alpha? Would they even have to?

What if the whole world decided it just wasn't worth fighting over a handful of freaks?

Sure, maybe a few would recognize how crucial the Shapers could be to detecting and resisting anything like the raknoth invasion in the future, and how much damage we could've prevented this time around, if only there'd been more of us, and if the Sanctum hadn't been busy hunting us like wild hounds. But there were only three raknoth left now, and I'd already given the Legion the cloaks they needed to beat them. My only other function, as envoy to Alton Parker, wasn't exactly overflowing with usefulness either.

What if Glenbark decided Elise and I simply weren't worth the effort anymore?

With cheery thoughts like that one floating around in my head, it was no comfort at all when we stepped from the wide open shooting gallery outside into Central Command.

Dillard posted Second Squad outside to bolster the building's already considerable guard detail, and was arguing with the security head about bringing First Squad inside with us when High General Glenbark herself parted from the perpetual chaos of the wide open operations room and came to meet us in the long entryway.

I eyed her warily, sure I was probably being paranoid. She looked furious. Or so I imagined she did, at least. Honestly, with Glenbark, I could rarely tell. She was a master of keeping her cool. Even when the scud hit the turbines, it somehow never seemed to fleck on her crisp, dark blue dress tunic and immaculately polished boots, or to ruffle her majestic mane of perfectly straight, golden-blond hair.

"Stand down, Ordo Durgen," she said as she approached the security head and Dillard, her voice somehow cutting through their argument and all the chatter without seeming particularly loud. Everyone snapped to attention. She ran an appraising eye across our group, and I couldn't help but feel she avoided my eyes. Or was that the paranoia talking?

"We could use as many level heads and loyal trigger fingers as possible right now," she added, looking to Dillard. "Accompany me to my office, Ordo Dillard. Bring your Hounds."

She turned and started back for operations while Dillard was still giving the, "Sir, yes sir." By the time First Squad was falling in on her flanks, she was already drawing up to one of the operations room consoles, and fixing the suddenly bolt-upright comms specialist there with her most serious gaze.

"I want General Auckus in my office as soon as humanly possible," she said, in a tone that was somehow as calm as it was commanding. While the specialist scrambled to follow the order and hail Gregor Auckus over the Haven comms, Glenbark glanced over her shoulder, and finally met my eyes with a gravity that momentarily sucked the wild winds out of my racing thoughts.

"We all have a lot to talk about."

6

NO SUCH THING

In High General Glenbark's spotless, well-furnished office, the mood was about as somber as the discussion was circuitous. Not that I was of a mind to actually follow everything that was said. My head was still spinning too fast for that.

You almost might've thought it was the first time someone had tried to assassinate me.

I sat between Elise and Johnny at the long hardwood table in Glenbark's office, trying to gather my thoughts and actually listen to Glenbark break the situation down with her small council—a pair of captains and one General Marcus Hopper, a strong-jawed man with dark hair and a pleasant enough demeanor beneath his resting frown. Franco was there too, as well as Four and his stone wall of a partner, Eight, who was still recovering from the round of fisticuffs she'd had with one of the Seeker-powered raknoth who'd fled Oasis during the assault.

Aside from General Hopper, his twitchy servitor, the two captains, and Ordo Dillard, there was a considerable lack of Legion presence in the room, considering the gravity of the topic. Or probably *because* of that gravity.

After the High Cleric's call to arms, who could we really trust? Scud, I wasn't sure I should even be behind closed doors with Glenbark, considering. Or that I could be reliably sure there was a "we" at all anymore. It was all just more fuel waiting to be cast on the fire. Because that hadn't just been a few hotheads taking a crack at me out there. This wasn't just more of the same old routine.

That had been the opening salvo of a war on all of Shaper kind. That cold truth was settling deeper in my mind with each passing minute, right along with the realization that such a war could quite possibly bring on the collapse of half the planet if the Legion truly intended to defy the High Cleric.

"The Sanctum simply doesn't have the jurisdiction to declare any war," General Hopper was saying, and world implications aside, I couldn't help but appreciate the indignation in his tone. "And especially not a war to commit genocide for inheriting the wrong, uh"—he glanced at me uncertainly—"traits."

To his credit, he genuinely seemed to hope that his word choice was inoffensive. Not that I was emotionally coherent enough to care what he called our gifts. He was a general, and he seemed to be on our side. That was all that mattered right now.

Well, that, and how many of his fellow generals felt the same way.

"It doesn't matter anymore what jurisdiction they have by law," Glenbark said. "The High Cleric knows that. He struck straight at their hearts today, fed into their deepest fears."

"Sir, he freely admitted the Sanctum's been lying to us for almost a thousand years," one of the captains said.

"That only makes his story stronger," Franco said, stroking absentmindedly at his thin black mustache. "Without admitting some fault of their own, it would've simply been name-calling. Name-calling from the man many consider the highest authority on Enochia, mind you. But name-calling nonetheless. Admitting the Sanctum's own culpability in the matter provides real authenticity. It will only deepen the public fear of Shapers all the more."

No one argued. Not really. Just talked their way through a few more circles to the inevitable truth of the situation. I half-listened, head bowed low over the table, the thick smell of the treated hardwood assaulting my nose in mocking waves, as if just to remind me that it couldn't be troubled to leave me in peace while the world threatened to burn down around us.

By now, word had probably reached the majority of the base, and I could only imagine there were several thousand conversations currently sparking —some openly in squad barracks, some privately in hushed whispers.

What's command gonna say about this?

I've never seen what all the fuss was about Raish anyway.

Whose side is Glenbark even on, anyway?

Whose side are WE on?

I glanced at the door, glad once again for the added protection of Dillard's Hounds out there. They, at least, were firmly on our side, as seemed to be the case for a good majority of the legionnaires who truly understood the role our "demonic" cloaking fields had played in retaking Oasis. But that was hardly everyone in the Legion.

Elise's voice snapped me back to the conversation.

"What would you have us do, High General?"

"We should leave," Four said, when Glenbark didn't pounce to answer. "All four of us," he added with a look at me and Eight. "Helping with the raknoth was one thing, but this is different. We just went from being murky gray areas here to being walking targets. Not to mention liabilities for anyone else who'd rather not see us get slugged for breathing."

It said something that I found myself wanting to nod along with Four, the Seeker who I'd all-too-recently rather despised for having spent years hunting and killing Shapers for the very Sanctum that'd just publicly marked him for death. I wasn't sure *what* it said, exactly. But definitely something.

"This is all kinds of gropped up," Johnny muttered.

That seemed about right.

"We can't leave," Elise said. Then, with a glance at Glenbark, "At least, I don't think we should. If we run away, where does it end?"

"With us not getting shot in the back, maybe," Four said.

"No," Glenbark said almost softly, shaking her head. "No, Citizen Fields is right. It doesn't matter if your being here paints targets on all our heads. Like it or not, this is about more than any one of us now. This is about the freedom of all Enochians, and about who—if anyone—wields the power to threaten that freedom. If the Sanctum says its death to Shapers today, who's to say it won't be damnation to cripples, or ebonies, or left-handed redheads tomorrow?"

"That's oddly specific," Johnny mumbled, frowning down at his left hand.

"Begging your pardon, sir," one of the captains said, "but don't you think that's a large leap? We're talking about individuals who can control minds without moving a muscle. It's not exactly the same thing as singling people out for their eye color."

There was a lot I wanted to say to that, but didn't. For whatever reason, I didn't really feel like I had any right to defend myself here, in this room.

Out there, against the Sanctum and the assholes who would've punched my teeth in for trying to save them, yes. In here, though, with Glenbark and Dillard and Franco, I was surrounded by people who'd sacrificed their own health and safety to help preserve mine. It was different.

"I understand what you're saying, Captain," Glenbark said, "but it's not a question of whether I think it's likely the Sanctum will actually come knocking for my servitor down the road. It's a question of whether we're comfortable allowing them to set this kind of precedent unchallenged."

"Sounds like a terrible idea to me," General Hopper said, leaning back in his chair. "Though I can't say it sounds like a very economical idea to try to stop them either."

No one argued with that.

I sat in the collective silence, turning over Glenbark's words right until I noticed her sharp gaze settling on me.

"Citizen Raish, you haven't said a word in all of this. What are you thinking?"

Mostly, I was thinking that I was surprised she'd think I had anything insightful to say at all. Between that and the shock of everything else, all I could do was shake my head at first.

"I don't wanna die, I guess, for starters," I finally managed.

General Hopper and one of the captains smiled a little at that.

Glenbark just nodded, still serious. "I'm glad to hear that. And?"

I swallowed. "And, I don't know. I'd rather not go back into hiding, but I don't want this planet to tear itself apart because of us, either. Especially not after we've all fought so hard to keep it together. And especially not when..."

"Speak your mind, Haldin," Glenbark said. "We're far past polite consideration here."

"It's just that..." I faltered, trying to organize my thoughts. "It's infuriating, how ready and willing everyone is to call us evil. Never mind that Shapers like me could've sniffed out the whole raknoth invasion years ago if they weren't busy hiding from the Sanctum's..." I glanced at Four and Eight. "Well, you know. But no. No one will talk about that. They throw up footage of me at the gallows to breed fear of the unknown, and it's like the whole world's forgotten that the reason I was up there was because Carlisle and I were the first people who actually tried to stop the raknoth."

I looked around the table and was unsurprised to see a mix of sympathetic nods from my friends and unimpressed looks from pretty much everyone else. *Yeah*, those looks said. *The world's not fair, kid. Get used to it.*

Only Glenbark and Hopper watched impassively, assessing.

"Look, I understand why the Sanctum is frightened of what we can do," I continued. "Scud, I've spoken with the High Cleric about it. And his personal hatred aside…" I glanced at Elise, and she nodded, squeezing my hand. We'd discussed this several times before. "I'm not blind. I see that Shapers can be dangerous. But they're twisting facts now, pretending like we're some kind of unholy raknoth consorts when we've really been leading the charge against the bastards all along."

By that point, I could've gone on for days about the injustices—how no one cared about how much I'd lost in this fight, or how the Sanctum had been keeping a few dozen of these so-called demons locked up in their own White Tower for personal use, or how I'd all but single-handedly been the reason the Legion had managed to retake Oasis and break the hybrid army at all. Luckily, some flutter of good sense—or maybe it was the pressure of Elise's grip on my hand—told me I'd said what I needed to say, and that the rest was less than useful.

"It seems to me that we're looking at an information war," Franco said. "And we're looking at it from an inferior position in terms of the most important resource."

"Holy righteousness?" I muttered.

"Authority," Franco corrected. "In the war of truth—and make no mistake, truth is a war—authority can absolutely conquer facts and good sense. And in the eyes of at least eighty percent of the population, there is no higher authority than the High Cleric of the Sanctum." He looked at Glenbark. "I clearly can't tell you how best to handle your military, but I can tell you that superior artillery and fortifications will mean little—will possibly even become a serious hindrance—if you're truly intent on winning the minds of the people and drawing a line for the Sanctum here."

"I'm well aware," Glenbark said. "What would you suggest we do?"

Franco considered. "Starting on the defense? I'd humanize our so-called demons. As Haldin points out, the people could use a clear reminder of all the good he and the rest of our friendly Shapers have done. But first we have to humanize them. Especially Haldin. He's plastered the reels for cycles now, but the world barely knows who he actually is underneath the teenage Legion discharge who's been at the root of multiple controversies and can accomplish physical feats no normal man could dream of. That's hardly a character to empathize with."

"I told you you needed a publicist, broto," Johnny murmured beside me.

I was too busy staring at Franco. "The High Cleric declares open war, and you want me to counter with an interview?"

"It's perfect," Franco said. He looked to Glenbark, who looked to General Hopper, who looked skeptically at me and finally shrugged.

"He'd better be an Alpha-blessed delight on camera if we actually want it to do any good."

For some reason, Four chose that moment to let out a derisive snort.

"Hey, it's not like it could do any *more* harm at this point, right?" Johnny asked. "What?" he immediately added at the array of frowns from around the table. "No such thing as bad reel coverage and all that, right? You know, except for… all those vids of Hal that… landed us right where…" He looked around, scrunching his face. "Yeah, I guess I'll stop talking now."

"I think that's a wise move, legionnaire," Hopper said, glancing at his own servitor, who was gaping at Johnny with some combination of horror and reverence.

"We simply need to see to it that Hal is properly prepared," Franco said. "And paired with a friendly interviewer, of course."

Of course.

It was just that finding a friendly interviewer—or getting significant coverage at all outside of emergency Legion channels—was probably going to be about as easy as tickling a haga beast's underbelly and living to tell about it. I was opening my mouth to point that out when Glenbark brought a pause to the discussion with a raised hand, touching lightly at her earpiece with the other.

"Acknowledged," she said, trading a look with General Hopper as she listened to some report. "Standby."

"He's here?" Hopper asked, looking none too pleased about it.

Glenbark's curt nod only sparked my curiosity. She turned to study our assembly like she was wondering whether or not to call it to an end.

"This is an internal Legion affair," Hopper said.

"True," Glenbark said. "But I'd say Citizen Raish has the right to face the man who's tried twice now to stab him in his sleep."

Hopper looked at me and my civilian friends and said nothing. I said nothing right back, pretty sure I knew *who* they were talking about, but not *what*. Glenbark was already touching her earpiece, decision made.

"Send him in. Alone."

Seconds later, the door slid open, and my suspicions were confirmed by the balding old man who appeared in the doorway, garbed in Legion general's tunic, his body as soft as his eyes were hard.

General Gregor Auckus took in the room with a casual sneer. "Ah, wonderful, the civilian brigade is here. Imagine my surprise. Freya." He spoke Glenbark's common name like a curse that somehow marginally seemed to sound like a greeting, then fixed his beady eyes on me. "Demon."

I said nothing, unable to imagine how any good could come of it, more concerned with what he was doing here now. Auckus had already taken his first strolling steps into the room before his eyes found General Hopper and narrowed suspiciously.

"Have a seat, Gregor," Hopper said. "It's been too long."

For a second, I almost thought Auckus might turn and run. "What is this?" he demanded instead, his glare shifting from Hopper to Glenbark. "Why are they here?"

"For the truth," Glenbark said. "Sit, Gregor."

Auckus teetered, clearly hesitant to even concede that much to her, but finally he sank into the empty chair at the head of the table, and quickly shifted gears to the task of trying to look like he owned the place.

Glenbark watched until he was settled, then crossed her hands on the table and spoke plainly. "I won't mince words, General Auckus. Have you been in contact with Sanctum personnel today?"

He didn't look at her, just stared straight at me. "Does it matter what I say?"

"Did you or did you not communicate classified operational information outside of sanctioned channels?" Glenbark asked, as if he hadn't spoken at all.

And that's when it hit me. Something about the way Auckus was staring at me, and the tickle of intuition that'd been nagging in the background since Johnny and I had escaped our first tavern brawl this morning to the tune of the High Cleric's sudden declaration of war mere hours later.

How had the WAN even known I was in the slums at all?

I'd assumed someone might've recognized Elise or Four from the reels, or might've even spotted the 51st Hounds, put two and two together, and made a lucky guess. I'd even bounced around a few hare-brained theories involving advanced scanners, telepathic spies, and Alton Parker's devious games.

But the much simpler explanation was that someone had simply told them where to find me.

"Sanctioned channels," Auckus practically spat, finally tearing his gaze away from me and back to Glenbark. "Sanctioned like this abomination of a meeting? Tell me, what worth are sanctioned channels when our own High General sits council with demons and civilians?"

"Check the records, Gregor," Hopper said. "There's not a single person here without the proper security clearance, civilian or otherwise."

Auckus showed him a snarl that might've made a wolf envious.

"The legality of this meeting is not currently in question," Glenbark said before he could actually speak—or bite. "General Auckus, did you or did you not communicate classified operational information outside of sanctioned channels?"

Auckus looked back and forth between her and Hopper before finally settling on me. "You've snuck into both of their minds, haven't you, Demon? Crawled right in and—"

"Answer the question, Gregor," Glenbark said.

He crossed his arms. "No. I will not. I will not stand trial in the presence of four established telepaths."

"You are not being offered the choice."

"No?" A slow, scud-eating grin stretched Auckus' mouth. "Then I call for an emergency meeting of the high command."

The slimy bastard.

Not that I hadn't already known that about him. In addition to being a crusty curmudgeon and an alleged womanizer, Gregor Auckus had also smuggled one of the Seekers, Siren, on base to fulfill her Sanctum orders to kill me during my post-Humility stay in the medica—the first of the two back-stabbings to which Glenbark had referred a minute ago.

He was a fully certified pain in our asses, that was for sure. But for him to resort to abusing the protocols and calling an emergency meeting just to get us out of the room...

His slimy bastard smile only grew as he took in Hopper's surprised look and Glenbark's resolutely blank one.

"You understand this does not excuse you from the current line of inquiry?" Glenbark asked.

Auckus raised an eyebrow, unperturbed. "Do you deny my right to call this meeting?"

"Of course not." Glenbark watched him for a few moments as if expecting he might rethink his childish move, then finally gave up and turned to us. "Very well. I'm going to have to ask you all to cede the room for an emergency convening of the high command."

We all exchanged a look, and rose from the table. Dillard and the two captains looked almost as discombobulated as the rest of us. Johnny and

Hopper's twitchy servitor both hopped to Glenbark's order to put out word to the remaining ten generals. The rest of us drifted toward the door until Glenbark turned to address us.

"If you could all wait outside, I'd like to finish our discussion afterward. This shouldn't take long," she added, with a meaningful look at General Auckus.

He ignored her, turning to shoot one last disdainful look at me and Elise.

"Do be careful out there, Demon," he said. "I'm told there's a war coming."

I held his venomous gaze, wanting to say something, to show him I wasn't afraid. Except I was. I could've broken the crusty old man like so many twigs, and yet in that moment, I felt more powerless than I could explain. Because what good would breaking him do? What good could I do at all?

The ball was already rolling. And it was a damn big one.

Glenbark caught my eye and gently gestured for me to step outside. I turned for the door, trying to reassure myself that Gregor Auckus was about to get what was coming to him. No matter how hard I tried, though, I couldn't quite ignore the sinking feeling that the slimy bastard had somehow just gotten exactly what he'd wanted all along.

7

PUBLIC OPINION

I refreshed my tablet for what must've been the hundredth time in the past fifteen minutes. Nothing. Well, not unless you counted the flood of replays and breakdowns of the High Cleric's impromptu confession and declaration of war. But no sign yet of the stories I was waiting for.

At least the High Cleric's bold performance had almost pushed my name —or the Demon of Divinity's—out of the day's top headlines. Almost. There were still a couple pieces about the mess in the tavern that morning, of course, but whatever. Small victories.

"Stop brooding and come hold me," Elise mumbled sleepily from the bundle of blankets beside me.

I set the tablet aside, unable to hold back a small smile despite everything. It never ceased to amaze me how, with just a few words, sometimes even with just her presence alone, Elise could simply yank me away from the darkness and straight to a place where I was floating at peace.

"I wasn't brooding," I said, burrowing in next to her and pulling her close. "Just waiting for Glenbark's statement to go live."

Elise made a noncommittal noise and snuggled into me.

"Besides," I added, "since when are you the one who needs to be held?"

"Maybe I'm scared," she said in what might've been a playful tone.

I stroked her hair, thinking. "Are you?"

She tilted her head a few inches to study me, and it wasn't playfulness I saw in her eyes. "We should probably figure out exactly what you're gonna say tomorrow."

"If I didn't know better, I'd say you were worried I was gonna mess this thing up."

"Well..." She kissed my cheek and sat up. "It's a very mess-upable situation."

I frowned up at those beautiful blue eyes. "If this is supposed to be a pep talk..."

She smiled down at me and gave me a firm pat on the leg. "Come on. Let's go."

"I thought I was holding you," I groaned. "Can't we just be happy we won today?"

She paused halfway out of bed to arch an eyebrow at me. "We both had multiple attempts made on our lives, and the High Cleric gave the go-ahead for all of Enochia to take another shot tomorrow. You call that a win?"

I shrugged, not really sure how to counter the point—even if Gregor Auckus *had* been discharged for insubordination, with immediate effect, during the high council's emergency meeting earlier that day.

"At least Auckus is gone," I finally said, but my voice sounded deflated even to my own ears.

The slimy bastard, I didn't add.

"Gone for now," Elise corrected me. "But I didn't like the look that slimy bastard gave us when he—What? Why are you smiling like that?"

"I just love you. That's all." The smile slid from my face as my thoughts turned from Elise's perfect choice of words back to Auckus himself. "But yeah, I didn't like it either."

"He still has too many connections here," Elise said, rising to pace the room. She didn't elaborate, but I understood just fine. I shared the same worries.

Summary Legion discharge or no, the day's "victory" might have come as more of a relief if the multiple counts of treason had actually managed to stick to Auckus alongside the charges of insubordination. Whether or not Gregor Auckus actually deserved to hang for what he'd done, as would've been the case for a condemned traitor, I couldn't say. But it hardly mattered now. He'd wiggled free from those charges on some bullscud technicalities. Not that I was surprised by that part. Honestly, I hadn't even thought to hope he would be discharged at all. The last time a general had been discharged—with the exception of Adrian Kublich, posthumously—had been well before I was born.

It was a big deal.

But even as relieved as I was, knowing Auckus wouldn't be readily able to sabotage our plans anymore, at this point, it was really only good news in the way that a dingy, hole-riddled raft would've been good news in the middle of a raging sea storm. Sure, it was something to hold on to. But it hardly meant you were safe from drowning.

From what little Glenbark had told us, the generals of high command had been furious about the entire incident. Auckus had been far from the most popular of their rank, but he'd also been general for a long time. He had allies among the twelve, and even if he hadn't, none of them were happy to see a general of the Legion brought to shame. I doubted they would have agreed to a full discharge if there'd been any choice—especially not when at least half of them probably privately thought his actions justified.

Glenbark hadn't said as much publicly, but I had a feeling General Hopper was in the minority by supporting her in her decision to draw a line and stand up to the Sanctum on the issue of Shaper genocide.

All that to say, the remainder of our war-room talk with Glenbark and the others had been rather grim following Auckus' heated departure.

As Franco had pointed out, aside from the defensive route of clearing up the facts and playing public relations for Shapers like me, the other option was pretty much limited to reminding the public that all law-abiding Enochians were sworn to be protected under Legion law—regardless of what the Sanctum said—and that genocide was explicitly *not* okay. Which probably should've gone without saying. But seeing as it apparently hadn't, there was really only one other option, short of storming the White Tower and pulling a full military coup of the planet.

If it was to be a war of truths and public opinions, the only other option was to attack the authority of the Sanctum and the High Cleric himself.

And that had been about all the further we got before the meeting had fallen to pieces. One of the captains had stood and stiffly requested to be removed from the small council, even should it be on pain of death or discharge. The rest of the room hadn't been much better. And even after everything, I wasn't sure I could blame them. I still couldn't help but wonder if my dad wouldn't have said the same thing. Scud, even after they'd made multiple attempts on my life, it still made me uncomfortable even thinking about publicly speaking out against the Sanctum.

They had a word for that kind of thing. Blasphemy.

I think it had been the first time I'd ever seen Glenbark's face betray real uncertainty, as she'd sat there, mulling over the situation. Finally, though, she'd invited the captain sit, and had drawn her own line in the sand.

"I assure you," she'd said, "there will be no smear campaign against the Sanctum. We will not fight dirty. But so long as this Legion is mine to command, nor will we ever willingly turn away from hard facts, even if those facts may be damaging to that which we hold dearest in our hearts. Our duty is to Enochia, to justice, and to Alpha—not to the Sanctum. The last two are not inseparable, no matter how much we might wish to believe it so."

I hadn't missed the look Franco had shot me at the part about never willingly turning away from hard facts. I hadn't needed to ask him what he was thinking, either, because I was pretty sure it was exactly what I'd been thinking about from the moment he'd first mentioned attacking the Sanctum's credibility: the ancient image we'd seen of the holy prophet Sarentus, facing down the last of the Emmútari, his eyes drawn in crimson that, even faded with age, all too closely resembled the eyes of a raknoth. The image that implied, however tenuously, that the entire gropping Sanctum might've been built on more than just the still-burning ashes of the ancient Emmútari peacekeepers.

It was ludicrous to think. Utterly ridiculous. So much so that neither of us had told anyone but Elise about the picture since having been captured back in Humility. Regardless, it was outside the scope of the plan at this point anyway. Glenbark had called a wrap on the meeting shortly after we'd hit our little existential snag. This evening, she would release a public statement to calm the waters—or to hopefully at least keep them from boiling into the streets tonight, thick with the blood of innocents. Tomorrow, I was to get in front of a camera and play nice.

Of course, none of us expected the WAN would be rushing to send over a friendly interviewer, but Franco had had an answer for that as well.

Barbara Sanders.

Barbara was one of Divinity's most beloved field reporters—the type of inquisitive but kind spirit who could deliver even the grimmest of stories with a gentle touch of dignity. She was also, as one of the captains had skeptically pointed out, a longtime associate of the WAN, which meant taking this job might well mean career suicide for her now that the High Cleric had declared war. Franco, though, had been sure that Barbara would be in. And he hadn't been wrong.

Barbara had jumped on the interview invitation with frightening speed.

I wasn't all that surprised. She'd been relentlessly trying to get my full story ever since we'd crossed paths at the White Tower, where she'd more than earned the right to hear it. Because that was the one part no one but us ex-renegades knew about that awful day: Barbara Sanders had saved my life at the Sanctum gallows.

But instead of taking her up on her generous offer to sit down with me and set the record straight for Enochia when it might've actually done some good, I'd spent the next cycles wallowing in a dark corner over the loss of Carlisle and my parents, right up until guilt and the resurgence of the hybrid army had jolted me into the action that'd seen my reputation burning, bit by controversial bit. Ignoring Barbara's standing offer all the while. Convinced I was dealing with the real threats. Outraged that the rest of the world couldn't see it that way, when really...

"I really gropped this up, huh?"

Elise paused in her pacing to look at me. "What do you mean?"

"Just... all of it," I said, not really sure how to encompass the entirety of what I was feeling.

Maybe it didn't matter. Maybe I'd already sat in my corner for too long, not bothering to do anything but fume as I'd been demonized again and again. At this point, I wasn't sure half of Enochia wouldn't simply power down their displays the moment I showed up and opened my mouth. But we had to try something, right?

Elise came and sat beside me, taking my hand in hers. "I think you need to give credit where it's due. It took a whole planet working together to grop things up this bad. We just need to remind the world that, at the end of the day, we all want the same thing, more or less."

I looked at her and wondered—not for the first time—if she shouldn't be the one to do this whole interview dance. I understood why Glenbark and the others thought it was best to start with me. I was the two-thousand pound haga beast in the room, so to speak—the dark hooded figure who had to be properly unshrouded before any of the Alpha-fearing people out there would even think twice about accepting the Shapers of Enochia as anything but the kin of the terrible Demon of Divinity.

They needed to see that even the worst of us could be good and kind.

Then again, if we wanted to put an empathetic face on the world of Shaping, I was also pretty sure we'd be hard-pressed to find a better face than Elise's. She was beautiful. Brilliant. Immediately likeable. More importantly, she was not me. She was better than me.

All that said, though, I also couldn't ignore the fact that putting her in the public spotlight in my place would effectively be the same as painting a few million Alpha-fearing crosshairs straight on her forehead. And grop that.

"I still think it's kind of silly," I finally said, "letting our hopes and futures ride on a gropping interview."

"Sillier than letting it all ride on a blade or a few choice slugs, you mean?"

And there was that charming wit that made her ten times better equipped than me for this kind of thing.

"Is it too late for us to just run away together?" I asked, stroking her cheek.

She stood, smiling, and tugged at my hand. "Come on, flyboy. We've got some empathy to go digging for."

Her smile was contagious, and this time I didn't resist. She pulled me into the living room, and we sat down to search for some usable scrap of the respectable, perhaps even charming tyro I'd once been, and to get that shiny veneer ready for the cameras.

It wasn't exactly how I'd ever imagined the push for Shaper liberty might begin, but I guess it wasn't such a bad start, either. Barbara Sanders, beloved reporter, was on board. General Auckus, miserable treacherous bastard, was sacked. And Elise was right here, looking at me as if she truly believed I could be redeemed in the public eye.

Brewing war aside, it seemed things were actually starting to look up.

At least until I saw the reels the next morning.

8

THE SCOOP

"Haldin?"

I snapped out of my reverie to find Barbara Sanders watching me with keen brown eyes. We sat facing each other across a low lounge table, stocked with two steaming cups of caffa. As if that little detail could force the weight from the air and settle this entire affair back down to a casual chat between two... not friends. Two people. Interviewer and interviewee. Barbara had specifically made as much clear upon her hasty arrival that morning, not because she actually felt unfriendly toward me— quite the opposite, in fact—but simply because she wanted this interview to be taken seriously.

And that, she had warned, meant she was going to have to press me at times.

"I sure hope I'm not boring you..."

From many other people, the words could have easily been a back-handed slight, but coming from Barbara and her genuine if restrained smile, it only sounded like a kindly jest.

"No," I said quickly. "Of course not. I was just..."

"There's something on your mind this morning?"

Slowly, I nodded. It was the first question I really wasn't sure how to answer.

So far, it had all been rather tame—a quick exchange of niceties and a short, simplified introduction to what a Shaper actually was, how they came by the gifts, and what they could and could not do with them. It had been more terrifying than I would've thought, revealing so much so freely to the people who wanted me dead. I felt naked, and I could only imagine half the Shapers on the planet would be cursing my name as they saw this.

But Franco had told me to trust that Barbara knew what she was doing, and I did. She was here to show the world who I was. And seeing as I had nothing to show but a long line of epic failures in that department, I wasn't about to fight her lead in any of this.

Besides, beyond hopefully calming the public's irrational fear of demonic powers, it wasn't like knowing the basics of Shaping was going to hand the people of Enochia any particularly useful tools for finding and eliminating us. The only truly useful tools in that fight had been the Seekers, and the Sanctum was sorely missing those now. Not that that had stopped the enraged masses. Hence my distraction.

"There was disturbing news in the reels this morning," I finally answered. "I guess I'm still getting over the shock of it. I apologize."

"You're referring to the first reported casualties of the Sanctum's war on demons?"

I nodded. "Yes. Though I worry that those casualties may have in fact been innocent victims."

"Do you mean that in the sense that you fundamentally disagree with the High Cleric's imperative?"

I shook my head. "Look, we all know I'd be lying if I said I agreed with the High Cleric's decision to declare war on gifted individuals, but no. When I say innocent victims, what I mean is that I'm worried we might be seeing non-Shaper civilians murdered by an overeager militia."

"A chilling notion," Barbara said gravely. "Though, as I understand it, many clerics have already been instructed to educate their worshipers in the detection and handling of demon kind. Are you saying that these teachings are ineffective?"

I bristled at the absurdity of the statement. I couldn't help it, cameras or no. It was just too ridiculous to think that *anyone* could buy into such bullscud. What were they telling them in there, that you'd just *know* the demons when you saw them? That you'd *feel* the evil taint in the air? And who in their right minds would honestly think mass worship halls of untrained civilians could be taught to handle dangerous hostiles by verbal instruction alone—and by gropping clerics, nonetheless?

At the edge of my vision, behind the camera crew, I caught Franco giving me the gesture to take a deep breath. I did, and the world settled just a touch. "What I'm saying is that the only thing capable of identifying a telepath is another telepath."

Barbara adopted the eyebrow quirk I was coming to read as her *tough question* face. "So when the High Cleric admitted that he and the Sanctum have been fighting a clandestine war against demon kind for decades now, are you implying that he was lying and that the Sanctum in fact lacks the tools to wage such a war?"

Deep breaths. Calm breaths.

I gave her my best apologetic smile. "I'm sorry, Barbara. I came here to try to set the record straight about myself and the Shapers of Enochia. I'd rather not make any wild accusations. If the High Cleric sees fit, I'm sure he can elaborate on what tools the Sanctum has or has not employed against people like me in the past."

Never had I felt so much like I was walking on eggshells.

"In the meanwhile, though," I pushed on, "I would just like to urge anyone out there thinking they've found one of these so-called demons to understand that there's an overwhelming chance they're going to end up murdering innocent civilians in the name of Alpha."

"A bold statement. But I wonder, are you able to quantify it? Do you know how many gifted—that is to say, how many of your kind—are out there across Enochia?"

I shook my head. "Sadly, as far as I know, the only real records that ever existed for people like me were destroyed many centuries ago."

Barbara's brow perked at the word, centuries, but she didn't interrupt as I continued.

"My teacher didn't know exactly, either, but he was under the impression that there likely weren't more than a few hundred of us on the planet, and that very few of those would ever reach a level of proficiency with their abilities to actually be much danger to anyone."

"You say that, and yet we've all seen the footage of the things you can do. Is this to say that you are somehow special among your kind?"

I tried to smile. "Is there a non-conceited answer to that question?"

She showed me the polite facsimile of a smile but was clearly waiting for a more substantial answer.

"Yes," I said. "At the risk of sounding tremendously arrogant, as far as I understand, my abilities have developed much more rapidly than most Shapers experience. My teacher was the only Shaper I knew who exhibited a similar... affinity."

"And does that fact alone not make you question the nature of your own abilities? How can you be so sure you are not playing host to demons?"

I swallowed. Alpha, was my mouth dry. I went for a sip of caffa, immediately started worrying the move looked suspicious, burnt the ever-loving scud out of my mouth, and sat back, trying to look thoughtful and not like I was about to scream.

"Well, it might be a bad comparison, but take someone like Tamar Reinski."

"The smashball world league superstar," Barbara clarified, clearly more for the audience than herself.

"Exactly. I haven't had much time to watch lately, but I know enough to know Reinski consistently pulls smashes no one else would ever dream of, and I don't see anyone questioning whether he's making deals with demons."

"Perhaps that's because he hasn't plucked any crashing Legion transports from plummeting to certain death with the power of his mind."

I tried to smile. "Well then maybe we should trade pay grades."

Alpha, how much more arrogant could I possibly sound? At least Barbara's smile looked genuine this time.

"You asked how I could be sure I'm not playing host to the demons. I guess I can't give any definitive answer that doesn't require some level of trust. But can anyone? What does a demon even look like? Can any of us say with full certainty that we're not touched by these things? What I do know is that there were twenty-six lives aboard that transport on the day you refer to, including the High General of the Legion. I did what I could to save them, and nothing inside tried to stop me. I can't prove an absence of evil in my spirit. I'm not sure anyone can. But I struggle to see how the number of lives I've bled to save is inconsequential in the discussion."

Barbara shifted back in her chair, nodding slowly as if digesting the thought. Behind the camera line, Franco gave me a dignified thumbs-up. That, at least, made me feel a bit better. I honestly couldn't tell how much of this interview was Barbara the WAN Reporter versus Barbara the Ally. Maybe they were one in the same. I didn't know. But whether her reactions and questions were completely off the cuff or carefully designed, she seemed to be leading me in the right direction.

"Let's talk about your teacher," she said, carefully picking up her caffa for the first time. "When did you first meet Carlisle?"

I was halfway into my standard reaction of steeling myself when I remembered what Franco and Elise had both emphatically coached. *Don't hide the emotion. Don't try to be a shiny hero. Let them see the pain.*

"I met Carlisle the night my parents were killed by the raknoth that had once been Adrian Kublich. Carlisle saved my life that night. Once from Kublich, then again from… one of the Sanctum's Shaper hunters."

Barbara cocked her head slightly. "The Sanctum came for you that night?"

"I think they were actually looking for Carlisle, but yes, they found me. I learned later that it was the trauma of losing my… of what I saw that night that flipped the switch on my latent abilities and put me in their sights."

"And even then, realizing that you had awoken something that put you in the crosshairs of the Sanctum itself, you didn't fear that these abilities of yours were born of darkness?"

"Of course I did. At first, I didn't understand what was happening at all. But once Carlisle showed me what he could do… Well, if I hadn't already witnessed my own High General growing scales and red eyes and… doing what he did to my parents, I don't think I would've believed it at all."

"Your world was shattered."

That drew my attention back to the present. I forced myself to meet Barbara's eyes, and something about the look she was giving me made me feel it all in a way that I hadn't since before the White Tower. "I guess that's a fair way to put it."

I actually felt the pressure of tears beginning to flirt with the idea of making an appearance.

Then Barbara's *tough question* look returned without warning. "Do you think it's possible that experience has in any way affected your grip on reality?"

I'm not sure if I actually rocked back in my chair or not, but I certainly did mentally—shuffling to gather my thoughts and pivot, and to remind myself that I shouldn't feel emotionally betrayed. This was her job, after all, and she'd told me she was going to press me at times.

"If I'd been alone in a dark room all this time," I finally started, "I admit I might still be asking myself that same question. For a while, I thought I might be losing it, that I'd had some kind of mental break. I mean, the High General of the Legion, possessed by some red-eyed monster? And then all this with the Shaping…"

Without really thinking about it, I fixed my senses on my caffa cup and telekinetically levitated it up to float between us.

"It was a lot to take in, you know?"

Barbara, who'd *actually* rocked back in her chair at the telekinetic demonstration, gave a slow nod, her eyes riveted to the floating cup and her fingers touching the sigil of Alpha that hung from a silver chain at her breastbone. I couldn't tell if the shocked display was for show or not.

"But the raknoth *are* real," I pushed on, hastily lowering the caffa cup back to the table. "Unfortunately, Enochia has learned that the hard way. So to answer your question, no, I don't think my experiences have impaired my grip on reality. I just wish we could've done a better job of convincing the rest of the world sooner."

And that the Sanctum hadn't been desperately trying to eradicate our only defense against them the entire time, I wanted to add, but that wasn't the name of this game. Play nice. Be human. That was the goal. Even if the Sanctum refused to acknowledge those rules.

"What about your parents?" Barbara asked. "What do you think they would say to you if they were still alive today?"

I shifted in my seat, hesitant to come right out with it. Unlike some of Barbara's questions today, I'd thought about this one frequently. Still did. It was probably one of the most humanizing questions she could've asked. And it was also the one I was least excited to open up about. If there was anything left that truly belonged to me and no one else, it was the memories of my parents.

But there wasn't room for such things to be sacred anymore.

"My dad… He was a man of faith. In Alpha. In the Legion. In all my years as a tyro, I don't think I ever met someone more disciplined." I smiled a little, remembering the way he used to sort of flip a switch when he'd arrive home and, with a relieved sigh, finally sink onto the couch with my mom and me—still disciplined, no doubt, but in a casual, fatherly-husbandly sort of way. I'd never realized back then just how good he'd been at flipping that switch.

I realized I'd drifted.

"I guess that's why it always seemed kind of funny that the one thing he used to tell me, above all else, was to always do what I thought was right, no matter the consequences. Trust in Alpha, he said. Follow your orders as best as humanly possible. Don't even think about second-guessing a superior because you think you know how to do the job better. But never let anyone force you to do something you know in your heart is not right." I showed Barbara a wan smile. "Coming from a decorated captain prime, I always thought it was kind of hypocritical. At least until I heard the full story about how he earned all those decorations."

"And how was that?"

"He did what he knew was right. He disobeyed a direct order that he knew would get his legionnaires slaughtered, found another way to accomplish the objective, and ended up delivering the blow the historians would come to agree was the turning point of the Durin Uprising."

I looked over, half-expecting Barbara to point out that maybe it wasn't as noble as I thought, having been taught life lessons by a man who, some still bickered, had technically been grossly insubordinate, but she only watched, waiting for me to continue.

"To answer your question, I don't really know what my parents would've thought of all this. All I know is that I regret it every day that my gifts awoke too late to save them. If I'd sensed what Kublich was sooner..." I shook my head. "I know it's too late now. But it's hard to ignore the fact that if there'd been more Shapers on Enochia to sound the warning bells, the raknoth might never have succeeded at sneaking their way into positions of power to start with. The number of lives that might've been saved..."

I fumbled, grasping for the right words, suddenly unable to find them now that I'd arrived at the most important of points. How did I make the world understand this? How did I make them believe?

The *tough question* look came out.

"Do you believe in Alpha, Haldin?"

A shot of panic hit. I'd known the question would likely be asked, but now wasn't the time—was the worst possible time. Still tangled on the point of proving the worldwide worth of Shapers, I looked to Franco for guidance. He laid his open hand over his heart, his expression solemn.

The truth. Just like we'd agreed.

I looked at Barbara.

"I thought I did. Still think I do, a lot of the time."

"But you're uncertain."

I stared at the table between us, wondering how best to put it in a way that the average Alpha-fearing worshiper might actually be able to understand—not simply the presence or lack of faith in Alpha, but everything that flowed from that one crucial factor.

It wasn't possible. It just wasn't. I ran through every variation of the answers we'd talked about last night, and they all came up sounding like polymer garbage. It was impossible to show them the truth within the confines of their even stronger beliefs.

And if it was impossible to show them the truth, I decided, I might as well just show them the impossible.

What could possibly go wrong? said Johnny's voice in my head, almost as clearly as if my redheaded friend had achieved telepathy and reached out to offer his encouragement. That alone probably should've cued me that this was a brash course of action, but I didn't know how else to save face from my lengthy silence at this point.

I reached out and floated my caffa cup off the table with telekinesis, then I went one step further and lifted the fluid itself up to hover over the cup in a lightly-steaming mass that held its shape when every law of nature said it should fall back to the cup and splash down to the table in a dark mess.

"Oh..." came Barbara's surprised murmur.

But I wasn't done. Even as much as I'd practiced, the next part wasn't effortless. I might not have called it difficult, but I did have to focus pretty carefully to hold the cup aloft while I shifted the mental construct holding the caffa, elongating, straightening, and then bending and adding details until the dark fluid floated in a singular replica of the sigil of Alpha. That done, I drained thermal energy from my liquid sculpture until it froze solid, then allowed the icy sigil to drift down to my waiting hand.

"I've seen a lot of strange things these past seasons," I finally said, offering the frozen sculpture to Barbara and allowing the empty cup to resume its place on the table. "Things that don't fit into the picture as they should. And maybe that *does* mean it's all demonic evil. But personally, I'm starting to think it might just be that we don't actually have the complete picture just yet."

Hesitantly, she leaned forward and took the dark sigil. It was already starting to melt a little where our fingers touched it—caffa not being all that prone to easy freezing. Barbara didn't seem to mind, though. She stared at the thing in open wonder.

"Not to downplay this admittedly marvelous spectacle," she said slowly, finally pulling her eyes up to meet mine, "but I don't believe you answered the original question."

I smiled and offered her my empty cup to relieve her of the melting sigil. "If you want the honest answer, it's that I don't know what to believe anymore. I know that I can do things that frighten a lot of people."

She plopped the sigil in the cup, still watching it attentively.

I set the cup down. "I know that we live in a universe where the raknoth exist. Whether we want to call them aliens and admit that there could be more like them out there, or if we just call them demons and leave it at that, the end result is still that they are real, and that they're a threat to this planet. A threat that needs to be stopped and safeguarded against for future generations. That's all I'm trying to do here. But it's not something we can accomplish without Shapers."

"And what would you say to those who argue the raknoth invasion only happened because of demons, or Shapers as you say?"

I swallowed the bitter insults that first sprang to mind and calmly spread my hands. "I'd ask them to consider the fact that the raknoth had already taken control of both the previous High General and the previous High Cleric before people like Carlisle and myself—people who are now being called demons—discovered their ploy and risked our lives to expose it. I understand that what I can do seems unnatural, but please, before you call for Shaper heads, please imagine what would've happened here if people like Carlisle had never existed. The raknoth were cycles away from completing an entire factory fitted to breed hybrids and drain human blood, and the vast majority of the planet had no idea about any of it. If that thought scares any of you out there half as much as it scares me, then please, let's talk about this before we turn to genocide in the name of a holy war. Let's see to it that Enochia is safe. I can't make you accept me or those like me. But I intend to finish driving the raknoth from this planet, and I'd prefer it if we could all pause for a moment and consider that the only way we can be sure the planet is safe moving forward is if we can all stand together and appreciate what each side can bring to the table."

Barbara let that sit in silence for a long stretch—at first, I thought, to simply allow the words to soak in. But then I noticed she was shooting furtive glances over at Franco and her crew.

"Well," she said, pointedly pulling her focus back to me, "whether or not you find the peace you're looking for, I think we can all agree the protection of Enochia's future is an admirable sentiment." She leaned in and offered me her slender hand. "Haldin Raish, it's been an honor. And quite an eye-opening one," she added, with a meaningful look at the now mostly melted Alpha sigil in my caffa cup. "Thank you for sharing your story with me and the rest of Enochia."

"Thank you for hearing it," I replied, shaking her hand. "I just hope it's worth something, and that we can all talk about this openly before any more triggers are pulled."

Barbara gestured to her crew to cut the feed. As soon as they did and gave her a thumbs-up, she stood, her polite smile darkening.

"What is it?" she asked, scanning her crew. "What's happened?"

So I *hadn't* imagined the looks. My stomach sank as Franco glanced over one of the crew members' shoulders and his face fell.

And here I'd been thinking that this had actually gone well. Certainly better than expected.

"I think we just got scooped, boss," one of the cameramen said, looking up from the tablet they were all huddled over.

"Scooped?" Barbara said, stalking over to them to see for herself. "What do you mean scooped?"

It was a fair question, seeing as it wasn't like there was another team here sneak-recording our talk. The cameraman handed Barbara the tablet. She read for a few seconds, muttered a curse, and looked to me.

"You'd better see this, Haldin."

I opened my palmlight and pulled up the reels, already pretty sure I knew what I could expect. It was truly starting to feel like the story of my life. If Johnny's adage about "no such thing as bad reel coverage" had ever been true for anyone, it sure as scud wasn't me. So, it wasn't with surprise or shock but simply with a dull, weary sickened feeling that I spotted the headline currently taking the reels by storm, complete with an Alpha-damned feature length storyvid.

Haldin Raish: The True Story of the Demon of Divinity.

9

POINT OF VIEW

Ever since I'd lost my parents and fled Sanctuary under Carlisle's protective wing, I'd seen my name—and the names of pretty much everyone I knew—dragged through all manner of mud, scud, and everything in between.

I'd been branded a terrorist. Accused of killing my own parents and burning my house down. I'd read stories that Carlisle and I were in fact criminal masterminds who'd simply fabricated the entire raknoth invasion. Carlisle was obviously still alive, some such stories suggested, pulling the strings from behind the scenes. Those red eyes? Lighted lenses. Those scaly hybrids? Cosmetics, broto. Cosmetics.

There'd even been spliced vids that made it look like it had actually been me and Carlisle batting down civilians and tearing out throats back when the hybrids had first been released on the Great Hall.

This was worse than all of that.

The Sanctum's feature didn't grasp at wild straws. It did much worse. It told the truth—or enough of the truth that I doubted anyone would know or care to spot the difference. It hit at every spot that hurt—my every flaw and weakness.

Point by point, the Sanctum deconstructed me for all of Enochia to see.

Barbara was sure that the timing wasn't a coincidence, and that someone, either on our end or hers, must've told the Sanctum what we were planning. Someone like a recently discharged and highly disgruntled Legion general, perhaps. Or maybe it had simply been Barbara's supervisor, looking to save her own skin before her daring little reporter earned the wrath of the Sanctum. It hardly seemed to matter at this point.

Once I'd gotten the measure of just how deep the thing was going to dive, I'd turned to leave, not really sure where I was going, only that I didn't want to watch my deconstruction alongside Barbara and a crew of complete strangers. Franco had reminded me that I couldn't just go strolling around base at my leisure—especially not now.

Which was how I'd wound up in a dark, cramped storage closet somewhere in the east wing of Central Command, staring at my palmlight in a kind of dumb stupor, just watching it all fall apart.

The so-called *True Story of the Demon of Divinity* had been shot in a series of presentation-style talks from multiple witnesses who'd been well-positioned to chronicle my every failure and shortcoming. We heard from the High Cleric about what a troubled spirit I'd been when we met in his White Tower quarters, and how he'd been wrong to allow High General Glenbark to wrestle me out from the Sanctum's grasp in the name of Enochian safety. We heard from Vantage guards and legionnaires I'd tangled with while on the run, who all unanimously attested to my savage nature, and from old tyro rivals about how I'd always been one to bend orders and stray from Alpha's path when possible. We heard from that lowlife, tavern-brawling bastard, Captain Man Glare, about how he and his brotos had tried to quietly alert the authorities to my presence and had suffered my immediate and gratuitous wrath.

The performances were all so good that I couldn't help but wonder if they hadn't been paid for by the Sanctum—or if maybe there wasn't a small grain of truth to them after all. To people like the men and women who'd diligently guarded the Vantage facility, ignorant to what was going on beneath their feet, I suppose I probably *hadn't* seemed like anything more than a violent criminal at the time.

It wasn't a comforting realization.

By the time the vid cut to the vengeful face of General Gregor Auckus, I couldn't even bring myself to feel surprised. I still felt plenty of other things, though, as Auckus proceeded to unload with a scathing and surprisingly surgical analysis of my value—or total lack thereof—to the Legion's wartime efforts against the hybrid armies over the past cycles. It was masterfully done, the way he painted everything from just the right angle. To listen to him, I'd basically let Alton Parker escape, endangered the lives of my assigned guard details more times than anyone could seem to count, disobeyed direct orders a similar number of times, and somehow sparked multiple hybrid attacks of unprecedented scope on both civilian and Legion targets. And all that just so I could spit on some pieces of scrap metal and tell High General Glenbark that I'd magically "protected" her legions from "unfriendly minds."

I almost started to believe it myself.

Never mind that there was well-documented evidence of widespread friendly fire chaos among the ranks prior to receiving my cloaking packs, and almost no such reported incidents since. My aid could hardly be counted in the retaking of Oasis anyway, Auckus argued, because I hadn't even cared enough to *attend* the assault. No, I'd been too busy sneaking off with my personal company of Hounds to rendezvous with the very creature who'd tried to kill the High General not two days earlier.

So whose side was I on? Alpha only knew. But I was clearly nothing but a danger to the Legion. A bumbling time bomb who had the High General firmly wrapped around my finger. Never mind all the lives that I had saved, or the fact that Glenbark had indeed put me on strict house arrest for bucking orders. To listen to Auckus talk, I did what I wanted, when I wanted, and Glenbark had unlawfully discharged him for trying to restore sanity to his beloved Legion.

The slimy bastard.

Tenuous as my hopes had been to start with, I had little doubt that Auckus' confessions alone would've been more than enough to drive the wedge of death straight through all my talk of peace in Barbara's interview. But that wasn't even the end of it.

I didn't recognize the legionnaire who came on after Auckus had finished speculating about how long it would be until I succeeded at handing the entire Legion over to the raknoth—one of whom I was routinely meeting with on Haven grounds, by the way. Whoever he was, I couldn't imagine he could do worse than Auckus just had. But then he began to explain how he'd been there the night his company had raided Franco's home after the attack on the Vantage research facility, seeking to apprehend the terrorists responsible. And that's when it hit me.

The one and only non-telepath I'd ever forced my mind on. And they'd found him.

I cringed as he described in vivid detail what it had felt like, sweeping an enemy hideout next to his fireteam one moment only to find that he couldn't move a muscle the next. For a second, he'd expected to fall. He'd thought maybe he'd been shot and his senses hadn't caught up, or that maybe he was even having a heart attack, or a massive brain bleed. But then he'd noticed his body *was* moving, by no will of his own. He'd tried to stop it, as the air had filled with a demonic flash, and he'd felt his hands reaching for the grenades on his vest. Tried to stop it as he'd felt himself pulling the pins and throwing himself at his own squad—his own little family. He'd tried to stop it as he'd listened to his friends screaming in shocked betrayal. And he'd been powerless to do a thing.

I felt sick.

I'd only been doing what I could to buy us time to escape Franco's, and the fact that he was alive at all should've made it clear enough that I hadn't actually killed anyone with the unsavory maneuver—that it had been thumpers, I'd used, and not lethal frags. But none of that made me feel any less despicable, seeing the pain on that poor legionnaire's face.

I'd crossed a line that night. One I'd been too new to Shaping to even realize I'd been about to cross. But now it was done, and here were the repercussions, come to collect their due.

Of course, the guy hadn't actually realized what had happened to him until after the raknoth had started pulling the same move on large swaths of Legion forces at Oasis. Still, though, he'd been uncertain. Because he hadn't been hunting a raknoth that night. He'd been trying to apprehend Haldin Raish and his partner, Carlisle. And how could Haldin Raish have pulled the same trick as a raknoth? Unless…

I paused the vid. It was all too clear where they were headed with this, and I couldn't take any more of it.

I sat in the darkness, trying to focus on my breathing and the dull background buzz of distant activity. Trying to focus on anything that wasn't the Sanctum, or General Auckus, or the raging scudstorm that was breaking across Enochia—more dangerous to my kind than any hybrid army.

And I didn't have the faintest clue what to do about any of it.

At the faint brush of a presence outside the door, I reflexively jammed the mechanism with telekinesis. Someone turned the handle.

"Let us in, Hal," came Elise's voice.

I released my hold and didn't even bother trying to look dignified as the door swung open. There were Elise and Johnny, standing in the hallway, and there I was, stuffed in a corner beside racks of sweeper bots and cleaning supplies like a moody stowaway. They didn't say a word. Just stepped carefully into the cramped space and pulled the door shut behind them.

Darkness enclosed us, thick enough that I could barely see Johnny and

Elise as they tried to situate themselves. For some reason, none of us spoke. None of us even activated a palmlight to illuminate the space. Elise wriggled into my corner on my left, her legs draped over mine, and Johnny found some arrangement that left him against the opposite side of the closet with his legs stacked over Elise's and more or less in my face.

"So glad you decided to join me," I muttered.

"It's actually kinda nice in here," Johnny said when he'd finally stopped shuffling around. "You've got your complete darkness, and your quiet, and your cozy little fit, and… hmm, not entirely sure what I'm touching right now, but that seems nice, too."

He continued on like that for a little while, saying a lot about nothing in particular, as he often did when he was especially uncomfortable. Elise just sat there silently running her hand through my hair all the while.

"So much for getting ahead of this thing," I said when Johnny's running narrative had finally died down.

"Yeah…" Johnny said. "But honestly, broto, were we ever *really* ahead of this thing to start with? It's kinda been mayhem from day one. Scud, I was even ready to shoot you back then, remember?"

"Aww," Elise said. "Back when we first met."

"Yeah, right? And look how that all turned out. We're golden."

"You were never gonna shoot me," I said.

"Well, yeah," Johnny said slowly. "But I thought about it. Like really, *really* thought about it. I even wrote you that message."

"Yeah, because *that's* what people do when they're gearing up to shoot their best friend," Elise murmured.

"Hey, you don't know me, lady. You don't know… Wait, you didn't let her read my secret best friend message, did you? Hal?"

"Honestly, I can't remember."

"Well, that's nice," Johnny muttered in the darkness. "Clearly, I made a strong impression with my emotional outpouring."

"I had a lot going on, Johnny. Franco and Phineas were captured. Carlisle and James were missing. The reels were saying they were all dead, and Elise and I were just…"

I trailed off, thinking about that terrible time, when Elise and I had hunkered down at Carlisle's temple hideout, two quivering children clinging to each other for the desperate hope that they weren't alone in a world gone mad. And now, sitting in a dark closet with Elise and Johnny, I couldn't help but feel like we'd somehow come full circle.

"Eh," Elise said, stroking my cheek in the darkness, "he's just trying to pretend like he didn't totally cry after reading it. You know, for whatever that's worth."

I felt Johnny's fist punch skyward. "Score!"

"Who invited you guys, again?" I asked.

A short but distinct silence fell between them, speaking more than their words could have.

"Look, you guys don't have to worry about me diving into the abyss again. I've got it under control."

"Really?" Johnny asked. "Because you're sitting here in a pitch black closet."

"*We're* sitting here in a pitch black closet," Elise said.

"Ah. Well-played, goodlady. But still, as far as designated mope zones go…"

"I just needed a gropping minute," I said. "Okay?"

"Totally understandable," Elise said.

"And totally under control," Johnny added, grunting and nearly kicking me in the face as he labored to readjust his position. "But you know, just in case, we're here to… Agh. Is that a boot in my ass, Hal, or…?"

I was fighting a smile and opening my mouth to tell him where he could find a boot when the moment was cut short by a light rap on the door. Someone knocking.

I frowned at the door in the darkness. "What, did you guys hang a sign out there or something?"

"Maybe we should have," Johnny said. Then louder, "Because we're having an important business meeting in here, and *I*, for one—"

"It's Franco," I said, focusing my senses past the familiar presence and on to a less familiar one. "And… General Hopper?"

Just as I said it, the door swung open, flooding the cramped space with light and leaving the three of us all squinting up at Franco, the good general, and half of Dillard's First Squad from our undignified tangle among the cleaning stores. As if Hopper or anyone else had needed any additional reason to wonder what Glenbark saw in any of us.

"Well met, sir," Johnny said, thumping fist to chest in a salute despite being packed into the storage closet too tightly to even sit up straight. "We were just discussing next moves in light of recent developments."

"Evidently," Hopper said, not quite smiling, but not particularly frowning either.

Franco offered Johnny a hand up first, as he was top of the pile. Once he was excavated, Elise rose lithely and hauled me up by one hand.

"Are we late for a meeting or something?" Johnny asked, glancing at his palmlight.

"Not exactly," Franco said.

"We won't be having another meeting like yesterday's until things settle down on base," Hopper added.

"How bad is it out there?" I asked.

Hopper's expression darkened. "I've seen more discipline and good sense in tyro barracks. It hasn't gotten past a few scuffles here and there, yet, but it's not pretty. I never thought to see the chain of command so thoroughly questioned. We have civies lining up in protest outside the gates. Half the legionnaires inside are calling for an official review of Glenbark's leadership. Others…" He shook his head. "Haven is ready to explode over this mess. Which is why I came to tell you to keep your head down where no trigger-happy heroes can see it."

"Of course, sir," I said, in no mood to argue. "But surely that message didn't need a general to deliver it. Was there anything else?"

"Oh no," Hopper said, shaking his head. "I just so happened to run into Citizen Fields a moment ago. As I'm sure you understand, it would be wise for the High General to keep her distance from you in the coming days. Same goes for me, of course, but I figured I could at least spare a moment to offer my support. Not that it's worth much at this point, but I happen to be one of the people who agrees that you've received the scud end of the stick, Citizen Raish."

"I, uh… Thank you, sir."

"Like I said, it's hardly worth spit in a can." He clapped my shoulder and leaned in conspiratorially. "But if you do happen to find yourself in need of the kind of support Glenbark might not be readily able to offer right now, I'm sure my servitor would like to hear about it."

That surprised me even more.

"I understand, sir."

"Good." He straightened and showed us all a grim smile. "Then I'd better get back to managing the madhouse. Be careful. All of you."

And with that, General Hopper marched off, well-polished boots clacking on well-polished tile.

"So what *is* the next move?" Johnny asked.

"Aren't you the High General's servitor?" I asked.

"Yeah, and she told me to keep our heads down. I thought your broom closet was a brilliant plan, honestly."

I stared at our vacated hideout, wanting little more than to crawl back in there—or better yet, into a safe bed somewhere—and to not come back out until the world made sense.

"Maybe we should try to contact Burton Kovaks again," Elise said.

Franco and I traded a glance. We'd already sent multiple messages to Burton Kovaks' public ID address since Humility, not really expecting he'd respond, hardly even positive what we'd do if he did. But now that innocent blood was being spilled with no likely signs of stopping soon, maybe Kovaks and his pasty friend would be willing to step foot out of their dungeon and do something to help the Shapers of Enochia. Maybe.

"Why not?" I said. "It'd probably be more useful than interviews and smiles at this point."

"I can compose another message through one of my proxies," Franco said.

"I'll help," Elise said.

Franco arched a thick eyebrow, softly smiling. "You don't trust your bumbling father to see it done properly?"

Elise shrugged. "I'm good at coaxing stubborn bastards into corners. That's all."

None of us saw fit to argue with that.

"Very well," Franco said. "In the meanwhile, it might be prudent to begin more seriously exploring what offensive weapons we have on hand in this battle of truths."

"Like the existence of the Seekers?" I asked.

Franco nodded.

"Four's just gonna love that," Elise said. "I can already hear him griping. 'Oh, sure, happy to be exploited. I'm sure Enochia will just take our word for it when we say the Sanctum had us doing their wetwork behind the scenes.'"

"So we're back to 'smear campaign on the Sanctum,' huh?" Johnny said. "Great. Maybe while we're at it we can start an awareness campaign to remind everyone that happiness is overrated and that there's really no such thing as pure altruism."

Franco shrugged. "If they're going to tell warped truths and outright lies to destroy our heroes, I don't see why we should withhold inconvenient facts to protect theirs."

"An eye for an eye, eh?"

"The facts," Franco said. "Only the facts."

Johnny pursed his lips, considering. "You do realize I'm gonna have to tell Glenbark about this, right?"

Franco showed Johnny the patient smile he always seemed to reserve just for him. "I wouldn't have said anything had I thought otherwise."

"Comforting," Johnny muttered, swiping a few commands into his palm-light before pausing to look up at me. "So what're you gonna do?"

I'd been wondering that myself, standing there listening to my friends marshal their plans. What was left to do? I'd already spoken my truth as best as I could. It wasn't like anyone particularly needed my help with talking to Four and Eight or sending yet another hopeless message to Burton Kovaks. When it came down to it, there was only one thing left that I was singularly equipped to do here, and much as I didn't want to do it, it sure beat the alternative of lying back down in a dark closet and trying to weather the storm.

"Well," I said, "I guess I'm gonna go kick Alton Parker until something useful falls out."

10

TO THE ROOTS

"You look terrible," Alton Parker said from the other side of the thick polymer window panel, his expression rather flat except for the faintest flicker of amusement. "Are you getting enough sleep, Haldin?"

I didn't bother wasting the breath on a comeback. For one thing, the effort probably would've done little more than please the raknoth—especially given that the salt-and-pepper bastard still barely looked ruffled despite having been without food or blood for seven days now. And for another, I didn't have much breath to waste.

"I had to go through a lot of scud to come see you," I said. He didn't need to know the full extent of how true that statement was—about how I'd had to beg and disguise myself in full specialist armor just to sneak over here like a freaking thief in broad daylight, heart thundering every step of the way.

"Consider me touched. What would you like to talk about?"

"This game of yours—"

"It is not a game."

"It's done," I pressed on. "We're out of time. If the legionnaires don't come for your head on Legion orders, they might just end up doing it in the name of Alpha instead, and sooner than later."

His smile was perfectly reptilian. "Feeling the pressures of a world on fire, are we?"

I tried not to let him see just how true that was. "I need to know what you know about the Sanctum and the Emmútari. If you give me that, I might be able to—"

"To what? Protect me? Please, you expect me not to notice that you're suddenly wearing armor skin under your clothes again, or that you arrived here alone, clearly not by plain sight, and took an extra minute in the antechamber outside to lose whatever disguise you were wearing? It hardly takes a cunning mind to see it. They're turning on you."

I wanted to argue—needed to quell his speculation and maintain my position here. But I couldn't seem to find the words. I just stood there, stunned.

"It was inevitable, Haldin. It is all inevitable."

They were just words. Ominous words, maybe. But also completely vague. Definitely too vague to explain why I suddenly couldn't seem to breathe. But something about the way he said them—the foreign, almost *gentle* tone in his voice… I think it was the most sincere thing I'd ever heard Alton Parker say. And it sent chills down my spine.

"Fine," I finally forced out. "Fine, you're right. If and when they come for you, they might just decide to make a grab for my head too. Maybe sooner."

"Maybe they already have, even," he said, studying me closely.

Alpha, was his stare disconcerting.

"Tell me about the Sanctum and the Emmútari."

"And what about my kin, and your hybrid cure? You were quite bent on both last time. It must truly be quite the ruckus out there if you've forgotten so easily."

"I haven't forgotten. I just… We need to know the truth about something I saw in an ancient text. An image of the prophet Sarentus and the last leaders of the Emmútari."

"You declare the time for games past, and then refrain from speaking your mind plainly. You wish to know whether Sarentus was one of my kin, do you not?"

I hung on the question, my breath halted for the second time.

"Was he?"

"Yes."

The floor rocked beneath my feet. I hadn't expected him to simply answer. But then again…

"Do you have proof?"

He seemed genuinely amused at that. "Not of the kind that would hold merit in the courts of the Central Justice."

My initial shock gave way to a ripple of disappointment

"But I could show you," he added. "Indirectly, at least."

Show me? Did he mean telepathically?

I eyed him through the thick polymer panel, positive that this sudden helpfulness was a bit too convenient. "What are you playing at, Parker?"

Trying to get me to disable the cloaks on his cell, maybe? Or to get me to step into the cell instead?

"How many times must I explain that this is not a game?" He said the words slowly and with immaculate annunciation, letting the perfection of his suave voice do all the insulting. "As I have told you, I am here for my own safekeeping until it is time for us to confront the greater threat facing your planet. As you yourself point out, my safety in this cell is presently a matter of increasing uncertainty. Hence, it is time for me to show you why I decided to surrender to these ridiculous accommodations to begin with. Do you follow?"

"You're a real pain in the ass, you know that?"

Calmly, the raknoth reached for the transfer port beside the door, pulled his hatch open, and laid his forearm down in the narrow rectangular space —a clear invitation to open the hatch on my side, take his hand, and physically short-circuit our way past the cell's cloaking fields.

I considered my side of the port, and the palm panel that clearly indicated the hatch was locked. I wasn't sure I even had access to unlock the thing. But that would hardly stop me, if I really wanted to open it. The real question was whether I was willing to reach into a narrow polymer shaft and take the hand of a raknoth who'd tried to kill me on multiple occasions.

"If I wanted to hurt you," Parker said, "I would've done it before now."

"You blew me off of a building two cycles ago."

"That was before I learned just how completely the hybrid initiative had failed, and decided that I needed you."

"Well if that's not comforting…"

"I'm a pragmatist, Haldin. You needn't trust me to at least trust that."

I looked from his eyes down to his offered hand. Back up again.

Alpha, I think I did trust that. Or at least trusted that he wasn't about to try to kill me through a six-inch-by-six-inch transfer port. But that was kind of beside the point anyway, because the truth was that I needed to see what was in his head. Which just left one problem.

"You expect me to believe you're gonna open your mind to me? Just like that?"

"I am not overly concerned by the notion."

That wasn't exactly comforting to hear, either.

In the days since he'd turned himself over, I'd considered more than once trying to break into Parker's mind by force, but that tactic came with a multitude of challenges—not the least of which being the physical contact required to circumvent the cell's cloaking fields, and the fact that I had no idea how strong a telepath Alton Parker actually was. I wasn't quite so arrogant as to forget how narrowly I'd succeeded at breaching Al'Kundesha's mind—and even then only because I'd caught him off balance. Alton Parker wasn't one to be caught off balance, emotionally or otherwise.

Glenbark, familiar with the feasibility of the act if not the precise details, had only asked me about the possibility once. As soon as she'd agreed that it sounded too dangerous, I'd all but put the thought from mind, thinking we had time to find a better option. Never once had it crossed my mind that option might turn out to be freely granted access to Alton Parker's mind.

Somehow, the idea of a free pass made me even more uncomfortable than the prospect of telepathically duking it out with the raknoth.

"You're not worried about what I could do in your head?" I asked.

"Not particularly. The time for secrets is passing, and I am not some fleeting human to be broken by any damage you could deliver." He considered me. "Not that I'd expect you to try."

"And if I decide not to relinquish control back to you?"

"Eventually, you will need to sleep. I will not." He showed me that reptilian smile. "It might actually be rather stimulating, relinquishing control for a time. It's been a long while."

"Yeah, you're not really making this any less creepy."

I kind of wanted to ask about the sleep thing, but it hardly seemed to matter now anyway. Raknoth didn't need sleep? Fine. Throw it on the list. I'd been mind-gropped a dozen too many times in the past seasons to feel excessively shocked by such things anymore. And why was I arguing anyway? Wasn't this exactly what I'd wanted all along?

He splayed his waiting fingers in the access port. "Come. Let us have on with it. Time, as you say, is dwindling."

Yeah. Exactly what I'd wanted. Sure. The world I'd tried to save wading straight back into the thick of war, and the raknoth who'd tried to kill me offering me his hand, inviting me to take a telepathic gander at what he seemed to think was the *actual* danger facing my planet.

Bring on the flowers and gropping sunshine.

I reached for the transfer hatch access panel. I was less than surprised when it flashed me a warning that my credentials had not been accepted. That was probably where a reasonable person should've stopped. But I needed to know. With one more wary glance at Parker, I sank into my extended senses and made short work of the hatch's internal locking mechanisms.

It was only once the hatch was open and I was contemplating grabbing one of the most dangerous hands on the planet when Parker decided to speak again.

"One more thing."

"Wonderful timing," I muttered.

"I ask that you defer to my guidance on what memories to explore, and when."

"So that you can keep your bullscud story straight?"

He smiled. "No. Because there are truths and tribulations in here that might break you if you stumble upon them by casual accident."

I couldn't decide if he was the worst salesman who'd ever lived, or the best one. Either way, I found my hand reaching for his as if it had a will of its own. I paused at the last few inches, then grabbed hold of his deceptively human flesh and tensed my telepathic defenses, more than half-expecting his mind to fall on me like a force of nature.

But it didn't.

I felt him there. It was impossible not to. But he kept his distance, so to speak, watching me calmly with his eyes as his mental presence settled down, shifting in pattern and density, preparing itself.

"At your leisure," came his voice in my mind.

As far as I could tell with a faint probe, his defenses were down—about as ready to bar my entrance as an open doorway. It was bizarre, to feel such vulnerability in a raknoth. But still, I wasn't going to take any chances. I focused my will, and threw my mind at his like one of the spiked bolts from Edwards' heavy pulse rifle.

And I punched straight in.

No matter how many times I did it, I doubted I'd ever truly get used to the feeling of diving into another living thing's head. Not that I hoped to try. Even putting the experience into words is difficult—words other than *disorienting* and *overwhelming*, at least.

At the heart of it, it sort of feels like you're standing on a rocky bluff, high above a raging river, solid and content in your own thoughts and sense of being. Then you jump. But you don't just hit the water. You explode into it, diffusing and merging so fast that, if you're not careful, you can lose track of what's you and what's the river before you have a chance to blink your telepathic mind's eye.

Did I mention it's overwhelming?

And none of that was even to mention the freaky level of sensory overload that came with taking up co-residence in a raknoth's head. Alton Parker's nose was so sharp we could still smell the scents of Johnny and Elise lingering on me in our shared headspace, right along with the faintest trace of cleaning supplies. His hand could practically scan the prints of my fingers, tightly clutching his. His ears could easily hear every beat of my heart.

Suffice it to say, it was unsettling. But I did my best to reel in my focus and point our thoughts at the prophet in question, Sarentus.

"Very good," Parker's voice came to me. *"Straight to business."*

Good was the last thing I felt, hearing Alton Parker whispering encouragement in my mind, but I was too busy maintaining my mental balance as we flashed through a rapid series of thoughts and memories, all pertaining to the holy prophet. There were a lot of them. But, then again, that wasn't surprising, seeing as you couldn't walk more than a mile in most cities without crossing at least a couple statues of the man. Or the raknoth, rather.

Because I could see it now, riding over every memory and reference of Sarentus in Alton Parker's mind—the smug amusement Parker felt at the fact that most of the planet had been all but worshiping one of his kin for the past thousand years, long before he and his clan had even considered coming back to Enochia. Parker hadn't been lying.

Sarentus, to the best of Alton Parker's knowledge, had been one of the raknoth.

Spoken aloud, the admission had rocked me. Realized within the winding depths of Parker's mind, it nearly sent me exploding into that raging river on the back of a thousand different questions. Worse, the raknoth's mind actually seemed perfectly capable of pulling full, discrete thoughts and memories to match every disjointed fragment of my shocked mind, piling them all on until I had to back almost completely out for fear of losing myself in the flood.

"The way we store and access memories is radically more efficient than the methods employed by human brains," Alton explained, apparently having noticed my near-overload, and sounding just as pleased as a sun-struck flower about it. *"A necessity, seeing as our lifespans are exceptionally longer."*

And now I was getting fun facts from a raknoth. Wonderful.

I resisted the curious urge to ask how long was exceptionally long, and instead returned to the matter at hand.

"Why was Sarentus here? How did he come to be on Enochia a thousand years ahead of your clan?"

"Because Zar'Faenor placed him here to act as a sentry during their first trip to Enochia. It was actually closer to fifteen hundred years ago, not long after we first scouted Earth."

Not that I had the capacity to process it, but I could only imagine my jaw was hanging as slack as my mind felt, trying to unpack everything Parker had just insinuated—and as casually as if he'd been paying compliments to the weather, no less.

Fifteen-hundred years? Zar'Faenor had come to this planet fifteen-hundred gropping years ago? And *we*… Parker had said *we*.

"You're…"

"Not some fleeting human, as I said."

"How old are you?"

The question conjured a confusing flutter of images I couldn't process and odd calculations I couldn't understand.

"I have lived for approximately two-thousand and eight-hundred of your years."

I tried to wrap my head around that, and failed. Miserably.

I'd already known from the brief glimpse I'd had in Al'Kundesha's mind that the raknoth lived a long time—that the one who'd paraded as Adrian Kublich had experienced other such lives before. But nearly three-thousand years?

It was inconceivable, and yet I could see in Parker's mind that it was the truth. But what had Zar'Faenor been doing on Enochia all that time ago?

I directed the question at Parker's mind, sinking back into our shared headspace, and we flashed to a memory in a lush clearing, well-forested on its perimeters. I spotted an odd collection of primitive huts off in the distance—made mostly from mud and branch and clay, I could see through Parker's sharp eyes. Only they weren't Parker's eyes, the memory told me. Al'Braka. That was his true name. And he'd occupied a different host in this memory. His first human host ever.

We were on Earth.

No sooner had I gleaned that fact from the memory than I recognized the raknoth prowling down the ramp from a long, bulbous ship like the one Parker had flown to Haven seven days earlier.

Zar'Faenor.

I recognized him readily through the memory, though he wore a fair-haired body I'd never seen. Which made sense, seeing as this memory was from well over a thousand years before the host in which I'd met Zar'-Faenor—Carlisle's old master, Cassius—had even been born.

In the memory, Parker—or Al'Braka, or whatever the scud he could be called—waited patiently as his clan leader reached the thick grass and stalked over. I could feel that Al'Braka was teeming with curiosity, and yet tempered in his questions by a deep-set fear. A fear of Zar'Faenor? Yes. Of Zar'Faenor. But also of the ones they maneuvered to deceive.

"It is done, master?" Al'Braka managed to force out as his clan leader drew up beside him.

Zar'Faenor didn't answer immediately. He gazed over the grassy clearing, over the rudimentary huts beyond, and finally skyward, toward something I couldn't see but could sense in the memory should be there, high above, beyond atmosphere. A world ship. Whatever the scud that was.

"The transplant was successful," Zar'Faenor said, bringing his attention back down to Al'Braka. "I have left Nan'Valen and Nan'Sarentus to oversee the humans' adaptation to their new world."

"And the world ship?"

"Will be returning to its designated task presently, none the wiser."

The first bit of hopeful relief blossomed, but still Al'Braka was afraid.

"It was a cunning idea, Braka. Risky, undoubtedly. And quite possibly foolish. But cunning. The seed has been planted. And for the first time, its fruit may well bear some inkling of hope for our people."

It was odd, feeling the emotion that rippled through Al'Braka at his clan leader's praise—not quite pride, maybe, but something like it, right along with a kind of inner warmth I had trouble imagining the creature that was now Alton Parker could ever be capable of feeling.

"May I ask, Master," Al'Braka said quietly, timidly. "What name did you leave this new world?"

Zar'Faenor's lip gave the faintest twitch—the closest thing to a smile Al'Braka had ever seen from him in five centuries of service.

"Enochia."

It all clicked then. Too much, too fast.

I swear to Alpha and everything else, my mind nearly exploded.

I yanked back. The world shifted around me, growing louder and yet more muddled. Then something hit me in the back. The wall, I realized, coming dazedly back to my senses in my own body. I'd released Alton Parker's hand and collapsed back against the wall.

I sank to my haunches, breathing rapidly, cold sweat running down my spine.

"Come now," came Parker's voice. "You didn't even make it to the upsetting parts." I didn't have to look up to know he was sneering. "That, as they say, was the good news."

I glared at him and stood, clenching my hands to stop the shaking. "What the scud is wrong with you? What was—What did…" I took a deep breath. "What Zar'Faenor said, about transplants, and this… this new world. Are you telling me Enochia is… that we were…?"

In the transfer port, Parker curled his forefinger in a *come-hither* gesture. "Why don't you see for yourself?"

As shocked and pissed as I was, I almost did go see for myself, just to show him I wouldn't be rattled. Luckily, some part of me was still alert enough to point out how stupid that would've been. Parker clearly saw that I needed a few minutes to get my head straight and try to wrap my mind around… actually, I wasn't even sure I wanted to try to wrap my mind around what I'd just seen.

So I settled for glaring at him a little longer. "How can you think any of this is amusing?"

"Oh, I don't know." He looked calmly around his cell. "Perhaps I'm simply getting bored in here." He cocked his head. "Or perhaps I think it's amusing because not so long ago, I stood fifteen floors above my best and only hope for this universe and listened to a human hatchling lecture me on the morality of my decisions, deliciously unaware that I've been alive longer than his entire civilization, and that I've experienced more pain and loss, more fear and raw, terrible knowledge than his sad little brain could possibly comprehend. You have no idea what is out there in the deep void, Haldin Raish. No idea how petty your planetary squabbles are next to…"

He tilted his head, the sneer sliding from his face to be replaced by a look of concentration.

"Dammit," he muttered, so quietly I barely heard.

"What?"

"Well, speaking of petty planetary squabbles, it sounds like we're about to have company."

I reached for my cloaking pendant. Company was fine, right? I was in the Haven brig, not slinking around behind enemy lines.

Except I *had* slunk over here, hadn't I? Because as far as half the base was concerned, I *was* behind enemy lines.

"They don't sound very friendly," Parker said.

I couldn't help but see what he meant as I dialed my cloak out and took in the scene with my extended senses.

At a rough count, it felt like a full squad. Fully armed. Filing quickly into the antechamber outside. No talking. Only gestures. That didn't seem good. Nor did the few fingers I had time to notice, shifting from trigger guards to deadly triggers.

I glanced dumbly at my palmlight, not really sure what I was hoping to see, other than some message or announcement that would explain the situation. Then the door hissed open, and legionnaires were sweeping into the room in breach formation before I could blink.

I didn't have time to be surprised. Not as they caught sight of me and charged forward.

Not as they raised their weapons, and opened fire.

11

THUMPED

Drills will save your life, tyro. I'd heard it over and over again. The less I had to think, after all—the more things happened automatically—the better my chances of survival in most any situation.

Of course, when your chances for survival start off at the level of *taking a hundred softsteel slugs to the chest*, "better" doesn't necessarily mean "good."

I nearly passed out before I fully registered what I'd even done. But there were my outstretched hands, lilting drunkenly in my dimming vision, and there were those hundred slugs, give or take, floating a few inches beyond—a veritable wall of softsteel that nearly blotted out my view of the stunned legionnaires.

The stunned legionnaires who'd just tried to *kill* me without warning.

And they weren't done.

Wobbly legs. Limited energy. Twenty hostiles, and too many tightening trigger fingers.

I threw their first softsteel barrage back in their faces without thinking. Not hard enough to kill or maim—I don't think I'd have had the energy for that if I'd tried. But plenty hard enough to add a splash of chaos as I charged forward, deflecting another few shots as I went, and smacked the lead rifle aside, wrapping the lucky legionnaire in a bear hug.

She headbutted me.

It hurt like scud, but I managed to hook in and pull her to the floor on top of me. Someone was barking orders. Something was slamming against Alton Parker's cell door. I cast my senses out, my mind reeling with drunken channeling fatigue, and a bad mix of screaming combat adrenaline and less-than-half-formed plans.

I focused in on the rearmost legionnaire, still out in the antechamber. Focused in on his gear vest.

"Free me, Haldin!" Parker cried somewhere to the right, just before another sharp crack on the cell door.

I might've half-considered it out of desperation if I hadn't already been too busy freeing the pull pins of half a dozen thumper grenades, scattered throughout the gear vests of my surprise assassination squad.

Something slammed into my side, sending a wave of fire through my ribs. I pulled back in time to see legionnaires on both sides, winding back for another round of rib kicks. The woman on top of me jerked her head back, ready to take advantage of the distraction with another headbutt.

I pulled a barrier up. Then the room exploded in a chain of low thumps and concussive waves that smacked my barrier aside and left me drifting somewhere dark, and heavy, and actually kind of pleasantly warm. Until the limp legionnaire on top of me shifted.

We both snapped to, her reaching frantically for something at her hip, me reaching frantically to stop her. I didn't have time to think about it. I was pinned, and there was no way I was killing her on purpose. I'd seen Carlisle drop men—even Seekers—straight from waking to unconscious with a light touch. I knew it was possible.

So I touched lightly at the struggling legionnaire's mind, doing my best not to plunge straight in, and willed her to sleep as resolutely as I could. Her head sagged, her eyes blinking dazedly.

"Wha...?" she mumbled.

I tried again, more insistently, and she collapsed on me like a hundred and seventy or so deadweight pounds of sleeping armored warrior. I let my own head collapse back to the hard floor, closing my eyes and panting for sweet, luxurious breath. I got about two inhales before I noticed the rustling and groans of the other legionnaires stirring around the room and in the antechamber.

"I think it's best you let me out now," Alton Parker's calm voice declared from somewhere overhead and behind me.

"Yeah, right," I grunted, rolling Lady Headbutts off and crawling to my feet. "I'm sure that would smooth over this whole..." I looked around at the kill squad, half of whom were stirring. "... whatever the scud this is."

As soon as I'd said it, I noticed one of the legionnaires who'd kicked me slowly raising a sidearm. I swatted it aside with telekinesis and descended on him to give him the shove to unconsciousness.

"You know what this is, Haldin," Parker said as I drew the legionnaire's stun rod and began putting it to quick work on anyone still moving. "They've made their decision. They're finished with you here. Now stop wasting time and release—"

"Will you just shut up and let me think?" I growled, jabbing the stun rod into the last legionnaire's neck.

I waited, senses extended, and felt nothing but shallow breathing throughout the room. No movement. And definitely no useful thoughts in my racing mind.

Allies.

Glenbark. Johnny.

I needed to tell someone. But even as I woke my palmlight, the brig amps clacked to life and planted the cold hard flag of death on any hope of that.

"Hear the call, Haven," came a voice I didn't recognize. "The demon known as Haldin Raish is loose on base without leave. Subject was last seen in the brig, secure wing, where he attacked an armed squad and resisted peaceful restraint. He is now to be considered an active combatant. Repeat, Haldin Raish is to be treated as an active combatant on sight, by order of Central Command."

"Does that clear things up for you?" Parker called, standing at his cell door like the Alpha-damned vision of calm dignity.

"They're..." I looked around at the squad that'd clearly been sent to kill me for several seconds before having the good sense to kneel down and check one's insignia. Haga Company. 323rd. The same damn company Auckus had sent to round me up when the hybrids had attacked Haven.

I looked numbly at Alton Parker. "Someone's trying to frame me."

"Succeeding too, I do believe. Now, if you'd be so kind as to get this door, I do think we best be vacating the premises."

I ignored him and looked at the door on the far side of the antechamber, trying to think. If I could just get clear, lay low until I could contact Glenbark...

"Whatever you're thinking, it won't be enough," Parker said. I rounded on him, but he already had his hands raised in peace, and demons to the wind, he actually looked for a second like a reasonable human being. "It *can't* be enough, Haldin, because you do not yet possess all of the pieces. The

Sanctum is far from the biggest threat facing Enochia if we should perish. Come, release me from this cage, and I will show you the rest of the puzzle once we are safely away from here."

Awfully convenient, I wanted to spit, *that you just need to be broken out of here before you can tell me the big dark secret you've been holding back.* But I'd already seen more in his memories than I could afford to process right now. I needed to get out of here and set things straight with the Legion. But I needed to see the rest of Parker's secrets even more.

If I'd needed any more convincing, the feeling of reinforcements prowling toward the antechamber door from the hallway outside did the trick.

No time to think my way out of this. The trap was already sprung. The damage already done. So I reached out, fried the door's access controls, and telekinetically reengaged the locks once the emergency override had had its say.

I turned back to Parker, who looked like he wanted to point out that my manually locking us in the room hadn't really improved our situation. Thankfully—or maybe unthankfully, as it might've actually knocked some good sense into my head—he refrained, and instead waited patiently as I drew up to the door.

This was madness.

"You kill anyone," I said quietly, "you even break a bone outside of what's strictly necessary, and I'll kill you, secret memories or no. Are we clear?"

He didn't look particularly pleased, but he nodded anyway. "Clear as your blinding sense of justice, partner."

The glib bastard. It was like he had a sixth sense that specifically knew when he could push me, when I was already too hooked to back away. Because that's exactly what I was right then.

I needed to know what he knew. No matter what.

Guessing his cell had no emergency override, I went straight to telekinetically unlocking each of the eight sizable deadbolts. That done, I kicked the heavy door open on its hinges, not particularly caring if it hit Parker.

He caught it in one hand, and stepped slowly out of the cell. Pissed as I was, and as much as it'd felt like he was at my mercy a moment earlier, I wasn't ready for the tide of fear that rose in me, facing him down without a foot of invincible raknoth cage between us.

I stomped down on that fear, reminding myself of my promise to him.

In the hallway outside, they were beating on the door now, muffled shouts coming through. It wouldn't be long before someone arrived with breaching charges.

"Did you have a plan?" Parker asked.

"Maybe," I said, sweeping the walls and the ceiling until I found a feasible break point and prepared to start excavating. "But I hope you're ready to put your back into it."

"Marvelous." His skin shifted a shade darker as he said the word. "In that case, I'd like to request we make one stop."

I swear to Alpha, the pounding on the door grew ten times louder and more urgent as I gaped at the raknoth. "A *stop*? This isn't a gropping Alphasday stroll to market."

The door-thumping legionnaires outside could attest to that. Remembering my good sense, I dialed my cloak off, reached out, and pulled as many thumper pins as I could sense out there. Shouts to *open up* and *hurry up* promptly turned to a frantic storm of curses, followed seconds later by a satisfying sequence of low booms. Relative calm returned. Relative *and* momentary, I reminded myself.

It'd only be minutes at the most until someone came through with proper breaching charges—and probably a few cloaking packs as well. My own shields, turned against me.

"We need to get the scud out of here," I said, reaching for the ceiling. The rest didn't matter right now.

"And what about your ailing hybrid friend?" Parker asked, catching me fully off guard. "One of the afflicted humans is important to you, are they not?"

Annabelle's sweet little face drifted through my mind, already pale and growing rough in spots from the beastly transition still happening inside her. "I… Now's not exactly the time to…"

But the words caught in my throat.

Now was not the time to potentially save Johnny's sister?

"Now may be the only time," Parker said. "I doubt they'll care to accept or administer our care package once we've escaped."

That was probably a fair point. It was just ten steps beyond disconcerting that he was the one to make it—that Alton Parker, cold-blooded monster extraordinaire, was the one who was suggesting we risk our necks to help an innocent life.

"Why do you suddenly care?"

He didn't answer, just looked at the antechamber door, where the sounds of activity were picking back up, and a few curling tendrils of black smoke announced the arrival of a phase torch.

"I think it's more prudent you worry about our imminent exit."

"Fine." I reached out and focused in on the first minor fault I found in the permacrete, trying not to pay attention to the burning smell of the phase torch or the sharp thud of the combat boot testing the door. "Then shut up and get those claws out, Parker."

1 2

———

BREAKOUT

If telekinetically deflecting rifle slugs was on roughly equal ground with physically swatting aside punches, catching a Raknoth Special sniper round with telekinesis was more or less like taking a groin shot. From a raknoth.

Then again, maybe I was just tired from tearing my way through multiple layers of permacrete ceiling. Not that I had done all the work. Maybe not even most of the work. As soon as I'd gotten the cracks started, Parker had sprung up with his inhuman strength, latched on with his creepy little claws, and started tearing off hunks of permacrete like he was shelling one enormous, dusty egg.

Still, whatever credit he deserved for his excavation work, I think I more than made up the balance when I caught the first three sniper rounds that came cruising for our heads the moment we leapt up to the brig rooftop. I staggered forward, half collapsing behind the nearest permacrete lip to at least provide cover from one direction. I didn't like what I saw before I dipped down.

To say there was an angry mob waiting for us outside the brig entrance would've been… well, completely accurate. Except for the fact that this mob wasn't sporting torches, impromptu clubs, and the odd firearm. They were all trained killers, all armed, and all catching on with military efficiency to the fact that we'd just emerged on the rooftop.

Parker, to his credit, didn't hesitate. He scooped me up like a helpless damsel and jumped.

Like, really *jumped*.

The only thing that kept me from screaming was that I'd seen raknoth leap before. Not quite this far though, I realized, as we continued ascending for longer than I would've thought possible. Too long. I twisted to look down at the ground as we reached our apex, and that scream nearly got me again as we started what must've been a seventy yard plunge, sailing through the bright noon air like our own version of a Raknoth Special.

"You may wish to slow our descent," came Parker's voice through the rush of wind and the cracks of gunfire below.

"You think?!" I shouted.

The reckless bastard. Then again, maybe I shouldn't have been surprised. We had both taken turns trying to kill one another, after all. Worst case scenario here was that he accidentally succeeded.

I fixed onto our combined mass and channeled off some of our downward acceleration, using the energy to adjust our horizontal trajectory leftward, toward a gap between two buildings.

"What are you—"

"Cover," I telepathically shot back.

He didn't argue.

I took another strong pull off of our descent velocity in the last couple seconds, but we still hit the permacrete with all the tenderness of a midspeed skimmer wreck.

"Alpha's wrinklies," I growled, shoving out of his grip and back to my own feet. "Would it kill you to lose a few pounds?"

"And here I thought you were powerful."

"You know what? I'm letting the next sniper round hit you."

He gave one of those too-suave-to-care Alton Parker eye rolls. "Which way is the research building?"

I double-checked my bearings, then set off running north between our two blocks of cover, too irritated to answer.

Parker was at my side in an instant, keeping easy pace. "Let me carry you."

"I can run."

"So can a sloth, technically."

I was considering whether to telekinetically trip him or simply tell him to grop himself to oblivion when the legionnaires caught up with us. They poured into the mouth of the alleyway where the two buildings ended ahead—what looked to be at least a full company. I could only imagine how many more were on the way up there, and the first gunshots from behind told me they weren't the only ones.

We ducked left into the cover of a shipping bay. I glanced at the doors that led inside, debating whether we'd be better or worse off cutting through the building. When I glanced back to see what Parker might think, the raknoth only turned to offer his back to me and lowered into a crouch, arms held wide.

"Climb on."

"You've gotta be kidding me."

He shot me a condescending look over his shoulder, his eyes beginning to shimmer with crimson raknoth fire. "Grow up, Haldin."

"Said the raknoth asking to play piggyback in the middle of a manhunt," I muttered. But I stepped forward and prepared to mount anyway, because the bastard was right. He was naturally far faster and stronger than I was, and I could devote a lot more energy and focus to playing defense if I wasn't busy pounding permacrete.

"Where is the lab?" he asked as I climbed on and scooted into a secure position, looping my legs over his hips and hooking my feet in the front.

"Northeastern quadrant," I said. "About a half mile in from the eastern wall and a quarter from the north. Three floor square building, right off an open shipping pad." Reluctantly, I wrapped my arms around his chest. "You picked a pretty scuddy time to grow a conscience, you know that?"

He only stood and snaked his arms around my legs. I could feel the strength in his body. There was no give, no strain. He handled my weight like I wasn't even there, and I was uncomfortably aware of just how easily he could probably snap my femurs—by accident, even, once the going got rough. Which it was unquestionably about to do.

"I trust you can protect yourself from gunfire?" asked my raknoth steed. Right before a pair of grenades sailed in through the bay doors and thunked down right next to us.

I plucked them up with telekinesis and sent them back out, and harm-lessly skyward. Or tried to, at least. They detonated a bare second after clearing the bay's entryway. I grimaced at the debris that showered down outside, but that was hardly my fault.

"Just go," I growled at Parker.

"Hold on tight," he said. "I won't restrain myself."

And as far as I could tell, he didn't.

We tore out of the loading bay with all the speed and momentum of a mag tram on scaly green legs, and Parker didn't stop there. He launched us for the wall of the opposite building. I watched in shock, not sure whether to slow our impending collision or not. Parker had it under control. He hit the wall running and promptly launched us again, across the gap to the opposite building.

Below, the legionnaires overcame their own shock and opened fire.

I tightened my grip on Parker and pulled a barrier around us just in time for the raknoth to nearly throw me off with yet another bounce to the opposite rooftop. I tried to cry out that breaking the cover of the buildings was a bad idea, but there simply wasn't time—or air in my lungs.

I almost wanted to be impressed that the snipers actually managed to peg us with a few would-be kill shots a scant second after we broke the rooftop line, but mostly I was just pissed at the extra strain on my barrier and my turbo-jostled body.

"Maybe don't abandon our only cover next time," I growled as Parker continued on, tearing across the rooftop with inhuman speed.

"Only if you prefer I cut through our bipedal obstacles down there," he sent back.

Then he reached the end of the building and dove off, rocketing us straight for the cover of the next set of buildings. I leveled out our landing with telekinesis, and almost broke into manic laughter at the looks of pure disbelief I glimpsed from our stunned pursuers.

Just that morning, I'd sat with Barbara Sanders, trying to humanize myself in the eyes of Enochia. And now here I was riding an Alpha-damned raknoth through Haven like some kind of demonic red-eyed hosa.

So much for showing Enochia my true colors.

Once we broke cleanly away from the initial mob that'd been waiting for us at the brig, though, things at least got a bit smoother. As in, I only had to catch or deflect a handful of stray slugs here and there, and the snipers only got a few more shots in between buildings.

But it couldn't last. Any lack of firepower now simply meant they were scrambling to get ahead of us. Stopping and giving them an extra minute to do so was probably a terrible idea. But I couldn't let go of the hope that Parker might actually be able to do what Therese Brown had been unable to. If he could save Johnny's sister, if he could give Therese a way to save all the half-turned hybrids the raknoth had left behind, doomed to die slow, violent deaths...

I couldn't turn away from that chance, however slim. Plus, I was starting to worry my hips were going to dislocate from Parker's mechanical, none-too-gentle sprinting if I didn't take a break soon anyway.

"Up there," I sent, pointing over his shoulder. "Just after we break cover. You should be able to make the door in one leap."

Throw that on the list of things I'd never expected to say to an ally.

Alpha, an *ally*? The word felt dirty. But I didn't have time to dwell on it. We broke cover to an emphatic welcoming wave of softsteel slugs. I sagged from my defensive efforts, then nearly lost my grip as Parker tensed and launched forward. Too far.

It took every bit of conscious willpower I had not to leap from Parker's back and throw my hands up in defense as we sailed straight toward the second floor of the engineering lab. Parker threw his legs and arms out wide, like he was planning to simply splat and stick onto the side of the building.

Instead, we hit like the massive bundle of stubborn man parts we were, crashed straight through a duraglass window—and, unless I was mistaken, at least part of the wall—and sprawled across the floor inside in an undignified mess of limbs.

"I said 'make the door,'" I groaned, rolling over and trying to assess whether I'd broken anything. "Not 'wrecking ball the gropping wall.'"

"There was a window," came Parker's voice. Then something strong and unyielding yanked me back to my feet. "And I sensed that the afflicted were located on this floor. No sense whining over unimportant details."

I glared at the back of his salt-and-pepper head as he stalked off down the hallway, crunching over broken duraglass on his bare, scaly feet and clearly in no need of directions. The worst part was that he was right: the hybrids *were* up here. Not that that meant the thirty seconds or so he'd "saved" us had actually been worth what felt like a mild concussion and a few bruised bones.

But what did a raknoth care?

I hurried after him, just hoping he could deliver the goods quickly so we could get the scud out, swap creepy, world-shattering alien memories, and then… Scud, I didn't even know what came after that. Couldn't afford to think about it right now. Whoever had sent that kill squad to the brig and sparked this whole scudstorm, I'd just have to hope Glenbark would still be willing to hear me out after all of this. If I was still alive to be heard at all, that was.

A scream from ahead broke through my whirling thoughts, and I realized with a curse that Parker had just found the hybrid cells.

13

THE OTHER SIDE

When I raced into the reinforced room after Parker, I found him standing with his hands held harmlessly—albeit still green and clawed—out to the sides. Therese Brown was backed into the furthest corner of the transparent cell in front of him, having apparently closed herself in for protection, and positively shaking despite the slug-proof wall between them.

"Hal?" she half-cried, half-croaked. "What's happening? What's he doing here? What's..."

"It's a long story," I said, hurrying to place myself between her and Parker. It was Annabelle's cell she was standing in, I registered. It looked like she'd been collecting samples. "A really gropping long story, but the short version is that he claims to have a cure for the hybrid victims, and we need to hand it over and get the scud out of here before they catch us."

Her wide eyes flicked rapidly back and forth between us, her tablet clutched to her chest like a shield. "You're... but he's..." I saw my words register in her eyes. "A cure? From him?"

"I did engineer these mutations," Parker said. "As you might recall."

"Shut up," I snapped at him before turning back to her. "I don't like it either, Therese, but unless you have a better idea, I can't turn away from a chance to save them. But we have to do it now, and fast. Do you trust me?"

"Haldin..." Parker said quietly behind me. I was holding up a hand to silence him when another low voice rumbled from the doorway.

"You sure you know what you're doing, kid?"

I turned to find Phineas standing there with a heavy pulse rifle and a perfectly bear-like glare trained on Parker.

"No," I admitted. "I might not. But I don't see any better options. I need what's in his head, and someone just sent a squad to kill me in the brig. We're working with what we've got here, which is probably less than two minutes before they storm this place."

Phineas considered that for a moment, then nodded and marginally lowered his weapon.

"Praise Alpha," Parker muttered as Phineas waved to Therese, who let herself out of Annabelle's cell and went to him, giving Parker a wide berth.

It might've warmed my heart a little more, seeing Phineas wrap her in a quick one-armed hug, if my heart hadn't been so busy taking that quiet moment to try beating out of my chest cavity with the screaming reminder of how much time we didn't have.

"What do you need to do?" I asked Parker, turning.

He was already striding for Annabelle's cell. "A quick look, first," he said, not looking back. "A receptacle for the serum I've prepared, as well," he added, glancing over his shoulder at Therese, who gathered herself, swallowed her clear misgivings, and went to the well-organized shelves of equipment on the far wall.

"Pulling them out of the chambers hasn't stopped the transition," she called as she picked a few glass containers. "It's only—"

"Destabilized it," Parker called, reaching down to gingerly take Annabelle by the chin and turn her head this way and that. "I know."

It made my insides squirm, seeing him touch Johnny's sweet, helpless sister. I tried to remind myself that she was already dead if someone didn't find a way to cure her of the raknoth disease creeping through her sedated system with each passing day.

Therese was saying something about their sequencing, and how they hadn't been able to properly determine some mechanism of action, but seeing Annabelle had reminded me that getting myself out might not be my only concern right now. I stepped closer to Phineas, who eyed me warily.

"I don't know for sure who sent that squad," I said quietly, "but it smells a lot like Auckus or one of his friends is pulling the strings out there."

Phineas scowled.

"I think we should get Elise and the Seekers out," I said. "Just in case things… in case this isn't an isolated attempt."

Part of me wanted to go charging back across base to Central Command to grab Elise and the others myself, but even Brash Emotions Hal knew that that was a tremendously stupid idea. You didn't send the man who was the acting slug magnet to rescue anyone. You got him the scud away.

Luckily, Phineas agreed. He was already nodding and opening a call with James on his palmlight. He looked at Therese, checking she was safe, started to step out into the hallway, then turned and grabbed my shoulder with one giant hand.

"Be careful, kid. I'll buy you a minute if I—"

"Hey!"

We both spun at Therese's cry, just in time to see Parker withdrawing his bloody fangs from Annabelle's wrist, which he held delicately in both hands, like a fine porcelain sculpture—or a delectable hand fruit.

Had the bastard just *fed* on her?

I was already pushing toward the cell, ready to do... I didn't know what. Not when he had the critical information and we had hostiles no doubt surrounding us from every direction. But Parker ignored us all and calmly began licking Annabelle's bloody wrist. I stopped at the cell's threshold, unsure what to do. Then he held up her wrist to show me. It was licked clean of blood, and the bite marks themselves were... healing?

I watched in shock as Annabelle's skin knit itself closed faster than human tissue had any right to mend.

"We don't have time for you to be indignant," he said, pressing past me and reaching to Therese for one of the glass beakers she was holding.

I was honestly surprised Phineas didn't shoot him then and there, but the big man seemed to recognize, like I did, that there was more happening here than we could readily understand.

"She should be primed to recover," Parker said, gesturing impatiently for the beaker. "Now, if you'd allow me to deposit the rest of my sample..."

"It's... it's okay," Therese said to Phineas, handing the beaker to Parker, who immediately closed his eyes and bowed his head over the receptacle.

Phineas swept his gaze across the room, his eyes settling on me with a heavy *I hope you know what you're doing* weight one last time. Then he was gone.

I looked back to Parker and recoiled at the thin layer of green *something* lining the bottom of the beaker. More was oozing down to join it. He was salivating the stuff, as far as I could tell, holding the beaker tight to his mouth and just letting it flow.

I'd known he'd said something about synthesizing the solution, but somehow I hadn't expected this.

"That's it for now," Parker said a few seconds later, withdrawing his mouth from the beaker and cleaning his lips with a few wet smacking sounds before offering the container out to Therese. "Administer this to the others once you confirm it's working in the girl. A few drops per patient should suffice."

Therese took the beaker, staring dazedly at the green liquid inside. "A few drops per..." She shook her head. "Alpha, this is so gropped up."

She could say that again.

I was looking numbly from Annabelle to Therese, feeling like I owed someone an apology for all of this, but Parker perked up before I could decide who.

"They're moving in," the raknoth said. "Ground floor. All entrances. I believe they have us surrounded."

"Rooftop?" I asked, clicking off my cloaking pendant to feel for myself. Parker shook his head just as my extended senses found the legionnaires sweeping down from above.

"Northern windows," Parker said, with what could only be described as a villainous, scud-eating grin. Then he turned and crouched to offer me my piggyback seat.

"Gropping scudbuckets," I grumbled, climbing onto the raknoth's back. I looked back at Annabelle one last time and said a small prayer before turning to Therese, who was watching us with that dazed look, the beaker clutched absentmindedly to her chest. "Sorry to put you through this, Therese. I just hope it works."

She couldn't seem to find her words, so I just waved goodbye.

"Stay safe, Therese."

That, at least, earned me a frantic bark of laughter from the frazzled scientist, which was probably fair enough, seeing as I was fixing to ride a raknoth into battle. And that raknoth was raring to go. No sooner had I said the words than Parker started running, not bothering to tell me to duck my head through the doorway.

"Be careful!" Therese's cry poured into the hallway after us—right as Parker began picking up speed, headed straight for the duraglass window at the end of the hall.

Careful. Sure.

This time, at least, I had a moment to think about softening the blow for us. I cast my will out, forming a mental construct not unlike my barriers, but exceptionally more pointy in all the right places. Probably, I should've communicated as much to Parker, but he wasn't slowing down to ask questions. If the advance wall of our mini lances surprised him, though, he didn't show it.

We punched through the window and emerged from the second floor of the engineering lab like one of those ancient black powder cannon balls. Normally, it might've been the kind of exit that would leave even trained legionnaires gaping—at least for a second. The forces surrounding the building, though, had clearly been warned to expect the ridiculous. And there were a lot of them.

The lot beneath us roared with gunfire, and I felt the smacking sting of multiple slugs testing my armor skin before I got our barrier in place. I almost wished I hadn't. I was half-unconscious with the effort by the time we crashed down on the next building over.

"If you could refrain from getting shot so much," I growled, trying to catch my breath in the ground fire lull, only to be rewarded with a few choice sniper rounds.

Parker—who wasn't doing so hot either, judging by how he'd handled the landing—let out a growl of his own and started pounding his way across the rooftop. *I would be happy to explain the limitations of controlling ballistic flight to you once we're—scud."*

I saw it an instant after he must've heard it, and my insides shriveled.

They'd broken out the heavy artillery.

The telltale flare of a missile streaked toward us from the northeastern watch tower, flying faster than even a raknoth could hope to match.

"Go faster!" I shouted anyway. Probably unnecessarily, as Parker gave up on sprinting and pounced for the end of our building in a low leap that carried us a good thirty yards and landed Parker right on the lip of the rooftop, tensed to spring.

"No!" I cried. "Not up!"

But it was too late. We were already sailing skyward in Parker's highest leap yet. A deafening boom and a slap of hot air from behind silenced my protests. We continued flying upward, high enough and far enough that we would clear the perimeter wall, I saw. High enough, a glance backward confirmed, that my protests hadn't been unfounded.

For the next three or four seconds, we might as well have been sitting targets for the ground teams. And they didn't waste time.

Another pair of missiles screamed after us from among the legionnaires on the ground, some of whom I could only imagine had been waiting their entire lives to blow a pair of demons out of the sky with a nice, big tracking missile.

Happy day.

"Stop them," came Parker's voice in my mind.

It wasn't hard to figure out which *them* he meant, staring back at those twin flares of death streaking toward us, tracking our trajectory as we reached the apex and shifted into the long descent. The question was how in the ever-loving scud I was supposed to do that.

"Overload the electronics," Parker snapped, apparently sensing my dilemma.

I didn't have time to question it. I aimed at a spot between us and the speeding projectiles, and I let loose with the most intense electromagnetic pulse I could channel. Whether it was a good shot or not, I couldn't say.

All I know is that the missiles were entirely too close when they detonated.

14

ALLIES

To say the world became a confusing blur after our friendly tracker missiles exploded halfway up our collective ass would've been an understatement. For one thing, it would've entirely missed the artfully varied and delectably exquisite collection of pains, aches, and general discomforts that pervaded my body over the next bleary *however long*.

For another, it would've failed to adequately explain how I eventually found myself once again draped over Alton Parker's arms like a helpless scudboots, staring up at a dancing canopy of leaves as the raknoth carried me into the forest.

The forest?

The Arkonian Forest to the northeast of Haven, my missile-shaken brain offered. Right. That made sense. Because they'd be chasing us, right? A glance past Parker's shoulder said yes. Especially since that indeterminable stretch of dazed, disoriented world-blurring had apparently only lasted a few minutes, tops.

We were barely fifty yards into the trees.

Close enough that I could still see bits of Haven through the trunks and branches and brambles. And close enough that I could just make out the first of the tracker's skimmers hovering up from the distant landing pads—most likely on their way to come see about that traitorous Demon of Divinity and his dastardly new ally figure, Alton gropping Parker.

All great reasons to run.

But there was something else, too. A voice echoing over the tall perimeter walls from the base-wide amps of Haven. A voice that lit a fire somewhere between my chest and my kill button.

"Auckus," I growled, rolling out of Parker's arms.

He didn't try to stop me, nor did he try to catch me when I collapsed straight to my knees, my head floating on thick waves of dizzy nausea.

"If you're done now," Parker said, "we really must be going. I don't think those skimmers are coming to say hello."

I held up a hand for silence, trying to listen in more closely. The sound from the amps carried well enough that I felt like I should've been able to make sense of it, but between the trees and competing echoes, the overall distance, and the steady ringing in my ears, Auckus' voice only came to me in snippets.

"—relieved of command… light of… including heresy and high treason, just to… interim, the high command… acting High General until such a…"

"Is he saying what I think he's saying?"

"To know that, I believe I would have to know what you think he's—"

"Parker," I growled.

He sighed. "It sounds as though High General Auckus has had quite an ambitious day. Perhaps we shouldn't allow him to add bagging our heads to the list of achievements."

Then I hadn't misheard.

High General Auckus.

I felt sick.

"Glenbark."

"Sounds to have been peacefully relieved of duty, pending trial."

"We have to go back."

He said nothing, just stalked over, clearly intending to scoop me up again. I scrambled to my feet and woozily staggered away.

"Don't be a child, Haldin. We have zero chance of doing any of your friends any good back there. We need to…"

But I was barely listening, busy instead with opening my palmlight, which thankfully still functioned, and swiping up my messages.

I breathed a sigh of relief when I saw Elise's name there, and then another one as I read the message.

<<Safe. With JJF. Meet where we first did in 2 days.>>

I read the first word over and over, trying to calm my breathing. Safe. She was safe. And with Johnny, James, and Franco? Probably. Clearly she'd been in a hurry in sending the message. That only made me wonder what

Phineas had told them, and if he and Therese would be safe as well—not to mention Four and Eight, and Glenbark herself.

Sweet Alpha, how had this happened?

"Answer," came Parker's voice from just behind me.

I looked at him, feeling off balance in a way that had little to do with my explosion-rattled brain. In the distance, I could feel the trackers approaching—not in my extended senses, but somewhere deep in my gut. Coming for us like the monsters in the dreams where you can never look back, only run.

"Answer her," he repeated, "and then we go, no palmlights."

It was downright annoying, how often he was right about these things. I knew for a fact the Legion could easily track my palmlight. There was no way I could bring it with us. For that matter, it seemed a slim shot that Elise had held on to hers once she'd sent that message, so I made sure to direct my reply to her public ID rather than to her specific device. Franco and Elise would both know more than a few ways to access it without getting themselves caught.

It was only once I had the blank message open and at the ready that I realized I had no idea what to say. What could I possibly say? I certainly wasn't safe. And after seasons of fighting to protect Enochia and dig ourselves out of the hole we'd landed in when the raknoth came, our entire world had just come burning down without warning.

"Haldin."

I looked at Parker, knowing that we had to move, and swiped out the basics.

<<*With Red. Be there in 2 days. I love you.*>>

Alton was already holding out his hand for my palmlight. I stripped the bracelet off and handed it over. He crushed the device in his bare hand like it was made of cheap plastwall.

It was only as I watched my palmlight bend and crack to useless scrap that I realized I wasn't even positive where Elise had meant by *where we first met*. Not Franco's old place. No way. Because that would be suicide if they were looking for us. It had to be somewhere else. Somewhere—

"Let's move," Parker said. I turned to find him facing me, arms held out, offering to carry me. Beyond the dense green canopy, I could just make out the sound of approaching skimmers.

I considered Parker's offer, then turned for the heart of the woods and started running.

"Too often, you confuse stubbornness for moral righteousness," came his voice beside me as he fell in, keeping effortless pace.

For a second, I considered channeling the energy to tap into the speed I'd discovered in Humility and remind him that I wasn't just another hapless human, but I was at least coherent enough to recognize how petty and pointless that would be. Especially since my stomach threatened to void its contents at the simple thought of channeling at all.

"Call it what you want," I grunted between breaths. "I need to know what's in your head, but I'm not gonna let a monster pretend like he's the good guy just so I can rest my tired legs."

He just shook his head at that, so condescendingly that I could've punched the glib bastard, but at least he didn't start prattling out loud about how a foolish little hatchling like myself couldn't possibly hope to understand the complexities of his superior experience and morality.

In fact, thinking about it as we plunged through the forest side by side, it almost seemed like a small kindness, the way the raknoth had bade me to answer Elise before the admittedly necessary act of destroying my palmlight. Almost like he cared. Almost.

Devious.

That was all I could think, ducking branches and vaulting fallen logs, the raknoth beside me every step of the way. Alton Parker was a devious serpent, and I'd be a fool to forget that his every breath was carefully calculated.

Still, this was all going to be for nothing if those trackers brought a legion down on our heads. It was hard to ignore the baying of the hounds back at the edge of the forest, maybe half a mile behind now, or the silent weight of the skimmers I knew would be overhead, making slow sweeps with their thermal scanners.

"This is foolish," Parker said a few minutes later, drawing to a pointed halt beneath a stony outcropping at the side of a burbling stream. "They'll be on us within the hour at this rate. Sooner." He extended his arms, offering again. "Do not be a child. There is far more at stake here than your pride."

So there it was. We'd made it about a mile before the shots at my intelligence and naivety came out. But there was no sense fighting it. He was right. I wasn't getting any less tired, he was a physically unparalleled alien being who was, by all appearances, indefatigable, and the hounds were getting closer by the minute.

Honestly, I was surprised he hadn't just attempted to snatch me up and make a break for it yet. Whatever he might think of my cognitive capacity, Parker at least seemed to be cautious of risking direct conflict with my abilities. Or maybe that was just what he wanted me to think.

Either way, we were running out of time to argue.

I pointedly stepped past his extended arms and hopped onto his back instead. Call me a stubborn human, but if I was going to ride a villainous raknoth through the woods, I was at least going to do it on my own terms.

If Parker took qualm with the small defiance, he didn't say anything. He just shifted to settle me in, told me to hold on, and took off up the stream bed like the Great Demon himself was nipping at our heels.

"So DID YOU HAVE A PLAN?" I asked some hours later, trying to hide my labored breathing as I stopped to tighten my boots. "Or were you thinking we'd just keep walking around in the woods until I starve, or those trackers finally catch up with us?"

Parker looked back from the rocky bluff overlooking the river we'd just reached, his usual smirk firmly in place. "Do I look like a man with a plan?"

"Only if I'm comparing you to Auckus and the High Cleric and whoever else was responsible for whatever the scud just happened back there. In which case, yeah, I'd say you look exactly like a... *person* with a plan."

It was the first either of us had spoken in a long while. After escaping Haven, Parker had carried me for at least an hour, maybe more, and we'd shared little but insults throughout. Insults, and Parker's steady insistence that we should go a bit further before slowing down. I estimated we'd covered a good twenty-five miles of woodlands at his daunting raknoth pace before he'd finally declared it safe for me to proceed on my own two feet.

My jostled hips and chafed thighs had been grateful for the news. The rest of me, on the other hand...

"So where are you taking us?" I asked, finishing with my boots and fixing him with a hard stare.

It'd seemed all along like he'd had some destination in mind. I just couldn't figure out where, especially not once we'd turned southeast a few miles back. Parker, of course, was being Parker about it, and saying only that he was trying to keep us out of the path of the trackers.

Had I not been on the run from the Legion and pretty much everyone else, with nothing but the clothes on my back and a shifty raknoth at my side, I probably would've put my foot down sooner. As it was, now seemed the perfect time.

Parker frowned at me and strolled over to sit on a smooth gray boulder before answering. Below, I felt the river flowing by, out of sight but still present in the roar of its waters and the refreshing kiss of the cool, misty air wafting over from the bluff's edge.

"I'll admit," the raknoth finally said, "I have been holding something back."

"Imagine my surprise."

He flexed his fingers, and I tensed a little to see his claws emerging. "Forgive me for not tripping over myself to share my every thought and secret with a child who bickers at even the simple thought of being carried. The information was not relevant until we'd cleared the trackers."

I held his gaze, refusing to flinch or rise to the bait. "And you're sure we are clear?"

He shrugged. "I haven't heard a hint of our pursuit since we changed bearing. As for your earlier complaint, if your poor body requires nourishment, perhaps you should go catch a hare and tend to that. I'm sure it's within your capabilities. This may take me a few minutes."

I wanted to ask him what the scud he was up to, but I was pretty sure he'd just enjoy the verbal exercise. Frustrating as it was, though, in some twisted way, Parker's slithery abrasiveness was almost comforting. As long as I knew we were still only a few short words away from a fight at any given moment, it almost felt like the world wasn't coming to an end around me. Almost.

"Parker."

He surfaced from whatever thought he was having and turned a serious look my way. I listened to the rushing water below, searching for the words, and not particularly wanting to find them. Would that I could simply relish the wonderful peace of this place instead.

"Was it you?" I finally asked.

His face gave nothing away as he cocked his head in question.

"The timing of everything," I said. "You turning up at Haven. You sending us to that tavern, sparking an entire world war on Shapers. And this… this mutiny of Haven, or whatever it was… I can't help but notice that suddenly everyone I care about is in danger, and you're here walking free, with me conveniently stuck to your boot treads."

He studied me for a long time, then finally raised one bare, dirt-blackened foot, as if to remind me that he didn't *have* any boot treads. "I won't claim I'm disheartened by the way events have turned out," he said, "but no schemer alive or dead could rightly take credit for setting all this in motion."

"And yet it's happening."

"Because your people have spent a thousand years stoking the fires of fear and good faith."

Because of your bastard pal, Sarentus, I wanted to snap back. But I still wasn't positive about what exactly I'd even seen in Parker's memories, much less its implications for Enochia. I was too busy worrying about my friends, who most certainly had not escaped the boot treads.

"What are they gonna do to Glenbark?" I asked quietly, not really expecting an answer.

Elise and Johnny would be safe enough with Franco and James, I thought. But the rest of my people, the ones who'd put themselves out there to help me these past cycles...

"I imagine you would know the answer to that better than I," Parker said. "It is a Legion affair, after all."

I scowled. "I'm not sure there is such a thing as a Legion affair anymore. Not with the Sanctum pulling all the strings. They must've helped Auckus pull this off."

"It hardly matters now."

"How can you say that?" I snapped, before I could remind myself who it was I was talking to.

"Because it is done, and because the situation is beyond our control now."

"Like scud it is. Just because you don't care about anything but your own hide doesn't mean I can't still out the Sanctum. Sarentus was a fraud. You showed me that much. And if that's true, then it's provable too. If we can just—"

"Haldin."

"What?" I met his patronizing look with a glare. "What the scud do you want? Why else even bother showing me these things if you don't—"

"I showed you because you asked," he said calmly. "And if we hadn't been so rudely interrupted, I might have finished showing you why a few petty squabbles over Shapers and Legion leadership are less than pressing in the grand scheme of things."

I gritted my teeth, not really sure why I bothered resisting the urge to telekinetically cast the raknoth over the bluff's edge and into the rushing river below. It's not like a little tumble would've been all that *pressing* for him, after all, in the grand scheme of things.

"I don't care what you think you know," I said slowly. "I need to protect my people. There's nothing petty about that."

Parker shrugged. "Perhaps not. But, setting aside the fact that you are all in fact hopelessly infantile blips on the journey to true maturity, your friends *are* all what you would call adults. They made their decisions. They will live their journeys. Perhaps they will even overcome the trials before them. It matters little."

I opened my mouth, but he cut me off with a sharp look, his dark eyes taking on a faint crimson hue.

"You wish to protect this planet of yours? All I can tell you with certainty is that you will fail unless you come to grips with the fact that you will never be able to save every life, or control every outcome. Not even close."

"That's bullscud," I said. "I'm not trying to control everything. I'm trying—"

"To butt heads with the strongest, most stable spiritual leadership this planet has ever known?"

"To tell the truth," I countered. "To make sure this planet sees justice and never has to deal with your kind again."

"Mmm," Parker said. "The truth. Well, then I suppose you had best learn the entirety of it before you…"

He drifted off, a light frown creasing his brow as he tilted his nose skyward and took a sharp sniff. I was about to ask him what it was when he rounded on me, eyes blazing with crimson fire. He opened his mouth—

And disappeared, rocketing from his perch and over the cliff's edge as if smacked by the hand of Alpha himself.

I saw nothing. No hostiles. Just the flash of a powerful mind appearing out of nowhere right above me, and the scream of my extended senses telling me to move my ass. I leapt aside the instant before the newcomer slammed down, shaking the rock beneath my boots. A raknoth. It had to be.

Another slammed down behind me, and before I could so much as twitch, a force fell over my body like a mountain of hardsteel, wrapping me tight until I could barely draw breath. I was hovering. Suspended a foot from the ground, completely paralyzed by the pressure.

Completely paralyzed by *telekinesis*, my shocked brain realized.

And no sooner had I stumbled through the implication of what that meant than I found myself rotating in midair to face the short, red-eyed raknoth whose face I'd never seen. But I didn't need to recognize that dark-haired, square-jawed face to know I was looking at the possessed body of one of the Seekers who'd been missing since Oasis. The one who'd been known as Five, I guessed. Which meant the sandy-haired, red-eyed woman behind me was the one who'd been Seven.

"Haldin Raish," said the former, drawing the name out as if it brought him no small amount of satisfaction. "The mighty Demon of Divinity, brought to heel with a snap of the fingers."

He actually snapped his fingers as he said the words, and what little breath I had was squeezed out, the invisible cage tightening until I thought my ribs would crack.

Five tilted his head to look at his partner behind me, favoring her with a reptilian smile.

"If only Zar'Faenor could see us now."

15

RIVERSIDE ROAR

Alton Parker had betrayed me.

That was the first thing—and pretty much the only one—that flashed through my mind as the Seeker-turned-raknoth prowled forward to end my life.

I couldn't have said why I felt so surprised. Certainly, Parker had never given me any reason to expect otherwise. He'd tried to kill me himself more than once. And trekking here through the forest, all the while pretending he was simply evading capture... All the while leading me to the slaughter...

And now there was nothing I could do.

Against Frosty, I'd barely managed to break free of her telekinetic hold. Against two of her supercharged kin, it was pointless to even try. Their raknoth bodies were simply too strong, too robust—capable of channeling far too much energy for my human flesh to ever hope to compete with.

I was dead.

Which is why I was properly, scud-to-sunshine flabbergasted when a dark green beast in a tattered brig jumpsuit came flying up from the edge of the riverside cliff and caught my first would-be killer in a ferocious tackle.

Parker and Five hit the ground in a growling mess of limbs, bouncing across the gray rock like skipping stones. Bound straight for me.

Some semblance of good sense caught up, and I telekinetically dialed my cloaking pendant in, close enough to cut me off from the raknoth still holding me. I hit the ground and dodged clear of the speeding double-raknoth missile—just in time to whirl around and find Seven rocketing straight for me, claws outstretched.

I rolled backward on the rock, kicking straight up to catch my incoming attacker in the stomach with both feet as she flew by. I rocked with her momentum, driving with my legs and adding a heavy hit of telekinetic force. She went flying. Literally.

Riding on the back of my telekinetic springboard, the raknoth had sailed a good twenty feet and was well on her way to plunging off of the cliff to the river below when her legs and hands shot out and she simply stopped right in midair. It took me a moment to register she'd caught herself with telekinesis. Then a wet crack and a stomach-turning shriek from behind yanked my attention away.

If Alton Parker had betrayed me, it wasn't working out well for him.

Parker was pinned, his foe holding his arm at an unnatural angle in both hands. As I turned, Five gave another wrench, digging his claws in at the shoulder, and Parker roared as something tore and his entire damn arm nearly came off. I reached out and ripped Five off of him with telekinesis, yanking the enemy raknoth right between us.

Just in time to remember I didn't have so much as a dinner knife to drive into his fiery red eyes.

I pivoted outside of the staggering raknoth's first swipe, planted a telekinetically-enhanced fist on his jaw, then tucked into a roll as my extended senses flared with a sharp alarm. I hadn't made it more than halfway through the maneuver when what felt like a loaded transport landed square on top of me, crushing me to the rock hard enough that it seemed a minor wonder I didn't simply splatter open.

Our flying raknoth had rejoined the party, I realized. And they had me pinned again, so firmly I couldn't even turn my head as the two closed on me.

At the edge of my vision, I saw Parker stumbling to his feet. I reached for my pendant with my senses, realizing even as I did that the raknoth were already too close for me to have any hope of effectively cutting myself off from their influence. For a moment, I clung to the hope that Parker would come lunging to the rescue. Then he slammed down to the rock beside me, clearly struggling against the same telekinetic restraints as I was.

I pushed harder, gathering my will, thinking to tell Parker to fight it alongside me—to put his Alpha-damned raknoth back into it. But a pair of dark boots stepped into view beside my head before I could so much as send the telepathic thought.

The thing that had been Five raised one dark boot, and I stared at the ridged treads, unable to think about anything but the fact that this must be some twisted joke of the universe—death by boot stomp not five minutes after I'd just made some smart comment about being stuck to Parker's treads. Maybe Alpha was paying attention. Maybe he'd sent these monsters to end me.

I stared up at that eager reptilian face, wondering what the holy bastard might have in store for the rest of my loved ones once I was gone.

Then the thing that had been Five jerked back, spewing a trail of dark ichor from the back of his head. He jerked again, and again, sagging limply to his knees before Seven threw her hand up, and three more sharp projectiles yanked to a halt a few feet in front of them. Pulse cannon bolts, I realized.

Legion bolts?

I didn't know whether to cry for joy or run for my life. I settled for throwing myself against my telekinetic prison with everything I could muster. Parker must've done the same, because after a moment of straining, we both bounced to our feet like we'd popped through an invisible membrane.

I didn't see the shooter, but the raknoth they'd hit was still sagged on his knees like dead weight, eyes dim and vacant. Seven whirled to meet us with a deep roar, the crimson fire in her eyes burning more than bright enough for the both of them.

More pulse bolts flashed in from the left as she tensed to spring, but they deflected off of whatever barrier she'd raised and pelted into the surrounding rock with a series of loud cracks and exploding debris. I reached out and telekinetically swept the raknoth's legs out from under her as she tried to launch herself at us. She collapsed like the rocks were slick with ice, and caught herself on her hands.

Parker lunged in for the kill and quickly found himself taking telekinetic flight into the nearest tree trunk, which gave way with a sound like a gunshot. More bolts from the left. Seven raised her hand toward me. I braced, preparing to counter her telekinesis. Then there was a flicker of movement to the right, and she whipped around—straight into a flying kick from a newcomer with glimmering red eyes and enough momentum to send the raknoth bouncing across the rocks with an aggravated snarl.

I took in our savior's green canvas jacket and violent smirk.

"Garrett?" I croaked. Right before our raknoth friend caught herself and lunged back in for revenge.

More by reflex than good sense, I telekinetically caught Seven before she could reach Garrett. In turn, Garrett stepped forward to take advantage of the opportunity, looking like he was ready to enjoy it. Alton Parker got there first.

I hadn't seen the raknoth jump from wherever he'd landed post-tree-crash, but Parker came down with enough velocity to tell me it had been a high one. I dropped my hold on our foe just as Parker crashed into his kin, feet first. The impact shattered the stone beneath them—which kind of seemed like it should have been the end of it.

It wasn't.

The enemy raknoth's hand shot up, and Parker took a blast of force that sent him flying back the way he'd come. I caught him before he flew too far, and dropped him back to his feet so he could try again. Garrett, meanwhile, was already stalking in to take his own shot at Seven. I charged forward to help him. Parker hit the rock beside me, and joined in without breaking stride.

For a second, I thought the three of us actually had her.

Then Seven reared her head back in a battle roar straight from demons' depths, and the air detonated with a brilliant flash of light and a concussive boom that rattled my entire being and sent us all flying. I only barely remained conscious enough to siphon some velocity off my own flight and bring myself to a shaky landing. Parker and Garrett didn't fare so well.

Frazzled as my eyes were, I felt more than actually saw them strike the rocky outcropping beside the river lookout, but the impact felt hard enough to make me cringe. When I finally blinked my eyes clear, Parker was shaking it off. Garrett, not so much.

And the enemy raknoth were gone. Both of them.

I scanned our surroundings, defenses raised, half-expecting a raknoth to drop down on my head or simply wink into existence behind me. But there was nothing. No sign of either of them. I shifted my efforts into maintaining the light barrier I'd raised, wondering next where our mysterious shooter had vanished off to. Because there had definitely been a shooter, hadn't there?

Even enhanced as Garrett was by whatever Parker and Frosty had done to him during his captivity, I was pretty sure he couldn't move fast enough to shoot from one side of the clearing and then attack from the other a second later. Which meant he probably had backup. And I had a feeling I knew who.

Before I could properly sweep the surrounding woods, though, a string of growled curses brought me back to the rocky bluff, where Parker was crouched down checking on Garrett, who clearly wanted Parker's help like he wanted another rock wall to the head.

"Back off, you son of a bitch," he was growling at Parker as I limped over to join them.

"Have it your way, then," Parker said with a dismissive shrug. The fire had dimmed from his eyes, and his features were already reverting from green and scaly back to standard human as he stood and shot a contemplative frown at his own mangled shoulder.

I almost asked if the two of them were all right before remembering that I probably shouldn't care.

"You look like scud, Raish," Garrett growled, somehow still managing to smirk up at me through his clear pain.

"Oh, be nice to the poor Demon," called a perfectly sultry voice from behind.

Siren.

I turned to find the dirty blond goddess strolling languidly toward us, a light pulse rifle braced casually over one shoulder. She showed me a smile nearly as glib as Garrett's.

"He's been having such a hard time lately."

SCHEMERS AND SCALES

I was too exhausted and shell-shocked—and plain old *normal* shocked, too, I guess—to do anything other than stare as Siren strolled right up and wrapped me in a warm, rather chesty hug. I stood there, looking confusedly at Alton Parker, of all people, until she drew back from the hug and patted my cheek.

"What," she said, "no hello for old friends?"

The memory of just how friendly she'd once tried to get with me finally snapped me back to my senses. I pointedly disengaged from her, taking a few steps back until there was nothing at my back but cold, trusty rock. As if that really made me any safer.

Hard rock at my back. Three people who'd each tried to kill me multiple times at my front.

Safe as safe could be. Totally.

"What are you doing here?" I asked, looking between Siren and Garrett. "How did you—Actually, never mind a second." I looked at Parker, deciding those answers could wait. "Is she still nearby?"

Parker shook his head. "I believe they've fled to lick their wounds for now."

And with that, he turned and walked away from us to go sit on his own private outcropping, as if that was simply that.

"They?" I called after him. "Five looked pretty dead to me after"—I glanced at Siren's pulse rifle—"you know."

She patted the weapon's stock affectionately. "I think I'm finally getting the hang of this thing."

"That thing was still alive?" Garrett asked, quietly enough that I didn't realize he was talking to Parker until the raknoth replied, loud enough that we could hear him.

"I believe so, yes. Now, if you'd allow me to concentrate for a moment…"

"Suit yourself, scudhead," Garrett muttered, accepting the hand Siren offered him and rising to his feet with a grimace.

I looked between the ex-Seekers and Parker, not sure what line of burning questions to follow. I settled on turning to the unknowns who were physically closer.

"What are you two doing here?"

"Breaking a few perfectly good ribs for your sorry ass, as far as I can tell," Garrett said.

"And protecting you," Siren said.

Garrett pointed at her, arching an eyebrow at me as if to say, *See? Told you.*

"You're welcome, by the way," he added.

I felt about as *welcome* as I did *safe and settled.* "How did you find us out here?"

They traded a glance.

"We followed the party," Siren said.

"Wasn't hard to figure out who they were after," Garrett added.

"We even found some fun new toys," Siren said, patting her rifle again.

My stomach sank. "You didn't kill anyone, did you?"

Siren touched a delicate hand to her chest as if to say, *Who, little old me?*

"We're not monsters, Raish," Garrett said.

"Said the ex-Shaper-hunter with the shiny red eyes," I muttered.

Garrett bristled at that, his coy smirk dropping for the first time to be replaced in full by hard fury. He took a step toward me, priming a finger to jab in my chest and no doubt make some point. Siren laid a hand on his shoulder before he could, and Garrett calmed, visibly and almost immediately, like her touch was akin to a low grade sedative for him—which, knowing what I did about her talents, it actually might well have been.

"We just borrowed a ride and kept our distance," Siren said quietly. "Judging by the way things were looking when we showed up, I'm thinking maybe you should be glad we did."

It wasn't so much that I didn't agree with what she said. It was just that it killed me, seeing the smug look on Garrett's face as she said it.

Somehow, I managed a calming breath. "Fine. You're right, I... Thank you. Both of you. I guess. We were in trouble before you showed up."

"I'll say," Garrett muttered, smirk firmly intact.

I clenched my jaw. "I guess I'm just wondering what it is you two are doing here."

"That's funny," Garrett said, "because I was just wondering what the scud *he's* doing over *there.*"

I followed his pointing finger and was rewarded with a jolt of alarm at the sight of Parker placing his clawed fingertips to his abdomen as if preparing to rip out his own stomach. His brig jumpsuit, he'd already ripped aside to clear the way.

"Alton! What are you doing?"

The raknoth looked up with a single arched brow. "It's 'Alton' now, is it? Well, if I'd known it'd be as simple as surviving one little fight together..."

He did it without warning.

One second, he was sitting there, looking like he was trying to remember where he'd left his coin purse. The next, he was buried to the wrist in his own innards. It was shocking on a number of levels.

And by "shocking," I guess I really mean "gropped up beyond words."

For starters, it was about as far from a pretty sight as I could imagine anything being. True, as far as plunging a hand into one's own abdomen went, I guess Parker had done a fairly neat job of it, but dark raknoth blood still flowed freely from the wound, running down his forearm and trickling from his elbow to the stone below.

And the sounds...

I'm not even sure where to start with the sounds, other than that they reminded me in the worst possible way of someone emphatically stirring a bowl of thick, saucy noodles. But the visceral disgustingness of the act was only the first in a long line of details that were making my skin crawl.

For another, after all the abuse I'd seen dealt—and sometimes dealt myself—upon raknoth hide, there was something highly disconcerting about seeing Parker's flesh give way so easily to anything, even his own claws. It looked fundamentally wrong, like a hardsteel blade inexplicably drooping. Like he was actually vulnerable. And making that thought worse was the look on Parker's face.

Once my brain got over the fact that the raknoth wasn't simply dropping dead, I processed the look on his face. It was an odd combination between discomfort and the focused look of someone rummaging through a bag for the item they couldn't see but knew exactly where to find.

Given the circumstances, it was pretty damn creepy.

"You forget where you left your shriveled heart?" Garrett asked, clearly trying to hide the fact that he was as rattled as I was.

Siren just watched with a soft grimace, her hand resting lightly over her own abdomen in sympathy or disgust.

After everything that'd happened in the past hours—the coup at Haven and the slug-storm of our escape, Parker's revelation about Sarentus, and Alpha, about the people of Enochia…

Even *before* I'd gone on the run with a gropping raknoth and been spontaneously attacked by two more, only to be rescued by two Seekers, I'm pretty sure I would've been justified in worrying I might've already lost it. When Parker's hand slid free from his own abdomen with a wet, sucking sound, bearing a fist-sized *something*, though, I decided it was more than justified.

The mystery object was dark—though that might've just been the raknoth blood I was seeing. Either way, the nauseous feeling in my gut took on a tingly chill when I realized the thing was shaped somewhat like an egg.

"What the scud…" I whispered.

Beside me, Garrett produced a more creative string of curses.

"You might want to keep your heads down," Parker said, closing his eyes and holding the odd egg aloft.

"Hey, wait!" I snapped, right as Garrett added his own, "Grop that!"

Something passed over me. I couldn't say exactly what. The faintest whisper of telepathic presence, like a barely perceptible stirring of wind. All three of us had taken a step forward, and I was reaching to remove the device from Parker's hand telekinetically when the raknoth opened his eyes and sat back, looking satisfied. Then expectant. Then confused.

The dark egg shot from his hand and came to hover a few feet in front of Garrett, who'd clearly grabbed it with telekinesis and was just as clearly hesitant to touch the thing. "What the scud did you just—"

I cried out and dropped to the ground before my mind could even process why. It was reflexive, an unthinking submission to the enormous mass quite suddenly floating over our heads out of nowhere. It was impossible, my senses cried as my tail bone hit hard rock and I gaped up at the dark apparition. But there it was. As real in my senses as it was to my shocked eyes.

It was Alton Parker's ship. The same slender, flowing vessel he'd flown into Haven on the day of his surrender. It floated twenty feet overhead, looming, its dark hull catching the sunlight with an iridescence that made it difficult to determine its actual color, beyond something vaguely purplish. It floated like it had been there all along, waiting, nearly silent but for a faint low hum.

"There we are," Parker said. "Splendid."

This time, Siren joined Garrett in his steady stream of cursing. They both had their weapons at the ready—Garrett with a long dagger in hand, and Siren with her pulse rifle aimed straight at Parker. I felt her glance my way as if to ask if there were any reason she shouldn't put a few sharp bolts through the raknoth's skull then and there. I was too busy sifting through the stream of indignant realizations rushing through my head.

"You had that thing the whole time," I said.

"Something told me the Legion might be reticent to hand the ship back over when it was time," Parker said, setting the... whatever it was down and reaching back for the open wound in his abdomen.

"Stop," I said, but without any real authority.

Parker stuck his hand back through the wound with a grimace, then summarily pitched forward from his rocky perch and flew through the air, corkscrewing around until he slammed to the stone at Garrett's feet. Garrett stared down at him with murderous eyes, keeping the raknoth pinned with telekinesis. After a moment's hesitation, I added my own strength to pinning Parker down, and moved over to stand above the raknoth as well.

"Any good reason I shouldn't kill this bastard right now, Raish?" Garrett asked as I joined them.

I was kind of surprised he even asked, much as he clearly wanted to do it.

Parker just gave him a bored look before turning a knowing expression my way. "Tell him, Haldin."

"I don't care how many answers you have buried in there, Parker," I said, kneeling down beside the pinned raknoth. "There are three of us now. We'll take your memories by force if we have to. Now tell me what the scud you're up to."

"Because he definitely won't lie," Siren said.

I ignored her. "What were you reaching for? What is that... thing?" I added, glancing at the dark egg-shaped device that'd fallen to the ground when Garrett decided to take a more active role in shutting down Parker's antics.

"That thing," Parker said, "is a kind of communications device. One that preferably shouldn't be dropped on hard stone," he added with a dark look at Garrett. "And as for what I was reaching for, it's merely—"

But Garrett dropped down and punched a hand into Parker's open gut before the raknoth could finish. The raknoth's eyes clamped shut, his jaw tight with pain, a low growl building in his throat.

"That's okay, scudhead," Garrett said. "We'll just see for ourselves."

"Those are my intestines," Parker grunted. "Agh… And that's the liver."

"Never knew anatomy lessons could be so much fun," Garrett said, rummaging on unperturbed.

My stomach felt about as comfortable as Parker's must've with the entire ordeal, but I said nothing, in no mood to defend either of them. Mostly, I just wished I could be anywhere but that ichor-stained rock, crouched over a lying raknoth and half-expecting our friends from earlier, or even the Legion trackers, to show up any moment. I looked up at the silent alien ship hovering over us and wondered how Elise and Johnny were getting along.

At least I could safely bet their day hadn't been stranger than mine, I decided as Garrett gave a satisfied grunt and messily yanked another bloody *something* from Parker's abdomen. It was larger than the egg device, and upon closer inspection, I thought it looked a bit like a high tech version of one of the automated food and drink hoppers people sometimes set out for their hounds when they were leaving their loyal pets alone for a prolonged amount of time.

The translucent container Garrett had yanked from Parker's abdomen was nearly empty, but I was pretty sure I knew what the small amount of dark liquid at the bottom was.

I felt my hands clench into fists. "You had this all planned the whole damn time. You had a way to escape."

"I couldn't call the ship until I was outside," Parker said calmly.

"You had the blood to survive for days."

"Do you blame me for hesitating to trust your people would be comfortable feeding me their own blood? I merely planned for the worst. I couldn't have hoped events would work out quite so perfectly as they ha—Agh!"

For a second, I almost thought it'd been Garrett who'd telekinetically lifted and slammed Parker's head to the rock. But it hadn't been.

"Oops," I muttered. "I didn't plan it. I swear."

"Yes, yes," Parker said. "Again with the righteous indignation. Have you forgotten what's happening out there to your precious world?"

"Happening because you let it," I snapped. "Because you started this entire gropping mess and led us all straight into it."

Parker scowled. "Grow up, Haldin."

At a motion from Garrett's direction, I looked over and found the Seeker offering me his dagger.

"If you don't," he said, "I will."

Parker shifted against our hold, probably preparing to fight. "This is hardly the time for—"

"Shut up," I said, taking the dagger. I didn't particularly want to use it. Or didn't plan to, at least. *Wanting* was a different thing completely. But either way, I figured it was better in my hand than in Garrett's.

And besides, Parker didn't need to know that I wasn't planning on killing him. Yet.

"If you didn't engineer all this, how did your kin find us?" I glanced at Garrett and Siren, realizing I still didn't really understand how or why they'd found us either, but that could sit another minute. I stared at Parker, waiting for his answer.

"I thought I was supposed to shut up," he finally said.

Garrett punched him.

I held up a hand to stop him from doing it again. "Now who's being the child?"

Parker shrugged. "Search my mind, then, if you would have the truth. I won't resist."

That caught me by surprise—not so much because it sounded to my logical brain like a trap, but rather because I actually found myself believing him. Garrett and Siren looked similarly uncertain, though probably for entirely different reasons.

Parker showed us a predatory smile, clearly enjoying our hesitation. "Whatever you decide, perhaps we should talk aboard the ship, where we won't be sitting targets."

"Yeah, because nothing blends in like a giant purple beardsplitter floating through the sky," Garrett said. "I'm not going in there."

"Comforting as it is to know that even alien men clearly feel the need to compensate," Siren added, "I agree. We're quite fine on the ground, thanks."

"Suit yourselves," Parker said. "Haldin, we should move."

Like scud, we should, I wanted to say, just like Garrett and Siren were obviously expecting me to.

"If you want to get answers out of his head," Garrett said, "then have at it. We'll help. But I'm not letting this bastard walk away alive."

"We stashed our skimmer nearby," Siren added. "We don't need this…" She looked up at the motionless ship. "… compensation."

On the ground, Parker gave a soft chuckle. Garrett cocked a fist, ready to shut him up again.

"What?" I asked before he could. "What's so funny?"

"Well," Parker said slowly, "for one thing, I'd like to point out that, aboard my ship, we *could* hide in orbit, as opposed to whatever rodent's den these two have crawled out of. No one on the planet will have any hope of finding us until we want them to."

Something about the way his satisfied smile kept stretching told me there was more.

"And?"

"Annnd…" He cocked his head as if listening carefully for some distant sound, and it was only then that I noticed it. The faintest hum of approaching skimmers. From the same direction, a hound's bark echoed to us from beyond the tree line.

"And it's possible my ship's appearance may have given our location away," Parker concluded, grinning at Siren. "Forgive me for compensating."

That did it for Garrett.

The dagger had flown from my hand into his and plunged halfway to Parker's right eye before I caught the weapon in my own telekinetic grasp. Garrett glared at me, incredulous. I opened my mouth to tell him I needed answers first.

Parker was ready.

No sooner had my focus shifted to the dagger than he exploded into motion, kipping up to his feet with inhuman speed and leaping skyward. Before either of us could blink, he'd landed in the open port that had mysteriously appeared in the side of the alien vessel, right above the boarding ramp that was unfurling from the ship like a living thing, inviting us to follow.

Siren opened fire. Parker ducked inside the ship.

I half-expected he'd fly off then and there, leaving us to deal with our closing Legion pursuit. Maybe just leaving the planet for good. But the ship remained exactly where it was, and Parker himself must not have retreated any further than behind the cover of the hull.

"Don't be foolish," he called down from the open port. "Get aboard and let us be done with this petty bickering."

"It that scudhead serious?" Garrett muttered.

Siren glanced at him for direction, her rifle still shouldered at the ready.

"I think we should go with him," I said, the words tasting like opa ash on my tongue.

They both stared at me.

"Is *this* scudhead serious?" Siren asked.

"We don't exactly have many great choices," I said, pointedly nodding toward the sounds of our pursuit.

By way of reply, Siren pulled her arcane vanishing act and disappeared from sight completely.

"Cute," I said. "But there's more at stake here than us getting caught and killed. Parker has information that could bring down the Sanctum, and maybe even exonerate our kind in the public eye."

"I doubt that," Garrett said.

"Well then sit here and pout," I snapped. I couldn't even say why I was suddenly so angry. "Or kill Alton Parker. Or run back to your hidey hole. See what good any of it does." I looked between them, prepared to evade the sucker punch I was fifty percent sure Garrett would throw my way.

"I'm guessing you two didn't come here out of concern for my personal wellbeing today," I said when it seemed my face was safe for the moment. "You wanna help me put a stop to the madness out there? I say our best bet is on that ship. That's all I've got, take it or leave it."

And with that, I turned and leapt for the floating ship, enhancing the effort with a heavy pull of telekinesis to land me on the boarding ramp twenty feet above. I was fuming, my hands shaking—though I couldn't have said why. Maybe it was that I was once again playing straight into Alton Parker's waiting claws. Maybe it was that I didn't seem to have a choice, or that Garrett and Siren were right, and I was making the wrong one. I couldn't tell anymore.

All I knew was that I was both irritated and relieved when I heard a thud behind me and felt the ship gently rock with the impact. I didn't have to look back to know that Garrett and Siren had made their decision and that, like it or not, my party of unsavory allies had just grown to three.

And as I stepped into the oddly angle-less, decidedly alien corridor of the ship, there was Alton Parker, casually leaning against the bulkhead with arms crossed, reminding me just what manner of treachery I might well be getting myself into.

"Welcome aboard," he said with a smirk.

"Just shut up and get us out of here," I said as Garrett and Siren stepped cautiously into the corridor behind me. "Then we're all gonna have a long talk."

17

ORBIT

After having witnessed the speed and agility with which Parker's ship had blown into Haven on the day he'd surrendered, I took it as a given that losing our Legion tracker pursuit wouldn't be much of a problem. I wasn't wrong.

The ship was beyond fast. Alien fast. And yet, somehow, the accelerations we were subjected to once strapped and secured in our flight seats didn't seem much more aggressive than anything I'd ever experience in a much slower skimmer.

It was a mystery, but hardly the biggest one. For instance, there was the fact that Parker seemed to be controlling the ship by telepathic influence alone. There was the generally similar but unmistakably *alien* architecture of the cockpit—or the flight room or whatever they called it. There was the fluidly responsive "viewport" at the front of the room, which had basically morphed from solid opaque purple wall to what resembled an enormous curved display that seemed to know exactly when and where to zoom, based on how we looked at it.

And then there was the deep, star-speckled black of outer space that utterly swallowed us as we cleared the last few layers of atmosphere only to find ourselves, I realized, still attached to the ship deck by some form of artificial gravity. In outer-freaking-space.

Just when I'd thought my day couldn't get any weirder.

"I think I'm gonna be sick," Siren whispered beside me.

I looked over to find her looking uncharacteristically clammy, her lips drawn tight. On the other side of her, Garrett looked a little green himself, but his pale reddish eyes were fixed on me.

"Lovely plan you have here," he muttered.

"Haldin is the only one of you who displayed even a modicum of logic back there," Parker called without looking back from his high-backed flight seat.

Parker's praise made me feel dirtier than any insult ever could have. Instead of wasting my breath arguing with either of them, though, I focused on controlling it and trying to calm my racing thoughts. I seriously needed a game plan. Or, at the very least, I needed to figure out what in demons' depths I was supposed to do until I could find the others and see what they'd come up with.

Lost as I was in my thoughts—not to mention in gaping at the wide open blackness of outer space, as Parker did whatever it was he was doing—I nearly jumped when Siren took my hand and twined her fingers in mine. At first, I thought she was just toying with me. She had seemed to genuinely enjoy making me uncomfortable in the past, after all. But then I glanced over and saw that Garrett was already holding her other hand, and I understood that the contact was intended only to circumvent my cloaking pendant.

Sure enough, Garrett's voice came to my mind almost immediately. *"We need to get this info you're after, figure out how to land this thing, and get rid of that bastard before he can do whatever the scud it is he's planning to do with us."*

I glanced at Parker's turned back, not necessarily disagreeing. Part of me wanted to say that I didn't think he planned any harm to the three of us— that he couldn't have possibly even known Garrett and Siren were coming at all. But the thought sounded hopelessly naive even in my own head. Parker had been scheming every inch of the way to get here. Which, for the thousandth time, just reminded me that I couldn't trust a single thing about the raknoth.

"What are you after, anyway?" came Siren's voice.

I eyed her, wondering if I could trust the two of them—or anyone else besides Elise and the others, for that matter.

"He showed me something before things hit the turbines back at Haven," I finally sent.

"I take it it wasn't what he's packing beneath that jumpsuit," Garrett sent.

"We all know you're a hard man to impress there," Siren added, which earned me a slightly sharper glare from Garrett.

Great. As if the man needed more fuel on his fire. Why *not* bring up the time his girlfriend had tried to sink her seductive fangs into me?

"He showed me something about the Sanctum's origin," I sent. *"Something that convinced me to break him out of there. Not that I had much choice after High General Auckus sent a squad to kill me."*

They traded a look.

"Is there a single tingler nest you haven't kicked on this planet, Raish?" Garrett sent.

"Yours, obviously."

He narrowed his eyes, and I swear the irises glinted slightly redder.

"What kind of secret's worth siding with a creature that's done the things he has?" Siren asked.

I was surprised by the depth of disgust in her mental tone. For a scant second, it almost sounded like she really cared. About everything. The hybrids. The war. The current predicament. And maybe she did. Maybe they both did.

"You never told me why you two decided to come looking for us in the first place," I sent.

"It's rude, you know," Parker cut in aloud before they could reply, "whispering behind closed doors, so to speak."

Ahead, he unstrapped and rose from his flight chair, apparently done with the navigation. By unspoken agreement, we all unstrapped and stood too. At the ready, just in case. However it was generated, the ship's gravity felt comparable to Enochia's.

I was still running through my assessment of our situation and Garrett was busy giving Parker a hot retort—something about the raknoth having some serious nerve—when the scene in the viewing wall began to shift. It started with a cool light at the bottom of our view, muting out some of the aggressive blackness of space. Then it grew, an enormous, hazy sphere of green and blue and white, cutting through the darkness, rising into view. Even Garrett fell silent.

Enochia.

The world rotated into view, all but filling the wall display with its tranquil beauty. Never in my lifetime had I thought to see my planet like this. Space travel had always been a job for those rare techs who worked installation and maintenance on Enochia's plethora of monitoring and communications satellites. That was it. They didn't go farther than orbit. What was the point?

As the Sanctum had reminded the world a hundred years ago when some pioneering adventurers had thought to go explore the moons, there was nothing out there for us in the cold depths of space. Alpha had already placed us on the finest utopia the universe had to offer, after all. So there we'd remain, worshiping his wisdom. To do otherwise would've been madness.

Staring down at the planet from on high, I really couldn't argue with the utopia bit. For several moments, none of us could seem to find words. Except for Parker, I gathered, when I finally tore my eyes away from the view and found him watching me with a smug grin.

"Nothing like traveling to see just how small your problems are, when viewed at the appropriate scale. Wouldn't you agree?"

I wanted to argue that our problems still seemed pretty damn big, and that it was bullscud to think what was happening down there was all right on any scale, but I was still too busy gaping at Enochia.

Besides, maybe he had a point. It was hard to imagine so much pain and chaos happening on a planet that looked so perfectly peaceful from far outside. I couldn't help but wonder how everyone else on the planet might feel if they could somehow all see what I was seeing now—not in the vids and the pictures, but here, drifting in space, staring down at the magnetic enormity of the planet that gave us all life.

How could those people all be so willing to live in fear and conflict and hatred when there was so much beauty down there? So much space for everyone to live their lives, free from fear?

Because the Sanctum won't let us, came the acidic reply from some dark corner of my mind.

I looked to Parker. "I need to see the rest of it."

To my surprise, he didn't argue or quip. Just nodded. "Yes, I think it's time."

Somehow, the lack of teasing and insults only reminded me that I should be furious with the raknoth for having once again played me like a harpa to get me aboard this ship. But I *was* aboard this ship now, and there was too much happening for me to worry about being pissed. I knew I couldn't trust anything I didn't yank directly from his mind—and that even *that* information should be treated with thorough skepticism. For now, it was enough.

Beside me, Siren tore her gaze away from the view. "If you two are gonna swap dirty secrets, I'm coming."

She looked defiant about it, like she expected us both to argue the point. I almost expected myself to argue too, but when I actually thought about it, I didn't really see any reason why the two of them shouldn't be aware of the truth about Sarentus and the rest of it. Sure, it was dangerous information. Extremely dangerous. And I was far from certain I could trust either of the ex-Seekers. But at this point, what was the worst that could happen?

For the first time since Carlisle had died, I was truly back on the outside —on the run from the entire planet—and while they hadn't said as much, I was pretty sure Garrett and Siren were here first and foremost because they sensed that staying on the sidelines would inevitably mean a short life, spent running from overzealous mobs.

"I think you should both come in with me," I said.

Parker said nothing.

"Grop that," Garrett said, looking between the two of us and then to Parker. "I'm not stepping into his head."

Parker quirked an eyebrow. "You don't secretly want to scour my thoughts and find out if I'm sorry for what I did to you?"

"Pretty sure I know the answer to that one."

Parker studied Garrett, and Alpha only knew what was going on in his head. "Many would call your alterations a gift, you know."

Garrett tensed, but Siren laid a hand on the back of his neck, and he settled long enough for them to have a short telepathic exchange—a less than ideal one, judging by the darkening expression on Garrett's face.

The ex-Seeker drew his dagger and touched the blade point experimentally before focusing back on Parker. "How about this one? I'll watch from the outside. And if I get the slightest inkling you're up to something, I'll cut our losses and jam *this* gift right through your thick skull."

To my surprise, Parker didn't have a snide comment. He actually looked a touch uncertain.

"The memories we are visiting… they are quite potent. I'd rather you not react hastily. Haldin and Alexia will in all likelihood have some external reaction to what I intend to show them."

I shot a confused glance at Siren, who looked startled and none too pleased herself. "Alexia?"

She scowled at Parker before turning to me. "Such a pleasure to meet you, Demon."

"Yeah." I looked between her and Parker. "I think I'll just stick with Siren."

She showed me a venomous smile. "I'd rather you did."

"Perfect," Garrett said. "Now if you two could focus on the raknoth telling me not to worry if he accidentally fries your brains…"

"He's not wrong," I said. "About us reacting, I mean," I added quickly at

Garrett's incredulous look. "What he showed me in the brig put me in a cold sweat and… well, it took a toll."

"Yeah…" Siren said. "Maybe we should start with a crash course on what I missed so far."

Parker just sat down to wait, but I didn't miss the way he rolled his eyes or the way he tapped his fingers on his crossed arms. Apparently, even a 2,800 year old alien could experience impatience. But he said nothing as I did my best to recount what Parker had shown me so far—that our holy prophet Sarentus had really been the raknoth, Nan'Sarentus.

"Bullscud," Garrett said.

I continued on until we reached the other, even less palatable revelation.

"What do you mean they *brought* us here?" Siren asked. "That's…"

"Bullscud," Garrett provided. "Complete, softsteel-sipping bullscud."

Parker yawned.

"I saw it," I said. "Or saw them talking about it, at least."

"Oh, right," Garrett said. "You mean you saw a memory you can't trust of the lying aliens talking about how they supplanted an entire Alpha-damned world population from some make believe *other* planet to start this one? Forgive my skepticism."

I did forgive his skepticism. It's not like it was unreasonable.

There was more I could have told them, I suppose. There were the memories of Earth I'd seen in Al'Kundesha's memories back before the White Tower catastrophe. There were the corroborating drawings from the Emmútari text to consider—the ones Franco and I had seen in Pasty's dungeon that showed Sarentus as a raknoth and also depicted a great mass of people debarking from an enormous ship at the base of the Bjornan Mountains. But we didn't need to open those additional drawers of messy complications right now.

"I'm not asking you to take my word for it," I pointed out, tilting my head at our silently waiting raknoth. "You know as well as I do that telepathy doesn't lie."

"In humans," Garrett amended.

"What will it hurt for me to see for myself?" Siren asked.

He looked at her like she'd just asked if he'd like to take a deep space stroll, which in turn prompted another round of private telepathic communication between the two of them. Again, Garrett didn't look happy when they broke the contact, but he didn't try to stop Siren. Mostly, he just glared at nothing in particular.

"We're ready?" Parker asked, taking Garrett's surly air of defeat as his cue. He spread his hands to the open deck space adjacent to where he sat, indicating we should join him in a more stable position—which, after my near-collapse back in the brig, didn't seem like such a bad idea.

I sat to Parker's left, folding my legs up and assuming a comfortable position. Siren sat to his right, closing our little circle. Garrett hovered behind her, patting the flat of his blade apprehensively against his thigh.

"Right, then," Parker said with a perfectly pleasant—and perfectly shallow—smile. "Let us get started."

18

HARVESTERS

If I could've chosen any one telepath on the planet to have my so-called back while invading the vast minefield that was Alton Parker's raknoth mind, Siren probably would've been somewhere around the bottom of the list. But she was here, and that was that.

Maybe I should've given her more credit. One near murder attempt and one nearly catastrophic attempt at seduction aside, she actually *had* been something of a reliable ally since she'd strutted into my life. At times. Sort of.

She'd seen fit to out General Auckus as the Sanctum's inside man in the first assassination attempt, at least. And she'd also probably saved my life and several others when she'd lent her strength to help me hold Frosty at bay at the canyon ambush.

Despite that, though, I wasn't about to consciously let her anywhere near my private mind.

We went in hard and fast, and with defenses fully intact—against each other as well as against Parker. As before, Parker made it easy, leaving himself wide open for us to stroll right in.

Even knowing what to expect, it was still a kick in the brain, adapting to the raknoth's alien mind, and to the extent of his intricately sharpened senses. I felt Siren floundering in the initial wave of it. Setting my better judgment momentarily aside, I reached out to her, thinking calming, stable thoughts.

She steadied, then gave me an abashed thanks.

"It's a lot to take in," I admitted. *"Just remember that we're in control in here."*

Together, we faced our attention toward the vast expanse of Parker's memories.

"Okay," I sent. *"We're here. What is it you want us to see?"*

"You're the one in control here," Parker's voice drifted to me from the darkness all around. *"Perhaps you should begin with what you'd like to see."*

He was still going to play it coy? Fine. I *was* the one in control.

So I pushed Parker down to the gutters of our shared mental space, bade Siren to hang on tight, and focused as clearly and willfully as I could on a singular thought: *What is this 'greater threat' Parker keeps rambling on about?*

In hindsight, it was a foolish move.

One moment we were adrift in the relative calm of Parker's mind, most of his active thoughts and feelings relegated to background noise. The next, there was nothing but a planet-shaking roar blasting me dead in the face, threatening to tear the flesh from my bones.

I could barely even fathom the enormity of the beast the sound came from, drowned as I was in the sensory overload of that roar, and the crushing pressure that came with it.

Pressure. That was the first word that flashed through my head, even if it was terribly inadequate. More accurate to say it was a telepathic onslaught, the likes of which I never would've wished on anyone.

It fell on us like a crashing ocean of boiling rage. It blasted all traces of Siren away from my side and set my nerves on fire until I forgot that it was a memory. It didn't matter that this was not my body, that I'd been in control only a moment ago.

For a second, I was there, alone. And I was terrified.

Then the moment passed. The flash of memory dimmed—by my doing or someone else's, I couldn't have said—and I yanked myself back. Away from the memory. Away from Parker's mind. Back to my own body, and sweet, blessed safety.

I surfaced to the ship deck just in time to see Alton Parker's hand shoot up, blindingly fast, and catch Garrett's descending dagger straight in the palm. It was a testament to Garrett's preternatural strength that the blade pierced all the way through to the back of Parker's hand, and a testament to raknoth pain tolerance that Parker didn't make a sound.

He just scowled at the dark blood dripping to the deck, then up at Garrett, then to me.

"Well, that was close."

Garrett's wild eyes flicked to me, assessing.

"It's okay," I said, raising my hands in peace. "Misunderstanding. We… We're okay." I looked at Siren, who was pitched back on her hands, pale, sweaty, and panting. "I think."

Garrett ripped the dagger free and dragged Siren back a few feet, ignoring her murmured protests. "It's not okay," he growled in response to whatever she said. "And you're not going back in there."

I actually felt for him. I doubt I would've reacted much differently if I'd watched Elise go through something like that. Not that I wanted to compare our relationship with whatever gropped up swive-fest was going on between the two ex-Shaper-killers. But still.

Parker was watching me. Not with his usual condescending superiority, necessarily, so much as with genuine curiosity.

"What was that thing?" I asked.

"That was Kul'Naga, oldest and strongest of those who call themselves our masters, the order of the rakul."

"Okay." I took a deep breath, looking around for I don't know what. Mental clarity, I guess. All I got, though, was a breathtaking reminder that I was orbiting my planet in an alien spaceship.

Misguided holy wars, alien ships, raknoth allies, and now freaking mountain-sized space monsters with atomic-level telepathic arsenals. The *rakul*, apparently.

Gropping sunshine and flowers.

"Okay," I repeated. "So there's… worse out there."

"That may be putting it lightly," Parker said.

I looked at Garrett and Siren, who were huddled together—Siren still trying to catch her breath, Garrett looking like he wanted to ask what the scud we were talking about, but was too pissed to form the words.

I turned back to Parker. "Is that thing… coming here?"

Parker sighed—a rather human affectation I was unused to seeing from him. "I don't know. It's certainly possible. Eventually."

"Why? What do they want? What do any of you want?"

"There are several long, deep answers to that question. But in the end, I suppose it might be grossly simplified down to what all living things desire. Safety and stability."

"Seriously?" Garrett asked. "You try to cannibalize our entire species for parts, then you claim 'safety and stability?'"

"That Kul'Naga thing didn't exactly look like a delicate flower," I added.

"I did say it was a gross simplification."

"Then maybe you can go one further," I said, "and simplify how we're supposed to rid ourselves of you and your… whatever they are."

"The rakul are our self-appointed masters," Parker said. "And as for how you might ensure Enochia escapes their eventual notice, I cannot give you a simple answer—nor any answer at all, save for that your planet would be the first to succeed in a long, long line of those who have failed."

"We never should've got on this gropping ship," Garrett muttered, skewering me with a hard stare. "There are real people down there, remember? Real problems."

I glanced at the viewing wall, toward *down there*. We were orbiting on the dark side of Enochia at the moment. I hesitated, wanting to agree with him, to get back to what I knew beyond the shadow of a doubt mattered in the here and now. But still. "You didn't see…"

"And you're sure you did?" Garrett shot back without hesitation. "He's a gropping alien, Raish. You can't trust what's in his head."

"I could show you more," Parker said. "Gently this time, if you'd prefer."

Fear gripped at my insides, thinking about revisiting even the memory of that terrible telepathic fury, and the feeling it had scorched through the center of my being—like every violent and emotional conflict I'd ever known had somehow been condensed down into one pulse-pounding nectar, amplified with a liberal pull of pure, feral animosity, and injected straight into my brain.

I didn't want to go back there.

"Don't," Siren said softly.

I looked at her, and she shook her head, silently willing me to listen. It was probably the first time I'd ever found myself wanting to, where she was concerned.

Alpha, what'd happened to the days when I was just trying to hide out from the Legion? Or just trying to stop the raknoth? Or even just trying to get ahead of the Sanctum before they could commit genocide on an entire planet's-worth of Shapers?

Where did it end? Save the planet, establish world peace, and then watch the giant space monsters fly in and accomplish what the raknoth hadn't?

I had to know what we were potentially up against here.

"I'll be careful," I said.

Garrett splayed his hands in a clear expression of exasperation. Siren just looked worried. And Parker?

"What are you so happy about?" I asked the smiling raknoth.

"It's rather cathartic," he said, "seeing you make this journey after all your time spent in your own little world, convinced that your problems were the worst problems, and that you were unwaveringly at the lead of your own little morality parade."

"Do you want me to come have another look or not?"

He shrugged and closed his eyes. "It doesn't matter what I want. Your planet stands in the path of inevitable destruction. The question I suggest you ask yourself is what you intend to do about it."

WHERE BEFORE I'D taken the entry to Parker's mind like a Legion breaching drill, this time, I eased in like... well, like a cautious telepath slipping into dark waters he knew could shift from calm to boiling with but a single misplaced thought.

"Tell me about Kul'Naga," I sent, only thinking the words this time, and granting Parker the freedom to guide me through his memories as he saw fit.

I tensed as the darkness around us flashed to bright landscape, but it was only that: empty landscape, familiar in the snowy tundra and the jagged rise of distant mountains, but also distinctly alien in a way I couldn't immediately put my finger on. Maybe it was just the oddly bright vegetation I glimpsed at the base of the mountains. Our perspective in the memory shifted before I could tell, Memory Parker turning around to take in...

"What the..."

It was like a winter village scene straight from ancient history—and tripping on radical deliriogenics. Odd, globular buildings of some amber, translucent material lined the wide, snowy paths. More of that bright vegetation sprouted here and there along both sides of the paths—big treelike plants that reared out of sizable snow drifts, their tops draped with something that more closely resembled partially unraveled balls of brightly colored wool than they did branches and leaves. And as bizarre as the village was, it paled in comparison to the creatures roaming the paths.

They were bipedal, but that was pretty much where any familiarity to human kind ended. Their flesh was sky blue, and most of them had a decent amount of it bared, despite the piercing cold—or what felt like it *should've* been piercing cold, at least. They didn't seem to mind. They were also huge. It was hard to say exactly how huge, without any familiar reference, but definitely far larger than humans. At first, I thought they were partially clothed, but then I noticed the wicked-looking horns sprouting from their heads and realized it wasn't clothes I was seeing but dark, bony spurs protruding from their bulky forms all along the legs, arms, shoulders, and backs.

It was like something out of an old fae tale. Giant gropping ice demons, marching about their bizarre village—on their respective ways, I could only imagine, to freeze young children solid for being naughty.

"Are these more rakul?"

"Hardly," came Parker's reply. In the memory, our perspective giant started off down the snowy path toward the village. *"I chose this memory because our occupation of this species marked the first time I saw Kul'Naga in the flesh."*

"You were... this is you? You were one of these things?"

"Once upon a time, as you say. This was my third occupation, nearly two-thousand years ago."

I quietly tried to wrap my head around and mostly failed miserably as I watched Giant Parker tromp along the snowy path, past dozens of his fellow blue giants, groaning and grunting in a strange, harsh language. Most of them were carrying large stones, I noticed—though *boulders* might actually have been a more accurate term, seeing as they must have been skimmer-sized on average, and definitely several thousand pounds. The giants carried them like sacks of grain.

Giant Parker looked over its massive shoulder to where its fellows were hauling their loads: a great clearing where the deep snow had been swept aside and several more giants were busy at work erecting an enormous shrine to what must have been a deity or a king of some sort.

I watched in disbelief as Giant Parker casually tore one of the thick, bright wool trees from the ground like a small weed and proceeded to take a big bite right off its stringy top. One of the giants in line bumped into his neighbor, who dropped his boulder onto another giant's foot. What sounded more like a foghorn than a cry of pain erupted from the injured giant's maw, then it whirled and clubbed the offender across the chest. The second giant staggered back, then caught itself and rushed its opponent in a full-on tackle. They hit the ground hard enough to cause tremors and tumbled around for position. One landed a solid kick, and its opponent crashed through the wall of one of the amber buildings.

Around them, the rest of the giants laughed as if this was all perfectly normal behavior.

"I don't understand," I sent. *"Who are these people? Why are you showing me this?"*

"I'm showing you this so that you can understand these creatures were just another version of life, not unlike you, trying to find their own safety and stability in the universe. I need you to understand what's about to happen."

"Kul'Naga?"

I didn't really need to ask. It was clear enough from his words that this wasn't going to end well for the giants. But the scene around us was already shifting in response to my question. It was a little later now—I'm not sure exactly how I could tell, but I felt it. Some giants were still at work on the shrine, but many of the boulder-haulers were taking a break to chomp down on a hearty meal of giant yarn trees. Everything seemed peaceful enough at first glance, but I could feel Giant Parker's apprehension bleeding through the memory like a permanent stain.

It was unsettling, feeling anything other than cold, reptilian calculation from Parker. But before I had time to dwell on it, a huge shadow passed overhead, and Parker's dread deepened.

They were here.

Around the clearing, the giants were exchanging uncertain glances, a few of them wearily lumbering to their enormous feet. In the distance, a ship descended into view and… No. Not a ship.

Massive wings flapped once, twice, three times, and even from a far distance, the rush of the air they displaced could be easily felt. And the thing riding those gargantuan wings down to the ground… It was a dragon. That was the only word for it. A creature straight out of the old fae tales. And it was the size of a gropping mountain.

The beast slammed to the ground in an explosion of snow, shaking the rock underfoot even from what I gauged to be a half mile away. Two fiery red eyes came to life, each at least the size of the huge boulders the giants had been lugging about. I understood now, the full scope of the monster my mind had been too shocked to register the first time around.

Then the thing roared, and I nearly lost it all over again.

The sound was deafening. The telepathic pressure was worse. It hit like a tidal wave of molten magma. I gasped, reaching for my defenses and—

"It's only a memory," Alton's voice came to me, not exactly concerned, but not quite condescending either. *"He cannot hurt you here. Yet."*

Somehow, I still had trouble relaxing.

The giants were all on their feet now, some ducking into their big, amber houses and emerging with a variety of brutal-looking clubs and other various melee weapons. Kul'Naga watched them patiently as they grunted and groaned their cruel language to one another and prepared to make war. The club-thumping continued, reinforcements pouring in from elsewhere in the village.

Then one of the shrine builders plucked a boulder from the waiting pile and hurled it at the waiting rakul, and the chaos began.

It was a mighty throw considering the boulder probably weighed in the league of ten thousand pounds. Kul'Naga swatted it out of the air with a massive forepaw and loped into a planet-shaking charge.

What followed wasn't a pretty fight.

The giants fought without fear, raining blow after heavy blow on the enormous rakul from all directions. The attacks weren't without effect, either. Soon Kul'Naga was oozing green fluid from dozens of ugly wounds, but the rakul took the punishment in stride and continued indiscriminately tearing his way through the giants' ranks with claws that must have been six feet long, and sharp as razors.

With each swipe, Kul'Naga hacked another giant to shreds like roast bova. The sky vibrated with their foghorn screams, on and on until I wanted to scream myself.

"Okay! I get it! Enough!"

The memory faded at will, leaving me trembling in our shared mental space. Slowly, almost gently, Parker prodded another memory forward. Reluctantly, I allowed it, and took in the final image of Kul'Naga standing atop a mountain of dead giants, covered in their dark blood, eyes ablaze with cruel red flames.

I couldn't imagine I was ever going to forget the sight.

"And that," came Parker's voice, *"is but one of the twelve reasons we are all doomed."*

19

REASON

"Twelve," I repeated softly in the quiet darkness of Alton Parker's resting mind, trying to comprehend just how much havoc twelve Kul'Nagas could wrought without thinking too specifically about the gory details of what I'd just witnessed. *"You're telling me there are twelve of those things out there?"*

"Twelve rakul, yes," Parker replied, *"but none quite like Kul'Naga. Kul'Mada is similar in scale, but the rest are dangerous in much different ways."*

"They're not all like... that thing?"

I hesitated to use the word, *dragon*, despite the outlandishness of everything Parker had shown me. Honestly, by that point, I was more surprised by my own hesitation than by the fact that there was apparently a living, breathing space dragon flying around somewhere out in the depths of the universe.

"Each rakul is a unique being," Parker said. *"Each one more or less a salute to the basic form of whatever species they last occupied before making the ascent to Kul. They are a collection of the twelve most dangerous species our kind have ever conquered, and they've been building the strength of their vessels for untold thousands of years."*

Twelve rakul.

The sacred gropping number.

It was all too much to process. All connected. The twelve nations of old Enochia. The rakul. The raknoth. Sarentus and his holy Sanctum... All of it.

Maybe Parker and Zar'Faenor and the rest of his acolytes had only returned to Enochia a decade ago, but their influence had been firmly entwined in the roots of our world all along, right from the start.

I felt small. And afraid.

There was anger too—at Parker, at the rakul. At the raw shock of finding out just how taken we'd all been, all of Enochian humanity. But it was an impotent anger. Hopeless. Because what hope could I have? I was fighting the last remnants of a clan that'd nearly brought Enochia to ruin, only to find out that they were the measly scouting party sent ahead by the true threat.

I felt lost.

"Do you understand now, why I scoff at the squabbles below?" Parker asked. *"The fight to protect a few cities' worth of humans? The holy war between Shapers and Sanctum? It's all an irrelevant flash in the pan measured against what the rakul will do when they find us."*

"You said you didn't know if they'd come."

"I said I didn't know if Kul'Naga would make the trip. He no longer troubles himself with the planets he deems unworthy of his attention. But it is inevitable. Eventually, the rakul will discover what happened on Earth, and it will be only a matter of time before the reaping of your sister planet leads them here."

Too much. It was just too much.

I backed out of Parker's head, drawing back into the safety of my own body. Only it didn't feel safe. Not knowing what I now knew. Not with our planet floating below, ripe for its inevitable demise by the masters of the very creatures who'd apparently put us here in the first place.

"He's back," someone muttered.

I looked up and found Garrett and Siren staring at me. They actually looked concerned.

"What is it, Raish?" Garrett asked.

Parker surfaced from his own trance and turned an expectant look on me. *Yes,* that look said. *Why don't you tell them what it is, Haldin?*

I was on my feet and heading for the corridor almost before I knew it. I'd never been one for panic attacks—well, not before the White Tower nightmares, at least—but I wasn't really sure what else to call the invisible weight crushing down around my chest and lungs as I staggered out of the flight room, gasping shallow breaths, ignoring the vague buzz of voices calling after me.

Some corner of my mind reasoned that, if I was going to have this reaction, I sensibly should've had it on the tail end of watching Kul'Naga slaughter an entire village of ice giants. But the rest of me just carried on, hyperventilating and not really caring why.

I hurried down the corridor, looking desperately for something to latch onto, anything to ground me. I needed Elise, or Johnny. Needed to hear their voices. Needed to see the face of someone who *hadn't* tried to kill me at any point in the past few seasons.

At the very least, I needed a dark, quiet room to sit and think.

Wired as I was, I jumped hard enough to hit the bulkhead when the solid corridor wall on my left inexplicably shifted—*slithered*, even—to reveal an oval opening, not unlike a doorway.

I stared through the suspicious hole to the open room beyond, my troubles momentarily forgotten as I retraced what had just happened. Finally, I arrived at a conclusion.

With careful focus, I sent a telepathic image, pretending the wall could hear me. I pictured the opening shifting back to solid wall. And it did. Somehow, the discovery didn't alleviate the unsettled feeling in my gut. But I'd wanted a quiet space, hadn't I? And at least I'd stopped hyperventilating.

I glanced back toward the flight room, then willed the wall open and stepped through.

Inside, the room was larger than the flight deck had been, the walls all sporting the same purplish hue, and flowing oddly from corner to corner without any proper right angles. The deck was a slightly darker shade, with a lightly grated texture, and filled up toward the back with an assortment of well-secured shipping crates.

It probably said something about my mental state, that I hardly even cared that I was exploring an alien vessel while in orbit of the planet I'd never thought to leave. The crates were clearly of Enochian origin, and silly as it might sound, that was about the most comforting thing I could have hoped to find right just then. I ignored the rest, sat down on my best link to home, and buried my face firmly in my hands, where I could pretend I wasn't on an alien ship, drifting through space on a sea of damning revelations.

What I wouldn't have given to go back to that cramped supply closet with Elise and Johnny right then… Had that really only been this morning? How had my entire world so spectacularly exploded in just a handful of hours?

Haven, Auckus, Glenbark. Parker and his Alpha-damned rakul. And the Sanctum, sitting on their devious haunches beneath it all, completely unaware—or maybe just not caring—that they were actively seeking to eradicate the only people on the planet who might have any chance at resisting another telepath invasion if and when it came.

I extended the fingers of my left hand, thinking to check for news from below, only to remember my palmlight was gone—smashed in the woods by Parker.

"I have spares aboard," came Parker's voice from the opening I hadn't felt confident enough to seal closed behind me. "And the ship will be able to access the reels from orbit, if you'd like."

I looked up at the raknoth, wanting to hate him, hating that I was beginning to understand what he was running from, and why he did what he did. Not that I would ever forgive any of it. But even understanding was bad enough.

"The hybrids," I said quietly.

"An army to overthrow the rakul," Parker said. He didn't sound particularly apologetic, but nor was there any illusion of grandness in his claim. "In all likelihood, it was a futile effort to begin with. But it was the best we had. I simply underestimated the problem of solving their eventual degradation. Clearly."

Underestimated, had he?

All those living, breathing people he'd been gambling with. Thousands and thousands of lives claimed for his little science project—millions more profoundly affected by the chaos he and his clan had spilled across the planet. And he'd *underestimated* the problem?

I wanted to scream at him. I wanted to slam him through the bulkhead and leave him to float in the cold empty darkness, reflecting on all the pain and death he'd wrought until the harshness of outer space finally took him. I wanted him to understand.

But he already did. He already knew everything I could think to throw at him. He'd understood full well all along what he was doing, what his actions would mean for the people of Enochia. He'd understood, and he'd done it all anyway. I could see it in his eyes now. And it made me gropping sick.

He was a monster. A monster fighting for his own survival, maybe. But a monster all the same. And nothing I said could make him feel it any more than he already did.

"Why?" I whispered, pointing my gaze back down to the deck. "Why tell me about the rakul? Why go through all this effort?"

I didn't look up at the sound of his approaching footsteps. It was only when he knelt down in front of me that my surprise got the better of me. I met his eyes, and his expression was more earnest than I'd ever seen.

"Because I want you to help me stop them, Haldin."

I just stared.

Everything he'd just shown me—everything he'd done to my people—and now this?

What else could I do but stare?

"I understand your hesitation..." he started.

And that was all it took to jiggle my shocked brain free and remind me exactly what I could do aside from stare.

It felt good, letting the energy ride through me in the familiar crackling rush. Even better to hear the thud as Parker slammed into the front wall of the room, twenty feet away. I rose and followed at a more leisurely pace, keeping him firmly pinned to the wall with telekinesis.

"I understand this reaction," Parker said.

I channeled deeper and fed him a solid telekinetic punch to the nose.

"And that one too," he grunted, as I closed in on him. "But none of it will change the facts."

"I thought changing facts was your specialty, Parker," came Garrett's wry voice from the doorway. I turned to find him and Siren both watching from the corridor—Siren looking wary, Garrett eager. "You need a hand with that?" he added, tilting his head toward Parker and fingering his dagger.

"No," I said. It came out harsher than expected. "We're just having a private talk."

"Well, all the same..." Garrett shrugged and stepped into the room, Siren following more hesitantly.

I didn't want them there. Didn't even want to be there myself. But it hardly seemed worth the breath to argue—or worth the exertion to keep Parker pinned, I decided, now that they'd interrupted. I dropped the raknoth. He didn't try to catch himself, just slid down the wall and settled on the deck, looking up at me. The manipulative bastard probably thought the position would be ingratiating or something.

"He wants help killing his old bosses," I told the ex-Seekers, mostly because I didn't know what else to say.

"Sounds like a *him* problem," Garrett said.

"I was kinda thinking the same thing," I agreed, still watching Parker.

"Then you are both fools," the raknoth said. So much for that ingratiating thing. "The rakul are a problem for all sentient life in the universe."

"Well as dire as that all sounds," Garrett said, "we've already got our fair share of assholes here trying to—"

He jerked at movement above, then ducked as a dark, serpentine something swept down from the ceiling for his torso without warning. Another descended. And another. Garrett growled a curse as one wrapped around his chest and yanked him up. Another caught Siren a moment later. Before I could blink, the two ex-Seekers were pinned face-first to the ceiling, shouting a steady stream of curses as more and more of the dark tendrils unfolded from the ceiling to circle their limbs and torsos.

"Let them go," I growled, slamming Parker back to the bulkhead with telekinesis.

"My kin are numerous," he said, unperturbed. "More numerous than the humans on Enochia. You've seen how strong we can become. And yet the entirety of my people live under the fear of the rakul."

"I said let them go, now."

"I am far from the first to dream of liberation. There have been revolts in the past. Direct challenge, too. All unsuccessful, but for one. Do you know what became of the first raknoth to defeat one of the Kul, eight-thousand years ago?"

I barely processed his words, busy as I was watching the slithering ship arms continue ensnaring Garrett and Siren until I could barely see them at all up there. I reached out with my mind, thinking to try manipulating them in the same way I'd done with the corridor wall.

"He simply joined their ranks," Parker was saying. "And so Zar'Gada, hero of the raknoth, became Kul'Gada, fierce and fanatic oppressor of our people. Long live the masters."

I tested one of the tendrils around Siren's leg and found my theory was accurate. The tendril quivered at my telepathic influence, but something still held it in place. Parker, I realized.

"So why do you think I can do anything about it, then?" I cried, trying and failing to keep the strain out of my voice as I threw my will indirectly against Parker's, first stealthily—a tendril here, another there—then all out.

No good. Garrett and Siren remained well-secured, their squirms subdued and their cursing muffled.

So I plucked the cloaking pendant from my neck, tossed it at Parker, and back pedaled away. As soon as I was clear of its range—and Parker was still bound by it—the tendrils parted to my will like fluid magic, so abruptly that I almost failed to catch the two ex-Seekers as they plummeted to the deck. Not that I would've been devastated to see either of them jostled.

Parker was on his feet now. I tensed, preparing to fight, but he was smiling. "I think you can do something about it," he said, nodding to where the tendrils had melded back into the ceiling with a satisfied expression, "because you never cease to surprise."

"I've got a surprise for you," Garrett murmured, starting forward, "you scudspouting—"

I'm not really sure why I felt compelled to stop Garrett from exacting his revenge, but my hand found his chest anyway. For a second, he clearly contemplated taking a swipe at me instead.

"It's all telepathically controlled on this ship," I offered, nodding to the ceiling and hoping it might diffuse some of the tension.

"Sure, naturally," Siren said, rubbing at her wrists where the restraints had left marks. "Thanks for the assist, by the way."

I nodded. Garrett bristled for a few more seconds before backing off and composing himself.

"It's not just Haldin I'm interested in, for the record," Parker said to the two ex-Seekers. "Your kind are the first I've ever encountered that might actually stand some chance of catching the rakul off guard. The more Shapers we can amass against them, the better."

"You can grop yourself if you think I'd ever help you after what you did," Garrett said.

"And I never said I'd help you, either," I pointed out. "Which I won't, by the way."

"Oh, I never expected you to help *me*," Parker said. "But I know you won't turn away from protecting your planet. That drive is in your blood, Haldin Raish. That much is clear. Just as clear as the fact that, if we do nothing, Enochia will one day fall to the rakul."

Siren and Garrett traded a silent look before Garrett turned to us. "Whatever bullscud you're proposing, we're out. Take us back down and we'll be on our way." He focused on me. "We came here to work on setting things straight for our people down there, not to play make-believe with Alton Parker."

"Very well," Parker said. "I can drop the two of you wherever you'd like, though it's probably best if we wait for—"

"The three of us," I said, before the fear and indecision could stop me. "I'm with them."

Garrett and Siren looked surprised, but also pleased. I'm not sure if it was everything we'd been through in the past hours, or just my own growing desperation to find a scrap of solid footing in all of this, but for the first time since they'd shown up by the river, I decided to trust that they were on my side, at least as far as the war on Shapers was concerned. It was all I had right then.

Parker, meanwhile, let out an exasperated sigh. "You don't understand the futility of what you're trying to do."

"Maybe not," I said. "Or maybe it's you who's too old and jaded to understand, for all your cold-blooded wisdom. You asked if I understood after seeing the rakul why you're not concerned about what's happening on Enochia."

He watched with a faintly arched brow, waiting.

"All I understand is that my planet has spent the past thousand years demonizing people like me, and that you and your clan kicked the tingler nest straight into the bonfire when you showed up. I don't care what planet we came from, or what might *theoretically* be coming for us one day. All I know is that this planet needs people like us to make sure things like you can never hurt it again. So I'm going to go find those two kin of yours. I'm going to kill them. And then we're going to show this world the truth, about all of it."

"There's the crazy ass plan I was expecting," Garrett muttered.

"I told you he wouldn't disappoint," Siren said.

Parker was only shaking his head—not in disagreement, but rather in abject disappointment. "I have half a mind to jump us to the next star system right now and give you all a few years to reflect on how ridiculously naive you're being." He tossed me my cloaking pendant. "I could do it with a single thought, you know. You'd never find your way back home."

I held his gaze, trying not to let him see just how terrified I was that he might not be bluffing. I had absolutely no way to know.

"Maybe not," Garrett said. "But we'd definitely kill the scud out of you as soon as we got there."

Parker showed us that reptilian smile of his. "Oh, I don't doubt it." He studied us for a long, tense moment, before finally letting out another uncharacteristically human sigh. "But what a waste that would be. Very well. I will take you back to your beloved planet. But first, might I at least suggest that you come up with something resembling a real plan before you march off against two of my gifted kin and an entire world religion?"

I turned my pendant over and over in my fingertips, thinking about the simpler of the two problems first.

"I think I've got a few ideas."

20

SHIP MATES

For all our collective bravado about getting ground side and back to the mission, it was hard to argue that there was a strong reason to do so right that very minute. For one thing, judging from what we'd seen in the reels, half the damn planet was currently looking for us—or for Parker and myself, at least. And for another, we were still working on that plan.

What little we did have was easily doable in Parker's ship, from the safety of orbit. And so, since we had over another full day before our meeting with Elise and Franco anyway, we reluctantly agreed to stay aboard the ship for a day, crafting, testing, and refining the tools that would hopefully help us take down the last two raknoth when we found them.

For the most part, Parker left us alone, aside from the occasional remark about what fools we were all being. I didn't even talk to Garrett or Siren all that much beyond the time we spent working on my newest rune creations. To say there was tension on the ship would've been putting it lightly.

I cringed at the footage of me and Parker escaping Haven when I finally saw it in the reels. Somewhere between fighting off supercharged raknoth in the woods and drifting around in Parker's memories of the rakul, I'd almost managed to momentarily forget just how deep of a hole I'd dug for my reputation back on Enochia. Deep enough that I couldn't help wonder if Parker wasn't right that I was beyond foolish to even attempt going back. But what choice did I have?

I knew the truth—about the Sanctum, and about why we were likely going to one day need every Shaper we could get our hands on. There were twelve rakul out there. There were apparently a whole scudload more raknoth. And even down below, there were more dark secrets than I could count, lurking beneath the surface. The origins of our beloved Sanctum. The origins of all gropping life on Enochia…

They needed to know. All of it.

If only that single resolve could've made me impervious to the rest of the crushing doubt. Because as good as it sounded—the truth and nothing but the truth—I honestly had no idea how I could ever hope to convince the world about any of it, much less what might happen if I somehow did.

It would be revolution. Maybe one of blood and violence. Maybe one of radical inner turmoil. It might be utter anarchy, pure and simple. But no matter what it was, I was pretty sure things would only be getting messier before they could possibly hope to get any better. After all the scud I'd been through in the past few seasons, to think that it had all merely been the eye of the storm, and that we were now preparing to fly into the true chaos…

It almost made me want to tell Parker right then and there to jump the ship across the stars and to never look back.

But that wasn't an option. It just wasn't. As much as it chaffed my spirit to admit it, Parker hadn't been wrong about my inability to turn away from the safety of Enochia. It was in my blood. Maybe it was an inherited trait, passed down hereditarily from Captain Martin Raish. Or maybe it was simply in the weight I still felt each and every day—the quiet reminder of what my parents and Carlisle had all sacrificed to keep me here.

Not too long ago, that weight had nearly driven me over the edge with guilt-ridden compulsions, grinding myself to the bone in a futile attempt to propagate their legacy. I couldn't count the number of times I'd let my actions be ruled by the singular question, *What would Carlisle do?* I still wondered about that plenty. What *would* Carlisle do? What would my dad say about this? I doubted I'd ever stop asking. But it had taken nearly losing Elise to finally accept the truth on the other side of that mountain of blackened guilt.

They hadn't died so that I could carry on mindlessly doing their will, accepting none of the responsibility. They'd laid down their lives to give me the chance to make my own mark on the world. They'd sacrificed themselves because they'd believed in me.

It was a terrifying realization.

But it only solidified my certainty in what needed to be done. I felt it clinging on, from the deepest depths of my gut to the farthest fringes of my conflicted thoughts. It needed to be done. And if the past cycles had taught me anything, it was that the intangible certainty tingling through my insides was the only pole to which I could orient my compass if I wished to maintain my sanity.

Alpha knew I needed all the help I could get in that department.

Given that none of us were exactly comfortable sleeping on an orbiting spaceship with an alien who, as far as I knew, didn't actually require sleep, by the time the second night rolled around, all of us were growing delirious with sleep deprivation. All of us but Parker, of course. The rest of us fluctuated erratically between *loopy-and-unusually-friendly*, and *moody-and-overly-aggressive*. It didn't help when the official news of the abrupt change in Legion leadership finally hit the reels.

Where the footage of me and Parker had made me cringe, the first official statement of the newly-anointed High General Auckus just made me nauseous. He apologized for the repugnant indecision the previous leadership had displayed in the Sanctum's oh-so-clearly righteous war on demons. He profusely condemned the actions of Freya Glenbark—who was to be put on trial immediately for high treason—as well as the actions of her supporters, who were soon to follow. And finally, with his most aggressively wolfish, scud-eating smile yet, he revealed the exciting prize he'd claimed in his takeover of Haven: two live-and-kicking demons, locked safely away in the brig, ripe for the slaughter.

Four and Eight.

"Son of a bitch," Garrett growled under his breath.

I tended to agree with the sentiment, for too many reasons to count. Near the top of the list was the fact that Four and Eight might not have even still been in Haven at all, if I hadn't pushed so hard for them to join the effort before Oasis. Right below that was the sinking feeling that the only way the Legion could succeed at keeping two Shapers locked up in the brig was if they were making use of the cell I'd designed for Parker. But that wasn't the end of it.

While Auckus hadn't said as much, his announcement of Glenbark's trial for high treason might as well have been an announcement of her own pending execution. It wasn't as if she had any chance of receiving a fair trial. How could she, when they were going to be weighing the decisions based on her relationship with "demons?"

"We have to get them out of there," I said.

Tired as we were, no one had anything to say to that, but I was pretty sure the feeling was unanimous, if only reluctantly so. My sluggish mind made a valiant effort to set in on the problem, but I couldn't seem to make it much further than that we probably had the tools for the job. We had an alien ship that could apparently teleport, after all—or something like it—and we also had a Shaper who could turn herself invisible. What more could we need?

A plan, probably. Including what the scud we'd do after magically yanking our friends out of Auckus' grimy clutches.

Even after all of this, Glenbark still had to have a strong base of supporters within the Legion. She was far too good of a leader not to. If we could find those loyal servants, get word to them somehow…

Tomorrow.

Assuming I'd actually guessed Elise's intended meeting place correctly, we'd meet with the others tomorrow. Franco and Johnny would know how to get it done from there, and who to get it done with. In the meanwhile, world burning or no, I needed to get some sleep if I wanted to be of any use to anyone.

Parker, having noticed our lack of sleep and apparently agreeing in his own superior way, announced with much eye-rolling that he was going to take us down to the expected meeting site under the cover of night so that we could sleep under our own stars instead of among them.

It almost seemed… not affectionate or caring, I guess. But at least mindful. Considerate.

Garrett must've read the thought on my face as we strapped into our seats in the flight room, because he reached over and took my forearm, his expression grave.

"Never forget what this bastard was willing to do to all those people."

I held his gaze, surprised not only by the lack of my irritation at his need to point out the obvious, but by the realization that I actually *appreciated* the reminder—that I was in fact starting to feel something like camaraderie with this man who'd obediently killed Shapers for years and had more blood on his hands than I ever wanted to think about.

It wasn't something I could recall having ever seen in the storyvids: the valiant hero persisting on, fighting the good fight with or without the blessing of the masses, until he one day looked around and realized that his only allies were the monsters and the killers he thought he'd been fighting. It was a sobering thought. But then again, maybe I wasn't the hero. Maybe none of us were.

In the scudstorm currently ravaging the once-fair planet of Enochia, I wasn't sure the situation even permitted for heroes anymore. There was only the truth, and the lies, and the people who were willing to kill for their belief about which was which.

I nodded to Garrett, and he released my arm as Parker brought us out of orbit and began the descent to Enochia.

Never forget.

I never would.

21

BY THE TOMES

After a particularly itchy incident with a puffscratch thicket at the vulnerable age of six, I'd never really been the biggest fan of camping in the wild. That said, by the time we'd made it groundside, found sufficient coverage for the big alien spaceship among the older, taller trees, and prepped a nearby hollow for sleep, the mossy ground beneath my polymer pad might as well have been made of clouds and pure sunshine. I was dead tired, far too tired to argue in the least when Garrett and Siren opted to stay up and sneak off into the bushes together for "first watch."

How anyone could be ready to swive through the advanced sleep deprivation after everything else we'd been through, I had no idea. Then again, it had been less than a mile from where I lay that Elise and I had first come to share our own pleasure after a long, tumultuous day spent on the run after we'd escaped the Legion assault on Franco's old home. So maybe it wasn't so unbelievable. In fact, if she were here now... The thought put a smile on my face and a pang of longing in my heart. Neither one lasted long.

I was dead tired, and I slept like it. But if I'd thought lying down had been the most wonderful feeling on this side of the planet, I'd been sorely mistaken.

Waking to Elise's loving eyes on mine, and her warm, strong hand on my cheek. That took the prize. So much so that I was certain at first I must be dreaming.

"Well isn't that just sweet as a demon's taint," came Garrett's muttered voice from somewhere nearby.

My eyes widened. Not a dream, then? I reached for Elise's cheek. Warm and soft. And real.

"Lise?"

She smiled and bent down to plant a kiss on my forehead, and another on my cheek, stopping at my ear to whisper, "I can't believe you went to space without me."

I blew out an airy laugh and wrapped my arms around her, overcome with relief. "I can't say it was part of the plan."

"Oooh," she cooed, squeezing me back. "You had a *plan*? Fancy."

"That's me. Fancy to the bone." We disengaged, and I sat up to look curiously around.

Garrett was sitting protectively over Siren's sleeping form a few feet away, watching us with a look I might've called amused disgust. Back in the direction of the ship, I spotted Franco, Johnny, and James talking to Alton Parker. Though talking might've been too friendly a word. Both Johnny and James were holding weapons at the ready, and Franco didn't look much less tense. I caught Johnny's eye and pumped the air in a sign to take it easy. He frowned but briefly touched his chest in an informal salute.

"You just got here?" I asked Elise.

"Pretty much. We went to our clearing first, but Parker must've heard us. He showed up, explained the basics, and guided us back here. Imagine my surprise when we found you camping beside a spaceship."

"Beats sleeping where he could theoretically whisk away at any moment."

Parker, clearly having heard the quiet comment even from fifteen yards away, shot me a frown. I focused back on Elise, trying to ignore the raknoth completely.

"What happened back at Haven? Are you all okay?"

"We're all fine," she said, then cocked her head, reconsidering. "Physically, at least. I think Johnny's more upset than he's letting on about the whole…"

"Sanctum-backed mutiny?" I offered.

"Yeah, that."

"Have you heard anything? Other than the reel bullscud, I mean?"

"A little," she said. "We've been in quiet contact with Dillard, and with General Hopper."

"Hopper? Is he still…"

"On our side?" Elise asked. "We think so. Can't really be sure about anything anymore, it seems like."

"But still, that's pretty good news, right?"

She gave a half-hearted shrug, looking reserved for some reason I didn't grasp. We had a ship. We had a Shaper who could turn invisible. And now she was telling me we had a strong ally on the inside. By all means, it sounded like the perfect recipe for a quick and relatively smooth rescue mission. And yet…

"Are there any plans to get our people off the noose?"

"There's plenty of talk," she said, still distracted by something.

I was about to ask what was bothering her when she shook off her daze and turned to me with a serious expression.

"There's something else."

I searched her face again, noting the bits of tension there that I'd over-looked in my raw excitement at simply seeing her here in front of me. "Tell me."

"Remember how I said I was going to help my dad compose a new message to Burton Kovaks?"

I nodded, suddenly uneasy about where this was going, though I couldn't quite say why.

"That was… Well, scud. I was sort of lying."

I stared at her, feeling unsteady. They weren't words I'd ever heard her say before.

"*Sort of* lying?"

She nodded slowly, biting her lip. "I knew there was no point in composing another cold message after your interview. Because Burton Kovaks contacted me three days ago."

"Oh…"

It was all I could think to say. I wasn't even sure what to think.

It wasn't like I could be angry with Elise for hiding something from me, could I? Much as I hated to admit it, my hiding things from her had been pretty much standard fare in our relationship up until only recently—first because I'd been told to keep her out of our business when we'd met, then because I'd simply been too wounded to tell her a lot of what I'd needed to after Carlisle's death. And she'd loved me anyway.

No, I couldn't reasonably be angry with Elise for this. But that didn't stop the hurt from churning in my stomach, threatening to evolve into something ugly and unreasonable.

"What did he say?" I forced myself to ask.

"In essence, that he feels they can't stay silent and watch from the side-lines anymore."

"Well, that's… good," I said. But good was the last thing I felt at the look on Elise's face. She'd done something. Something she felt was necessary, I thought, but also something she was reticent to tell me. But why?

She met my gaze. "I'm going to meet with him."

"Like scud you—"

"Hal…" She didn't need to say my name loudly or harshly to draw me up short. She just let her tone settle the scales, reminding me with that one word how much love and support she'd never stopped showing me, even when I'd done my best to push her away.

I tamped the ugly feelings down as best I could and forced myself to breathe before I spoke again.

"I'm sorry. It's just… Well, you know what happened when Franco and I met with the guy."

"Which is why I was scared to tell either of you about any of this."

"Because Kovaks is dangerous."

"No. Because you're both kind of overprotective beardsplitters when it comes to giving me space to handle things on my own."

I opened my mouth and hesitated, knowing she had a point.

"I love you," she added. "But you can't really tell me that's not true."

I sighed. "You're right. Of course you're right."

She took my hands in hers.

"Can I at least come with you?" I asked quietly, already pretty sure I knew the answer.

"He asked me—"

"To come alone."

She eyed me uncertainly. "No. To specifically not bring you."

"Well that doesn't sound suspicious or anything," I said.

Elise only looked thoughtful. "I kind of get the impression they're afraid of you, though I'm not really sure why."

"Maybe they just decided to get with the times," I muttered.

I had a sneaking suspicion it actually had something to do with that bizarre test they'd given me—the one that had involved me opening my mind to a rune-worked helmet, of all things. I hadn't forgotten the way Kovaks' pasty-faced friend had recoiled from me after whatever the helmet had shown him. Like I was a wild animal, liable to lose control at any moment.

I still didn't understand what that had been about. And I wasn't sure I wanted to.

I focused back on Elise and was swept by an odd mix of fear and guilt at the conflict written across her face.

"When?" I whispered.

"Today."

I swallowed, resisting the arguments that tried to escape my mouth. It felt wrong, just nodding along. Felt wrong even thinking about letting her stroll into danger alone when we'd only just reunited, and when the world was churning faster than an industrial waste processor out there. But where had my patronizing hero act gotten any of us?

For the sake of Enochia, we needed those Emmútari records. I was more sure of that now than I ever had been. And if that hawk-nosed bastard Burton didn't want me to be a part of it…

"Just… if he yanks one of those little wands on you," I said, standing and offering her a hand up, "don't try to yank back with telekinesis."

It still made me blush on the inside, thinking back to how I'd dived straight into that trap and put myself out cold upon my first meeting with Burton Kovaks under the Penitent Pass.

Elise smiled as I hauled her up, patting the collapsed spear strapped across her back. "I'd rather stick to the basics, if it comes to that."

And that was my raven-haired warrior girlfriend for you.

I pulled her in for a kiss, and only relented when we were interrupted by an appreciative noise from Siren, who'd apparently woken up.

"Well, isn't that just as sweet as goja pie?" she said.

Elise stiffened against me, adopting the disdainful look she normally reserved for serpents and other wriggly creatures. I turned and looked between Garrett and Siren.

"I think you two have been spending too much time together."

"I think we've all been spending too much time together," Garrett said, shooting a dark look toward Alton Parker.

Siren laid a hand on his thigh, and some silent communication must've passed between them, because he perked up like a hound at the dinner bell, eyeing the bushes where they'd had their "first watch" last night.

"Again?" I asked before I could remind myself that I probably didn't want to know.

Siren rose from her blankets and arched her back in a languid stretch, full yawn and everything, before innocently turning for the woods, away from the ship. "I think I need to stretch my legs a little." She shot us a smile. "Wake myself up."

Garrett stood to join her, shooting me his signature smirk, with a clear overtone of, *That's right, Raish. You jealous?*

That smirk wavered, however, when Siren turned back to us, her eyes turning positively mischievous as they flickered over me then roamed much more attentively along the length of Elise's body. "The more the merrier, by the way."

For the second time that morning, I found myself completely at a loss for words—albeit for entirely different reasons. Elise might've been similarly caught off guard, but she regained her senses much more quickly.

"I typically refrain from casual strolls with people who've tried to murder my boyfriend."

Siren just made a slight pouty face, then shrugged, took Garrett's hand, and turned for the woods.

"There's something wrong with that woman," Elise said quietly, frowning after the retreating pair.

"There's something wrong with that man," I added.

She smiled, and kissed me. "Come on. Johnny looks bored over there. Let's see how the meeting of the minds is going before someone starts shooting."

The meeting of the minds, it turned out, was mostly spinning in neat little circles, with no clear sign of moving forward.

"There's nothing to be gained by it," Franco was saying as we approached. "And in all likelihood, a civil war on the other side of things, assuming she truly retains as much support as Hopper believes."

"We can't leave her to stand trial with High General Ass Grabber in there," Johnny said. "We all know how that one turns out."

"If you would simply listen to what I'm telling you..." Parker started, then turned at our approach. "Or perhaps you'd prefer to hear it from your chosen messiah."

They all turned to face us, except for Johnny, who was frowning at Parker, his rifle not quite pointing at the raknoth, but still held ready. "Our chosen *what*?"

Parker rolled his eyes. "Never mind."

"Yeah," Johnny muttered. "Because I'm the idiot for not understanding your made up raknoth words."

"Did something happen?" Elise asked as we joined the tense circle in the shadow of Parker's ship.

"Nothing of note," Franco said. Then, with a glance at Parker, "Or of human compassion." He turned to me then, and looked like he was about to express some of that human compassion and say hello when Parker cut in.

"Will you tell them, Haldin? I tire of this pointless chatter."

"Tell them which part?" I asked.

"The part where none of our petty human concerns matter, apparently," Franco offered.

"That's definitely his favorite," I said.

"Tell me about it," Johnny said, still watching Parker suspiciously. "Shouldn't we, like, put this guy in some shackles or something? I dunno about you, but I don't trust the superpowered planet-wrecker here to play nice. And why are Smirks and Lady Lust with you anyway?" he added before I could answer, shooting a frown off in the direction the two ex-Seekers had disappeared for second watch. "You didn't happen to accidentally join the League of Evil Bastards overnight, did you broto?"

"I'm standing right here," Parker said.

"Exactly my point," Johnny said.

Parker looked at me. "I explained that the Seekers offered unexpected aid during our escape, and that circumstances dictated we bring them with us. I'm not sure where the confusion is."

Johnny, Franco, and James all turned to me, clearly exasperated.

"We got into a scrap in the woods."

"With them?" Johnny asked.

"With the raknoth," I said. "The ones that took Five and Seven and escaped Oasis."

Everyone in the circle gave a start.

"You got jumped by reekers?" Johnny asked.

"Are you okay?" Elise added.

"Clearly we survived," Parker said. "At which point, I summoned the ship and we made our escape."

"After your summoning the ship brought the trackers down on our heads and left us no choice in the matter," I added.

"Convenient that you left all these little details out," Johnny said, tapping the side of his rifle with his trigger finger. "Almost as convenient as the fact that the reekers found you in the middle of the woods at all."

"I wouldn't call anything about the situation convenient," Parker said, looking to me as if for confirmation.

"Parker fought alongside me," I admitted, aware as I did so of how much all of this could easily be interpreted as my having fallen for Parker's grand manipulation. Not that I could prove with certainty that I hadn't. I decided to stick with the facts instead. "The two were strong, though. They had us pinned when Siren shot one from the trees. Garrett charged in afterward, and we managed to drive them away." I looked at Parker. "I was hoping the one was down for good once he took a bolt to the brain."

"Alone, he might have been in trouble. With Nan'Vala's aid, though, he will likely survive."

"See?" Johnny said. "Alien first name basis with the enemy? Convenient."

"They were my clan mates," Parker said.

"Yep. That's pretty much what I'm getting at, right there." Johnny frowned. "And you're telling me a pulse bolt to the head wasn't enough to finish a reeker? Smirks got Frosty with a gropping dagger. What're us normal folk supposed to use?"

"Two bolts, perhaps," Parker said with his most reptilian smile.

"Also, reekers?" I asked.

"Yeah," Johnny said, finally breaking his stare on Parker to look at me. "That's what we're calling 'em."

"I thought we agreed that's *not* what we're calling them," Elise said.

"You agreed that's what *you're* not calling 'em, lady. I don't know about you, but I refuse to die because I'm busy shouting, 'Look out, here comes that Seeker-turned-raknoth-turned-meat-puppet guy!'"

"Or girl," Elise said.

"Or girl," Johnny agreed, tilting his head. "It's ridiculous. As opposed to 'reeker,' which is clearly syllabolically superior."

"Now who's making up words?"

Johnny spread his hands. "Well, there wasn't a word for Seeker-turned-raknoth-turned—"

"I meant 'syllabolically,'" Elise said. "Obviotudinally."

Johnny scrunched his face up in thought.

Alton Parker cleared his throat. Or maybe growled lightly. It was kind of hard to tell.

"Perhaps we should get back to the question of prudent next steps," Franco said.

"Which is exactly why I want Haldin to confirm what I have been trying to tell you all along," Parker said, with the kind of tone normally reserved for children.

Franco and the others ignored his attitude and looked to me.

I wasn't even sure where to begin.

"We've got some problems."

"Ha!" Johnny barked. "Problems, he says."

"Sarentus?" Franco asked, drawing confused looks from the others.

"Was actually a raknoth," I confirmed. "According to Parker's memories, at least."

"Wait…" Johnny looked between us, then to Parker, then back to us. "No. You're not… You're serious? *The* Sarentus?"

"You saw it?" Elise asked.

"I saw Parker's memories of the raknoth Nan'Sarentus back on Earth, and I saw Zar'Faenor telling Parker that he'd left Sarentus on Enochia."

"So this Earth place is, like, actually *real*?" Johnny said.

"And Zar'Faenor visited with Sarentus," Franco said.

"Over a thousand years ago," Elise concluded.

"Yeah, it's…" I looked around at them, and decided I might as well have out with it all. "Yeah. You guys might wanna sit down for all this."

22

HARD TRUTH

Never in my life had I seen a group listen with such rapt attention to words that felt so utterly ridiculous coming out of my mouth. Though, now that I thought about it, maybe that was how I would've felt about a standard worship hall sermon, now that I knew what I did. Or thought I did, at least.

"So basically," Johnny said when I'd finished, "you're telling us that our entire world's a lie, we're actually sorta aliens, the Sanctum's basically a mad cult, and even if we somehow manage to sort any of this scud out, Parker's beardsplitter bosses are gonna come eat our planet whole. Did I miss anything?"

"The part where we're wasting our time talking about this," Parker called from where he was sitting over on his ship's boarding ramp.

"Are you positive this isn't all bullscud?" Johnny asked. "Because it kinda sounds like bullscud."

"Unless raknoth minds are playing by totally different rules of telepathy, yeah, I'm pretty sure."

"And what are the chances they are?" Franco asked.

"Playing by different rules?" I traded a glance with Elise, then looked over at Parker, wishing I had something other than gut feelings and a few ancient drawings to corroborate any of this. "Slim. I'm pretty sure what I saw was real."

Franco studied me for a few seconds, then nodded. "Then I think we all know what must be done."

"Damn straight," Johnny said. Then he took in Franco's somber air. "Wait, you're not saying… You don't actually think we should move on this scud?"

"I think we should attempt to find some demonstrable evidence, and embrace the facts."

"That's real noble and all, coming from an information broker, but—"

"Do you remember how your High General intended to treat the Legion's relationship with the truth?" Franco asked. "Before the Sanctum pushed her out?"

Johnny's jaw tightened, and it was in that moment that I first saw just how much was *not* okay right now. "I remember. But what we're talking about… it could tear our planet apart. And that's *if* there's actually any truth to all this, and Alton Parker isn't just playing another one of his games, trying to get us to throw fuel on the fire." He looked at me. "You didn't actually see Sarentus on Enochia, raising Alpha's sigil with glowing red eyes, did you?"

"No, but—"

"That's why we should focus on finding some evidence," Franco said. "On tapping into the Emmútari records, getting more than one side of the story." He gave Johnny a meaningful look. "And on getting Glenbark and the rest of our allies clear of this madness long enough for reason to have its day."

"Reason…" Johnny muttered.

"If you refuse to trust my memories," Parker said from right behind Johnny and James, who both jumped at his sudden appearance, "perhaps you can at least trust that I do not particularly care what happens to this planet. Certainly, I have no strong desire to watch ignorance drive a species to self-destruction. Perhaps I'd even rather see Enochia find peace and prosperity. But you needn't trust my word on any of that. Trust simply that I am governed by my own self-interest in escaping my own vengeful masters. What happens to Enochia has little to do with that anymore."

"Yeah, super comforting," Johnny said.

I could see him warring with whatever thoughts were in his head, and I completely understood. Even having seen all this for myself, and even having had a day and a half to chew on it all, I still wasn't really sure what to think about any of it. And any time I tried too hard to figure it out, it all just felt… insurmountable.

And I was pretty sure that was exactly the thought I was seeing on the others' faces.

"What if none of this matters?" Johnny finally asked. "What if it's just all, you know…" He looked around at us, assessing. "Well, I never thought I'd be the one to say this, but what if we're just all gropped sideways no matter how we play this? What if we've already lost?"

"The thought has occurred to me," I admitted quietly.

"And the logical thing to do in that case," Parker said, with a pointed look at me, "would be to simply move on to a new problem. A more pressing one, with a more well-defined solution. But what do I know?" he added at the round of unappreciative stares he got. "I've only been around a few millennia longer than all of you."

"Are you sure we can't at least find a muzzle for this guy?" Johnny asked.

"Perhaps you'd be more grateful for my bite," Parker said, "if you knew what I've done for your sister."

Johnny went rigid, his gaze flicking to me. "What's he talking about?"

My mouth went dry.

Parker turned his smug attention on me. "She *was* this one's sister, was she not?"

I couldn't find the words.

As explosively insane as our breakout had been, I hadn't had time then or since then to really assess the decision I'd made to lead Parker to Annabelle—to let him sink his fangs into Johnny's ailing sister to Alpha knew what end. Thinking about it now, though, seeing the disbelief in Johnny's eyes, I felt sick. What had I been thinking?

"Hal, what's he talking about?"

What if Parker had actually made things worse?

"I developed and delivered a solution I believe will undo the hybridization process," Parker said, before I could find my tongue. "A biological entity not unlike what your parvobiologists would call a retrovirus."

Johnny's face was a mess of emotion. It shifted from confusion, to gradual comprehension, to tentative hopefulness. Then to dark realization. "You believe?" he growled.

Parker scowled at him. "I never imagined I would find myself needing to undo the process. It wasn't a simple solution. But, I imagine the treatment should begin to—"

"Wasn't… simple?" Johnny was shaking in a way I'd never seen, his face red, his eyes wild, and riveted to Parker. "You used my sister as a…"

Parker's knees were hitting the soft forest undergrowth almost before I registered that Johnny had just put a pulse bolt through each of the raknoth's legs. Johnny stepped forward, rifle leveled at Parker's head, too caught up in his rage to realize a pair of holes in the legs wouldn't keep a raknoth down. Elise was already darting forward to stop him even as I reached out and held Parker down with telekinesis.

"You bastard!" Johnny roared, struggling against Elise's bear hug, his eyes still locked on Parker, whose face was fixed in a snarl of either violence or pain.

The raknoth's skin had taken on a dangerous tint of green, and he was beginning to struggle against my telekinetic hold.

"That's enough," I said, shoving Parker back and stepping between him and Johnny.

To the right, Elise stepped back from Johnny, who'd stopped struggling but now turned his glare on me.

"What did you let him do, Hal?"

A thousand answers ran through my head, none of the them right. None of them sincere.

I faced my friend and told him the only thing I could. "She was dying, Johnny. We both know it."

His jaw clenched. His face working like it couldn't decide whether to scream or cry. I'd never seen this look in Johnny's eyes—the depth of the pain and despair.

"I wish there'd been time to talk about it," I said. "To let Therese run the tests, or figure out some other way. But there wasn't time. The entire damn base was trying to kill us, and something told me that even if we survived, that was the last chance we'd have to see Annabelle before it was too late. I'm sorry, Johnny. But I only did what I thought was best for her."

He just stared at me with lost eyes, trying to process. Elise was still standing there with her hand on his shoulder, not quite blocking him from me and Parker, but there all the same. Johnny's gaze shifted from me to Parker, and I could see what he was thinking. That if things took a turn for the worse, he'd like nothing more than to be the one to put a few bolts through Parker's head.

But he wouldn't. I could see it in my friend's face as he backed away from Elise and turned to stomp off into the woods. He was just too good on the inside. Myself, on the other hand…

"Pull a move like that again," I sent to Parker. "And I might just kill you myself."

He didn't respond with words, just climbed back to his feet and regarded me with a bored, unimpressed stare. Some corner of my mind pointed out that maybe I should be glad I could still feel this level of distress and revulsion over a matter of a few individual lives after seeing the scope of the destruction that had so clearly jaded Parker to such relatively trivial matters. But the fact that any part of me felt the need to point that out at all was nearly as disturbing as if I'd already gone full cold-blooded.

I needed to get my head grounded. I needed a clear mission to sink my teeth into.

"What'd we miss?" called a voice from the direction of the hollow. Garrett. "Why'd the mouthy ginger look like someone just shot his—Oh. "

The ex-Seeker drew up short at whatever he saw on my face as I rounded on him. He had an arm slung around Siren's waist, and they both looked half drunk on whatever it was they'd just concluded in private.

"So serious," Siren whispered conspiratorially to Garrett, who looked notably less amused, like he could sense there'd been real fighting here only moments ago.

I couldn't deal with them right now. Or anything else, for that matter.

"Ten minutes," I said, starting off after Johnny without a backward glance. "And maybe someone could figure out what the scud we're supposed to do next."

I FOUND Johnny sitting on the thick trunk of a recently fallen oak tree, staring sullenly at the quiet forest beyond. He hadn't gone all that far from our shipside circle, nor did he look up with his red-rimmed eyes or seem particularly surprised when I walked up and sat down beside him. For a while, we just sat in silence. Even if I'd had any idea where to begin, something about the weight of the moment made me feel like it wasn't my place anyway.

Finally, Johnny gave a wet-sounding sniff and straightened up. "Well this is a first, huh?"

I glanced at him, not needing to wonder about which part of our mess he was referring to. The situation here was simply backward, no matter which way we looked at it. Throughout the years, I'd always been the one to lose it, and he'd always been the one to come set me straight. And now... it felt wrong, seeing my unshakable friend break like this.

"Johnny... whatever you're feeling, whatever you need to say to me... you can say it. I probably deserve it."

He looked at me in earnest for the first time like he wasn't quite sure what I was talking about.

"I'm sorry," I said. "About all of this. Parker. Annabelle. Glenbark."

He thought about that for a little while, then shook his head and muttered to the trees, "There you go again. Hal versus The World."

"No." I shook my head in kind. "I'm not saying this is all on me. Or that I could've changed the way things played out. But I'm sure I could've done better. And I'm sorry if I made the wrong call."

"I hate that smug bastard," Johnny said after a while.

"I'm not a fan either. Trust me."

The look Johny gave me left little need for words. It was a look that said he wasn't buying my bullscud, nor was he amused I'd even try to ship it his way.

"I didn't have a choice, Johnny."

"We always have a choice," Johnny said. "I'm pretty sure you've told me those exact words before."

He wasn't wrong. In some form or another, they were the words my dad had told me time and time again, and the same words I'd echoed to Johnny during any number of our debates about the proper place of rights, wrongs, and good old-fashioned discipline in service to the Legion.

"All you had to do was leave him in that cell," Johnny said. "Why didn't you?"

"Because Auckus' attack hounds came to kill me before I could finish extracting what was in that bastard's head," I shot back before taking a breath to cool my head. "The things he showed me, Johnny… words can't adequately describe it. All I know is that my gut's telling me we can't ignore these rakul any more than we can allow the Sanctum to move ahead with this bullscud war."

He stared into the chittering forest, saying nothing.

"You don't believe me?"

He frowned. "Of course I believe you. If I honestly thought you'd let that monster slaughter good men and women…" He shook his head, apparently unsure as to what he'd do in that case, and the quiet settled back between us.

"Are you okay?" I finally asked.

"I'm fine," he muttered.

It was my turn to give him the *no-bullscud-accepted-here* look.

"I *will* be fine," he amended. "It just hasn't been easy. With Bells. And

Glenbark. With any of it, really. And if that scaly bastard's *solution* doesn't work…"

"It will," I said. "I really think it will. He didn't offer the cure out of the goodness of his heart."

"No scud."

"I'm pretty sure it was a bribe," I continued. "Just another calculated move to win some of my trust."

"Also, no scud."

"Point being, I don't think he would've offered at all if it wasn't going to work."

"Yeah, I pretty much figured the same. I think that's the only reason I didn't pull the trigger a third time back there." He looked at me, serious. "But Hal, we should probably talk about why he's willing to do all this just to earn your good favor. I don't know if you're aware of this, but mass-murdering sociopaths aren't really…"

I heard the cracking twigs and thudding boots at the same time Johnny did, and we both turned, expecting the worst. Thankfully, it was only Elise, jogging toward us at a pace that suggested she had something important to say, but not quite life-threatening.

By our current standards, we might as well have called that good news.

"What happened?" I asked as she reached our log, eyeing us to gauge the emotional air of the conversation she'd interrupted.

"We just got news from General Hopper," she said a little breathlessly.

Johnny was already on his feet. "Freya?"

"Has been safely extracted from Haven," Elise said.

"Where?" Johnny asked.

"He couldn't say. He'll send word again when they've established a secure location, but—"

"What happened?" Johnny said. "I thought we were going to…" He trailed off, frowning like he was trying to piece something together.

"We offered our help when we first managed to contact Hopper," Elise explained to me. "He didn't like the way things were shaping up with the high council moving into Glenbark's trial."

"No kidding," I said, hardly needing to imagine. Even if some of the Generals had been favorable toward Glenbark's plight in the coming trial, I didn't want to think about the level of depraved threats Auckus would've been willing to level at them to get everyone in line. With the Sanctum at his back, the greasy scudball had already committed nothing shy of mutiny, after all.

"Well, I guess he saw an opportunity and took the shot," Elise added to Johnny, who nodded absentmindedly, still lost in thought.

"We need to find them," Johnny said.

I couldn't say I disagreed, though I wasn't entirely sure what use we'd be if and when we did. Aside from adding fuel to the imminent fire, of course.

Even before Auckus' mutiny, the alignment of the Legion had already been in danger of fragmenting into several disparate factions. The open attempt on my life in the middle of a Haven crowd had made that clear enough. Now, though, if those Legionnaires who'd been rubbed wrong by recent events saw Glenbark out there, surviving against hostile forces with her band of loyal soldiers… I'd bet hard coin there'd be more than a few companies throughout the Legion willing to break ranks and follow after their true High General.

The thought stirred up hope and dread in equal parts. Because as nice as it'd be to have Glenbark and a few thousand friendly guns watching our backs again, I couldn't exactly jump for joy at the thought of escalating from the Sanctum's war on demons to a full-blown Enochian civil war.

"There's something else?" I said to Elise, reading as much in the wrinkle of her brow.

"Yeah," she said, her gaze falling to the dirt. "It's Four and Eight. They couldn't get them out, apparently. And seeing as Auckus just lost his most important prisoner, I guess he felt the need to make a public gesture."

My stomach fell. "What did he do?"

"He's moving them to Divinity. It's all over the reels." She gave me that look she still used sometimes, when she was afraid something she was about to say might set me back to the Dark Place I'd barely crawled out of after Carlisle's death.

"They're planning to execute them in front of the White Tower," she said. "Today, at sunset."

2 3

ON THE HOOKS

If I'd lived to be as old as Alton Parker himself, I still would've been more than happy to never so much as glimpse the White Tower again. Before all this had begun—before Al'Kundesha had killed my parents, and I'd been pulled headlong into an ongoing alien invasion—the gleaming Tower had been something to look to for reassurance. A stalwart symbol of Alpha's grace and strength. An always visible reminder as to why we tyros did what we did, forsaking normal childhoods so that we could be ready when the time came to defend Alpha's domain, and the good people of Enochia.

But that had been then.

Now, as I stared at the White Tower from the congested air traffic lanes, all I saw was a gaudy monstrosity, erected by thousand-year-old lies and kept in order by a long history of oppression and self-service. Of course, it was entirely possible the Sanctum's mounting pile of attempts on my life had left me somewhat embittered toward the establishment. But I'd also seen the unholy splendor of the High Cleric's *temporary* quarters—the ones he was relegated to while they rebuilt the Great Hall proper.

So maybe my disgust was at least a tad warranted.

"Makes you think, huh?" Johnny asked beside me.

I turned away from the skimmer window to face him. Ahead, in the driver's seat, Garrett was also eyeing Johnny in the mirror. Beside him, Siren was lost in her own thoughts.

"Makes you think what?" Garrett asked.

Johnny loudly and pointedly cleared his throat. "This was actually intended to be a private conversation. You know, for people who haven't tried to kill us both in the past."

Garrett rolled his eyes. "What is it with you kids and hanging on to the past? And I wasn't even trying to kill *you* back at the hydro plant," he added toward Johnny.

"I think I still have some internal bleeding that disagrees with that statement."

Garrett shrugged. "Maybe you should learn to handle yourself in a fight."

"Maybe you should stop trying to kill people," Johnny countered.

Garrett turned his gaze out toward the White Tower. "That doesn't seem likely in the near future."

"So this is what it's like, huh?" Johnny asked me. "Being an outlaw, and whatnot?"

I studied him. "You seem oddly chipper about all this."

"Hey, I sorta missed out on the whole renegade hero kick last time around. Can you blame a guy for getting excited? Plus, we might even get to take a shot at High General Creepy Pants. What's there to hate?"

"Overwhelming odds," Siren muttered in the front. "Innocent bystanders."

"Sanctum Guard," Garrett added. "Onyx Guard."

"WAN cameras everywhere," Siren said.

"And the fact that we received this intel too late to hit them in transit," Garrett concluded.

"These two kinda suck," Johnny whispered to me behind a raised hand, loudly enough that everyone could plainly hear.

"Still better than Parker," I said, before I could think about it.

That sobered the mood in the skimmer cabin right quick. No one wanted to think about our undesirable ally, and how he was drifting high in the atmosphere, ostensibly watching us at this very moment, ready to protect his assets—or to do whatever the scud he decided might suit him best in the moment. Who knew? All I knew was that we'd do just as well to try to forget he was there at all. Because if scud hit the turbines with this rescue mission and it came to Alton Parker sweeping down to carry us off in his clearly alien ship, I was sure I could kiss goodbye to any chance of ever clearing my blackened public image. Assuming I hadn't already done so and just failed to admit it.

"Let's just not grop this up," Garrett said, and I had the feeling he was having similar thoughts—though maybe more out of repulsion for Parker in general than out of any concern for how this was all going to look to Enochia. But who knew there, either?

I missed Carlisle.

But, I reflected as we closed on the White Tower, at least I had Johnny here. One person I could trust without reservation. I could barely bring myself to think about the others right now. The thought of Elise, Franco, and James currently on their way to Humility to meet Burton Kovaks with no backup…

I closed my eyes, breathing deep and focusing on bringing my thudding heart back under control.

"Holy scud," Johnny muttered beside me.

I opened my eyes, followed his gaze out the window, and saw what he meant. And not just saw it, but *heard* it as well.

We'd expected the crowd outside the White Tower would be packed. The Sanctum's ongoing war being what it was, I could only imagine there weren't many people in the city who wouldn't like to see a pair of alleged demons strung up in the name of Alpha. But this was more than packed.

It looked like the entire city of Divinity had gathered. They stood in the shadow of the White Tower, packed shoulder to shoulder. Thousands of them. Maybe tens of thousands. I could hardly tell, other than that they were spilling out of the massive courtyard and into the surrounding streets.

The air buzzed with the dull roar of their collective voices, easily rising above what I'd originally mistook for the sounds of the air-jammed skimmers all around us. The skimmers themselves were beginning to run out of airspace. Hundreds had already thrown caution to the wind and were illegally hovering over the courtyard, staking their spots for the show to come. The tides of enforcers and Sanctum Guard present didn't seem to particularly care about the technical traffic violation—either because they'd been ordered to allow it, or simply because they had more pressing issues in trying to keep some semblance of order in the oceanic flow of pedestrians below.

"So about that escape plan…" Johnny said.

None of us had to ask what he meant. We'd all known this was going to be hairy. But seeing the sheer mass of it, hearing tens of thousands of good Enochians roaring for demon's blood and knowing they'd be even more ecstatic to see it be mine… Much as I hated the weakness of that little voice in my head, it was impossible not to acknowledge that we could still turn back—that there was nothing at all stopping us from simply flying away, just another skimmer in the chaos. Nothing but Four and Eight, and the heavy certainty that their deaths would haunt us all if we didn't do everything in our power to save them.

Well, that, and the naive little voice that puffed up in my chest to remind me that we were the good guys here, the ones in the right, fighting the good fight. Somehow, the reminder didn't quell the icy apprehension churning in my gut. Because we were also the good guys who'd come here out of necessity with barely more than a scrap of a plan, and no backup to speak of—aside from an emergency raknoth, of course. There hadn't been time for anything more.

By some combination of aggressive maneuvering and a steady stream of cursing, Garrett managed to wrap us around the back of the White Tower and squeeze into a spot among the growing throng of hovering skimmers, more or less above the main stage. At least we were close. Closer than any of us had expected, seeing as we'd planned to land on one of the many high rise buildings that formed the edges of the courtyard. So there was that.

And there, down below, were Four and Eight, on a wooden stage that had been constructed so that a few of the courtyard's regal stone columns could rise straight through and provide a handy and elegant means by which to secure waiting prisoners. Four and Eight were each bound to their own columns with thick ropes, and judging by the way they looked to be slouching against their restraints, I guessed they'd either been beaten or drugged until the powers that be had felt safe betting they wouldn't be able to make any miraculous escape attempts.

Around them, squads of Sanctum Guard and enforcers held a tight perimeter between the roaring crowd and the stage, which I could see now was in fact a double gallows by the throw levers and the lines of the trap doors beneath each of the ex-Seekers. Luckily, I couldn't see any nooses on their necks yet, which was going to make my job a lot easier.

"Okay…" Garrett said, flipping the autopilot on to keep the skimmer hovering in our tight spot. He didn't have anything to add, apparently, but that one word expressed the sentiment just fine, as did the look he and Siren exchanged before they shared one last kiss.

Again, I had that unsettled feeling like I'd left my bearings far behind—back in Alton Parker's cell, maybe, or maybe even all the way back at Carlisle's funeral pyre. Because here I was getting ready to risk everything to save two veteran Shaper killers, and every bone in my body told me it was the right thing to do. The lines just kept getting more and more blurry.

Quickly, I dialed my cloaking pendant off and reached down to attempt contact with the ex-Seekers only to find that it was as we'd expected.

"They've got at least one cloaking generator down there," I said. "Maybe more."

My own tools, forged to fight the raknoth, now being used as weapons against me and mine. I'm sure there were a few tomes' worth of lessons to be learned in there, but for the moment, we'd simply have to press on.

Johnny leaned over me to glance out my window, then settled back to his seat with a noncommittal grunt. "You guys don't happen to uh… know their names, do you?"

Garrett and Siren parted to shoot Johnny a double stare.

"Why?" Garrett asked.

"Oh, I don't know," Johnny said. "Just seems like, you know, maybe we should know the names of the people we're about to throw ourselves on the angry mob for."

Garrett and Siren traded a look that told me what I'd come to suspect: true, given names were not something the Seekers disclosed on a whim. Or at all, maybe.

"We don't know their names," Siren said.

It probably could've told me something about the oppression of the lives they'd led, that they could've worked alongside their fellow Seekers for years and have not even learned their names. But I couldn't think about that now.

"Right…" Johnny shrugged. "Well, I guess let's go save Four and Eight, then. Go team."

"Like you have anything to worry about," Garrett muttered.

"Oh, I'm plenty worried," Johnny said, eyeing the swarm of people below before turning back to me and hurriedly clapping my shoulder. "You got this, broto."

"Are you ready, Demon?" Siren asked, looking back at me with none of her usual coy air.

I nodded.

"Raish," Garrett said, his voice suddenly thick. "If you don't get her out—"

"We're getting out," I said before he could finish whatever threat was on his tongue.

Something in my voice must've convinced him I meant what I said, because he drew his lips tight and gave me a curt nod.

"Sexists," Siren grunted as she started climbing over the divider into the back seat and slid in between me and Johnny.

I cracked the door open on my left and looked up at Garrett one last time. "You're ready to play catch?"

He grunted an affirmative. I traded one last look with Siren. Then I swung the door open and scrambled onto the roof of the skimmer. Even knowing that I could telekinetically catch myself from pretty much any fall, the sight of the sprawling courtyard crowd far below, coupled with the rush of skimmer-churned air and the lurch of our own vehicle beneath my weight, all added up to one seriously unhappy stomach. I turned before it could get worse and focused on helping Siren climb up after me.

"Holy scud," she whispered, clutching to me as she took in the fall.

"It's okay," I said, gently turning us toward the front of the skimmer and scooting forward for the windshield. "I carried four of us down from the Great Hall the night it went up. Two of us is nothing."

"Well," she said, scooting down the windshield beside me, both of us clinging together and moving slowly, "aren't you just my big strong hero, then."

"Just trying to make you feel better," I muttered.

"Even though I poisoned you that one time."

Scoot.

"And stunned you the other."

Scoot.

"And—"

"Can we just focus?" I muttered, edging toward the end of the skimmer hood.

"Sweet Alpha, you're actually blushing? Ready to dive feet first into certain death and you're blushing because you once saw me naked."

I drew up to the edge and stopped, mouth hanging open with half a dozen different replies, from a clearly untrue, *I'm not blushing,* all the way up through, *Can you just shut up and be happy I'm still ready to throw myself into the ring for you people?*

Before I could say anything, she leaned in and kissed my cheek.

"Never change, Hal."

"Yeah," I said, wiping my cheek off and practically feeling Garrett's death stare from behind us. "You had to make it weird, didn't you?" I turned to her. "And since when do you call me that?"

She shrugged. "Now seemed like one of those *just in case we die* kinds of moments."

"No one's dying here today."

She searched my face, serious once again, and finally gave a slight nod. "Okay."

It was the first time I saw it for sure written across her features, but there it was. She was every bit as terrified as I was.

I wrapped my arm around her waist, and she slung her arm over my shoulders. "Okay."

"Anytime now, scudhead," Garrett's voice crackled in my ear. "People are starting to notice."

I resisted the urge to look around and distract myself with the sight of confused and maybe even concerned Enochians point at us from skimmer windows and the crowd below, wondering what in demons' depths we were thinking. Of course they were starting to notice. But it hardly mattered now.

I kept my eyes fixed on Four and Eight, and my mind focused on the plan. The plan that was really so simple it bordered on stupid. Scud, maybe it *was* just stupid. Come to think of it, I wasn't even positive it qualified as a plan.

But it was all we had.

"Ready?" I sent.

By way of reply, Siren leaned forward, gathering her legs beneath her. I did the same, keeping my eyes locked on Four and Eight, doing my best to ignore the explosive pounding of Siren's heart as I gripped her tighter, or the hammering in my own ears.

"Take me for a ride, Demon."

Every muscle in my body tightened.

And we jumped.

2 4

CHOKE

side from the preposterous number of armed men below and the sight of the rapidly approaching gallows stage, there were a few distinct facts that stood out to me as Siren and I fell. For one, there was the cleric I hadn't noticed from the skimmer—the one apprehensively pacing the stage right behind the stone columns Four and Eight were bound to. For another, there was the dazed look of horror in Four's eyes as we passed through the invisible boundary of a cloaking field generator and entered his and Eight's sphere of telepathic awareness.

And then, as I gathered my will to catch the energy of our fall and hurl it into phase one of our master plan, I saw the real kicker. Two thin, dark collars, strapped one each to Four's and Eight's throats. Explosive collars.

"Don't!" Siren all but screamed in my head.

Flustered as I was at the sudden change in plan, I barely managed to catch our fall at all, much less to do anything useful with the energy. We hit the wooden stage hard. Hard enough that we tumbled forward in our efforts to catch our invisible balance while maintaining contact with one another. Hard enough that I lost over half the energy I'd just channeled in a useful rush of hot air.

And hard enough that Siren's illusion flickered.

For a moment, I wasn't positive it had really happened, quickly as my limbs once again disappeared from my own sight. Then the scream went up from the crowd, and spread like a wildfire.

"*Scud,*" came Siren's mental growl. "*What do we do?*"

"Just hold the shroud."

Beyond that, I had no idea what came next. I didn't need to scan our surroundings to know a full squad of Sanctum Guard were detaching from the perimeter to sweep up onto the stage, or to see that the twitchy cleric was now holding a small black device in his hand, brandishing it in our general direction like a weapon. And that confirmed exactly what I'd feared the moment I'd seen those collars.

The plan had been so simple it bordered on stupid.

Siren and I would fall, covered by her arcane shroud. If Four and Eight were untethered, I'd use the energy of our fall to launch our friends straight back up the way we'd came. Equal and opposite. If they were bound, I'd instead use the energy of our fall to free them, then I'd brute force them up to the skimmer with telekinesis. Either way, Siren and I would be free to slink off stage in the chaos under the cover of her shroud.

Except now, the plan that had been so simple it bordered on stupid, had just gone plain stupid. Stupid, and suicidal. Because now, even if we got Four and Eight out, they'd still only be the press of a button away from instant and explosive decapitation.

Stupid.

But there was nothing for it now. So I reached out and telekinetically yanked what I prayed was the only detonator from the twitchy cleric's hand straight to my own.

"What're you—"

"*Move,*" I snapped, starting us toward the back corner of the stage before Siren could finish berating me for the risky decision.

"*Slowly,*" she snapped back, crushing my hand in her tight grip.

It was surreal, walking slowly across the wide gallows stage, invisible in plain sight, trying to pretend like the crowd wasn't positively roaring behind us now, trying to ignore the Sanctum Guard rushing up the steps on either side. I fixed my mind on Four's bindings and started in on freeing him, letting Siren lead us.

"*How do we disarm those collars?*" I sent as I finished yanking the first knots loose.

She seemed too occupied to answer. With everything happening around us, I didn't really blame her. I felt Four's mind sluggishly reaching out to us now—almost definitely drugged—and the Sanctum Guard were storming onto the platform, their impersonal golden faceplate sweeping back and forth for any sign of us. Down in the courtyard, the sea of civilians was pressing in on the perimeter like they had every intention of throwing demons to the wind and coming to join the Sanctum Guard in the hunt.

This was going nowhere good, and it was headed there at breakneck speed.

I was caught between reaching out for Eight's bindings and telekinetically shoving some of the Sanctum Guard back down the steps into their fellows when a strong voice boomed out.

"Demon!"

The word sliced through the growing panic of the crowd and yanked me out of my focus, straight to the decorative dais from which is had been shouted. It was almost unbelievable, how quickly the roaring courtyard fell silent. But I was far more fixated on the man who'd spoken, looking down on us from his pedestal, his robes of gold and cream positively radiant in the midday sunlight.

"Reveal yourself, Demon," the High Cleric called, his voice booming from dozens of amps throughout the courtyard. He raised one hand, and I didn't need to ask what it was he was holding. "Reveal yourself, or prepare to watch your fellow demons perish before your eyes."

Another detonator.

The holy bastard had another detonator.

"Stay hidden," I sent to Siren, letting go of her hand.

"You have five seconds, Demon," the High Cleric called.

Siren held on tight, tugging me closer. *"Hal, we can't—"*

"As soon as I get that thing out of his hand," I sent, "I need you to have Eight lose."

"But how—"

"Three seconds!"

"Secure those knots!" one of the Sanctum Guard called from beside Four's column.

"Two."

There were too many. Too many Sanctum Guard swarming the stage. Too many frothing civilians beyond. And the collars…

We'd had one shot at this. And we'd missed it. Completely.

"One."

I wrenched my hand free from Siren's—right as she dropped her illusion anyway. The two of us winked into sight, side-by-side less than five feet away from the closest four Sanctum Guard.

They whipped their rifles around just in time to catch a telekinetic blast that sent them thudding across the planks and tumbling over the edge along with a few of their friends. Across the stage, another team opened fire. I caught a thick burst of softsteel on my barrier before we ducked behind the last stone column. Not like it could offer much protection.

They had us completely surrounded.

And yet the gunfire had stopped. Looking back to the High Cleric's dais, I saw why. His holiness held his non-detonator hand high in a closed fist, signifying a momentary cease-fire. Even at a distance of thirty yards, I felt the heat of his stare. He looked at least mildly surprised to see me. Or did, at least, before that surprise caught fire under the weight of his utter contempt.

"Raish…" He handled my name like a particularly nasty strain of throat fungus.

Out in the crowd, I heard a few shouts go up that it was Haldin Raish, that it was the Demon of Gropping Divinity. One excitable zealot began screaming exultations to Alpha for having delivered me to their justice.

For a second, I thought the High Cleric would silence them, that he might continue his prattling with dignity. Instead, he dropped his fist, pointed straight at us, and bellowed, "To arms, loyal servants of Alpha! Let us have done with these foul demons once and for all!"

As he said it, he raised his detonator, clearly not intent on missing his chance in the name of waiting for a more prim and proper conclusion to the ceremonies. I rounded out from the small cover of our stone column, barely conscious of the slug that immediately slammed into my barrier. No time. Not to reach the detonator. Not to save Four and Eight. I stood frozen, watching the High Cleric's thumb plunging for that switch in slow motion, feeling a depth of helplessness I never would've imagined possible for such a brief instant.

Then four solid black figures slammed into the High Cleric, tackling him from his dais.

Onyx Guard, my stuttering brain realized.

Right before the raknoth that'd once been Five slammed to the dais like a falling meteor. The elegant structure imploded under his speeding mass like a cheap toy, then exploded into the thick crowd of Sanctum personnel around it as Five ripped loose with a shock wave of telekinetic force.

No sooner had I registered what'd just happened than Seven came thudding down to the gallows stage, hands splayed wide like deadly weapons. The air exploded with a deep thrum, and at least a dozen Sanctum Guard went flying off the stage, half of them clearing the perimeter and the first several rows of the crowd before coming to messy landings. The rest, nearly outnumbered now, skirted toward the stairs, opening fire as they bought space and time to rejoin their allies.

Seven turned to me with a smug grin, of all things, paying little heed to the retreating Sanctum Guard or to the incoming hail of slugs pelting into her ready barrier.

"The detonator," Siren hissed.

I nearly jumped, so focused on Seven that I hadn't even noticed her behind me. Immediately I tensed, expecting the raknoth to pounce on my moment of distraction. She didn't.

Just turned and launched herself at the closest mass of retreating Sanctum Guard.

I didn't understand. Nor did I understand the screams coming from the direction of the White Tower, where Five was now ripping indiscriminately into the crowd of clerics and acolytes and terrified worshipers, working his way after the High Cleric, who was being rushed from the area by four Onyx Guard while others joined the Sanctum Guard in the futile exercise of trying to stop Five.

Someone grabbed my hand—Siren—and she was frantically trying to tell me we needed to shroud and find that detonator when ahead, Five spontaneously turned from his onslaught and tossed a small, dark something through a high arc straight toward us.

I caught the thing out of telekinetic reflex more than anything. I was too shocked to do anything but stare.

It was the detonator.

I wasn't sure how or when he'd snatched it from the High Cleric. I wasn't sure it mattered. Not nearly as much as why the scud one of the reekers had just—

My senses buzzed a warning, and I dipped and spun just as someone thudded down to the gallows stage beside Siren.

"Nice going, scudhead," Garrett growled.

A swell of gunfire from offstage slammed into my failing barrier before I could even try to answer. I threw my focus into reinforcing the shield my stupefied brain had nearly forgotten about completely. I didn't have to worry about it for long.

The squad below barely had time to squeeze off a few rounds before Seven came soaring over our heads like a guardian falcon and crashed into their ranks, cracking bones and golden faceplates, sending half the squad scampering for cover while the rest charged in to try their luck with blades.

"What the scud is going on?" Garrett snapped.

"They're… helping," Siren said, looking every bit as confused as I felt.

"Like scud, they are," Garrett said, even as I thought it.

I held the two detonators out to Siren. "Get those collars off of them. Now."

"Where are you going?" she asked, looking more frightened than argumentative.

I looked back over to where Seven was dismantling a Sanctum squad only to find that she'd finished the task and moved on. To the perimeter line.

"Just get those collars off these two!"

I turned and took off running for the edge of the gallows stage before they could argue, staring in horror at the scene unfolding ahead as I went.

Whether the civilians pushing the front of the perimeter line had seen what Seven had just done to over a company's worth of Sanctum Guard, I didn't know. All I knew was that they were mounting the dividers and surging over like they were certain they had the holy light of Alpha's grace at their backs.

And they were all about to be slaughtered.

The enforcers and the few Sanctum Guard left at the perimeter were left in dumb awe, gaping back and forth between the oncoming raknoth and the suicide militia. Then Seven plowed straight through the perimeter line and let loose like a natural disaster.

I reached the edge of the stage and leapt with all my strength, and then some. Channeled energy crackled through me, and then I was soaring high over the now empty space between gallows and perimeter, headed straight for where Seven was tearing into the crowd.

Only she wasn't *tearing* into it, I realized, as I began to arc down. She was punching and kicking, and blasting away with telekinesis. But there were no bloody raknoth claws and fangs at work. Her eyes weren't even showing the crimson fire that had to be lurking just beneath the surface.

I didn't have time to wonder why. I just pulled more energy and came down on Seven hard enough to crack the courtyard stone with her scale-free face. I rode her all the way down, catching her wrist and yanking her into a tight shoulder lock before she could out-muscle me. She growled. Energy spiked in my extended senses. Then a wall of force slapped into me —enough to send me staggering backward, but not as much as I would've expected. Like being smacked full body by an enormous pillow, rather than the mag train's worth of energy Seven had just channeled.

The runes were working, then.

I might've smiled if I hadn't been standing knee-deep in the broken sea of the victims I'd already been too late to keep this reeker monstrosity away from.

"What the scud are you doing here?" I growled as she climbed to her feet and turned to face me.

Her grin returned, even smugger than before, and my senses buzzed a warning from behind even as her eyes flicked over my shoulder. I felt Seven drop the telekinetic curtain on me, aiming to pin me in place for whatever was coming. It made it all the sweeter when my new anti-crusher runes kicked in and allowed me to keep moving, much to Seven's confusion.

What I hadn't expected though—as I turned control over to my senses and pivoted to the right, sweeping around with an elbow strike—was to catch a wild-eyed civilian in the act of trying to stab me in the back. I'd caught his wrist and broke his humerus before I had time to process that it wasn't one of the Sanctum Guard. He staggered back with a cry, knife clattering to the stone. Behind him, dozens more looked on the verge of charging in and letting the sheer weight of numbers win the day.

Then Seven gave a throaty scream of, "Alpha will not defeat us!" and charged—not toward me, but straight for the densest bunch of onlookers.

And that was when I understood.

25

OVERLOADED

It was something I'd never wanted to remember again after the White Hall: just how breathtakingly quickly a raknoth could deal out death to a crowd of unarmed civilians. Seven gave me no choice but to remember.

Three more lay dead by the time I caught the raknoth with telekinesis and smashed her to the ground. I slid my sole dagger free from the sheath, darting forward through the field of abandoned belongings and fallen civilians. Seven didn't stay down willingly. Or long.

Keeping her pinned for more than a few seconds would have already been hard enough on its own. With the steady stream of true believers rushing forward to bring me Alpha's divine justice at the point of a dagger, or the blunt face of a makeshift club, though, it quickly became impossible. I dodged and slogged my way through the mess as best I could, desperately trying to catch Seven as she broke free from my hold and leapt back to the slaughter.

"She's a raknoth!" I shouted at the top of my lungs, batting aside one poorly-aimed cane, telekinetically yanking another's dagger to my own hand. "Get the scud out of here, you idiots! She'll kill you all!"

They didn't listen.

But what I lacked in crowd-turning ferocity, Seven was clearly more than making up for. When I parted through the last few zealots and into a pocket of open space, I almost thought the opposite. Seven was splayed out, still standing but held immobile by what must've been at least ten civilians practically piled on top of her, gripping desperately at any limb or part of her they could manage to get a hand on.

I wasn't sure how the strength of ten panic-crazed humans might match up against a raknoth's. Seven, tilting her head back in laughter, didn't seem all that interested in finding out.

A woman charged in from the crowd and plunged a dagger toward Seven's heart.

The air detonated with a booming shockwave before the blade fell, and every one of Seven's brave captors went smashing into the pale courtyard stone, or rocketing into the crowd like human ballistics. All of them but the woman with the dagger, who Seven had caught by the throat and now held aloft for everyone to bear witness as she broke the poor woman's neck with one hand.

That did it. After that, even the wild-eyed zealots eyeing me like it would've been the highlight of Enochian history to pick up where their compatriots had failed and sink a dagger through my demonic heart turned and ran for their Alpha-loving lives in the wake of the raknoth's mad spree.

I was shaking, overcome with the raw violence of it all, flinching away from the growing pile of bodies, and the memory of Al'Kundesha breaking my dad's neck as Seven had just done with that poor woman. I clutched at my mismatched daggers, barely aware of the cuts and throbbing aches I'd accumulated from my slog through the crowd. Barely aware of anything but the burning need to bury those daggers through Seven's head and end this madness.

I started forward, and Seven stepped to match, seemingly content with her work on the crowd for now. I broke into a run. Stumbled as she dropped a mountain of telekinetic force on me. The crusher runes did their thing, mitigating the falling wave of telekinesis, and I staggered forward with the sensation that my armor skin was simply lined with a couple hundred pounds of softsteel.

It wasn't perfect, but it was better than being smashed to the stone, completely immobile. And even better when I saw the confusion and uncertainty spreading across Seven's face.

I charged forward with a wordless battle cry, infusing my body with channeled energy as I'd done in Humility—caring little for what it might cost me, so long as I could end Seven first. Her eyes widened, and whether it was a testament to the power I conjured or just her sheer surprise at the fact I was still moving, she went down when I slammed into her with mind and body alike.

We hit the stone with enough velocity to go skidding several yards. A pair of her lifeless victims drew our trip up short, and I allowed the sharp halt to carry me forward. I landed with a knee on each of her biceps, pinning her arms down as I raised a dagger.

Unseen force smacked me in the chest, nearly unseating me, then the dagger tore free from my hand. I tried for my other dagger, then tucked and rolled as my extended senses screamed a warning. Something whooshed through the space I'd just occupied, and I felt the arrival of a second vast telepathic mind even before I rolled back to my feet and saw Five thudding to a landing in the courtyard.

Almost absentmindedly, the raknoth plucked a hunk of stone debris from a fallen statue and hurled it with deadly speed into the retreating crowd. I flinched, too far and too slow to do a thing as the projectile stone cut down two people. Five turned back to me, mirroring Seven's smug grin as she hopped back to her own feet. Like Seven, Five's eyes were devoid of raknoth fire. And that's when I knew for certain.

They were deliberately playing human, hiding their obvious raknoth features for Alpha knew what purpose. I hardly had time to wonder about it right then. Not with Five and Seven facing me down, arms crossed, favoring me with those unsettling smiles as if inviting me to do something about their wanton slaughter.

"Do you think they'll pull it off?" Five asked, his gaze shifting to something over my shoulder.

"Oh, I think something's coming off, one way or another," Seven replied.

Warily, I shot a glance back toward the gallows stage, where Garrett and Siren had freed Four and Eight from their bindings and were currently kneeling in a tight huddle with their fellow Seekers, all four of their heads bowed in concentration. Our skimmer sat waiting out front of the stage, but I saw no sign of Johnny. To the sides of the gallows, the few Sanctum Guard and enforcers still standing—and they *were* shockingly few—paid the Seekers no mind, instead watching me and the two raknoth from the divider line, weapons at the ready. Maybe they'd swallowed the fact that we were on their side at the moment.

Or maybe they were just too frightened to draw any of our demonic attentions.

The Legion transports forcing their way through the onlooking air traffic and the golden ranks of fresh Sanctum Guard emerging from the White Tower beyond the High Cleric's ruined dais suggested it hardly mattered. I had no idea what the raknoth were trying to accomplish here, but whatever their aims, we had about a minute before we were drowning in soldiers.

So I turned back to the raknoth, preparing to push my system into overload.

There were too many forces converging. Too much congestion between the air traffic and the mass flood of the tens of thousands still trying to flee the courtyard through insufficient channels. I didn't see how any of us were getting out of there at that point. And if this was my last shot at killing these reeker bastards, I wasn't going to take it lightly.

I swept Five's and Seven's legs with a hard telekinetic kick and charged, letting the energy roar into me just like back in Humility, when I'd kicked off the brakes completely and channeled enough to nearly outrun a transport on foot. The raknoth didn't fall flat from my sweep attack, both catching themselves and springing back to readiness. But I was flying across the gap faster than they'd expected. Faster than humanly possible, my crackling body informed me.

I flung my dagger at Seven, shifting my trajectory toward her, then yanked to a halt and spun to drive the hardsteel toe of my boot straight into the side of Five's temple when he lunged forward to seize the opening. Even amped as I was on channeled energy, it still felt like kicking a permacrete wall. But I'd kicked *through* my target, and it showed.

Five hit the stone like a sofsteel brick, and I wasted no time in telekinetically ripping back the dagger he'd stolen and whirling on Seven, who was nearly on top of me. She jerked clear of my rising stab and caught the blade on her cheek rather than through the bottom of her jaw as I'd intended. Then she swung her inhumanly strong fist straight for my head.

I dipped to the outside too quickly and staggered off balance, then something smacked down on my back, and I crumpled to my knees. The stone around me shattered like an invisible transport had just crashed down. It wasn't until a dark tendril of smoke wafted up from my chest, carrying a sharp burning smell that I registered what'd happened. Another attempt at a telekinetic smackdown—one that had apparently pushed enough energy through my crusher runes to ignite my tunic. But there wasn't time to gape.

I rolled from my little circle of unbroken stone a second before Seven slammed down and rectified it's smooth surface. Stumbling to my feet, I spun just in time to catch Five's incoming rush. I caught him by one wrist, then dropped my center of gravity and rotated into a hip throw—which, in hindsight, wasn't the wisest move against a raknoth.

Fusing telekinesis with my own strength might've let me manhandle the beast for a moment, but it seemed a minor miracle my hip and shoulder were still in their sockets when Five finished his ride and smacked down in front of me, belly up. I saved the prayers for later, drove a pair of vicious stomps down on his head, yanking his arm for leverage, then darted clear as Seven came rushing in.

I twisted clear of one blow. Ducked another. Stumbled as subdued telekinetic forces slapped at me this way and that. Launched into an off-kilter corkscrew to dodge a speeding hunk of stone.

For a few seconds, I moved with a sure-footed grace that would've made Carlisle proud. When the pair finally succeeded at corralling me back between them, I gathered my strength to leap clear—and fell without warning, the ground beneath my rear foot inexplicably opening up to swallow my leg whole.

Seven sprang forward with a lunging punch, victorious snarl firmly in place. There was no dodging it. Not with my leg trapped.

So I opened my body to the energy completely, and caught her fist in my open palm.

It felt like catching a sledgehammer from a pulse cannon while my insides played conduit to the city power grid. Something broke. I couldn't have said what. I let the pain in, feeding it straight to that whimpering part of my brain that begged me to stop. Seven's eyes, already saucer-wide, flickered crimson for the first time. I fed on that too, telling my body to hold on just one more moment.

Then I gathered everything and ripped her down to her knees, face to face with me. I drove my dagger straight for her left eye as it lit in full with red raknoth fire. She caught the blade straight through her palm then, with a garbled shriek, caught my wrist with her other hand, fighting against my enhanced strength, squeezing tighter and tighter. Bones cracked. I screamed and abandoned the physical effort, throwing myself fully into driving the blade with telekinesis.

I was dimly aware of Five rushing in from behind, of his ground trap constricting on my leg like an organic trash compactor. I took it all and pushed harder, screaming straight into Seven's face even as she roared in mine.

Five's shadow fell over us. I felt him closing, felt the end kissing at my back.

Then a spray of black ichor spattered the stone beside me, and Five let out a strangled shriek, staggering past us. I pushed harder. No room to break focus and look. My vision darkening. Someone shouting behind me. Dark shapes rushing past. A raknoth roar ahead.

I pushed the dagger harder. Seven fought right back, her flesh beginning to ripple with green, her eyes positively blazing now. She dropped her unpierced hand from the blade and reached for my throat. I tried to take advantage of the opening, to drive the blade home before it was too late. But I had nothing left. Nothing but dull resignation as her sprouting claws came for my life's blood. Less than nothing.

I remember thinking that at least I'd never have to push my body that hard again.

Then a pulse rifle muzzle touched the side of Seven's head and coughed three times, spewing the stone to the left with dark, gooey hunks of raknoth matter. I stared at the gory mess, uncomprehending, as Seven's eyes dimmed and she crumpled in front of me, her fanged jaw agape and lifeless. Somewhere in the distance, there was a terrible raknoth roar. But I couldn't bring myself to care. My vision was swooning, my thoughts jumbled and disoriented. Somewhere in the depths, my nerves were only just beginning to send word of how badly I'd gropped up.

And then there was Johnny, dropped to one knee in front of me, pulse rifle slung to his side. He was saying something. Something I couldn't seem to register until he took my face in both hands and gave me a shake.

"—e've gotta get your leg out of there. Come on, broto, help me out here."

I tried to wrap my muddled head around his words. It wasn't easy, but the pain at least cut through some of the shock when he scooted beside me and pulled my broken arm over his shoulders.

"Scud," he growled, spinning around and instead wrapping my torso in a bear hug from the front. "Come on, Fly Boy," he said, starting to heave. "You can pass out after we get the scud out of here."

Passing out sure did sound nice right then.

"You… you killed a reeker, Johnny," I mumbled.

Alpha, why did it feel like I'd been chewing permacrete dust?

"And that's…" he grunted, heaving with each word, "… exactly… the story… we're sticking to!" With one last mighty pull, my leg tore free of its underground prison. Johnny fell on his ass, pulling me along with him. "After we get the scud out of here," he added, panting as he patted my chest. "Thanks for the help there, by the way. Not like you weigh two hundred gropping pounds with all this gear."

"Sorry," I said. Or tried to. The words died as I took in the descending

Legion transports above and the squads of Sanctum Guard spilling down from the White Tower to help wall us into the now mostly-empty courtyard. Twisting around, I saw our skimmer landing nearby—right where Garrett was duking it out with Five.

Judging from the cuts and tears on his face and clothes, it wasn't going well. Four and Eight were there too, though neither looked steady on their feet after whatever they'd been through. Four hurled a gout of flame at Five, buying a moment's distraction in which Eight closed the gap and drove a hard front kick into the raknoth's chest. Both the ex-Seeker's looked on the verge of collapse from the effort, but at least I didn't see explosive collars at their throats any more.

At least something had worked.

But even that victory turned to ash when the Legion transports began touching down around the courtyard. A lot of them.

"How the scud are we getting out of here?" I whispered.

"That *is* a question," Johnny said quietly, clearly not even sure where to point his pulse rifle. It was the look on his face, though, that told me we were well and truly gropped.

Apparently having arrived at a similar conclusion, Five smacked the ex-Seekers away with one of those radial telekinetic shockwaves, then shot for the nearest rooftop in a mighty leap. Or tried to, at least.

Twenty feet up, the raknoth yanked to a midair halt like he was tethered. And so he was, I realized. Tethered by Garrett, who stood with his clenched hands outstretched toward Five as if he'd physically caught onto the raknoth and was preparing to rip him back down to the courtyard.

But Five didn't fall.

Garrett held on, trembling with the effort, as Siren hopped out of the skimmer and hurried toward him, probably thinking to lend her own strength. Then the first gunfire cracked through the courtyard, and Siren jerked and fell, clutching at her shoulder.

"Alexia!" Garrett cried, falling to a knee and casting a hand out just in time to deflect a hail of incoming slugs.

Above, Five broke free from Garrett's invisible hold and rocketed skyward in what must've been pure telekinetic flight, up through the wildly scattering sea of skimmers and over the northern building line, disappearing from sight in seconds flat.

"Any chance you can do that too?" Johnny asked.

I can hardly lift my own head right now, I might've said, had I been able to conjure even that much energy or willpower. But I was fried—my body shutting down, my wrists screaming in pain with every tiny movement. If there'd been some hope at that point, any inkling of a feasible escape plan, I'd like to think I would've found it in me to rise above it and find my feet again. But there was no hope, watching Garrett and the others clamber to protect themselves and form a barrier around Siren, watching the Legion open controlled fire on our skimmer, grounding it for good.

We'd made a mistake coming here.

Beside me, Johnny was already setting his pulse rifle down and raising his hands in surrender. They were all around us, slowly approaching from the courtyard perimeter. Johnny shifted, deliberately positioning himself so that the nearest legionnaires would at least have to shoot through him and his peacefully raised hands to hit me.

Futile as it was, the gesture put an aching in my chest. Because I doubted they'd hesitate to gun down either of us, peaceful surrender or not. I was fully expecting they were about to when the closest two legionnaires gave a pair of sharp jerks and dropped to the stone, clutching at their necks, where they'd been hit by...

Stunner bolts?

Stunner bolts from whom? my tired mind asked.

Right before the thumpers detonated.

At first, I thought I might've taken a softsteel slug to the brain stem, and that I was merely experiencing some kind of sensory system overload in my final moment. The detonations were that unexpected. And that synchronized.

The entire courtyard pulsed with one massive boom that jarred my body from toes to teeth and left my brain feeling like a warm bowl of fabricator sludge. Then there were more noises. More thumps and booms, and the sounds of large ship engines. Beside me, Johnny was muttering a stream of what could've been prayers or curses. I tried to pull the hazy swirl of smoke and stone and blurry shapes back into focus, and my senses begrudgingly began to respond.

Around the courtyard, dozens of legionnaires were down—some sprawled and clearly incapacitated, others hunkered by their transports for cover, or looking exactly like I felt. Thumped. Disoriented. And—

I followed the rising aim of their rifles to where more Legion transports were descending.

Descending, I realized, with hatches wide open, and with dozens more legionnaires raining mayhem down on their brothers and sisters in arms. They kept a steady stream of stunner fire pouring down, others hurling thumper after thumper to keep the ground squads from regrouping. From the surrounding rooftops, I heard the thunder cracks of heavy sniper fire, and I watched in disbelief as shooters rapidly and methodically cored one enemy transport engine after another.

Maybe it was a testament to the depth of my despair, or simply the level of abuse to which I'd just pushed my mind and body, but it was only then, watching Johnny pounce to his feet, waving and shouting at the nearest descending transport, that it dawned on me these might in fact be friendly arrivals. Ahead, the transport swooping down to cover Garrett and the others from the soldiers who'd been firing on them seemed to confirm that notion. Especially when the transport's ordo appeared at the top of the boarding ramp, waving furiously for the ex-Seekers to climb aboard.

It was Ordo Carter. Dillard's second in command.

"Go!" Johnny was shouting at them, his rifle back in hand now. "Go!"

He whirled to me, dropping down to grab me in a bear hug, preparing to lift again. "C'mon, broto. We're not done yet."

No, I realized, looking up at the companion transport coming for us. We weren't.

This time, I didn't struggle to find the will. It was already there, stemming from that tiny blip of hope. I got my feet under me and stood with a little help from Johnny. On the closest side of the courtyard, some of the hunkered legionnaires took notice, and wasted no time in taking aim, too.

Channeling sounded about as appealing at that moment as flaying my own skin, but it didn't matter. I reached down and found the will to catch the incoming fire anyway. I kept the barrier intact behind us as we turned for the landing transport. I held on, knowing that this was not the end, that our allies had not forsaken us.

The transport yawed around, offering us admission to the rear boarding ramp as it set down.

And there, at the top of the ramp in all her indomitable glory, was Freya Glenbark, dressed in full battle garb for the first time I'd ever seen, flanked by Ordo Dillard and big, burly Edwards.

I could've laughed. I could've cried. Could've fallen to the ground and melted into a sniveling oblivion, content in the knowledge that there was still someone on this planet who believed in us.

Instead, I just held on to Johnny and ran for our salvation.

2 6

———

UNEXPECTED PLACES

"I thought you were on the run."

They weren't the first words I meant to say to Glenbark once we were safely clear of the White Tower courtyard and the Hounds' medic, Calvin, had given me and Johnny the *not dying right this moment* once-over. There were about a thousand and one better options. *Thank you,* for instance. Or maybe even, *I'm so happy to see you I could just die.*

But as I sat drinking in her commanding presence and the oh-so-welcome knowledge that we weren't going to die in that Alpha-damned courtyard, trying all the while not to wince as Calvin splinted my wrists, *I thought you were on the run* was just the first thing that popped out.

"He means thank you," Johnny said, giving my head an affectionate pat as if to say I wasn't of any right mind to speak. He probably wasn't wrong. "And I'll second that," he added. "Right along with a praise Alpha's merciful ass you showed up when you did, sir."

Glenbark rested her head back against the seat, looking tired and like she wasn't quite sure whether to smile or frown. "You're quite welcome," she finally said. "Both of you. Though I'm not sure I'd call any part of Alpha merciful these days. As for my fugitive status," she added, looking at me, "I imagine that depends on who you ask at the moment. Personally, I have no intention of running from any of this. Call me old fashioned, but I swore an oath to protect this planet, and I will not allow bent rules and corrupt cowards to bar my way."

"How did Auckus even manage to—Agh!" I grunted as Calvin adjusted the splint too tight for comfort. The combat medic just held my indignant gaze, silently daring me to complain.

"Thank you," I mumbled.

He smiled.

"I don't need to tell you how pervasive the Sanctum's presence is throughout Legion ranks," Glenbark said. "Even among those they haven't deliberately taken into their fold. Asking my people to choose between my word and the High Cleric's…" She frowned, as if she'd already decided her next words were not to her liking. "It's beyond asking the children to side with mommy or daddy. It's not a harsh word or a firm hand that's at risk. It is our very spirits that are on the line."

"And ours are with you, sir," Calvin said, finishing his work and standing. "To whatever end."

If I hadn't gotten to know Glenbark as well as I had in the past cycles, I might've missed the emotion trying to fight its way out from her composed visage. She gave the combat medic a grateful nod, then dismissed him with a crisp salute. He returned the gesture at attention, then turned for the steps to the main cabin below, where Dillard had just emerged. The ordo gave his man a firm grip on the shoulder, and a look of deep approval and genuine respect.

It was the moments like that that swept me with an intense gratitude for having had the luck to end up with such a quality company watching my back. Gratitude, that is, and the intense remorse that they'd somehow wound up sucked into my world of dangerous problems.

"Good to see you in one piece, Raish," Dillard said, taking a seat beside Glenbark and across from me and Johnny. "Or mostly, at least."

Mostly good, I wanted to ask, *or mostly in one piece?* But I was pretty sure I already knew the answer. Because Dillard and his Hounds hadn't been passively pulled into this fight. At first, maybe. Back at Vantage. But they'd shown up willingly since then, time and time again. And I'd do well to remember that. Because they weren't stuck *with* me, coming along for the ride. It was all of us who were actively choosing to be here, to fight for Enochia in what way we thought best. I wouldn't have been here without them.

And for the first time, that somehow actually felt like a comforting thought.

"Pardon my interruption, sir," Dillard was saying to Glenbark, who dismissed the apology with a benign shake of her head.

"At any rate," she said, turning back to us, "crisis of faith alone might explain much of why the majority of Haven was willing to stand by while Auckus and his companies took Central Command. But it was more than that. He was a general for nearly three decades. He knows his fellow officers. Knew exactly how to make each one bend and break to his will."

"He threatened them?" I asked.

Glenbark gave a slight shrug. "Hard to know what was said for certain, or to whom. But Auckus was never particularly loved by his peers in the high command. Even among the generals who vocally disagreed with my every move, there are at least four I'm certain would never have stood for mutiny. Not if they'd had any choice. I'm assuming there was good reason General Hopper wasn't willing to act until his wife and two children were safely off base. It's hard, I imagine, to worry about the sanctity of one's spirit when one's family is in danger. "

"That slimy bastard," I muttered.

Glenbark didn't see fit to disagree.

"I'm sorry, sir," Johnny said softly beside me. Aside from a few quips, he'd been uncharacteristically quiet since our fleet of transports had blown out of Divinity, and when I looked at him now, his head was bowed like a hound who'd been found out snatching food from the table.

Glenbark studied him. "Whatever for, Wingard?"

"For leaving. For breaking communication and vanishing without... If I'd known what that slimy... what Auckus was planning..." He shook his head. "I would've come back, sir."

"And then General Hopper would've had to liberate two of us from the brig," she said. "Or, just as likely, I would be mourning the death of a good servitor who'd had the unlucky disposition to step between Auckus and his target. You chose to proactively protect Legion assets—and innocent civilians, no less—when circumstances did not allow you the time to seek clarifying orders. Moreover, in my opinion, you did the right thing. And you need never apologize to me for that, Wingard."

Johnny looked like he might actually get choked up.

"Did you just call me a good servitor, sir?"

"Did I?" Glenbark thought about it. "Hmm. Well, I suppose you haven't been without your uses."

"And he did just kill a raknoth," I added.

I think that was the most surprised I'd ever seen Glenbark look.

"Truly?" she asked, looking back and forth between us with wide eyes.

Dillard looked equally taken aback. In the fray of getting the scud out of

Divinity before the crippled Legion ships could take up pursuit, I realized we hadn't actually gotten around to that single piece of good news.

"Well," Johnny said, "I'm not sure it'd be decent, me taking credit for the deed when He of the Twin Broken Wrists is sitting right next to me…"

"Lefty's only sprained," I pointed out.

"Ah, right." Johnny shrugged. "Well yeah, in that case then, I guess I did just kill half the reekers on Enochia." He frowned at me. "Assuming three bolts did the trick."

"I didn't feel any lingering presence there when we left," I said. "I think that's one down."

I wasn't accustomed to using words like *happy* or *excited* to describe Glenbark's demeanor, but in that moment, they might not have been such a stretch. I guess we all needed some good news.

"Well then, tidy your organizational and administrative skills, Wingard," she said, with an honest-to-Alpha shining white smile, "and perhaps we can make a suitable servitor out of you yet."

"Sir, yes sir," Johnny replied, positively beaming, and more than a little red in the cheeks.

"Excuse me, High General, sir," one of the pilots called from the cockpit. "I don't know how to say this, but we, uh, seem to have an unidentified craft trailing us."

"Seem to?" Glenbark asked, rising and striding up to have a look.

"It's flying unusually high, sir. Outer atmosphere. And its signature is… finicky. Like nothing I've ever seen before."

A spark of recognition lit in my mind.

Dillard was already approaching the cockpit, hopping straight into the rapid-fire series of questions and possibilities that began spilling out.

"I think I can explain that," I called before they got far.

They all turned to look at me—Dillard curious, the pilots genuinely confused, and Glenbark narrowing her eyes in recognition.

"Alton Parker," she said.

It was more a statement than a question, but I nodded anyway. "With everything going on, I honestly forgot…"

And now that I wasn't tripped up on unexpected explosive collars and surprise reekers, it occurred to me that Parker had taken a rather steep approach to our *only in dire emergency* contingency plan. Maybe he'd simply seen Glenbark's forces on the way. Or maybe this had just been another one of his infernal tests.

I realized that Glenbark was staring at me. "You forgot you had an alien ship on standby?"

I held up my dual splints. "It's been a pretty hectic few days if I'm being honest, sir. I know this might sound rich coming from me, but I actually thought I might die down there."

"He did have to go fisticuffs with two reekers for a few minutes before we could get to him," Johnny agreed.

"Damn," Dillard muttered, bobbing his head appreciatively—until Glenbark sobered him with a look.

"How did you even get that thing out of the shipyard?" she asked. "Even in confinement, I heard the rumors floating around, good soldiers claiming the thing had disappeared without trace or warning."

"Parker had some kind of device," I said. "A beacon, or something."

"Hidden in the woods?" Dillard asked.

I shook my head, not bothering to hide my disgust. "Hidden in his abdominal cavity, along with several days' worth of feeding blood."

"Slimy bastards on our left," Johnny muttered. "Slimy bastards on our… Sorry."

Glenbark turned her sharp stare from him back to me. "You're telling me that ship can teleport and that Alton Parker had the remote the entire time he was in our custody?"

"As far as I know, yeah. That pretty much sums it up. Parker's…"

"Slimy?" Johnny asked.

I started to agree, then aborted at the look on Glenbark's face. "He has information," I said instead. "Information that might be critical to this planet's long term survival."

"How convenient," Dillard muttered.

"That was exactly what I thought, until I saw it," I said, fixing Glenbark with a serious look. "There are more raknoth out there, and worse. And that's not even the entirety of it."

I didn't miss the sigil of Alpha Dillard furtively drew over his heart at the news of additional monsters lurking in the dark. Glenbark didn't look too pleased either, though she hid her reaction better. Still, she also didn't miss my unspoken suggestion that we should probably discuss the rest of the matter in private.

"We're going to need to have a long discussion about this information," she said, her brow furrowing. "And about your decision to break Alton Parker out in the first place. For now, though, let's start with what he wants, and why he's following us."

"He wants my help," I said. "And the help of any other Shapers he can get his hands on, I guess. That's why he's following us."

"Your help," Glenbark repeated, studying me with those eyes that always seemed to see a few levels too far. I nodded.

"He's got a pretty scud recruitment strategy if that's been his goal all along," Dillard said.

"I think it kind of became Plan B when the hybrid armies proved to be unstable in the long term," I said.

For a few seconds, by the look on her face, I was sure Glenbark was about to ask what he'd really been building an army for. She must've either arrived at a satisfactory answer herself or decided she'd find out soon enough, though, because she said nothing more about it.

I took advantage of the opening to ask Johnny if he'd had word from Franco, seeing as the two of them had drawn the lucky honor of wearing the two ID-clean palmlights Franco had kept on hand for just such emergencies. I tried not to worry too much when he told me he hadn't. Pasty and Kovaks' dungeon hideout was probably well out of Light coverage, after all. And Elise was more than capable of handling herself.

But try as I might, I couldn't rid myself of the incessant fear that something had gone wrong. Maybe it was simply my own brush with death tinting the lens of my expectations. All I knew was that I would've given just about anything to have her sitting with me right just then.

I'd give it another hour, I decided. Then I'd talk to Glenbark about borrowing a ride.

I could only imagine that would be a happy conversation. Especially as Glenbark and Dillard stood there quietly debating the question of what to do about the alien ship tailing us.

"Will he listen to you?" Glenbark finally asked, turning to me.

It was a little concerning, how close I came to saying yes before the truth of the matter surfaced to give me a condescending slap across the face.

"If it suits him."

"Wonderful," Glenbark said.

"For what it's worth…" I hesitated, not quite believing that I was actually about to say it—much less say it to Freya Glenbark. "… I think he might actually be done waging war on this planet."

I wasn't surprised that that earned me stares all around. Scud, even I would've been staring at myself for that one. It sounded ludicrous. But I also couldn't completely ignore what my gut was telling me. Glenbark, at least, seemed to read as much.

That, or she just hid the rampant skepticism much better than the others.

"Well then," she said, "I think we'd better try to hail that ship and let Parker know that, whatever his angle or allegiance, he's not to bring that ship anywhere near our base unless he wants to find out how its hull handles heavy artillery fire."

I didn't argue. "If we can get him on the lights, I'll do my best to make it clear he needs to stay away from… where are we going, by the way?"

She looked at me, and for a second, I could've sworn she was internally running the odds on whether I could actually be trusted, if maybe I hadn't been turned spy—or something more sinister—by Alton Parker. I guess I couldn't blame the suspicion after the betrayal she'd experienced at Haven. The raknoth had all but taken over the world not so long ago, after all. But the look passed, and she relaxed a fraction, apparently deciding I was the same Haldin Raish she'd already risked so much for.

"I told you I have no intention of running," she said, dead serious. "I meant it. To General Hopper's infinite displeasure, we've set up camp right where they can see us. Right where our people laid down their lives and used your creations to finally turn the tide against the hybrid army."

"Oasis." It was my turn to stare in disbelief. "That's… a bold move, sir."

"Now seemed an appropriate time."

That was true enough. And after I got over my initial surprise, I started to realize just how much sense the choice of locale actually made if Glenbark's aim was to present an open, honest front for the case against the Sanctum's holy war on Shapers—or on anyone else, for that matter. She wouldn't be alone. I was almost certain there were loyal companies out there that would flock to her banner in these troubled times just as Dillard and his Hounds had clearly done. And with a proper Legion fortress to defend—a fortress that stood in testament to the potential strength of an alliance between Enochia and its Shapers…

For the first time in days, I felt the true stirring of hope.

It was far from over. The Sanctum would be coming for us with everything they had, as would their false High General Auckus. I had no doubt about that. But it was more than I'd had when I'd gone to sleep in that chilly hollow the night before, and it was sure as scud more than I'd ever hoped to have again as I'd fled Haven through a hail of gunfire, riding Alton Parker like a scaly green hosa.

"Okay," I said, finding a slow smile pulling at my lips despite the pain in my wrists and the worry for Elise gnawing at my gut. "Well I guess I'd better get a hold of Parker, then."

2 7

FALLOUT

I hadn't been wrong about the loyalty Glenbark commanded throughout her Legion.

As optimistic as I'd first felt about Glenbark's choice in base of operations, when the pilots had announced we were beginning our final approach to Oasis, the true apprehension had finally set in. I'm sure some part of it had simply been my lack of faith that Parker would actually hold to his grumbling, condescending word after our brief talk and keep his distance for the time being. But mostly, I'd been afraid. Afraid that I'd been wrong to put such blind trust in Glenbark's magnetic leadership. Afraid that we were about to fly into an empty shell of a base that would welcome us with little more than an eerie creaking and a soft whisper that we were indeed bound on a fool's quest, the likes of which even its previous occupants would've laughed at with their beastly growl-hisses.

When I finally caught sight of Oasis, though…

It still might've been a fool's quest we were on. Only time would tell for sure. But at least I could say we had the men and women to see this quest through to the end.

All told, I estimated there might be as many as a thousand legionnaires in Oasis. Two full legions. And that wasn't counting whatever support staff had come along—cooks, medics, technicians, and the like. That still left the odds at about a-hundred-to-one in terms of raw numbers against Auckus' Legion—and even worse than that if we took into account the

Sanctum Guard and the various ancillary forces of Enochia, like the enforcers.

But with good soldiers, they were exactly the odds we could hope to survive inside a strong fortress.

And true, after everything Oasis had been through in the past cycles, it'd probably take a few thousand man hours of work before the place was once again a shining example of the lean and clean Legion aesthetic. But the foundations still looked as sturdy as the soldiers manning them, and for now, that was all that mattered.

I just hoped it'd be enough to discourage open warfare.

General Hopper greeted us at the landing pads, looking about as excited about the entire ordeal as my mom had looked on my first day of tyro training, when she'd taken a good thirty seconds to stop hugging me at the door, and tried her best to hide her tears when we'd finally parted. Clearly, the rescue had not been the good general's plan, and judging by the tension on his face during their quick exchange at the base of the boarding ramp, I was guessing he'd been vehemently against Glenbark's personal inclusion in the mission.

And, given the dark look he shot my way as they stepped aside to clear the ramp, I was pretty sure I knew who he blamed for the whole thing. Which was bullscud, of course, because we'd had no communication with Glenbark. I'd assumed she'd moved on the Sanctum execution out of a sense of duty to save Four and Eight from the fates they might've escaped had they joined their people in hiding, as they'd originally intended, instead of remaining in Haven to help her with the raknoth.

If anyone had told her we'd been planning to crash the party, it must've been Hopper himself. He'd been the only one to know, aside from Elise and the others. So maybe the good general was really just pissed he'd inadvertently lured Glenbark out of her Haven imprisonment and straight into a dangerous mission. That might explain the furtive glances he kept shooting her as the transport began unloading.

"Is it just me," I muttered to Johnny as we started down the ramp, "or does it seem like you might have a potential rival for Glenbark's affections?"

He frowned at me, gave up preemptively on trying to deny my allegations, and instead turned his frown to Hopper.

"Whatever," he muttered. "Guy didn't kill half the reekers on Enochia today, did he?"

"You're the undisputed champion, broto."

"Damn straight."

"I'd give you a high five," I said, holding up my splinted wrists, "but…"

He narrowed his eyes at me but said nothing as Glenbark waved us over to her and Hopper.

"Straight to the medica with me?" I asked.

"Actually, I'd prefer we discuss the matter of Alton Parker's intel immediately." She glanced at my wrists, her expression softening a few degrees. "If you're up to it, of course."

"I think Calvin gave me enough painkillers to make a haga go huggy. I'll be all right."

"It's good to see you in one piece, Citizen Raish," Hopper said, laying a hand on my shoulder. His words sounded sincere enough, but I couldn't help notice his smile looked a bit strained. I wasn't sure why, or even that I hadn't simply imagined it.

After Johnny and I took a moment to once again give our thanks to Edwards and Dillard and the rest of the Hounds, we departed the landing pads with the two generals, listening attentively as Hopper filled us in on what was happening around Oasis.

The damage and disrepair wrought on the base from two major battles and a violent—albeit short—hybrid occupation were far from insignificant. Not that that came as much of a shock. Still, as I'd suspected, the foundations of the base still held plenty strong, and Hopper's crews were well on their way to restoring what critical infrastructure had been lost. My estimations on troop counts hadn't been far off either.

Everything else considered, it seemed a not-so-small miracle that they'd managed to marshal such a serious presence in Oasis on such short notice.

But, as Glenbark pointed out, that was exactly how well-executed leadership often ended up looking: a seeming miracle from the outside, and a long, carefully managed set of checks and smart questions from within. She favored Hopper with a warm smile as she said it, and he returned it with interest, his earlier tension forgotten.

I didn't miss the dirty look Johnny shot at the back of the good general's head during the exchange. There might've even been a muttered something or another about married men, but who knew.

The short trek to Central Command was more of a relief than I'd expected. Hearing numbers was fine, but it was good to actually see the men and women going about their duties with my own eyes—an irrefutable hustle to their step, and a brimming pride to their movements as they stopped to salute their generals. These soldiers believed in what they were doing. You could practically taste it in the air. And while true belief certainly wasn't a hard requirement for disciplined soldiers to get their jobs done, I would've taken a single fireteam of these legionnaires over a squad who knew damn well their High General was a corrupt, lecherous bastard.

It didn't hurt, either, that none of them tried to shoot me this time.

That's not to say they didn't look wary as they took me in. Afraid, even. But considering the depths this mess had slid to in only a few short days, that was perfectly reasonable, in my mind.

Soon enough, the four of us were through the vocal chaos of the still-coming-together central command room and settling down in Glenbark's new office. It wasn't the well-polished darkwood museum her Haven office had been, but then again, I wasn't so sure she'd ever particularly cared for that decor anyway. This office was smaller, the furniture and aesthetic more reminiscent of what I'd expect to find in a Legion encampment out in the field—effective and utterly without gaudy flash.

It suited her, I decided. As did the dark blue armor she'd swapped her High General's tunic for.

"Right then," Glenbark said, taking a seat at the room's single battered table and gesturing for us to join her. "Let's have it all at once, Haldin. What has Alton Parker been hiding?"

As I had with Elise and the others, I started with what Parker had shown me in the brig and pushed on from there—though I may have spent a little more time with this audience making it particularly clear why I'd had little choice but to run for my life and drag Parker with me. Aside from several open gapes and a few stutter starts from Hopper, who was summarily waved to silence by a stern-faced Glenbark, they listened without interruption to Parker's disturbing revelations about Sarentus, the rakul, and our very existence on Enochia.

When I finished, they were both silent for a while, staring off

"You both seem to be taking this pretty well," Johnny said.

General Hopper stirred, blinking. "I think I might've had a brain bleed ten minutes back." He looked at Glenbark, but she was still lost in thought, staring somewhere just over my shoulder and about a thousand miles away.

"We can't just take this on faith," Hopper continued, turning back to me. "You call this intel, but we're talking about, what, memories? Memories from an alien mind that *you* can't even tell us is reliable with any certainty. Without anything more…" He just shook his head, spreading his upturned palms as if to say, *What do you expect us to do with this?*

"I understand," I said, trying my best to actually mean it. Because much as I wished I could somehow just show them what I'd seen, clearly as I'd seen it, I would've been crazy to expect them to swallow any of this without some kind of proof. "I'm just reporting what I've learned to the best of my ability."

Hopper opened his mouth like he'd been expecting an argument, then closed it, surprised, and gave me an approving nod. "Very well. Thank you, Citizen Raish." He looked at Glenbark again, silently inviting her to weigh in.

"Why didn't you tell me about the Emmútari's depiction of Sarentus after your capture at Humility?" she finally asked.

My stomach sank. Out of all the questions she could have asked…

"He didn't tell me either, for what it's worth," Johnny said, maybe because he wanted to clear his own name in Glenbark's books, or maybe because he was still a bit miffed about it. Maybe both.

Glenbark said nothing and continued watching me for an answer.

"Franco and I agreed it was unnecessarily volatile information to bring up without having first tried to verify it," I finally managed. "We didn't want to automatically discredit everything else that'd happened."

"That sounds like a Francesco Fields answer," Glenbark said. "What's yours?"

I swallowed. "I was afraid of what it might mean. For my own credibility. For my already strained relationship with the Legion and the Sanctum. And I guess maybe I was afraid it was true, too. I'm sorry for holding it back, sir."

She watched me closely.

"Is there anything else you're holding back at this point?"

As many dark secrets as I'd been carrying around lately, I genuinely had to stop and think about it before I could shake my head. "That's everything, sir. Though I worry that…"

"Go on," she said.

"He's worried us mere mortals can't understand how big of a deal this space dragon guy is," Johnny said when I was slow to answer.

Glenbark shot me a questioning look, and I tipped my head, not arguing his point.

"I'm not sure I can stress enough just how strong the rakul may be. Think of what the raknoth were able to do to our legions. Then imagine the telepath who can hammer armies of raknoth into submission. It was…"

"I understand, Haldin."

I looked up and was almost surprised to find that that's exactly what I saw in Glenbark's eyes. Understanding—not for the exact nature of what I'd seen, necessarily, but at least for the weight it had left resting firmly on my chest. The weight of knowing full well what doom was headed for our people.

"Rest assured," she continued, her tone gentle, "I hear you. And we will not ignore this intel," she added with a sideways glance at Hopper. "Though we must tread carefully, of course."

"Carefully?" Hopper asked. "Sir, if there's even a fraction of a chance that the Sanctum… that Sarentus was…"

He trailed off, either unsure what to think or unwilling to share it with us.

"If everything you'd ever believed was a lie," Glenbark said slowly, looking at no one in particular, "would you want to know?"

Hopper's jaw and brow worked through half a dozen expressions before he finally settled on a stubborn scowl. "Of course I would."

Glenbark waited a few seconds, as if offering him the chance to change his mind, before she finally spoke.

"Good. Because we're going to proceed as if these are all viable tips, pending confirmation."

Hopper closed his eyes but said nothing.

"I don't wish to see any of this prove true either, Marcus. But we were also told we were alone in this universe, and because of that belief, we nearly lost the entire planet before we even knew the fight was upon us. I will not ignore a reliable source questioning our beliefs any more than I will stand by while the Sanctum seeks to commit genocide."

"Reliable?" Hopper frowned at me. "He just admitted he's lied to you. General, I stand by you in our duty to Enochia, in protecting the people and in checking the reach of the Sanctum. You know I do. But questioning the history of our prophet? Of our entire planet? Where does it end?"

"With the truth, I should hope," Glenbark said.

"And what of Alpha, sir? What of that which we may never prove, even if we all know it to be true in our hearts?"

Glenbark was silent for a long while before she finally turned to me and Johnny.

"That's all for now."

Johnny and I traded a look, but she pressed on before we could voice our objections.

"Get yourselves to the medica and get some rest. Both of you. We'll gather the Seekers and speak soon about how to deal with the fallout of what happened today."

None of us had to ask what fallout she was referring to. Even if our moronically simple original plan had panned out earlier and we'd somehow managed to rescue Four and Eight and escape the White Tower without a single casualty, I had no doubt that, within the hour, the reels would have been teeming with horrid accounts of demonic raids and terroristic attacks. But our plan hadn't panned out. And people had died.

The Sanctum was going to unleash everything short of the fury of Alpha himself on us.

Submitting to the medics and resting up was the last thing I felt like doing at the moment. But Glenbark clearly wanted a moment alone with her right hand general, and I had my own people to check in with anyway.

For a second, I considered asking Glenbark for aid in checking on Elise's status in Humility, but my gut told me not to, and for once I listened. I stood instead, and Johnny joined me.

"Raish," came Hopper's voice as we moved for the door.

I turned back, waiting.

He looked uncertainly at Glenbark before continuing. "I think we can all agree it's best if you don't spread these reports too far before we're able to formulate a proper plan here."

I didn't particularly love the unspoken implications beneath his words, but the request itself seemed earnest and reasonable enough. Glenbark seemed to agree.

"Until we say otherwise," she said, "please treat the information we discussed here as classified."

We acknowledged that we understood, and left them to privately discuss Alpha knew what. Maybe their relationship with Alpha himself, if our earlier breakdown in conversation had been any indication. The thought made me a little uneasy, though I couldn't say why—or couldn't narrow it down from the few thousand obvious and unsettling possibilities, at least.

Out in the hallway, Johnny looked even less thrilled than I felt—at first, I assumed, because he was indignant about being let out like children so that mommy and daddy could discuss the big grownup things. But he didn't say a word about it.

"You okay, man?" I asked.

"I don't know, broto," he said quietly, absentmindedly shaking his head. "That stuff wasn't really any easier to listen to the second time around. And…" He shook himself out of his funk and sighed. "I don't know, man. I just need to get ahold of Therese and check on Bells. It's all I can think about right now."

I laid a hand on his shoulder and was a little surprised to feel a wave of relief when he didn't shrug it away. That was probably just my guilty conscience talking, though. Much as it seemed like Johnny was angry solely at Alton Parker for what had happened to his sister, I couldn't pretend like I hadn't played a part in the whole situation. I had a feeling there was more for us to talk about than we'd had time for since our woodland meeting, but for now...

"Call Therese," I said, giving his shoulder a squeeze before I let go.

"Yeah." He nodded dazedly. "Yeah, I think I will."

"I'll give you some space," I said, starting down the bare bones hallway toward the dull roar of the main operations room.

"Hal," he called before I'd made it far.

I turned, expecting maybe a thanks or a friendly jab—hoping that maybe he'd tell me to grop off with the sensitivity and come listen in. But he was just standing there, looking pleasantly surprised, his palmlight held up for my inspection.

My heart surged. "Franco?"

His grin was all the answer I needed. I hurried back to him. The device buzzed with a new message, and he turned it back to himself to read. "Ah. Pretty sure it's Elise, actually."

The palmlight buzzed again, and again, and Johnny's expression shifted from relieved to amused to guilty as he skimmed through. I pushed in to look over his shoulder, and he angled the display to give me a better look at the stream of incoming messages.

<<Are you two okay?>>

<<For the love of Alpha, tell me you two are okay, Johnny.>>

<<Six hours. I let you two out of my sight for six hours and the reels explode.>>

<<What happened to Lady Lust going invisible and slipping them out? Were those reekers Hal was fighting? >>

<<Please be okay.>>

"Guess they got back to the Lights," Johnny murmured, shooting me that knowing look that was half-amused, half-guilty. "You think maybe we should tell her we're okay?"

I was already reaching to jab at the icon to connect us in a call. "Yeah, Johnny. I think we should probably tell her we're okay."

I could've laughed or cried, or maybe both. The sight of Elise's words—the knowledge that she was safe and that my growing worries had been baseless... it was too much relief to process for a moment. Maybe I was just still too wired from the White Tower courtyard. Either way, I nearly lost it when Elise's face filled the palmlight display.

"Oh, thank Alpha," we both sighed at the same time.

"Warms the heart," Johnny said, shaking his head.

"Are you okay?" I asked.

Elise shot me an exasperated look. "Are *you*? I just had a pair of eccentric shut-ins to worry about over here—no offense, guys—but you? I saw the reels, Hal. I…"

She kept going. Something about knowing a reeker when she saw one, bullscud headlines be damned. But I was still caught up on that one little detail. *No offense, guys,* she'd said. Like those two eccentric shut-ins were sitting within earshot. Which meant…

"Wait, are you… Is Kovaks there right now? Are you—where are you?"

Elise glanced surreptitiously at her surroundings. "We're safe."

"As in safe in the creepy torture dungeon, safe?" Johnny asked.

In the background, I heard the grumble of a gruff voice that took my mind straight to unpleasant memories of arcane wands, hawkish noses, and greasy dispositions. Burton Kovaks. I might not have recognized the voice out of the blue, but in the moment, I was sure.

"We've… established contact," Elise said slowly. "Yeah." She looked up at something, and I thought I heard Franco's voice in the background. Elise nodded at whatever he said, then looked back to us and let out a heavy breath. "Yeah… I guess we have a lot to talk about."

28

FLUNKED

"What happened today, Hal?" Elise asked once Johnny and I had found a private room with a working wall display and settled in for that long talk. "Why did the reekers crash the execution? And why the scud were you out there by yourself trying to go full Carlisle on their asses?"

"They were going after civilians, Lise. It was a slaughter. I think… I don't know. You said you saw the reels."

She nodded.

"Did you notice how the sneaky bastards kept the scales and the red eyes under wraps until the very end?"

Elise looked up, presumably at Franco. "We noticed. And you should know that the red eyes never made it onto the reels. The vids all cut before it happens."

"Imagine my surprise," I muttered.

Of course they would've nixed that part from the footage. I felt stupid for even assuming Elise might've seen it.

"So the reekers and the Sanctum are both trying to make it look like this was all just Shaper-on-Shaper violence?" Johnny asked.

"Seems that way," Elise said.

"Showing the whole world what happens when demons roam free," I said.

Johnny was frowning at the floor, looking disturbed. "They couldn't be working together, could they?"

"I find that unlikely," came Franco's voice, a second before he stepped into the display frame over Elise's shoulder. "Believing that the raknoth would wish to further destabilize Enochia by perpetuating the demon crisis, though… that seems quite within their operational parameters. They must have their reasons." He focused a meaningful look on me. "Perhaps you should consult your own domesticated raknoth as to what those reasons might be. If we understand their game, we'll have a better chance of predicting their next move."

I wanted to point out that Parker was about as domesticated as a brain-touched haga beast, but it wasn't as if Franco didn't already know that. Plus, Parker had begrudgingly accepted my orders to steer clear of Oasis and wait for further instruction, hadn't he? Just like he'd begrudgingly complied with pretty much every demand I'd made since busting him out of the brig. He'd even adhered to my *no killing* rule during our mad dash out of Haven, which by itself seemed like a small miracle.

And all of these things, I firmly reminded myself, he'd almost certainly done for the explicit goal of convincing me that he *would* listen—that he *could* be trusted to play by my rules when it mattered.

As if.

"I'll talk to him," I said, already not looking forward to it.

"And it's not *their* next move, by the way," Johnny said. "It's *his*. Singular."

Surprise rippled across Elise's and Franco's expressions, both their gazes turning to me.

"You killed one?" Elise asked.

Johnny cleared his throat, his hand rising as if by its own accord to jab a finger at his own humble visage.

"Oh," Elise said.

"Oh?" Johnny shot me an indignant look. "*Oh,* she says! Because since when can Johnny hang with Haldin Raish, in all of his mighty gropping…"

He kept on going, but I only half-heard the rest of what he said. I was too caught up wondering if Franco was right about the disparate motives of the raknoth and the Sanctum. It seemed like a safe enough bet. Much as the High Cleric despised me and every other Shaper on Enochia, I couldn't believe he would've cut a deal with the raknoth.

And yet he had survived Five's initial attack, hadn't he? Perhaps I could chock that up to the reflexes of his Onyx Guard, or to Five's indifference for who and what he'd been slaughtering back there. But it still felt a little hard to believe that we'd actually managed to keep Four's and Eight's heads attached to their bodies when the alternative had only been a button press away. Had the High Cleric hesitated on purpose, sensing an opportunity to put a damning spin on the unfortunate interruption of a perfectly good execution?

It probably didn't matter now.

People were dead. And the footage was out there, no doubt making it look like it was the fault of Shapers alone. Of course, anyone who knew the first thing about Shapers and raknoth would be able to understand that the ease with which Five and Seven had torn through the crowds was simply beyond what any human could've done. But pretty much anyone who knew that was probably already in Oasis with us. Which meant we'd probably just slid another few miles into demons' depths.

The sound of Elise's voice drew me back to the conversation.

"None of this explains why you thought it was a good idea to duke it out with two superpowered raknoth."

"I *didn't* think it was a good idea," I said. "But I didn't really have a choice. They were out of control, and everyone else was tied up trying to make sure Four and Eight didn't lose their heads to the clerics' bomb collars."

"Which was kind of why the plan fell apart in the first place," Johnny pointed out.

"You mean *after* you decided to go rogue and crash a public execution with half of Divinity in attendance?" Elise asked.

"I think you both did an admirable job, for what it's worth," Franco said, earning himself a frown from his daughter. He shrugged. "I didn't say a smart job."

"Nice," Johnny said. "Thanks a lot. Good to be appreciated."

Franco tipped his head obligingly.

"All right," I said. "That's enough judgment for us. Your turn. What are you doing calling us from the kidnap lair? What, did they invite you in for cookies and caffa?"

By way of reply, she shrugged and held a glazed clay mug up in cheers.

I just gaped.

"Mmm, caffa," Johnny murmured, looking envious. Then his brow furrowed. "Wait, don't drink the kidnap caffa! That's like…"

"Good manners?" Elise asked. Franco, for some reason, chose that moment to wander off the edge of the display.

"Not what I was thinking," I said, trying to rein in the burst of nervous energy fluttering through my chest.

"Yeah, well, give a girl some credit, will you?" Elise said, glancing up to where I assumed Kovaks and his pasty friend must be lurking. "There might not be any cookies, but I think it's safe to say our induction went a teensy bit smoother than yours."

"I wonder why," I muttered before I'd even managed to figure out what the scud I meant by that.

"I dunno," Elise said, arching an eyebrow. "I think it might've had something to do with me using my words instead of attacking on sight."

I scowled. "Whatever. I don't know what Kovaks told you, but he was the one who whipped out his wand first when we met."

"And there you have it," Elise said, smiling in spite of herself. "Boys and their wands."

"Ha!" Johnny barked. Then, noticing my dark frown, he quickly covered his amusement and narrowed his eyes at Elise. "I mean, that's totally not fair. Emasculating. That's what it is. Degrading, even."

I let out a deep breath and turned back to Elise. "What's the situation over there. Are they ready to help out and share those records?"

For some reason, those questions seemed to rattle Elise more than anything we'd discussed so far. She dropped her gaze from us, taking the time for a long but shallow pull of caffa before answering at all.

"We're all on the same side, here," she finally said.

"And you're suddenly being weird becaaause…?" Johnny asked.

Elise bit her lip. "Because the question of sharing those records is a little more complicated."

"Complicated how?" I asked.

"They umm…" She looked up again, as if checking with someone. Kovaks? "Well, the Watchers—umm, Kovaks and Omelius, I mean—were originally tasked with—"

"Watchers?" Johnny asked.

"Omelius?" I added. Did she mean Pasty?

"Did you join a cult?" Johnny asked.

Elise looked back and forth between us in a rare moment of tongue-tied indecision.

"Sweet Alpha," Johnny said. "She joined a cult. And she says she can't leave *us* alone for six hours…"

"I didn't join anything," Elise said in a huff. "Look, it's just… these two are part of a long line that's been tasked to basically wait for the right time and place to get this information back into the hands of the Shapers in a way that might actually let us avoid repeating all the mistakes that led to the first thousand-year downfall of our kind."

"And they're serving you caffa where they served me arcane stun prods because…?"

"Because the gravity of that duty has apparently left them a bit picky about who they're willing to talk to." She dropped her gaze. "And because you didn't pass the test."

"The test?" Johnny asked, looking between us. "Like, that psychic helmet thingy you told me about?"

I was too busy staring at Elise, trying to wrap my head around what she was telling me. "And you did pass?

"So they tell me," she said. She didn't sound particularly happy about it.

I wasn't sure what to think—still wasn't even really sure what the scud that test had even been about, or what they possibly thought they could've gleaned from a few flashing runes on a thousand-year-old helmet.

"Well that's… That's good then, right?" I asked. "I mean, if you're in the club now, you can find out what we're looking for and we can just go from there, right?"

It probably made more sense than the alternative anyway. Because while I might be a stronger Shaper at the moment, Elise was exceptionally better than me at this kind of detective work. It definitely made sense, I decided. And yet I couldn't help but notice the subtle tightness in my gut. I couldn't have said what it was or why it was there—only that it felt like the seed of something that past experience told me might well grow ugly and problematic with time.

And the look on Elise's face didn't really improve matters.

"I'm going to see what there is to see," she said slowly, as if half-expecting I'd object. "And I'll keep you guys posted as best I can."

"As best you can?" I asked, not loving the sound of that.

"I don't really know anything yet. I just know Omelius is very… apprehensive about what's in these records. Apparently there's some pretty dangerous stuff buried away. The kind of stuff the Emmútari didn't want to see falling into the wrong hands."

And there it was. A little spritz of water for that ugly seed in my gut.

"And you're saying my hands are the wrong hands," I said. "Because of a thousand-year-old helmet."

"No. That's not what I'm saying, Hal."

"But it's what *they're* saying, isn't it?" I felt my fists tightening. Felt the tide of anger rising. Knew I should just take a deep breath. "Who gives a scud what a gropping little helmet has to say about it? They don't know the first thing about me. The Sanctum is trying to wipe us off the face of the planet, and you're telling me those two are scared I might learn a few old Shapers' secrets?"

I was practically shouting by the end. Enough so that I would've been embarrassed even if Johnny hadn't been sitting there, watching me with a look that said I was taking it a bit far, even if my frustrations *were* understandable.

Elise was just silently bobbing her head in mechanical agreement, not meeting my eyes. "That's pretty much exactly what I told them, Hal." She looked up, and the compassion in her eyes only made me feel that much worse at having lost my scud like that. "I'm still on your side, here," she said. "You know that, right?"

I blew out a breath, dropping my eyes to the permacrete floor in shame. "I'm sorry, Lise. That was... I'm just glad you're okay, and that that stupid helmet was wise enough to recognize you're the right choice for this thing anyway."

"Thank you," she said softly. "Now will you two go get some medical attention? I'm going to get back to... whatever we wanna call it over here."

"Orientation?" Johnny asked.

"Why not," she said.

"Ahhh..." Johnny clapped a hand to my shoulder, shaking his head. "They just grow up so fast, don't they?"

That, at least, got Elise to smile a little, which in turn made it easier for me to find my own.

"I love you," I said.

"And I, you." She looked to Johnny. "I'd ask you to make sure he doesn't do anything reckless..."

"But I'm just far too important these days to be bothered with babysitting the B team?" he asked.

"Something like that. You two be careful."

"Only if you are," I said.

She gave her eyebrows a little waggle and ended the call, leaving me and Johnny alone in our quiet little meeting room, contemplating what we'd just learned.

"Well scud," I finally said.

"Yeah, I'll say..." He looked over at me. "Wanna go get some food and talk about it?"

I *was* starving. But I also had two wrists in need of a heavy dose of nanites, and the last thing I felt like was talking about... whatever this was. I just needed to think. And maybe to sleep a few winks. But first...

"I think I should call Parker," I said. "See if we can get any insight as to what those reekers were thinking, and what Five might do now that his partner's gone."

"Yeah…" Johnny stood, clearly not wanting any part of talking to the raknoth. "I'll call Therese while you're at it. Feel free to tell Parker I'm praying extra hard he chokes, though."

I gave him a tired smile. "Will do."

He paused halfway to the door and turned back. "You okay, broto?"

"I'm fine."

He studied me for a stretch, and I thought he was going to adhere to regulation broto code—if a broto says he's fine, he's fine, even if he's clearly not—and leave it at that.

"You're wondering why you didn't pass the magical helmet test," he said, "aren't you?"

"No," I said out of some tired combination of denial and sheer stubbornness.

"Yeah, me neither. I mean, it's not like you're the most famous, maybe even the strongest, Shaper on the planet. Why would you have any reason to expect you would've been the one to pass the mysterious arbitrary helmet test anyway?"

I finally turned to meet his eyes. "Did you have a point under all that ginger snark?"

"Who, me?" He shrugged. "Eh, I dunno. Seems like it'd be wasted if I did, seeing as neither of us is burning with curiosity about the thing anyway."

I rolled my eyes and came back to find him watching me with a more serious look.

"Don't let this thing fester in that big pretty head of yours, broto. We have no idea what any of this means yet."

I looked back to the empty display, at a loss for anything useful to say, and not all that sure I'd want to say it even if I'd had it to say.

Johnny crossed back over to me and clapped a hand on my shoulder. "Besides, Lise is way better at the book stuff than us barbarians. That helmet probably just counted concussions and came to the conclusion your poor brain is hopeless at this point."

I scowled up at him. "I thought this was supposed to be a comforting pep talk."

He made a face. "Alpha knows what gave you that idea, man."

I watched my friend go, not quite sure whether to scowl or smile.

2 9

HEROES

When Alton Parker appeared on the wall display, he looked bored. And not just in the *I'll stand here and roll my eyes while you pathetic mortals try to keep up with my massive intellect* kind of way that I was coming to expect from him during difficult conversations. But genuinely, mind-numbingly bored. Or maybe it was subdued defeat hanging across his well-chiseled face. I couldn't really tell. Suffice it to say, he wasn't a ball of sunshine and flowers.

"What can you tell me about those two raknoth?" I asked without preamble.

"Aside from that Nan'Vala appears to be quite dead?"

I watched him, wondering if that thought would stir something in him— anger or sadness or anything else. But his expression remained flat. Subdued.

"Why were they there? Why attack a public execution? Why protect Four and Eight?"

"There are several potential explanations," Parker said. "Several of which you've no doubt already arrived at yourself, leaving me to wonder why you'd expect I would have any more accurate information than you."

"They are your kin."

"As Auckus and the High Cleric are yours," Parker said. "Tell me, have they never once acted in a way you hadn't expected?"

I watched him, setting aside the validity of his point and allowing the paranoid skeptic in my head to have its day.

"Did you send them there?"

He studied me right back, a slow smile spreading his lips. "No. But I'll admit I enjoyed watching you stop them."

"Enjoyed it so much that you left us to die down in that courtyard?"

And there was the composed exasperation I'd come to expect from the raknoth—the flagrant eye roll that still somehow managed to come off as elegant and casual. "Spare me your indignation, Haldin. You were quite emphatic in your conviction that it would be devastating to your goals to be seen in collusion with this ship. I was watching you fight from several miles above. Did it not occur to you that I was also able to observe your shining High General flying in to the rescue?"

It *had* occurred to me. But that didn't exactly lessen the harrowing intensity of what we'd survived through. Even if Parker had technically been adhering to my orders...

"You just wanted to see if I could win against two of those things, didn't you?"

He cocked his head noncommittally. "Once again, your resourcefulness in the face of hopeless odds has prevailed."

I pointedly held up my splinted wrists, demonstrating what my success looked like. He just shrugged, as if the matter of broken bones was a non-issue. I sighed and lowered my wrists, which were properly beginning to throb again on the waning edge of the pain meds Calvin had given me.

I needed to wrap this up and get to the medica.

"Why were they there, Alton? What do they want? Your best guess."

He frowned at me as if I'd said something mildly unexpected, but pushed on before I could register what or why. "Based on the past two encounters, I think the safest assumption is that they were hoping to see you neutralized. My best guess is that they correctly assumed you would make an appearance at the execution, and that that appearance would in turn offer them a chance to eliminate you while simultaneously dealing a public blow that would give all of Enochia every reason to embrace the Sanctum's war on Shapers. Because once your kind are gone—"

"There'd be no one left to stop them from taking the keys to the planet right back into their scaly little hands," I said.

"Not exactly how I was going to put it," Parker said, nodding, "but yes, that is quite possibly the crux of it. With Zar'Faenor gone, I imagine they would've liked nothing more than to claim rulership of their very own private planet. As to the why, well…" he quirked an eyebrow. "I imagine it is primarily because those two have always been complete morons. They were power drunk even before they claimed their shiny new Seeker vessels."

"This coming from the guy who helped his clan take control of Enochia in the first place."

"This coming from the guy who had a coherent plan and reason for doing so," Parker countered.

"Yeah," I said, "if by 'coherent plan,' you mean 'obliterating the human population to raise your own hybrid army.'"

"I said coherent. Not compassionate."

I glared at his calm smirk, glad for the reminder that, no matter what else might be going on, I would never be without good reason to despise this creature. It felt good. Good in a way I doubted many soothsayers would deem "mentally healthy," maybe. But good all the same.

"Haldin."

I stirred from my inner hate fest and took in the serious look on Parker's face.

"I understand you're not ready to hear this, but I ask you to at least consider that it may be time to—"

"To what?" I searched his calm, calculating eyes. "To forget about my planet and help you instead?"

"That is a supremely shortsighted way of looking at it. If you honestly believe you can still hope to affect the tide of this—"

"You can stop right there," I said, standing to leave. "Because if *you* honestly believe I could ever run away and just forget about all this, you haven't been paying close attention."

"So that's what he wants, huh?"

I jerked around at the unexpected voice to find Johnny standing in the doorway, staring past me with unseeing eyes. He looked like he was in shock. But not at what he'd just heard, I thought. He looked like…

"Johnny? What happened?"

"It's… It's Bells," he said, his absent gaze momentarily flicking to Parker on the display before returning to the thousand-yard stare. "She's… Therese says she looks… better today. There's still a bunch of tests to run, apparently, but…" He finally stirred from his funk and fixed his eyes on me. "Therese says she thinks the treatment… she thinks it's working."

I stood there staring, trying to wrap my head around the news—and moreover around the fact that I didn't find myself jumping for joy. Why? Because it sounded too uncertain? Too good to be true? Or was it because the treatment in question had come from Alton groping Parker, and the thought that it might actually be genuine, and not some dirty trick, chilled me to the bone as much as any bad news ever could have?

That moment stretched on forever—me hovering there, all too aware of the silent weight of Parker's presence on the display beside me. Johnny staring at the raknoth's image, thinking Alpha knew what. Parker just standing there, lost in his own quiet thoughts.

I waited, wondering if I should say something, expecting any moment that Parker would finally let loose some snide comment, or that Johnny might even thank the raknoth—or at least threaten him about what would happen if this turned sideways. But no one spoke.

Finally, Johnny roused from his reveries, shot a dark look at the display, and turned to me. "We should get to the medica. Freya might want to call that meeting sooner than later."

And with that, he was gone.

I glanced at Parker, then turned to follow my friend, not trusting myself to talk right then, much less to sort through the raknoth's bullscud.

"Consider what I said, Haldin," Parker said before I'd made it three steps.

I hesitated, then killed the connection and followed Johnny out into the hallway. He was propped against the opposite wall, arms crossed, looking like he was trying to decide whether to be happy or angry, or to simply give up and allow himself to melt into the permacrete floor.

"It's good news about Bells," I said, not knowing where else to start. "Therese wouldn't have gotten your hopes up if she didn't mean it about her getting better."

For a second, he looked like he wanted to say something, but the somber silence only stretched.

"I take it Therese and Phineas are still safe in Haven?" I finally asked.

Still nothing. He just stood there, lost in some point on the opposite wall, his face an emotionless mask.

This wasn't right. Any of it. That Annabelle had ever been dragged into this nightmare at all. That the entire situation had gotten so gropped we couldn't even share a moment's happiness over the news that maybe she was going to be okay. But this wasn't just about Annabelle, either. I could see that much on Johnny's inexpressive face.

He also felt betrayed. And it wasn't hard to guess why.

"I told you he wanted my help," I said.

"You just forgot to mention the part where it included an invitation to leave the planet," he said flatly, not looking up.

"It didn't seem worth mentioning."

"Because you've already got it all figured out."

"Because it's gropping ridiculous."

He finally looked up. "So you're not thinking about it? About leaving?"

"No." I shook my head. "No way. It's… This is my home, Johnny. Our home. I'm not gonna go flying off looking for monsters when we've already got a perfectly good scudstorm in need of tending here."

"And after we've tended that scudstorm?"

I opened my mouth with decisive certainty, only to find that I didn't have an answer. I wanted to tell him that I'd be right here, ready to defend the planet from the next one—or, Alpha forbid, to finally just enjoy the peace beside him and Elise. But the rakul were out there. Kul'Naga was out there. I'd seen him. Felt his power. And if that creature was truly on an inevitable collision course for Enochia…

Johnny quietly shook his head at whatever he saw on my face. "Come on." He pushed himself off the wall and turned to leave. "There's no way I'm gonna win servitor of the year if I don't get your bruised ass to the medica."

"Johnny, I'm not gonna—"

I fell silent at his look.

"I might not know what you're gonna do, Hal, but I know you well enough to know that you don't really know at this point either. I see that bastard's words turning in your head. I see you actually starting to consider it. Because that asshole knows what makes you tick. He knows exactly how to appeal to your deepest desire."

"And what's that?" I asked, irritation rising in my chest.

Johnny dropped my gaze. "That you need to believe you're the hero of this story."

His tone was flat, but he might as well have slapped me. My insides turned over like gravity had momentarily reoriented itself, and I stood there, staring at my friend, wondering how he could say such a thing. I wanted to argue—that I didn't think that at all, that that's not what was happening here, that I *was* the hero of this story, dammit…

But my brain didn't want to form the words. It was too concerned with the insidious chill worming its way through my insides. Such a simple, harmless statement, and yet it'd left me so stunned. I didn't understand it. Especially not when it wasn't all that different from the warnings Johnny had given me before—to remember that this fight didn't belong to me alone, and that the men and women who chose to support me against the Sanctum were fighting not for me, but for what they believed their planet should be.

They were words I'd tried my best to keep close to my heart. But something about the way he'd just said the words, *hero* and *believe*, like maybe Johnny was less than certain himself what to believe anymore...

"Come on," Johnny said, still avoiding my eyes. "We're wasting time. We can talk about this when we're not both ready to collapse."

I didn't argue. Just fell in beside him as he turned for the operations room.

We walked down the hallway side-by-side, the silence hanging like a softsteel anchor between us. He was probably right. With the fire growing in my wrists and the incessant hunger pangs growing in my belly, now was hardly the time for a serious inward look. We'd both almost died, I'd just found out my girlfriend had filled my boots as envoy to the freaking Emmútari, and Johnny was clearly dealing with the emotional ride of his sister's progress. We probably both needed a few minutes to clear our heads.

But that didn't stop his words from playing through my head over and over again as we marched off for the medica, silent as the urn.

Much as the shared silence bothered me, I didn't argue when we reached the medica and the medics immediately split us up—taking Johnny off for a quick once-over of his cuts and bruises and guiding me to a room for overnight admission.

There'd been a time not so long ago that every part of me would've rebelled at the thought of lying around while the world was burning out there. But now, after everything that had happened, and after what Johnny had just said, I found I was actually kind of looking forward to the idea of a little quiet peace. At least until my medic swept me into a room, and I realized I was going to have roommates for the night.

"You've gotta be kidding me," I grumbled.

"Funny," said Garrett, looking up from Siren's bedside to scowl at me even as Four and Eight roused in their own beds. "I was just thinking the same thing."

BAD COMPANY

Even with a full stomach, a cush medica bed, and a heavy dose of painkillers and nanites circling through my blood, the afternoon did not pass particularly pleasantly.

Mostly, I blamed the company. And not just because half of the room's occupants had tried to kill me at one point or another. It was more that I just desperately needed some time alone with my thoughts. If the medics hadn't been so clearly understaffed in Oasis, I might've worked up the audacity to ask for a separate room.

Truth be told, though, the ex-Seekers weren't really all that abrasive, aside from the few casual jabs Garrett had thrown my way as I'd settled into the room. Four and Eight had been rather courteous, even, in the light of what we'd all gone through to pull them out of the White Tower square.

For the most part, though, we all stuck to the solitude of our own thoughts, which was fine by me. In a way, it was almost comforting, sharing the heavy silence with four other individuals who were arguably as deeply entrenched in the scud as I was. *Almost* comforting. Even if they were all murderers.

Some part of me gave an inward and very Alton-Parker-esque eye roll at that hard condemnation, pointing out that maybe I could finally admit that they'd been through a little more than I understood, and that maybe it wasn't fair to just slap that label across all their foreheads. But maybe that was just the past days' madness and the warm honey-brain kiss of the painkillers talking. They *had* all killed people, after all. Lots of people. And it probably said a thing or two about my mental state that I had to actively remind myself that was still a big gropping deal, raknoth invasions and Sanctum incursions be damned.

What I would've liked more than anything was to simply sleep the afternoon away in blissful ignorance. But tired as I was, sleep refused to come. There was just too much to worry about. Elise and the Emmútari. Johnny and Bells. Glenbark and the gropping Sanctum. It felt like everyone I knew was waging their own private war at this point, and that I'd somehow managed to stick my would-be heroic head into every single one of them.

The thought reminded me of something Johnny had once said to me about my chronic inability to resist sticking my fingers into every single problem I saw, never trusting that maybe, just maybe, someone other than the mighty Haldin Raish could be trusted to handle business. And maybe it had been that bright moods and low-hanging innuendos had distracted us from the heart of the matter that day. Or maybe I simply hadn't been ready to hear it. But now, as much as I thought I'd already taken Johnny's advice to heart, I couldn't avoid it.

He'd been more right than I'd known.

More right than maybe even *he'd* known.

Just like I was growing more and more certain that he'd been right about what he'd said back in Central Command earlier: that I was falling straight back into my fae tale delusions of heroic grandeur, and that Alton Parker was gleefully tugging my leash every step of the way.

Since the hybrid armies had fallen and the Legion had retaken Oasis, I thought I'd been doing better. I'd listened to what Glenbark and the others had said. I'd resisted my myriad urges to try to take every matter into my own hands. I'd been a team player. Or so I'd told myself, at least.

And then along came Alton Parker, feeding me the secrets that only I could see, that only I could use to save Enochia. He'd placed me right back up on that valiant pedestal where I'd been the only one who could take the necessary steps—the only one who could even *see* the steps that were needed to protect our planet.

He'd left me no choice.

Or so I'd told myself.

"What do you think over there, Raish?" came Garrett's voice, tugging my attention back to the medica, where my four roommates were all watching me expectantly.

"About what?" I asked.

"About *what?*" he repeated, scowling at me. "Alpha, have you heard a word we've said in the past five minutes?"

"Should I have?"

"This is why no one likes you," Four muttered, shaking his head.

I frowned at him. "What happened to all the *thank you for saving my life* stuff from earlier?"

Four shrugged. "I never said I liked you."

"I like him just fine," Siren said sleepily.

"She doesn't know what she's saying," Garrett said, with a pointed look at the drug infusion pumps that were no doubt giving Siren her own case of the honey brain.

"No, he's got spunk," Siren argued. "Like a…"

We all watched, waiting for the follow-up until I thought she might've actually nodded off.

"… like a three-legged hound," she said, blinking dazedly, and slurring a little. "You never know quite how he's going to pull it off, but you're never disappointed."

"Uh, thanks?" I said.

Siren just smiled contentedly.

"As I was saying," Garrett muttered, adjusting her blankets for her, careful not to agitate her shoulder where she'd been shot in the Legion's initial push.

"We were asking whether you think the High Cleric will command an attack on Oasis tonight," Four said.

"Oh." I looked around at them. "Do you?"

"Alpha," Four said. "You honestly didn't hear a single word, did you?"

Siren stirred. "He's too busy thinking about his sexy little…" She trailed off. Then, seeming to re-notice Garrett for the first time, she made an appreciative purring sound and tugged him down by the front of his shirt.

To our collective unease, Garrett's lack of regard for Siren's drug-brained declarations did not extend to her romantic advances. I swallowed and did my best to look away and focus on Four and Eight while Garrett and Siren filled the sterile-smelling room with the wet smacks of sloppy kisses.

"It never ends with them, does it?"

"How should I know?" Four asked, openly staring at the lip-smacking pair. "This is forbidden. *Was* forbidden. They would've been killed for this back in the Sanctum."

Eight cleared her throat loud enough to cut through the pheromones. "And they still might be."

That, at least, got the two to cool it for the moment. They broke apart, Siren with a breathless little giggle, and Garrett with a glare that said he might've considered killing all three of us if it meant he could finish what they'd just started.

"Fine," he growled. "Let's get back to the part where we're all going to die because you people can't stop pissing off the entire world."

"Us?" I asked.

He ticked us each off with a pointing finger. "I'm counting three assholes who've ended up on the gallows." His finger paused on me. "And one who can't seem to eat his morning grains without starting a gropping war."

"You think this is my fault?" I stared around the room. "You think there's any version of our history where this wasn't eventually going to happen anyway? Your Sanctum is a pile of steaming hypocrisy sitting on a mountain of lies."

"It's not our Sanctum," Four said. "It never was."

No one argued. Garrett's gaze fell to the floor, a dark look settling on his face, his hand drifting to the spot on his throat where I knew there'd once been an explosive collar—the ever-present mark of their enslavement.

Because they had been slaves, hadn't they?

"What lies do you speak of?" Eight asked in her reserved tone.

A weary weight settled over me as I remembered Four and Eight hadn't received the full extent of Alton Parker's world-shaking truths. I wasn't looking forward to wading through it all yet again to the open disbelief of Four's swarthy stare and Eight's stony one. Luckily, Garrett was willing to do the honors—albeit with a good amount more eye-rolling and open skepticism than I might've employed. Still, I was happy to sit back and let him go.

"You trust a raknoth in all of this?" Four asked me when Garrett had finished.

"I was inside his mind," I said. If any roomful of people on the planet understood what that meant, it was this one. "But even if he somehow misguided me in any way, I am sure of one thing. There was a time when people like us were seen as respected keepers of the peace rather than unholy fiends to be mobbed down and strung up."

By the uncertain look Four and Eight exchanged, I was pretty sure that they, like Garrett and Siren, had also never heard of the Emmútari before.

"And what happened to these respected keepers of the peace?" Four asked. "You're not telling us that…"

I nodded. "Sarentus united the twelve nations against—"

"Against an army of manifest demons," Eight said, her jaw rigid and her brow as stern as that of any cleric reading from the old texts. "An army the likes of which Enochia has never again seen since the Sanctum came to power and Alpha's light—"

"Permitted Sarentus and his Sanctum to develop their own private kill squad," Garrett provided, "and to start snuffing out whatever demons remained."

Eight clearly wanted to argue, but there was also hesitation there.

"It's a convenient story," Four said. "Neat and tidy. But why should we believe any of this?"

I hesitated, then decided there was no reason to lie.

Like it or not, we were all in this together now.

"Because we found the remnants of the Emmútari," I said. "Elise is with their record-keepers now, looking for anything that might help us move forward from this demon-hunt bullscud."

Garrett did a double-take. "*That's* where your lady went? I thought they scattered from the party to meet one of Fields' intel contacts."

"Yeah, well maybe you would've caught the full story if you two hadn't been too busy swiving in the woods."

Four and Eight turned shocked stares on Garrett, who opened his mouth to counter, then glanced down at a sleeping Siren and gave a shrug as if to say, *Whatever. Worth it.*

"But…" Four shook his head clear of whatever woods-swiving thoughts he was still on and turned to me. "Move forward? From this? The High Cleric hates us. Deeply. And so does the rest of the world, now. There's no moving forward from that. What are you possibly hoping to find that could change that?"

I didn't have an answer. Never had since we'd started all this.

Even if Elise found hard proof of these stories, even if it was strong enough to convince the public to question the Sanctum's word…

"Grop moving forward," Garrett said. "Surviving this scudstorm is the best we can hope for. Eventually, the mobs will forget about us and go back to their lives. It's not like they can spot us in a crowd."

"Which is why they're probably gonna murder another few thousand innocent people before they give up," I said. "You're okay with that?"

Garrett shrugged. "If the dumb bastards wanna kill each other out of superstition, I don't really see how it's our job to stop them. I'm all for protecting our own. Scud, I'm even for protecting harmless civies, too. But I'm not about to stand up waving and shouting just to keep the angry mobs from incurring some friendly fire."

"And when these rakul show up? What do you think's gonna happen to those harmless civies when Enochia's facing an invasion of the creatures that make the raknoth look like common foot soldiers?"

"Something tells me we'll all be long dead by then, kid," Garrett said. "Assuming these things even exist at all."

I wanted to argue. Wanted to show him the raw power of the beast in my memory. Wanted to tell them all to imagine what we could do if there were more of us, if we didn't have to hide our abilities. But I couldn't seem to find the words. Couldn't seem to find anything but the walls themselves pressing in on me, telling me that I was a naive child, and that Johnny had been right, and that I'd been deluding myself ever thinking I could stop what was happening.

"The planet doesn't want us, Raish," Four said, as if reading my thoughts. "There's nothing we can do about that."

"What we should be focusing on," Garrett said, "is how we're going to keep our people safe, and what we can do to find the gifted who are out there lost in the crowd right now."

The conversation livened somewhat after that, Four and Eight perking up now that the subject had shifted from my childish fantasies of world peace to something tangible and practical: our survival.

Maybe I shouldn't have been surprised that a trio of ex-Seekers couldn't see much hope of us ever escaping persecution for the simple fact of our existence. They'd spent their lives doing the hunting, after all. But that didn't make it any easier to swallow.

I listened half-heartedly as they discussed the logistics of the isolated retreat the other ex-Seekers had apparently established somewhere near the Faol Mountains—how many Shapers were already there. What defenses were in place. How many more they could likely take on before they grew beyond their capacity to hide and supply the settlement. Where else they might begin to establish similar bases.

Bit by discouraging bit, I drifted back into my own thoughts, wondering how I'd ever thought this had been anything other than a grab and rescue mission. Somehow, when Garrett and Siren had showed up to pull my ass out of the fire, I'd assumed we were all on the same page. That our rocky alliance was a necessary first step in some grand Shaper revolution.

But it was all just one more instance of me trying to play the hero, I realized now. Spouting out my ideals and charging into battle without looking back. Because if I had—if I'd bothered to take a good hard look at the situation, if I'd been honest with myself from the start…

Would it have changed anything?

I rolled over on my side and closed my eyes, trying to shut it all out, wishing more than anything that Elise were there to take me in her arms and tell me that it was going to be okay. To tell me what was right. To center me, as she so often did.

But she was off on her own journey now, delving into the knowledge I'd been deemed unworthy to receive.

And maybe that's what was really bothering me, underneath everything else. Not that Elise had passed the test that I'd failed. But the realization that maybe that stupid little helmet had been right, and that maybe that was exactly *why* she'd passed: because she *could* center me in a way I could never seem to accomplish myself. Because without her and Johnny, left to my own devices, I probably would've already fallen off into madness by now.

Because somewhere along the line, I seemed to have lost myself amid the chaos.

What was I anymore, aside from a walking bag of raknoth secrets and arcane power that was as likely to detonate any situation I touched as I was to defuse it?

I didn't know the answer. Nor did I know how I'd ever had the audacity to think someone who didn't know that answer could be the one to bring an end to a thousand years of systemic injustice.

So I lay there in the medica, trying to find sleep as Garrett and the others finally lapsed back into a thoughtful silence that was broken only by the hums and rhythmic whirs of our various pumps and monitors—all of us awake with our abject listlessness, none of us saying a word. Not until Four perked up in his medica bed, brandishing a tablet.

"High Cleric's going live," was all he said before he diverted the feed to the room's main wall display with a flick of his fingers.

I wasn't particularly interested in what His Holiness had to say about the day's events, mostly because I'd been through the mud in so many bullscud cover-ups by this point that I was pretty sure I could've written the High Cleric's monologue myself. Still, I couldn't help but listen as he gave his heartfelt prayers for the victims who'd fallen in what had clearly been the latest and most devastating attack in an escalating pattern of demonic violence. There was no mention of the raknoth. I didn't need to pull the reel vids to know there'd be no evidence of Seven's red-eyed slip up at the end of our fight, either. It was all pretty much as I'd expected.

At least until the High Cleric began outing the attackers by name.

Not that I was surprised to hear my own. I was the Demon of gropping Divinity. Everyone knew my name. But no one—myself included—knew the names of Adam Drove, and Enid Trugden.

"Scud," Four said.

No one knew the names of Garrett Fellwood and Alexia Arkova.

"Son of a bitch," Garrett growled, clutching a sleeping Alexia's hand.

The names Radnor Brattuck and Lilith Gretchen were also thrown out there, but judging by the lack of sharp hisses in the room, I was guessing those names must've belonged to Five and Seven.

And besides, I was too busy watching as Garrett turned to Four and Eight with the oddest demeanor. If I had to put a word to it, I'd say he almost looked ashamed—not unlike Siren had looked when I'd first found out her real name—but I couldn't begin to understand exactly why.

"Nice to meet you, Adam," Garrett muttered. "Enid."

Four and Eight traded a glance, and they looked more rattled than I think I'd ever seen them.

"Garrett," Four finally said, tilting his head.

"I don't like this," Eight said flatly, as if the look on her stony face had left any doubt about the matter.

It was a strange moment. Almost strange enough to distract from the High Cleric's closing remarks. But not quite.

"Allow me to make one thing perfectly clear, my children," the cleric was saying on the display, gazing out at Enochia with the sternest of looks. "Those good citizens of Enochia, those loyal children of Alpha who continue to serve and abide by His law, have nothing to fear. We will protect you. We will apprehend the creatures responsible for this vile attack, and they will be brought to know the swift justice of Alpha's Might. To my loyal children, I bid you rest easy tonight, and steel yourselves for the work ahead.

"But to anyone else hearing this message, to those who would dare to harbor a demon or indeed even to lend one of their ilk the slightest of aid, I give you this warning. We will no longer tolerate your perverse treachery. We will no longer show you and your dark masters the decency of mercy. Not when the stones of our own White Tower stand slicked with the blood of the innocent. Not when factions of our own Legion maneuver to conspire against us. Not when the very sanctity of our spirits stands imperiled.

"So to those of you who would think to oppose our holy right to uphold the Will of Alpha, to those of you who would raise arms against us in defense of these seven demons and those like them, be you a broom maiden or a High General, hear me now: lay down your arms, withdraw your aid from your dark masters, and you may yet find your way back to Alpha's Light. But resist, and you *will* suffer His almighty wrath."

With that, the broadcast cut to standby.

"Well that wasn't oddly specific or anything," Garrett muttered, swiping the display off.

"You know," Four finally said after a long, heavy silence, "I think I preferred it when no one realized yet that they wanted me dead."

"Welcome to the club, Adam," I said, then immediately regretted my careless words.

It felt wrong somehow, worrying myself over upsetting any of these people, but I couldn't help it at the pained, almost frightened look that touched his face at the sound of his own name coming from my mouth.

"Four," I corrected myself. "Sorry. I didn't mean to…"

I trailed off, uncertain as to exactly *what* it was that I'd done to the ex-Seeker, but Four was already shaking off my apology, his expression grim.

"No, you're right. I don't see any good reason to cling to the name *they* gave me," he said, jutting his chin at the display. "I don't belong to the Sanctum anymore. I don't see why my true name should either."

He turned to Eight and reached a hand over the space between their beds. "I'll be Adam if you'll be Enid."

"I hate that name," Eight said quietly. Her jaw hardened. "But I hate them more." She nodded and reached for his hand. "Adam it is, then."

"Enid," he replied, his face breaking into a soft smile. "It feels strange, doesn't it?"

"Feels stranger watching," Garrett muttered, "trust me."

I expected that the salty remark would kill the moment, that Adam and Enid would release one another's hands self-consciously, and that the ex-Seekers—or scud, I might as well just say it, my allied Shapers—would return straight back to their solemn bickering. But Adam laughed instead— a light chuckle that started in his lungs and spread through the medica room like a jovial infection, catching on Enid's lips, alighting in Garrett's eyes, tickling at my own chest.

Before I knew it, we were all laughing, and I couldn't for the life of me have said why.

It was an odd kind of laughter, tinged with an almost frantic, desperate quality. It gripped us until my battered sides ached with it and it occurred to me that it really *was* an infection of sorts—a kind of respiratory virus that had invaded our innards and now sought to shake them loose of all the pain and fear and near-death realizations that we'd all been through earlier that day.

When Siren stirred and tried to murmur a bleary question about what she'd missed, we just laughed harder.

"Grop them," Garrett said when we'd finally regained our sobriety.

He didn't have to explain which *them* he meant. It wasn't hard to guess from our position on the pointy end of the mob's collective demon skewers. And maybe Garrett had the right idea. Maybe it really was time to say *grop them*—to say farewell and good riddance to the Enochian masses, to turn instead to the challenge of preserving and even building the ranks of Shapers from the uncrowded corners of our fair planet. Maybe it was time to tell Alton Parker to space off with his vaunted secrets and his doomsday predictions. It had always been a fool's errand to think I could do anything about them anyway. I saw that now.

All this time, I'd been fighting to protect what I'd thought were my people.

But maybe it was time to accept that *my people* were a much smaller tribe than I'd originally thought, and that my grand efforts to kick start the Shaper Revolution of Enochia would be infinitely more useful, applied to the simple but monumental task of survival. Because no matter who thought what about our plans moving forward, and no matter how much we wanted to pretend like any of us were tough enough to rise above it all, I was pretty sure we all agreed on one thing.

We'd survived the day, but we weren't even close to being in the clear.

UNHOLY OATHS

By the time Glenbark summoned us to Central Command the next morning, I was just about ready to swear off my powers of responsibility completely, lay down at her feet, and acquiesce to whatever she deemed was right. Because if there was any one thing I was certain of after an evening mired in my roommates' cynicism and my own self-doubt, it was that I sure as scud wasn't qualified to make the call anymore—not about anything more important than my breakfast choice, at least.

"You doing okay?" Johnny asked me quietly as we approached the small gathering of officers and ex-Seekers outside Glenbark's office.

"Are you?" I asked, thinking of Annabelle.

I half-expected him to withdraw, but by the playful way he scrunched his face up, I knew I had my friend back from the haze that'd understandably claimed us both the previous day. It lightened the load in my chest by a few slivers, but that hardly brought me back up to *sunshine and flowers* status.

"Hal, what I said yesterday was—"

"Pretty spot on, as far as I can tell," I said.

"Oh no." He glanced past me to Garrett and the others. "They didn't drag you back down to the dark place, did they?"

"I've been an idiot, Johnny." I looked from him to Garrett and back. "Someone had to tell me. Might as well have been all of you on the same day."

"So that's a yes, then," he said, frowning in their general direction.

"They really weren't that bad," I said. "We even kind of bonded, I think."

"Well, isn't that wonderful?" he said, turning back to me with his fiery red brows held high. "Clearly it worked wonders for your sense of self-worth."

I shrugged. "Like it or not, I'm pretty sure you were right yesterday, Johnny."

His eyebrows reached higher. "I didn't know what I was saying yesterday, Hal. And yeah, maybe there was some truth to it, but…" He shook his head. "Look, broto, I know things have been looking pretty bleak lately, but—"

"If you say the night is always darkest before the dawn…"

"I was gonna remind you that, heroes or not, we might all be raknoth food right now if it hadn't been for you and Carlisle. And that there's still hope as long as we're here with Freya, and Lise is off doing her thing with Captain Creepy Nose." He cocked his head. "Also, the night is always darkest before the d—"

"Okay, okay," I said, shaking my head and failing to suppress a small smile. "Thank you for all that. But seriously, you saw the High Cleric's broadcast last night, right?"

He nodded, clearly not liking where this was going.

"What if we've already lost?" I asked. "I'm running around worrying about an alien threat that may or may not ever find this planet, and I think it's time to accept that maybe I've just been too blind to see that maybe there was never any winning at all."

"Okay," Johnny said, nodding slowly to himself and looking around as if he were physically searching for one of many counter-lessons he'd prepared for just such an emergency. "Look around us, Hal," he finally said. "What do you see?"

I said nothing, waiting for him to get on with it and make his point. But he only watched me expectantly , waiting for me to answer what I thought had been a rhetorical question.

I sighed, looking around. "Walls. I see walls. And a bunch of rebel apostates manning them."

"Exactly," Johnny said with a clap of his hands. "Apostates. Rebels. We've got nearly two-thousand people on this base alone, all flying the Team Enochia flag, all doing it even after Freya made it clear that you and the murder squad over there are part of that team. And what's that tell us?"

I scowled at his playfully patronizing tone, resisting the urge to point out that it hardly mattered, all things considered.

"It tells me that that's two-thousand people who are willing to give your demon ass the benefit of the doubt," he continued, unperturbed. "Now, I know it might not seem like much when you stack it against Team Stabby-Stab's numbers, but that's still two-thousand victories by my count. Two-thousand more victories than it sounds like you woke up with this morning. And that's not half bad for a day's work, right?"

I stared at my friend, waiting for the arguments to come—that even with a sturdy fortress around us, two-thousand people couldn't compete against the entire world. That reframing the hard facts with bullscud positivity wasn't going to do anything to pull our collective ass out of the fire. That we were living right smack in the middle of a fae tale if we believed for one second that any of this could make a difference when the Sanctum, and most of the planet with them, had already made up their minds.

But each argument fell short on its path from my brain to my tongue, each one running up against a tiny obstruction, so small and simple that it seemed almost laughable it could halt any thought at all. But there it was.

Two-thousand victories.

It was a nonsense distinction, calling it anything other than a single rebellious uprising. But it was *also* two-thousand victories. Two-thousand separate victories that Glenbark had won simply by standing tall and following her own compass. Two-thousand men and women who were willing to fight for an Enochia where people like me were subject to the same rights and laws as anyone else, even if we were a royal pain in the ass.

And if Freya Glenbark could convince two-thousand to follow her, then why not twenty-thousand? Why not *two-hundred* thousand?

"I think Freya's starting to rub off on you," I said quietly.

"If only," Johnny murmured, a wistful expression touching his face before he shook it off and focused a frown back on me. "But why do you say that?"

"Because you're starting to make a habit of making more sense than I'm ready to deal with."

"That's an insult as much as a compliment, you know, " he said, tapping thoughtfully at his jawline. "But I'll *choose* to take it as the latter. Because that's what we can do, see, when someone gives us a hard bit of blunt opinion."

"Yeah, yeah," I muttered.

Glenbark's door hissed open before either of us could say anything more, and General Hopper appeared to invite us all inside. Johnny and I filed in behind Garrett and the others. I exchanged a brief hello with Dillard and a few polite if not quite friendly nods with some of the other ordos and captains gathered.

All told, there were fourteen of us. More than enough to make Glenbark's recent downgrade in office space rather noticeable, but we filed in and found our seats around the table without complaint.

"Red," Johnny said, settling down beside Garrett, who favored him with the narrowed eyes one might normally reserve for a particularly aggravating pimple.

"I trust you all saw the High Cleric's cease and desist warning last night?" Glenbark asked from the head of the table before the chatter could pick up.

Unanimous nods around the room.

"I was kinda surprised not to wake up under siege," Johnny admitted.

"Rest assured, they're out there," said General Hopper. "They haven't found the stomach yet to close the perimeter and establish a proper siege, but I doubt it'll be long before they do. We received another legion of supporters from the southern outposts at first light."

That earned him several surprised looks and a few excited murmurs among the officers. I felt a little flicker of hope myself. Five-hundred more victories wasn't bad. But the room sobered quickly enough when Hopper added, "Even Gregor Auckus isn't fool enough to allow this to continue freely."

"What do we intend to do if they press further than a perimeter siege, sir?" asked one of the captains.

The question was obviously intended on a higher level. Every officer in this room knew exactly what tactics and actions to apply if Oasis came under attack. But as to whether to order triggers pulled when it was legionnaires and Sanctum Guard on the other side of the barrels...

"I spoke to the High Cleric this morning," Glenbark said, rescuing Hopper from the council's focus. "The contents of that conversation are what I called this council to disclose."

That didn't sound overly promising. Immediately, I wondered if anything I'd told her about the Sanctum's origins had come up, but now was hardly the time to ask.

"As you're all aware," she continued, "we are assembled here outside of what the High Cleric and the acting High General Auckus have deemed our lawful right. They say that I am a criminal and that any man or woman acting under my orders will likewise henceforth be treated as such. That said, I want you to all understand that you are not bound here today. If you share my loyalty to the Legion oaths we swore, and if you agree that it is our duty to defend any and all law-abiding Enochians against any threat domestic, foreign, or divine, then I welcome you by my side gladly. If, however, you wish to leave, you may walk away from this table and this fortress without fear of punishment. The High Cleric himself has claimed you may return to your former stations in the same fashion, if you choose to trust his word. I leave it to you."

The silence that followed, while undoubtedly grim, did not feel like one of hesitation so much as one of mutual respect, each assembled member allowing his or her fellows the chance to speak first.

"We're with you, High General," one of the captains finally said, to the solemn nods of all her peers.

"You already know where we stand, sir," Dillard added.

Glenbark looked around the table, waiting to see if anyone would say otherwise.

No one did.

"Then I am proud to serve with each and every one of you," she finally said. "And you should know, first and foremost, that after my having talked with the High Cleric, I genuinely believe peace to be untenable with his regime. Indeed, at this point, I suspect that, even if we were to turn over every gifted individual currently in our protection, the High Cleric would not rest until he'd seen each and every one of us stripped of our power— and possibly of our lives as well."

A tangible wave of unease passed through the room, carried around the table on the backs of nervous glances and uncomfortable shifting. General Hopper frowned at Glenbark, apparently not approving of her candor in front of the troops.

"I do not make this claim lightly," Glenbark said, unfazed, "nor will I pretend it to be anything more than my personal appraisal. The High Cleric did not say as much directly. But from what I have seen of this man and his fervent zealotry to uphold what he deems to be the Will of Alpha, it is my honest belief that he would kill outside of our worldly laws to see to it that the Sanctum remains unchallenged, even by the Legion. Which is exactly why he supplanted me with Gregor Auckus, a man who has resided deeply in the Sanctum's pocket for some time now. Perhaps it is melodramatic of me to say, but it seems in our efforts to pry Enochia from the clutches of the raknoth, we've allowed it to land squarely in the grasp of two men who would see the world serve their will rather than any other alternative."

She paused to look around the table, allowing time for argument, or maybe just to process.

"Forgive my bluntness, High General," said the captain who'd spoken earlier, "but how do we aim to rectify the situation?"

"You needn't apologize for bluntness here, Captain Tennin," Glenbark said. "And as for the *how*, we will begin by taking back Haven."

That caused the first real stir among the officers—all of them, including Hopper, exchanging worried looks, like they'd just received the confirmation they'd secretly been fearing all along: that their High General had indeed lost her mind.

"Don't mistake my simplicity to mean I expect it will be easy," Glenbark said. "It will not be easy. But it is possible. I was awake through the night, speaking with dozens of officers stationed in Haven and elsewhere. Today, I will speak with dozens more, and I expect the consensus will be much the same. There are those who firmly believe in what Auckus and the Sanctum did to me at Haven. Some refuse even to speak with me. But for each of those non-allies, there are many more who are disturbed by what's happened. They are afraid and conflicted. And they might well be willing to do something about it."

"Sir," one of the captains said, "even if we were to resume control of Haven…"

"You wonder how it would be any different than before."

The captain gave a curt nod, avoiding her eyes. "Yes, sir."

Glenbark looked around the table.

"I failed you all before. I underestimated the High Cleric's resolve to act so boldly right at the heart of our power. For that, I am sorry. Lives were lost. And Enochia was shaken. And for all of it, I claim my due responsibility. But I promise you, on the sanctity of the office that I swore to execute, I will not make that mistake again. We will take back our Legion. We will offer our brothers and sisters the same choice I offered you. And most importantly, we will open our doors and offer protection to anyone and everyone who would be persecuted outside the bounds of established law by the Sanctum or any other powers that be."

"Freya…" Hopper said, rousing from his silent reflections with a startled expression. By the look on his face when she turned to him, I'm not sure he'd meant to speak at all.

"It is an exploitable vulnerability, yes," she said, not flinching from the fact. "One the Sanctum may well try to use against us, even. After everything that's happened to Enochia, though… Call me idealistic, General, but I think we've had enough of world powers neglecting to espouse the very values for which they claim to be fighting. And so, when I say this Legion will uphold our oaths to Enochia, what I mean is that we will protect those in need—not once we have the power, not once circumstances favorably permit, but from now until such time as Alpha himself descends with hard proof that these men and women are anything less than rightful citizens of Enochia." Her lip quirked. "And even then, I might still have a few questions."

Whether it was the words themselves, or just the cold fire with which they spilled out of her, that earned a round of thumps on the table from the officers. Johnny and I joined in, as did Garrett and the other Shapers.

Only General Hopper refrained, watching Glenbark with a critical stare. It was only when she turned his way that he gave her a conciliatory tilt of the head. The gesture seemed to cause him physical pain.

"What of the High Cleric himself, sir?" Dillard asked. "If he can't be met in peace, what are we to do when the time comes?"

"We could kill the bastard," Garrett muttered. "Theoretically," he added at the number of heads turning his way. Siren even shot him a look, though I'm positive it was more for him to shut his mouth than out of any moral disagreement.

"What?" Garrett asked. "He knowingly pressed the kill switch that was supposed to remove eleven of our heads. And that was just a Juveday morning for the guy."

"He *has* condemned many Enochians to death behind closed doors," Adam said. "Both before and during his short time as High Cleric."

For a second, I almost thought Enid was going to pitch in as well, but then she relaxed in her chair, apparently satisfied with what had already been said. She and Adam both looked immeasurably better than they had the day before—though that wasn't saying much considering they'd been beaten and tied up for a public execution yesterday. Siren, too, looked markedly more composed after a good night's rest, though she still visibly winced with every small movement.

Much as the thought of having these ex-Shaper-killers sharing in our inner circle still bothered me on an idealistic level, I had to admit it was actually kind of nice, not being the only Shaper at the table. It gave someone else a chance to draw all the furtive glances.

"Even if he has committed worthy crimes against Enochia," Glenbark was saying, "which is not the topic of this council, killing him is the one thing I am sure we cannot do. Such an act would leave our Legion irrevocably tainted in the eyes of the Alpha-fearing public."

"What if we could show Enochia his true colors?" my mouth asked before I'd given it proper permission.

So much for letting those other Shapers draw the glances.

"You've seen what's inside of him," I pushed on, meeting Glenbark's eyes —that piercing gaze that never waned, never seemed to miss a thing. If I'd seen the darkness lurking in the High Cleric, there was no way she'd missed it. "There's violence in him. Hatred. All the things a High Cleric is said to have transcended. If we were to somehow show that to the world…"

I wasn't sure how it might be done, or whether it would make a difference, or even if that difference would be in our favor. It was a figment of an idea. And one I wished I'd have thought out more thoroughly before speaking, as I felt the weight of thirteen stares holding on me.

"How would you propose to do this, Citizen Raish?" General Hopper asked.

"Well…" I shrugged. "I know he despises me. I doubt it'd be that hard to get him to show it in person if he thought no one was—"

"No," Glenbark said.

It came so suddenly and with such authority that, for a second, all I could do was stare.

"For now," she continued, turning back to the rest of the small council, "we will focus on…"

Her voice trailed off in my mind as I sat there, waiting for the indignant frustration to come. There I'd been, trying to offer myself up for the cause again, only to be shot down before I could take off. And I was grateful, I realized with a flicker of surprise. It wasn't anger that came, but relief. I felt like a weary traveler who'd unexpectedly reached the top of the climb when he was sure there'd been miles left to go.

Because I *was* weary.

I didn't want to face that man down again. I didn't want to find out if I could fight my way clear after the fact. All I wanted at that point was to fall into a comfortable bed with Elise, and to never leave it again.

I looked self-consciously around at the gathering, sure that they'd see my red-faced shame at sitting here on the brink of a revolution, grateful that I'd not actually been tasked with the worthy sacrifice I'd so hastily thought to offer up. But no one seemed to be paying attention to me at all. And that was a relief as well.

When had I become a tired coward?

"Your assignments, accordingly, are equally unorthodox," Glenbark was saying. "We will meet again this afternoon to begin stress-testing the campaign plan, but between now and then, I want each of you to reach out to your most trusted peers. Mention nothing of our specific designs on Haven, but do not hesitate to converse openly about what has happened to our Legion, and why we seek to restore the integrity of our oaths."

A few of the officers, Dillard included, looked like they'd have rather been given orders to march straight on the White Tower than to play diplomat, but no one said a word.

"I recommend you take some time before you begin," Glenbark continued. "Reflect on what it is you're fighting for, and why you believe it matters. Talk to your soldiers if you so wish, or reflect privately. It matters not, so long as you can look your colleagues in the face and tell them with conviction why we are doing this, and why we have run afoul of those claiming to represent the rule of Enochia."

She looked around the table, favoring each of her officers in turn with an expression that was hard to describe. Not a smile, but a kind of stern pride with just enough of a hint of friendly camaraderie to make good soldiers hop to. And so they did, each ordo and captain sitting just a little straighter as Glenbark's gaze found them.

"That is all for now," she finally said. "Thank you. All of you. You are dismissed."

Compared to the tidy salutes and the crisp movements of the officers rising to clear the room, I must've looked like a drunk. I rose to join Johnny and the Shapers in filing out of the room, still wondering what critical error had occurred in my base programming to have left me feeling like this.

I almost jumped when Johnny unexpectedly grabbed my arm out in the hallway. He frowned down at his palmlight for a second, then nodded we should go the other way, toward the unused office we'd used the day before to talk to Elise and Alton Parker. I didn't argue. I did glance back over my shoulder as we parted from the small traffic stream. As had been the case in Glenbark's office, no one seemed to notice or think twice about what I was or wasn't doing. No one but General Hopper, who watched us go with a curious frown but said nothing.

"What's up?" I asked when Johnny pulled us into the empty office. "If this is about what I said back there..."

He shook his head and brandished his palmlight. "Just following orders like a good servitor. I think she wants to talk to you in private."

"Oh."

That was… unexpected.

"Though, for the record," he added, "I didn't love where that High Cleric stuff was headed either."

"Yeah, me neither," I said, suddenly kind of wishing Johnny had pulled me in here solely to have words about what I'd said in there. For a second, I even wanted to point out that I'd been relieved to have been shut down by Glenbark. Then I realized I kind of just had, and that Johnny was staring at me like I'd just coughed up a hairball.

"Are you okay?" he asked.

"Yeah, I'm just… Bad night's sleep, is all. I'll be fine."

"Right, sure." He eyed me speculatively, clearly not taking me at my word. "Well, just wait here a minute either way. I'll be right back."

32

DAMNED IF YOU'RE DAMNED

I didn't argue as Johnny slipped out of the meeting room, nor did I manage to assemble my thoughts into anything resembling "tidy" or "coherent" before the door opened a few minutes later, and Glenbark slipped into the room alone. I caught a flash of Johnny outside as she pulled the door closed behind her. Then it was just the two of us.

That didn't bode well.

"What you said about showing the High Cleric's true colors," she said slowly. "Did you have a plan?"

My stomach fell. "No."

She cocked her head slightly as if to say she could hardly believe that.

"Not a good one," I clarified.

"Sadly," she said, "I think the time for good plans might be behind us."

"But then why did you…" I considered what I was about to ask, and sank into the closest chair with the weight of my own answer. "You don't trust that council?"

She took a few steps closer, speaking in a voice that would not be overheard, even by Johnny outside the door.

"If we are seriously going to consider putting you back in harm's way, I'm not going to take any undue risks."

"Sir, I… I didn't think before I spoke in there. I don't have a real plan. I'm not even sure it would matter if I did."

She was watching me intently enough that I felt the need to bow my head just to escape her scrutiny.

"Wingard told me what he said to you yesterday," she finally said.

"He did?" I spouted, looking up before I could contain myself. More calmly, I added, "Well, that was… just a friend being a friend. I'm pretty sure we have more important things to worry about."

She looked unconvinced. "He seemed quite worried his words might affect your judgment moving forward."

And there it was—the tiny flicker of irritation that was the first sign of life I'd felt inside all day.

So now Johnny was playing part-time soothsayer and reporting back to Glenbark on my mental wellbeing?

"Well," I said, "I opened my mouth in there today, didn't I? Clearly I'm not too rattled to spout off half-cocked bullscud plans."

"So there *is* a plan."

"No." I scowled at her. "There's just me, starting another war because I was stupid enough to think I could solve the world's problems."

Glenbark took a composed breath, preparing to deliver a no-doubt equally composed reply. And then she did something I'd scarcely seen before. She hesitated. But not in the way I'd seen her do on a few choice occasions, when circumstances had called for a particularly challenging decision. This was different. This wasn't just the cogs turning in her head. This was her emotions bleeding through at the edges. Her ever-present defenses peeling away, layer by layer, until I almost felt as if it were just another human standing before me, and not the fearsome High General of the Legion.

It was Freya Glenbark as I'd never seen her, and I didn't understand why I was seeing it even then.

She hovered there, hesitating, withering, until finally she sank into the chair beside me, her gaze fixed on something buried far away in her mental landscape. I watched her in the stretching silence, at a loss for what to say, or for what I'd even done.

"Do you think I'm afraid, Haldin?"

No, I wanted to say reflexively. *Of course not.*

How could she be? I'd never met anyone so fearless, so single-mindedly disciplined and composed under pressure. No one but Carlisle, at least.

And yet, as I looked at her, and as I thought about the way Carlisle must've felt on his final flight into Divinity, and about the way I felt now, I found myself slowly starting to nod.

"Yes," I whispered.

She showed me the pained ghost of a smile. "I am terrified. But no one outside this room can ever know that, can ever so much as suspect it. The minute they do…" She shook her head, leaving the obvious unsaid.

I swallowed. "Why are you telling me, sir?"

She just looked at me like she expected I already knew somewhere deep down. And, on a more careful look, I guess it was kind of obvious, if I simply forgot for a minute who it was I was dealing with. She was telling me because, deep down, Freya Glenbark was human like the rest of us. Maybe she was tougher. More disciplined. More everything. But not enough to transcend that one simple fact of humanity, and the accompanying fact that, at some point, these things needed to be said to someone. To anyone.

And for some reason, she'd apparently decided I was that person.

"Wingard is right in a way, you know," she said quietly. "Most of us have little choice in casting ourselves as the heroes of our own little stories. That's human nature. But believing yourself the hero of something bigger, something that by all rational means should stand outside your circle of control… There's an unmistakable danger in allowing yourself to fall for such a fantasy. But also, I think, an unmistakable strength. A strength I'm not sure one can find anywhere else. The strength I always thought it must require to take the weight of the world on one's shoulders. But do you know what I've come to understand, in all my years of service?"

She straightened, rousing from her thousand-yard stare, but not quite looking at me.

I watched, silently waiting for her to continue.

"Sometimes," she said, "the smallest things can be every bit as meaningful as the great heroic feats. Sometimes, the ordo who takes the extra second to calm one shaking greenhorn can have just as much impact as the captain who goes down with the carrier to buy his legion more time. Sometimes, both of them can share far more impact than the general who deludes himself into believing that he is the one to decide the day simply by merit of which plan he assigns a 'yes' or a 'no' to." She shook her head, rejecting the idea. "The smallest actions, executed at the right times, and for the right reasons, can be every bit as heroic as a defiant High General making a grand stand, or a young Shaper saving a full transport of legionnaires from certain death."

She looked at me then—looked at me as she never had before—and I'm not sure if I felt twenty years older or she looked twenty younger. All I know is that, in that moment, I felt connected to her in a way I couldn't rationally explain, like she'd shared a sacred part of herself with me. A part that might well take me years to truly understand, but that was no less powerful for it in the moment.

"I'm not asking you to be a hero, Haldin. I'm not even asking you to have the courage to do what you think is right. I already know you have it. All I'm asking is for you to believe in yourself, just a little longer. Believe in yourself, and in what we're doing here."

"Following my heart is part of what's led us into this mess," I said, dropping her gaze.

"Yes, and also a part of what's given us hope through it, and what's allowed us to overcome what well could've been a world-ending invasion. I won't claim your actions have been without flaw, and nor should you. But that hardly means you've failed."

"I know that." Of course I knew that. But I also knew now that I'd meddled in affairs laughably far beyond my mortal—and admittedly naive —grasp, and that things were only going to get worse from here before they got better. Doubly so, I could only imagine, if I was actively involved.

"I just don't know how to help anymore," I concluded, opting to leave out the additional, *Short of scrubbing lavatories, keeping my cursed demon head down, or flying off across the galaxy to confront Alton Parker's problems instead.*

Given the direction the conversation was taking, I expected she was about to tell me exactly what I should do to help anyway. Only, for the second time, she got that hesitant look in her eyes, like even after everything she'd just disclosed to me, she still hadn't gotten around to the real thing she didn't want to have to say out loud.

"Do you believe the Sanctum is evil at its core?" she finally asked.

I thought about my answer, making sure I meant it. "No. Not really."

I wanted to, of course. This all probably would've been a whole scudload easier if I had believed it. But even beneath the foundation of lies, and after everything I'd been through at the hands of two High Clerics, it simply wasn't fair to discount every other good deed the Sanctum had ever done, or every well-meaning believer who'd ever etched Alpha's sigil over their breast.

Not that any of that made the answer less sour on my tongue.

Glenbark, at least, looked marginally relieved. "Nor do I," she said. "I admit, my faith in Alpha has been somewhat shaken by what we've learned about the Sanctum's origins, but I sense we are in agreement when I propose that an entire people's worth cannot be so easily summed by the actions of a powerful few over the years."

I didn't particularly feel like agreeing out loud, so I said nothing, waiting for her to get to the point. She took her time.

"You said you don't know how to help anymore," she finally said.

"I just meant that—" I started, feeling the reflexive need to defend myself.

She raised a hand for pause before I was faced with the awkward proposition of explaining what exactly I *had* in fact meant.

"Do you know why everyone considered your father such a stellar leader?"

That caught me off guard.

I studied her expression, looking for whatever test I expected must be afoot. "Because he was willing to do whatever he had to for his legionnaires," I finally said, trying not to make it sound like a question. "Even if it meant pissing the wrong people off."

She nodded. "That was certainly a large part of it. Undoubtedly the loudest, most widely observed part. But do you know what most people failed to take note of once those heroic moments had passed?"

I shook my head slowly, curious as to where she was going with this, and not especially loving the feeling of being quizzed on my understanding of my own dad.

"Your father knew when to stand up for what he believed in," Glenbark said, nodding. "That much is irrefutable. But what many of my colleagues seem to take for granted is that he also knew when to sit down and allow others to take up the charge, so to speak. It is a rare skill indeed."

I thought about that, trying the idea on for size. It didn't sound right at first pass. My dad had never sat back a day in his life. He'd worked tirelessly, without complaint. Every bit the ambitious, driven leader. Except I couldn't deny that his ambition had always been a source of confusion for me.

For instance, I knew for a fact that he'd once turned down an offer to be considered for the seat of the retiring General Danton—a seat that most of his fellow officers would've killed for, and one that everyone had assumed would be his if he would only accept it.

I'd wondered more than a few times over the years why he hadn't accepted that offer. Everyone who knew about it seemed to have had an opinion on the matter, though most of them did their best to avoid letting his son hear about it. Still, it'd been impossible to miss a mutter here or there at the time. He'd simply been afraid, some had said, scornfully. Or he'd obviously been hiding something. I vaguely remember a few of the older doceres, Mathis included, treating me oddly at the time. Not kindly, exactly, but... different. I'd never understood why. I'd worked up the courage to ask my dad once—why he'd turned down the offer, why everyone seemed so upset about it.

To my shame, I couldn't even remember now what answer he'd given me.

So maybe Glenbark had a point about people taking that side of him for granted. If this was even what she was getting at.

"You mean because he passed up General Danton's seat?" I asked.

She tilted her golden head in partial agreement. "Again, certainly the most bold example of his philosophy. But it's not as simple as that." She paused for a few seconds, searching for the right words. "For all mortal servants, the time eventually comes when the highest possible contribution they may make is to step aside, and to allow their legacy to flourish absent their guiding hands. If your father had pushed forward and become a general, if he'd tried to more directly impose his spirit on the Legion from a position of higher power, he might well have soured the many hearts he'd already touched, corrupting the foundations of his contribution. Or he might not have. That outcome was beyond his control, you see. And I believe he understood that. So instead, he showed the world his truth—brilliantly, decisively—and then he allowed them to do as they would, always continuing to serve, but never thinking to impose his beliefs on any who did not come to them willingly. Indeed, never thinking at all that he knew better than anyone else to begin with, only that he was dedicated to serving the world in a way that felt true to himself."

She gave a sad smile, shaking her head at some thought or memory. "In the end, it's not such a wonderful example, seeing as I truly believe your father would have made an exceptional general. But that hardly cheapens the honor and value of what he accomplished with his life. In a world that too readily derives discipline from power, authority, and fear, your father led by true inspiration. He was a great man."

For a long time, I couldn't do much more than stare down at my hands, turning her words over, trying to quell the longing ache in the back of my throat.

"Are you saying you want me to step aside?" I finally asked, pretty sure I already knew both parts of the answer.

"Not yet," she said.

"But soon," I finished, feeling the heavy weight of the certainty in my own words.

Because soon, no matter what else happened with the Sanctum and the Legion, and with the war on Shapers itself, I was probably going to have to face the fact that I was no longer welcome in the eyes of Enochia. Because I'd become too much of a liability. Because I'd scorched their collective nerves one too many times for the world to ever do anything but eye me warily from across a wide, empty room.

I searched Glenbark's expression for any sign that I'd misread her meaning, not really expecting to find it, not really expecting anything but a look of grim apology in the face of the inevitable. But she didn't look grim. Or apologetic.

She studied me thoughtfully, looking—if anything—mildly amused, silent respect brimming in her eyes. She looked at me like we'd already been through the worst of the scud, and now it was simply time to finish the thing, so that we might one day sit back and share an incredulous laugh over the fact that we'd somehow survived the journey to demons' depths and back.

"You have more truth to show the world than possibly anyone in history, Haldin," she said. "Hard truth. And while it's possible, with time and care, that the magnitude of your service to Enochia might come to outweigh the fear—"

"I'm also the Demon of Divinity. And I always will be in their heads. Or in enough of them, at least."

I'm not sure why I expected her to argue the point. I guess I didn't, really. Whatever else she was, Freya Glenbark was not a light-handed scud-spout. But a part of me still hoped that she'd correct me anyway. That she'd suddenly reveal the magical insight she'd been sitting on this whole time— the one that would allow us to set the records straight, end all of the wars, and give me my life back, once and for all.

But all I got was a sad smile and a tired sigh as she rested heavily back into her chair beside me, both of us staring at the blank display on the wall in companionable silence.

"You are the Demon of Divinity," she finally agreed. "And here I am disclosing my deepest, darkest fears to a teenager who just so happens to be the most wanted man on the planet." She shot me a sideways look. "Can you promise me you'll remember that part next time you find your resolve waning?"

I opened my mouth to tell her I would, but nothing came out. I couldn't even seem to nod. It was just too much in that moment. No surprise. Nothing I hadn't seen coming from a hundred miles away. And yet in that moment I felt like a little kid who'd just found out his first hound had died.

"This has never been your fault, Haldin," she said. "No more than it's been mine, or even the High Cleric's. What we're looking at is the inevitable shifting after a thousand years of building a world on faulty foundations. Perhaps events could've unfolded slightly differently. Perhaps the damage could've been better contained. But this conflict was always bound to happen as long as those in power were willing to lie to keep it."

She looked at me, and I could see the innumerable layers of her armor beginning to pull back into place, marking the end of the rarefied moment of Freya Glenbark's vulnerability.

"Agreed?" she asked.

I swallowed, and nodded.

"Good," she said. "So tell me, then... What will you require for this half-cocked non-plan of yours?"

33

DARK STARS

I t was a quiet night in Humility.

The air behind the Dark Star Tavern was as still as it was thick. Dark, too, almost like a small singularity had opened up and swallowed every scrap of streetlight and every sound of clinking glass attempting to permeate the dampened space of our surroundings.

All in all, it was a great place for a crash landing.

Not that the landing itself was all that bad, really. With three Shapers in our free-falling huddle, there was more than enough telekinetic juice to go around—even with the extra raknoth in tow. It was more just the indignity of having to sneak into the city slums at all, acting like covert specter skim-divers, minus the glidesuits. Given the general haze of disgruntled irritation hanging in the air between me and my companions post-landing, I gathered we were all more or less on the same page there.

"This feels like the beginning of a scuddy joke," Siren grumbled from beside her dumpster of choice.

"Hiding out behind a scuddy tavern like a pack of frightened rodents," Garrett said. "That's the joke."

I felt more than saw him glance at Siren in the darkness, no doubt wanting to add that bringing her into the field when she'd been shot only yesterday was also part of this not-so-funny joke. She reached up and cupped his cheek before he could, sweetly and silently daring him to say it. He was too busy melting to her touch, as he always seemed to do.

It never ceased to weird me out, how cuddly the two ex-Seekers were around each other when either one of them probably could've killed a man for sneezing wrong. But then again, maybe I wasn't in any position to judge, dragging us all into harm's way just to find Elise.

I certainly wasn't in any position to comment on the matter of braving the field while sporting significant injuries. My tender, splinted wrists were testament enough to that. None of us were quite crippled after a day-and-a-half's intensive healing at the medica, but nor were we anywhere close to prime fighting condition.

Well, none of us but Alton Parker, at least.

I glanced at the raknoth's silhouette in the shadows, half-expecting him to weigh in on Garrett and Siren's exchange with some glib remark of his own, but he said nothing. Somehow, that irritated me even more. I looked around in the darkness for the thousandth time, resisting the urge to check my palmlight and create any unnecessary light. I would've felt the vibration from Elise's message if it had come.

I sank deeper into my extended senses instead, surveying the drunken inhabitants of the Dark Star Tavern and trying not to give over to the bitterness eating slowly at my insides.

Even when I'd been on the run with Carlisle, and all of Enochia had thought us apostate terrorists of the highest order, I'd never felt so hunted and on guard. Back then, we'd been frightening criminals—an unpleasant sideshow thought that would undoubtedly be handled by the authorities sooner or later. But now...

Now we were Alpha-damned demons, and all it would take was one unlucky glance and a few alarmed cries before half of the good people of Humility took to the streets and flooded into this alleyway after us with whatever crude weapons they could find.

Even getting picked up from Oasis that night had felt like a tremendous risk, what with the thousands upon thousands of Auckus' twitchy legionnaires gathering for the siege out there, watching Glenbark's base through Alpha only knew how many different scanners, scopes, and good old-fashioned eyeballs.

Under the cover of nightfall, though, Parker had seemed confident enough that his ship was capable of making the pickup without detection. And given that they hadn't been hounded down by an entire armada of Auckus' fighters within thirty seconds of takeoff, it appeared that the raknoth had indeed been correct.

Unless we were still being followed.

It seemed impossible. We'd taken every possible precaution, including an extra orbit around Enochia and a liberal use of Siren's propensity for arcane camouflage. But you never really knew for certain. Especially not when the entire planet was on the lookout for you and your friends.

I frowned over at Siren and Garrett, whose silhouettes were meshing together rather closely in the dark now, and lamented having even thought the word. Friends? Friends with the people who'd tried to kill me? And not just tried, but tried *emphatically*? Somehow, with the exception of Elise, Johnny, and the others, that was about all I had left on this Alpha-cursed planet right now.

"If you two can't keep your hands to yourselves for a single mission..." I started, before promptly realizing I had no idea what exactly I had left to threaten the two swive fiends with.

I'd already dragged them out here, after all.

Not that "dragged" was really the right word for it. Once I'd clued the ex-Seekers in on the plan back at Oasis—or, more specifically, the moment I'd mentioned the name, Burton Kovaks—Garrett had been rather insistent on coming. Insistent to an extent that had only raised my initial hesitation to the idea all the more. Adding more volatile variables to this walking firebomb of a plan had hardly seemed a smart move. Moreover, Garrett hadn't exactly been forthcoming about his interest in meeting Kovaks—only that he had something important to tell the man. Something personal.

None of it helped quell the nervous wriggling in my stomach. But the ex-Seekers were our allies now, no matter how I wanted to look at it, and Elise's messages had specifically indicated that I should bring two of them along.

If that was what the keepers of the Emmútari remnant had decreed, who was I to tell them how to do their jobs?

"She's close," Parker said quietly, breaking the tense silence.

I pulled my mind back to the present and swept our surroundings. There was no immediate sign of Elise's presence, but on closer inspection, I could feel the trace hints of her—the faintest trail of her scent and her warmth, caught through my extended senses rather than from the embrace of my arms, as I would have preferred. Like catching the first smell of home, I couldn't help but think.

So maybe Garrett wasn't the only mushy one out here. But that was just fine, I decided, as Elise dialed her cloaking field out further and enabled me to bask in the welcome comfort of her approaching presence.

"Three Shapers and a raknoth walk into a tavern..." came her voice in my mind.

My lips quirked in a grin. "Pretty sure Garrett's dying to hear the rest of this one."

She said nothing, but I knew her mental touch well enough to recognize the ebb of fading humor. So maybe I hadn't been the only one with reservations about bringing two ex-Seekers and a raknoth along. But we were well past the point of no return now. The sight of Elise's lithe silhouette sliding into the alleyway ahead swept all the negative thoughts aside for the moment. Right up until the moment a second shadow ghosted into the alleyway behind her—the lanky, hawk-nosed shadow that could only be Burton Kovaks.

Joy.

I forced myself to take a breath, resisting the urge to sweep my senses over the man and risk triggering that silver-gilded knockout wand of his, and whatever defensive runes had shut me down the last time we'd met. Instead, I focused on the sight of Elise moving to me at a dignified but crisp pace. Dignified, that was, until she drew close enough that we both broke down and dashed forward into a rough hug.

Alpha, did it feel good to hold her in my arms. So good that it seemed a little obscene in the moment that I could ever even consider letting her go again—especially out here in this mad world of ours. If ever there was a reason to recommend a nice near-death experience to someone, I'm pretty sure there's something to be said about the sheer magnitude of relief and gratitude one might experience after the fact, upon being reunited with the one they love.

In that moment, I could have died happy.

In that moment, I kind of wished we would have, together. Because I knew that the moment was leaving, just as soon as it came. And because I knew what lay on the other side of it.

"You didn't say you were bringing *him*," came Burton Kovak's haggard voice.

I didn't have to look to know who he was referring to. I glanced around anyway, and was unsurprised to see Kovaks staring at Alton Parker with wary loathing.

Alton was supremely unperturbed by the tangible ill will.

"I figured it was kind of implied," I said, reluctantly parting from Elise, "seeing as there was no way we were getting out of Oasis otherwise."

"Then you shouldn't have come at all," Kovaks said. "Especially not you, Raish. Not after—"

"I think that's enough posturing," Elise cut in, firm but somehow still amicable. Every bit the daughter of Francesco Fields. "We're all here because we want the same thing. What we should be focusing on is getting off the streets before a band of merry do-gooders happens by and recognizes one of us."

As if to punctuate her statement, a pack of overly rambunctious tavern-goers shambled past the mouth of the alleyway, singing a disjointed chorus of an old tavern classic. They might not have noticed us at a glance—especially not with how quickly we all scurried into the shadows like Garrett's frightened rodents—but it was more than enough to drive the point home.

More than enough for most of us, at least.

"Not a chance," Kovaks said when the civilians had passed, shaking his head emphatically. "We're not taking the raknoth. And we shouldn't even be—"

A sharp slam sounded right behind us. I whirled in time to see the Dark Star's shoddy back door fly fully open and smack into the wall with another unpleasantly attention-grabbing *crack*. A drunken belch poured out of the open doorway, shortly followed by a shuffling mountain of a man who had the clear look of a drunkard looking for a place to empty his bladder.

Instead, he stumbled out into the alleyway and found himself a shadowy congregation of six illegals.

He froze, drunken eyes squinting at us in the dim light of the door, trying to decide if he was indeed seeing what he thought he was.

I felt Alton Parker ghosting forward, preparing to pounce. I reached out, thinking to stop him. Then the mountainous drunkard collapsed in front of us—strings cut like magic. He hit the ground hard. I glanced back at Kovaks, expecting to see that arcane wand of his in hand, but he looked just as surprised as I felt. Then I looked back to our unlucky intruder, and understood.

Siren had materialized from the darkness just behind him, her hand still raised to the spot where his head had been, her nose wrinkled in disdain as she surveyed the undignified heap of a man at her feet.

For a few seconds, we were all frozen too.

Then Garrett rounded back on Kovaks. "And how about now?"

Kovaks shook his head again, his dark scowl just barely visible in the dim light. "Not a chance, Garrett Fellwood." He glanced at Siren. "Alexia Arkova."

They both bristled at the brazen use of their names, but Kovaks pushed on before they could say a thing.

"Much as I would like to say I appreciate your change of heart, I can't let anyone—especially a pair of Shaper killers—see the way in until they've cleared the test. Which, honestly, I'm kind of doubting either of you ever could, considering, but I guess that goes to show you just how far we've fallen."

Alexia straightened at that, puffing her chest out like she was about to fire back, and then some. But Garrett coaxed her down with a raised hand and a shake of his head. Maybe it was just the dim lighting to blame, but I could've sworn he almost looked guilty or apologetic as he turned back to Kovaks, silently inviting the grungy Emmútari envoy to continue if he pleased. It was odd. But not odd enough to make me miss Burton Kovaks reaching for a coat pocket.

I tensed, expecting the worst, but instead of a wand, he only drew out a handful of metallic bracelets. "You three put these on," he started, tossing one each to me, Garrett, and Siren. "And—"

He cut off as I sidestepped my incoming bracelet and let it clatter to the alleyway floor.

It had happened by reflex more than anything—reflex born of the dark, helpless memory of our last meeting, when I'd reached out to defend myself and promptly found myself face-planting into the permacrete, vision darkening, powerless to move.

The pair of metallic clatters on my left flank told me Garrett and Siren had been paying attention when I'd warned them to be careful around Burton Kovaks' hardware.

For several long seconds, we all stared at each other, Elise hovering uncertainly beside me.

"Put them on," Kovaks said slowly. "Put them on, and the raknoth stays behind. Otherwise, this meeting is over."

I glanced suspiciously down at where the bracelet had landed. I could barely see the thing in the dark, and I wasn't about to reach out to inspect it with my senses. Not after what'd happened last time. But either way, I didn't trust the bracelet, and I had even less interest in finding out what would happen if I actually followed Kovaks' instructions and put the thing on.

"I can control the raknoth," I said, looking back up at Kovaks. "And I'm not putting that thing on."

"Then you stay too," he said flatly, turning away from me like I'd ceased to exist, and instead focusing his expectant stare on Garrett and Alexia. "What about the Seekers? Have you all come here just to waste our time tonight?"

"I came to talk to you, actually," Garrett said, earning himself an even more suspicious look from Kovaks.

"Then put the bracelet on," Kovaks said, "and demonstrate that you are safe to talk to."

Garrett glanced to the bracelet at his feet, seeming to consider it.

"Or maybe I just scream *demon* right now instead," Siren said, turning her frown from Garrett back to Kovaks. "You want to see how many of us make it safely back to our little hidey holes once that happens?"

Beside me, I felt Elise's impatience growing on pace with the tightness in Kovaks' jaw. It made me wonder—not for the first time—exactly how much authority she'd been granted in this outfit now that she'd apparently joined up as head Shaper to Kovaks' and Pasty's creepy record-keeper act.

"Your friends are being difficult, Herald," Kovaks said, with a sideways glance at Elise.

So maybe she had *some* clout. And maybe Kovaks even had a point, I decided, now that my nerves were beginning to settle. Because, much as I didn't want to ever experience another round of arcane knockout, I also couldn't believe that Elise and Franco would've both been taken in and fooled by men who truly intended to harm us. Alpha knew they were both better than me at reading people. So maybe it was time to stop arguing and put the first foot forward in this game of trust.

I was opening my mouth to say as much when Elise raised a hand to silence me.

"Our allies are being prudent, Keeper," she countered Kovaks. "I don't need to remind you how few of them we have in total, approved or not, so maybe we can afford to respect that prudence. I don't know about you, but I don't think I really fancy the idea of trying to keep a low profile out there while leading three blinded—"

Kovaks cut her off with a strangled noise somewhere between a growl and a hiss that I could only assume translated loosely into *Shut your Alpha-damned mouth, girl,* while also more or less confirming what those bracelets might do. And just like that, my goodwill evaporated, right along with the good sense that had made me think twice about smacking Kovaks' grimy ass around with telekinesis. Before I could do that, though, and before Kovaks could even find the words to properly express his irritation at Elise's openness, Garrett spoke up, taking us all by surprise.

"I came here to talk about your brother," he said, as if they'd never been interrupted earlier. He bent down to pluck the bracelet carefully from the ground, studied the shiny artifact delicately between thumb and forefinger, then finally tossed it back to its now slack-jawed owner. "I came here to tell you what I know about Andre Kovaks' last days. If you'd like to hear it."

I was too busy gaping to properly register that the bracelet hadn't even stunned his ass into oblivion at first touch.

Andre Kovaks... What in the scud did Garrett know about Andre Kovaks?

The memory of the man's final frantic moments at the gallows played through my mind, as they had so many times before. I didn't have the faintest clue what Garrett knew. But I was pretty sure I'd just gotten my answer as to the nature of his personal business with Burton, here. And as much as I wanted to be irritated by the fact that he hadn't thought to mention this secret knowledge to me in advance—or to Siren either, judging by the look on her face—I couldn't deny that he seemed to have picked the perfect moment to reveal his intentions.

Perfect, that is, or perfectly catastrophic.

Burton Kovaks might've been a statue or a time bomb. Mouth ajar. Eyes dull and lifeless, and locked firmly on Garrett. He held the bracelet that the ex-Seeker had tossed him absentmindedly against his breast, where he'd reflexively caught it, and that infernal little wand of his had found its way into his right hand like it had been waiting right up his dark sleeve the whole time.

For a long moment, no one spoke. Elise and I didn't need telepathy to establish that neither one of us knew what Garrett was playing at, or whether we should try to intervene. But then Kovaks finally stirred, and the time to decide was past. He looked with those apathetic, dead eyes from Garrett to me, then to Alton Parker, and finally to Elise, who gave him a firm nod but refrained from words. Which, given the volatility in the air, was probably a wise choice.

Kovaks stared at her for a few seconds, assessing, then finally blew out a bitter huff and shook his head. "Scud, what do I care? It's your extinction, anyway." His sneer hardened back into something dead serious. "But the raknoth stays."

Elise didn't look like she particularly disagreed with that sentiment. I turned toward Parker, not quite sure what I thought myself, just in time to see the raknoth spring into a silent leap that carried him out of the alleyway and up onto the building across from the Dark Star. He effortlessly vaulted the rooftop lip and disappeared into the night without a backwards glance.

"*Go*," his voice came to me before I could reach out and ask him what the scud he was doing. "*I will wait here, for a time.*"

I considered asking how long that time might be, and whether he would still be in for what we had in mind after I'd procured what help we needed. But it wasn't like I could take him at his word. That was the Holy Rule of dealing with Alton Parker. And I sure as scud didn't want to come across like I was actually worried about losing him as an ally. Aside from it being complete bullscud, that notion made me feel sick on multiple levels. But there were far more reasons than that to think twice about letting a raknoth wander off into the dark.

"*Don't kill anyone,*" I finally sent. It seemed to cover most of the bases.

"*Do not tarry,*" he replied, "*and I doubt I will have to.*"

Wonderful.

What in demons' depths had my world come to, that I could actually sit back and let a creature like Alton Parker roam freely in the heart of a civilian populace?

I looked back down to the dark alleyway with an uneasy feeling in my gut, and realized everyone was watching me.

"He'll hide until we're done," I said, somewhat weakly.

Kovaks' frown darkened. "And you wonder why we're wary of you," he muttered, shaking his head.

I looked to Elise, not really needing an explanation for Kovaks' disgust, but kind of wanting one anyway—or at least some reassurance that I hadn't completely lost my mind. She only shook her head, indicating I should drop it and count the win for now. I tensed reflexively as Kovaks reached for his pocket again, then remembered it hardly mattered anyway. The guy already had his weapon out, after all, following Garrett's unexpected truth bomb.

What Kovaks drew from his pocket looked to be little more than a smooth stone, small enough to sit easily in the palm of his hand. I doubted it was anything so simple, and indeed, he moved with deliberation, pausing only to pocket the bracelets from the ground, and give each of us a pointedly disdainful look as he did. He said nothing, though his gaze did linger especially long on Garrett—dark and distrustful, and more than a little angry beneath the surface.

That done, he turned and walked a short distance down the alleyway, moving with specific purpose.

Again, I glanced at Elise for explanation, but she was frowning after

Kovaks with her own confused look. Ahead, Kovaks shot one last dark frown at the rooftop Alton Parker had disappeared onto, then he leaned in close to the dirty permacrete wall, brushed its surface clear with one hand, and thrust his odd little stone forward with the other.

Understanding dawned with the sound of faint clicks and shifting stone, just before a door-sized section of the old alley wall swung inward on hinges I couldn't see or hear, revealing the unlit way to what I could only assume was some manner of secret passage. I chided myself for not having noticed it earlier in my senses. Of course, it might have been protected by whatever arcane mechanisms had responded to Kovaks' little key stone. But still, it was just a good reminder that, even with all the practice I'd had, it was easier than not to miss the things I wasn't specifically looking for in the flood of information that was my extended senses.

"I knew there was something you weren't telling me about this spot," Elise said, as we all drew up to Kovaks and his mysterious new doorway.

He gave her a kind of sickly sweet scowl that said that his omission was hardly the worst of the transgressions to be counted there that evening, then he turned and stalked silently into the opening, darkness swallowing him whole.

"It's okay," Elise said quietly beside me. "He's like this all the time."

I traded an uncertain look with the two ex-Seekers. Or with Siren, at least. Garrett was busy staring after Kovaks with an uncharacteristically troubled expression. I glanced at the doorway, then back to the rooftops, still not loving the idea of Alton Parker roaming free out there, and wishing more than a little that Johnny—and maybe even Dillard's Hound Company—were here right now, too.

But they weren't. And they wouldn't be. Not like they used to. Not until I'd done what I had to do. Maybe not even then.

"Okay then," I said, carefully setting those darkening thoughts aside and looking back at my companions. "Who's ready to follow the dangerous stranger down the creepy dark passage?"

Garrett started forward after Kovaks without a word or a backward glance.

Siren frowned after him, looking worried, but she covered it up well enough as she turned to us. "Dangerous strangers and dark passages?" She reached up and patted my cheek affectionately. "I used to call that a Juveday night, sweetling."

Then, with a wink at Elise, she turned and followed her man into the darkness.

I found Elise's hand and held it tight, allowing myself to wonder for a few precious seconds what our life would've been if the raknoth had never come to Enochia, and none of this had ever happened—if my abilities had remained dormant, and I'd simply bumped into Elise out on leave from Sanctuary, like a normal legionnaire.

"Still too late for us to run away from all of this?" I asked quietly, giving her hand a squeeze.

She didn't return my feeble attempt at a grin. She just looked tired and worried. Afraid. Whatever feelings she'd been bottling up in the face of our clandestine meeting finally creeping out, now that we had a moment to ourselves.

But the echo of boisterous voices approaching the end of the alleyway reminded me that even this moment was not ours. Not completely.

"Come on," she said, pulling her hand free from mine and starting forward after the others. "We wouldn't wanna be left behind."

"No," I muttered quietly, watching her go with the sinking feeling that, as per usual, she'd intuited entirely more about my intentions than I'd thought possible. "No, I guess we wouldn't."

I took one more glance back at the alleyway—back at the city of Humility, and at the world of Enochia, and all its millions of good, Alpha-fearing people. People who would've sworn on their children's eternal spirits that they wanted nothing more than for us to *be* left behind. People who had no idea what might befall their children's children if we were. I took one more look at it all, reminding myself that it all might still happen even it we weren't, and that I was but one more infinitesimal blip in the roiling ocean of Enochia's fate. It wasn't up to me to decide any of it, I reminded myself. All I could do was what I believed to be right in my heart, and then get the scud out of the way of my own shadow.

Holding that thought in mind, I turned and followed after Elise.

We had a lot to talk about.

3 4

CHILDREN OF ENOCHIA

"Remind me again why you were worried about blindfolding us?" came Siren's voice from the flitting dance of handheld artificial lights and dank shadows ahead. "As if any of us can actually tell where the scud we're at right now."

Past her and Garrett, Kovaks said nothing. Only turned left down the next narrow passageway—which, honestly, given the fact that we had to go single file and sideways to even squeeze through, felt more like an architectural accident than an intentional avenue for travel. Not that Kovaks seemed to mind. Given the timing of the turn in relation to Siren's comment, I wasn't sure it wasn't simply done out of spite, just to throw another wrinkle in our already winding way.

Scud, I wasn't even all that sure we hadn't just been walking in circles for the past twenty minutes.

Initially, I'd assumed Kovaks' hidden passage would lead more or less straight to his and Pasty's secret dungeon. I'd been wrong. And now, a dozen or so turns and mismatched, unlit passageways later, I wasn't really sure of anything beyond the fact there were entirely more abandoned tunnels beneath Humility than I ever would've guessed. Which probably shouldn't have been all that surprising, considering how old the city was. Still, my Legion-trained sense of direction wasn't used to being this thrown, and even my extended senses weren't all that much help.

The fact that Elise was there, and that she didn't seem particularly worried about Kovaks' navigation was the only real comfort I had. She certainly wasn't going out of her way to reassure me otherwise. In fact, she'd been... well, not distant, exactly. Not even cold-shouldered, really. In fact, she'd given me little but what would likely be considered perfectly civil behavior between most lovers. But none of that quite dissuaded me from the feeling that something was up.

Maybe it was just a touch of insecurity over one thing or another. Or maybe there was something going on that I hadn't even thought about. I'd intended to ask as soon as we got to some privacy, but given that that didn't seem to be happening anytime too quickly...

"Are you okay?" I finally sent as we exited the narrow "passageway."

Smooth as ever, I was. But it was something, at least. And after twenty minutes of silent tension, something sure felt better than nothing.

"No," she sent back. *"And neither are you."*

"No," I agreed, seeing no reason not to. *"Not really. But I'm, uh, also not entirely sure what I've done to upset you."*

"Who says you're the one I'm upset with?"

I looked at her, squinting to get a good read on her expression in the dim reflections of our handheld lights. She didn't particularly look like she was trying to back me into a trap. Elise had never really been one to play such games, or to beat around the bush when she had something to say.

That said, I was still hesitant to bite at first. At least until she took my hand in the dark, and I felt the caring in the way her fingers closed around mine.

"You're going after the High Cleric, aren't you?"

I took a steadying breath, resisting the urge to verbally backpedal. We were past all that.

"Maybe. That's what I wanted to talk to you about."

"Oh, good." I felt her sideways glance. *"Well, in that case, I don't think it's a good idea."*

It might've seemed a small thing, but I couldn't overstate how grateful I was for what she *didn't* say in that moment: that going after the High Cleric of the Sanctum was suicide. That I'd be beyond a fool to even think about trying it, never mind the rampant neglect that doing so would clearly demonstrate for the loved ones I'd be leaving behind. That I wasn't going to do it, dammit, and that that was that, and I should just forget about it.

I still felt some of those sentiments lingering there beneath her words, of course. But that was only because Elise wasn't delusional. She understood exactly how dangerous it would be for me to go anywhere near the High

Cleric, but she also wasn't going to insult my intelligence by acting like I didn't understand it too. Instead, she was calmly inviting me to explain myself. It only made me appreciate her all the more.

"I don't like it either, Lise," I admitted, "But he's the single biggest obstacle to ending this war, and I'm pretty sure I—

"Hey, what's the holdup back there?" Kovaks called from ahead, where he was waiting at what looked to be our next turn.

"They're passing secrets," Siren said, in one of her mischievous tones. "Rude."

"Something you need to tell us?" Kovaks asked as we caught up to the rest of the group.

"Not yet," Elise said, glancing at me to see if I had anything to add.

I didn't. Definitely not yet. So I remained silent until Kovaks finished skewering me with his distrustful stare and rounded back to his navigation.

"Come on," he called, not looking back. "We're here."

"We'll talk about it soon?" I sent to Elise, giving her hand a squeeze.

She nodded, not looking especially excited about the prospect. *"I expect we will."*

We followed Kovaks into the next passageway, down a side chute, and finally to an old, sturdy-looking darkwood door that opened with a rich creak to the familiar sight of the dungeon I'd so rudely awakened to only a few cycles ago.

Kovaks waved us in, standing by the door so he could give us each one last warning glare as we entered. I stepped through the doorway behind Garrett and Siren.

The room was large, but fairly cozy on account of the wild variety and volume of its contents. Ancient-looking stone walls and floors, set all around with hand-carved wooden furniture—chests and chairs and tables and shelves, the latter filled to the brim with books upon books. Tomes so ancient-looking, it seemed a mystery they didn't simply disintegrate into thin air.

What shelves and surface weren't covered with books were mostly occupied with a host of mysterious runed devices, not unlike Kovaks' knockout wand and blindfold bracelets, all of them neatly ordered, and meticulously clean like the rest of the room. By comparison to the ancient furnishings and the unquestionably arcane artifacts, the far side of the space—the portion that housed several node workstation displays, as well as a fab, a self-contained hydrocycler, and a few other modern amenities—felt like an odd juxtaposition. A flash of the new, tainting the once-pure memory of a people long-since passed.

It was an interesting sight, to say the least. As were the room's inhabitants. Or two of them, at least.

Franco and James, I'd expected, and was more than a little bit relieved to see. Then there was Pasty—or Omelius, as Elise had called him—a silent curiosity as he hovered in the corner, hands clasped nervously in front of his worn brown robe, studying the new arrivals, bald, barefoot, and portly as ever. Him, I'd expected. But not the fourth.

She was an older woman. Bushy, graying hair, and eyebrows to match. Those eyebrows were restless as she studied our group, and between her slightly mismatched state of dress and the dazed, somewhat dreamy look in her eyes, I got the impression of someone who was chronically frazzled, but also perfectly at peace with that fact.

She looked friendly enough, I decided. And membership issues and syrup-thick tensions aside, I saw no reason not to make myself as harmless as possible in their eyes.

"Hello, everyone," I said. Or started to say, at least, before Kovaks pulled the dungeon door shut and touched that key stone of his to a silver rune on the wall.

It was exactly the kind of kick I'd been tensed for the entire time. Like someone had turned off my lights. Like they'd jammed a cloaking pendant straight down my throat. Only this was different. Not just a partitioning wall on my extended senses. They died completely. I couldn't feel a thing, inside or out, and it happened so quickly, I didn't even have time to think before I'd dropped into a fighting stance, rounding on Kovaks even as he raised his wand at my face.

"It's just a precaution," Elise said quickly, grabbing my arm.

At her touch, the world stopped spinning, and I regained enough higher function to note that she was directing her words at Garrett and Siren, who'd tensed as well, albeit not quite as violently as me.

"An unnecessary one, I'd argue," Elise continued, with a sideways frown at Kovaks, "but one that'll make them feel better until you two are cleared for—"

She cut off like she'd just realized what she was about to say. I might've put that together with the uncertain look she shot me if I hadn't been too busy trying to calibrate to the world that had so suddenly collapsed down to little more than mundane sight and sound, and the grip of Elise's fingers on my arm.

None of it felt right. Like the connections between my brain and my sensory organs had been frayed. Was this how things had always felt before I'd mastered my extended senses? I wasn't sure, but as my heart rate started to come down, I recalled that I'd had a somewhat similar sensation the last time I'd been here. It had just been less alarming then, I guess, given that I'd been too groggy and disoriented to really process it.

"You two, with me," Kovaks said, gesturing to Siren and Garrett before I could even think to ask exactly what he'd done to us. "Get the Judge, Ome. Let's get this over with."

I wasn't sure what he meant by the last bit, but Omelius obviously was. The pasty mute hopped to immediate action, darting with surprising gusto over to a darkwood chest in the corner, bare feet slapping against the stone with each step. From the chest, he withdrew an object that I recognized all too well, even if I still wasn't rightly sure what in the scud it actually was, other than the arcane brain scanner that had apparently convinced Kovaks and Omelius that I really *was* the Demon of Divinity, with a capital D.

Omelius, apparently recalling the same episode, glanced from the runed helmet to me, then down to the floor, like he was afraid to even look at me. He turned and pattered after Kovaks, who was headed for the arched hallway I hadn't even been able to see last time from my stationary vantage point bound at the round wooden table in the center of the room.

"Come on," Kovaks called over his shoulder. "You're either in or you're out."

Garrett and Siren traded a look, then glanced my way. As the apparent supreme leader of the "out" crowd, I gave them a clueless shrug. Siren quirked an eyebrow, then frowned and looked at Garrett, as if she'd just remembered telepathic communication was off the table.

Garrett, still having barely said a word this entire time, turned and followed after Kovaks and Omelius, making me wonder all the more what in Alpha's name he had to tell the brother of Andre Kovaks.

"This is gropping weird," Siren muttered, turning to tag along with Garrett. "Even by my standards."

We watched them go until it was just the five of us in the main room, standing with a healthy helping of pregnant silence.

"It's good to see you in one piece," Franco said, coming forward to give me his habitual clap on the shoulder. He frowned thoughtfully at his own words. "Seems like I've been saying that a bit too often lately."

"It's been a rough few days," I agreed. "Glad you're all, uh..."

I was deliberating on the word, "safe," when I noticed our bushy-haired, dreamy-eyed spectator was moving closer to me. Too close. She leaned right in, getting a good look, like I was little more than a particularly fascinating museum display.

"Hi there," I said uncertainly.

Her brow furrowed, but the silent scrutiny only continued.

"Nala," Elise said, "do you remember what I was saying about personal space?"

My bushy-haired spectator—Nala, I took it—studied me for another moment, then gave an exasperated huff and turned to Elise. "What's wrong with 'im?"

"He's not a lamp, you know," Elise said. "He can talk."

"Right, then," Nala said, turning her dubious stare back on me, still too close for comfort. "What's wrong with you?"

"Uh..." I looked to Elise for help, not really sure what to say to that.

"Nothing's wrong with him, Nala," Elise said, her tone overtly patient.

"Well there must be, mustn't there, if'n those two and the Judge all say so. Do ya not agree, Herald? None of the others have been reportin' any blue-blue-reds, now, have they?"

"Nala..." Elise warned, unmistakable tension in her body now. She shot a quick glance at me, then looked to her father for some help.

"What's going on?" I asked before Franco could step in. "What does she mean, others? What others? And what the scud's a blue-blue..."

I trailed off at the sinking expression on Elise's face.

"Well," Franco said, looking back and forth between us. "That was fast."

"What was fast?" I demanded. "And can you please back up?" I added, turning to Nala, who if anything was leaning closer now that I was showing signs of life. "You're... making me nervous."

"Ha!" Nala recoiled with one wrinkly hand to her chest and a look of pure indignation on her face. "Me, makin' 'im nervous? You hear that? A blue-blue—"

"That's enough, I think," Franco said. "Nala, would you mind terribly if I asked you to make us some of that lovely hattica leaf tea of yours?"

The old lady shot him a dirty look. "I'm not an invalid yet, you know. I can tell if'n someone's tellin' me to bother off."

"Not at all," Franco said. "I simply think this conversation might call for a soothing beverage." He turned. "James, perhaps you wouldn't mind?"

James, who'd been watching the entire interaction unfold with all the relaxed ease of an over-stressed tension cable, practically bounced off the ground at being called on. "Uh, yeah—Yeah, I can, uh..."

"Oh sit down, my shiny little biscuit," Nala said, brushing past us and stopping to lay an affectionate little pinch on James' cheek. "We can't well have you goin' and makin' the tea, on account'n that it would be just too sweet, comin' from ya."

"Duhhh thanks, Nala," James said, rubbing his pinched cheek and looking like he wasn't quite sure whether to be flattered or terrified.

Apparently, someone had an admirer. I might've been amused, if not for the serious looks on Franco's and Elise's faces. I looked between them, my uneasiness growing with each passing second they didn't speak.

"Guys, what is it? You're freaking me out."

"It's..." Elise started.

"Probably going to upset you," Franco offered.

"And we all know what happens then," Nala called from over by cycler where she was drawing water for tea. "Don't wanna go upsettin' a—"

"Yes," Franco said firmly. "Thank you, Nala."

"Hmph," she said, turning back to her kettle.

"I literally have an entire planet trying to cast me back to demons' depths," I said, watching them. "I think I can take it, whatever it is."

"Right," Elise finally said. "Well, for starters, Burton and Omelius aren't the only surviving remnants of the Emmútari."

"Oh." For a long moment, that was all I could think to say. "Well, that's... That seems like good news, doesn't it?"

"We certainly thought so," Franco agreed out loud. On his face, though—and on Elise's as well—there seemed to be an abundant lack of excitement.

"How many others are out there?" I asked. "And where have they been...?"

I trailed off at Elise's subdued head shake.

"Look at 'im, diggin' straight for the gold," Nala commented—quite loudly—to herself over at the kitchen unit, shaking her head while she measured out tea leaves.

"Those two are gonna be pretty pissed we told you anything at all," Elise explained. "Well, I mean Burton is, at least."

"Well, that sounds like business as usual for the guy," I said, not particularly caring at this point, what with all the heavy looks and the Emmútari secrets floating around. "I mean, if you guys all know already..." I looked to Franco and James. "No offense, but why would they let you two in on all of this if they don't even want another Shaper to know?"

The two traded a look before Franco took the lead.

"Because they don't find the two of us terribly threatening, I suspect," he said, in a tone that made it all too clear that that sentiment didn't extend to me. He pursed his lips, clearly not eager to say the next part. "And because we both submitted willingly to that Judge of theirs."

I looked around the room at the four sets of eyes, all attentively watching me. All waiting to see what I'd say.

"You passed," I said quietly. "You all passed?"

"Of course we passed, ya kook!" Nala cried, spreading her hands wide. "Whadaya think'n we're all doin' here?"

I blinked, trying to process the random outburst. *She passed?* I mouthed silently to Elise when my efforts failed, and Nala had turned safely back to her tea leaves. Elise only gave me an apologetic shrug.

"At any rate," Franco said, with a soft frown in Nala's direction. "I don't think it's something we should overly worry ourselves about."

"Yeah," James agreed. "It's nothing, really."

"None of us even actually understand what that thing does," Elise added. "It's practically a religion for them at this point."

"A religion that just so happens to mark me as a demon?" I asked. "The *second* religion that just so happens to—"

I cut myself off, distantly aware of how bitter and childish I sounded. This was exactly why they'd been afraid to tell me anything. Because they knew I wouldn't be able to set something like this aside. Of course, I wasn't so sure any one of them would've handled things any differently, in my place. I imagined it was a lot easier to dismiss the mystical spirit test when you were among the four-fifths of the people in the room who'd been Judged worthy.

But remembering the way Omelius had looked at me after my own test —like he was facing down a feral wolf—and finding myself the odd man out now, and in a group that included this Nala lady, no less... Given all that, it was kind of hard not to wonder what exactly I'd done to so clearly tarnish myself in the eyes of their divine Judge.

But that question also did us no good right now, I firmly reminded myself. What I needed to do was get my scud together and take this news like a big boy, if for no other reason than to get them to all stop looking at me like they were, with those same damned wounded-animal looks I'd gotten so much of after Carlisle had died. Like I was some kind of tragedy, and they only wished they knew how to fix me.

"So these other remnants..." I said.

"We're scant on the details ourselves," Franco said. "The network was arranged so that no one person, not even the Keepers, could compromise the other cells. But we have been in limited contact with a few of the other recruits."

"Shapers?" I asked. "Or more like our buddy Kovaks?"

"A bit of both," Elise said. "I get the impression the Keepers only agreed to begin bringing Shapers back into the fold recently. Right around, well…"

"Right around when I went and blew the lid off of the big secret on live WAN vid?" I asked.

Elise gave an innocent shrug. "Maybe somewhat around then."

"Things seem to have been moving rather quickly here ever since the White Tower," Franco said. "Doubly so these past few days. I think everyone senses we're approaching a critical moment for the future of Shaper kind."

"You mean *more* critical than the Sanctum declaring war on us?" I asked.

"Possibly," Franco said, perfectly seriously.

That caught my attention.

"Up till now," he continued, "we've been looking at a so-called holy war on demons that, oddly enough, has been waged almost exclusively between the Sanctum and Glenbark's faction of the Legion. At best, we might call it a proxy war for Shaper kind. I would simply call it a political power struggle, and one so clouded by religious idealism that few could probably even articulate exactly what it is that's even being fought for anymore. Whatever name we call it by, though, the outcome will likely be the same. Unless the Shapers of Enochia are prepared to begin standing up and making themselves known to the public eye in a meaningful way, they will be forced by default to stand by and watch as their collective reputation and their rightful place in this world are inexorably consumed in the fire of the Legion and Sanctum's war."

We all chewed on that in silence for a small time. It felt like more of the same. The same problems we'd been discussing this whole time. The same insurmountable obstacles. Us against the world. Except now it wasn't just us, apparently, but us *and* this secret underground network of Shapers that was apparently already growing. Even so…

"Glenbark is fighting for *us*, not for political gain," I said. "She's given everything for us."

Franco nodded empathetically. "I know that she is, and I know that she has. I don't question any of that for a minute. But others will. And that's what we're really up against here."

"Fear and blind ignorance," Elise said. "Willful or not. The world has been looking for answers about what's happening to the planet they thought they knew…"

"And all they've been seeing is me," I finished. "Me and a bunch of red-eyed aliens."

"That," Franco agreed, "and also the High Cleric pointing to the trail of destruction behind you."

Destruction the Sanctum had caused, I wanted to say. Collateral damage of the raknoth invasion, and of the concomitant wars I'd never wanted a single damn part of. But there were no words. Nothing to explain away the heavy certainty settling across my chest, telling me that it simply didn't matter anymore who had started it, who had given this flaming ball of scud the first push down the mountain. It never had.

I hung my head, suddenly too ashamed to meet their eyes.

"It was foolish of me to ever think we could wrestle public opinion back under control with a fresh spin and a few nice words," Franco said, speaking slowly. "We should have known better. *I* should have known better. I'm sorry, Haldin."

He was sorry? Him—the man who'd lost his home and willingly thrown away pretty much everything but his own family to take care of me? The man who'd practically become a father to me?

It wasn't Franco who should've been sorry. I wasn't entirely sure *who* it was. Me, maybe. Me and the High Cleric. General Auckus and the raknoth. The Legion. The Sanctum. The unruly masses of Enochia, all howling for demon blood. There was hardly any limit to the people who should've been sorry about all of this. But I was damn sure Franco wasn't among them.

So I straightened up, shaking off what shame I could, and gave his shoulder a reassuring clap as he so often did to me, hoping that that alone was enough to say whatever it was I couldn't seem to find the words to express. The look in his eyes told me it was.

"So does this outfit have a name for all of Shaper kind?" I asked after a moment's silence, hoping to move us on.

At that, Franco and Elise traded a look of wry amusement, even if it didn't quite reach their eyes.

"They were literally calling themselves The Remnant when we got here," Elise said.

"Well, if that doesn't sound like a radical terrorist organization..."

Elise brightened a shade. "Right?"

"So I take it there's a new name in the works, then?"

She nodded. "We were thinking we should call them the Children of Enochia."

I chewed on that for a moment.

"It's... good," I finally said, truly meaning it, though I couldn't have said precisely why at first—only that the name rang like a hammer-struck bell somewhere deep in my chest, for reasons I didn't immediately understand. "It sounds... hopeful."

"And humanizing, we hope," Franco said.

"That too," I agreed, nodding. "There's just one problem."

Their eyebrows adopted almost identical slants—father and daughter, side by side.

"You're talking about this like you aren't a part of it," I explained.

"And that's not even ta mention the fact that'n we ain't all children 'round here, right?" Nala chimed in, before Elise could respond.

I looked over, having nearly forgotten about Nala, and realized she'd laid out five steaming cups of tea at the table. The same table where, not so long ago, I'd woken up as a bound, helpless prisoner.

Tumultuous times, to say the least.

"I'm surprised they're not finished in there yet," Franco said, glancing in the direction Kovaks had taken Garrett and Siren as we all settled down around the table to take our cups.

"They're probably talking," Elise said. "Garrett said he had something to tell Burton about his brother's last days."

Franco looked curious about that, but he let it pass.

"Hal," Elise said, turning back to me. "What you were saying earlier, about the High Cleric..."

Tension returned to my insides, reminding me of what I still had left to do. All I could do. It only felt all the more important now that I knew what Franco and Elise and their Children of Enochia were up to. Even so, I hesitated, not really sure I wanted to have this conversation anywhere but with Elise, in private. But telepathy was apparently off the table until Kovaks turned the lights back on, and this was probably something Franco and James would have useful input on anyway.

And then there was Nala to consider, too, but I guess you couldn't win them all.

"What about the High Cleric?" Franco asked, in a tone that told me he already had a decent guess.

"Hal wants to go after him," Elise said.

"Go... *after*?" James asked slowly, tapping at his tea cup and pretty clearly wanting to ask if I'd made the weighty decision to murder a man.

"Not like that," I said. "It's just... Given how our last talk went, and everything that's happened since, it occurs to me that I might be uniquely suited to, uh, weaken his position, if I could get close to him and..."

"Expose his true colors?" Franco offered.

"That was the general idea," I agreed. "Do you think it can still work?"

"Showing the world that their holy beacon is flawed and fallible just like everyone else?" Franco said, stroking his dark mustache thoughtfully. "Casting doubt on the foundations of everything he's done. I think that, in principle, it all sounds well and good."

Elise bristled a little at that, clearly not liking the direction this was headed.

"I also think," Franco pressed on, before she could interject, "that I'm missing some crucial part of this plan. I don't imagine the High Cleric is going to invite you to tea and agree to a live feed debate, given the current state of affairs."

"No," I agreed. "I don't think so either. Which is why—"

"You were thinking of just flying straight into the White Tower, guns blazing?" Elise finished.

"Demons to the scudding wind, there's a thought!" Nala cried, slapping at the table with a wrinkled hand. "Guns blazing right into the belly of the beast, eh? Blue-blue-red, indeed!"

Again, I wanted to ask what the deal was with the colors. But I was a little distracted by the way everyone else at the table had fixed me on the ends of their expectant stares, awaiting my response to Elise's question. I opened my mouth and closed it more than once, working through a few false starts before settling on the simplest answer.

"I wasn't planning on taking any guns, actually."

"Ha!" Nala cried, clearly having the time of her life with this conversation—just as clearly as she was the only one at the table doing so.

"No guns," Elise echoed softly, shaking her head and paying no mind to Nala. "Just a raknoth, right? Alpha's blackened hands, Hal, you know what I meant."

I knew what she meant, all right. What I couldn't even begin to understand, though, was how *she* knew. As always, it was a little frightening how easily Elise could see into my head, even without telepathy.

"You want to take Alton Parker on your mission to discredit the holy authority of Enochia?" Franco asked.

Somehow, he managed to say it without adopting the tone of one speaking to a complete moron, though the words alone still carried enough of that weight. Nala, on the other hand, didn't attempt to hide her incredulous delight.

"I expect he'll be need'n a cameraman to be hold'n the camera while he shakes all the dirty little secrets outta that holy scudder, eh?" she cried, slapping at the table. "Cough'n up about the Seekers and all..." She rose from her chair and shambled off toward the kitchen unit, shaking her head and mumbling to herself about holy scudders and crazy bastards.

I turned back to find Franco and Elise studying me with expressions that said they understood there was more to the story, and that I hadn't in fact gone completely softsteel-sipping mad.

"Why Parker?" Franco asked quietly. "What trick are you hiding up your sleeve, Hal?"

"Well," I said, eyeing the Omelius' darkwood chest, and the assorted array of runed Emmútari artifacts, "that's kind of what I wanted to talk to the Children of Enochia about."

35

LEAP OF FAITH

When the time came to say goodbye, I left with a full rucksack, and a heavy heart.

"You don't have to do this," Elise reminded me quietly, holding me tight in her arms just outside the door of their underground hideout.

"I know," I said, squeezing her right back, trying my best to breathe her in and store away every last fleeting detail, just in case. "But it's the right thing to do."

She drew back and searched my face. In the reflected light of my palm-light, I saw tears brimming in her eyes, and I felt my own not far away.

"I love you," she whispered.

Before I could answer, she drew me in for a kiss—the kind of kiss that made me forget about answers, and words, and pretty much anything else beside the indescribably loving girl in front of me, and the precious sensation of her lips on mine, and her hands on my cheeks. The salty wetness of tears found our kissing lips, and we parted with a shaky breath. I planted one last kiss on her forehead, then forced myself to turn and take the first step. Then another, and another. Step by heavy step away from the person I loved most on this world, refusing to believe this might be the last time, yet unable to shut the thought out completely.

I fought the intense desire to turn back for one more look, one more precious moment. I'd never be able to leave if I did.

That said, I couldn't contain my extended senses from reaching back to her. I didn't even try, really. And I was relieved to find that neither did she. Our minds met in a silent, ethereal embrace, and I held onto that contact, only distantly paying attention to my physical surroundings and Burton Kovaks' wary frown as he turned to lead me back out of their labyrinthine hideout. I held on for a quarter of a mile or so, until the cold voice of reason grew too loud to ignore, and I was forced to acknowledge that we would soon be out of range, and that I might as well get it over with while we could still communicate effectively.

"Come back to me," she sent, seeming to have arrived at a similar thought. *"Come back to me when it's all over."*

I wanted to tell her that I would. Wanted to believe it more than anything.

Instead, I opened my mind and showered her with all the love and gratitude I felt, not bothering with words, holding nothing back. It was all I had to give. And we both knew it. I hesitated, then, knowing I should end it, but not quite able to bring myself to flip the switch on my cloaking pendant.

Elise was stronger than me.

One moment, we were hanging there in the bittersweet telepathic abyss, and then the next, she was gone, and I was alone with Burton Kovaks, slogging through the dark, winding ways.

Luckily, our trek back through the maze of tunnels was as silent as it was uneventful. I don't think I could've stomached anything other than the silence right then, with the ghost of Elise's kiss hanging on my lips, and the colossal shadow of my next challenge looming ahead of me, inescapable.

It wasn't until Kovaks drew to a halt in front of me that I realized we'd made it back to the hidden door behind the Dark Star Tavern. Kovaks was watching me in the glow of our lights, his hand frozen halfway to the key stone activation rune, like he'd fully intended to boot me out the door without a word, but had lost the battle against his own infernal curiosity.

"Why are you doing this, kid?" he finally asked, lowering the stone and turning to face me like it was all my fault.

"I guess I feel like it's the only way left to help."

The words came out without my really thinking about them—not that I could've found the mental space to think of much else to say if I'd tried. At any rate, the answer seemed to suffice.

Kovaks pondered my words for a few moments, then turned back to the rune-gilded wall, opting to keep whatever thoughts he had to himself. I didn't worry about it. Guess I was lacking the mental space for that, too. In fact, aside from Elise and the shadow of what lay ahead, the only thing that remained in my mind, as Kovaks pressed his key stone to the door runes, was the fact that Garrett and Siren weren't with us.

They'd remained behind with the Children of Enochia. Had been free to do so, as far as I could tell. The details had been frustratingly scant. Kovaks hadn't said much when they'd finally emerged from the room where they'd gone to administer their Judge to the two ex-Seekers. None of them had said much, for that matter. I'd only gathered that Garrett and Siren had been tested, and that they apparently weren't to be thrown out like a pair of feral, dark-spirited wolves. Not like me.

That, more than anything, chilled me to the bone.

Maybe I should've been glad. I'd never intended for the two ex-Seekers to accompany me on the next leg of this journey, after all. Besides, unquestionably dark pasts and rough edges aside, they were both adept Shapers, and fairly charismatic to boot, when they put their minds to it. If they truly intended to help the cause, I wasn't sure Elise and Kovaks and the others were going to be finding many more vastly superior candidates among the long-hunted dregs of Shaper kind.

That said, I was still a little hung up on the fact that two honest-to-Alpha murderers had apparently managed to pass the test that I'd so spectacularly failed.

If taking human lives in cold blood wasn't enough to rule someone out in the arcane eyes of the Judge, then where the scud did that leave me?

I'd thought about asking. About the Judge itself. About Nala's talk of blue-blue-reds, and what in the scud this divine test of theirs was even testing at all. I'd thought about it a lot. So much so that I'd probably missed half of what'd been said in the past couple hours.

In the end, though, I hadn't asked. Mostly because I figured I'd have only gotten more vague non-answers from them. Or so I'd told myself at the time. Now, though, if I was being completely honest with myself, I couldn't quite ignore the idea that it hadn't been a lack of answers holding me back, but rather the fear that I might learn the honest truth.

Whatever that arcane helmet had seen inside of me, I wasn't sure I wanted to know. And given the way Burton Kovaks was staring at me as I came back to the present, it seemed more than a little unlikely I was missing out on anything good.

I stepped out to join him in the still shadows of the Dark Star Tavern's alleyway, wondering one last time if I shouldn't demand some answers anyway.

"You sure you'll figure out how to use that thing?" he asked before I could, gesturing to the rucksack slung over my shoulder.

I shrugged. "Guess I'll have to."

There wasn't really anything more to be said about it. Not now. And least of all to Burton Kovaks.

He seemed to feel the same way.

"Well," he said, "don't grop this up." Then he turned and disappeared back into the dark passageway, swinging the rectangular patch of perma-crete closed behind him.

I watched with some interest as the door blended back into the wall—not just by mere illusion and tight engineering, as far as I could tell in my senses, but rather by actually physically weaving itself back into a cohesive whole.

It was damn impressive runework, to say the least. Especially when considering it must've been laid down by Shapers now several centuries beyond the pyre. As far as I'd come with my own abilities, my head spun just trying to imagine how I'd even begin the task of arranging and empowering the runes to pull off something that complicated. And that wasn't even to mention the rest of the ancient Emmútari tech lying around in there—knockout wands, next-level cloaking fields, that thrice-damned Judge, and Alpha only knew what else.

I couldn't even imagine how many lifetimes of collective work had gone into crafting such things. And, lucky for me, I'd probably never find out, either. Not until I purged my blackened spirit in the eyes of the Judge, at least.

That cheery thought brought me back to the dark alleyway, where I was alone, and starting to get a little cold.

"Well?" came Alton Parker's smooth baritone, even as I reached out to begin searching for his presence.

Not quite alone after all, then.

Parker was right where I'd left him. Literally. As far as I could tell, the raknoth hadn't moved an inch from his rooftop perch.

Worse, I realized, I was actually *relieved* by that fact.

Because at least I wasn't the only freak in this outfit. And also because, like it or not—and I didn't, not one bit—I needed the slimy bastard to pull this off.

And that was the *other* part that chilled me to the bone.

"I've got something that should work," I sent back, wishing more than

anything that I could simply curl up under a thick blanket with Elise, and never think another troubling thought again.

"*Should?*" Parker asked.

I shrugged, even though I could feel he didn't have a line of sight on me. "*It's probably been a thousand years since anyone used this thing. There might be a little troubleshooting involved.*"

And that might've been the understatement of the millennium, too. But we wouldn't know until we tried.

"*Very well.*" Parker's dark outline appeared at the edge of the rooftop like a wraith in the night. "*We'd best get outside the city limits, then. I'll call the ship.*"

AN HOUR or so of sneaking, a few inhuman acrobatics, and a covert countryside pickup later, we'd made it back to the ship and safely into orbit, where I was finally free to kick back and start worrying about the next part properly.

A few hours after that, we'd managed—with only a few choice insults back and forth—to establish some passable operation of the souvenir Kovaks and Omelius had agreed to leave to me, almost as reluctantly as they'd agreed it was probably for the good of everyone. And only then because I'd had Franco and Elise arguing my case. I'm not sure what I would've done otherwise. Though I also wasn't sure why, out of everything in their arcane arsenal, Kovaks and Omelius had been so hesitant to give me this one.

It was a weapon of truth, after all. Not exactly the kind of thing a vile demon should seemingly have much use for.

Which only made it that much more deliciously rich that it was Alton Parker, of all creatures, who was most effectively equipped to wield the thing against the High Cleric and against his holy vendetta against all of Shaper kind.

Maybe the world truly had gone crazy.

"You knew this was going to happen, didn't you?" I asked quietly, as I tucked the arcane headpiece back into the rucksack and Alton began the task of bringing us down from orbit. "You knew from the moment you showed me the rakul. Even before then."

Alton studied me for a stretch before answering, maybe debating the same thing himself, maybe just deciding how extensively to twist the truth to suit his narrative.

"You've been damned in their eyes ever since the WAN reels pronounced you back from the dead and branded you a terrorist," he finally said. "There is no coming back from that. Not ever. Not truly. Even if you'd been a unanimously shining paragon of good. Even if the High Cleric himself had blessed you, declared you Alpha's Chosen. Somewhere deep down, you know there always would've lived a shadow of fear in the heart of the people."

He was right, of course. I understood that now. And what was even worse, was that he'd somehow picked up on exactly what I'd been asking, possibly more clearly than I'd known myself.

"You say that like it's all said and done already."

"Well, if it wasn't before..." He nodded toward the rest of our cobbled-together recording rig, as if to ask how I could ever expect to be forgiven for what we were about to attempt. Which was a fairer question than I really cared to think about right then.

Luckily, Alton chose that moment to indicate I should strap into a flight seat for descent, which conveniently pulled my mind away from the gloomy haze of the Enochia that had forsaken me, and back to the beating heart, twitchy nerves Enochia that was probably about to try to kill me, one last time.

"At the risk of infantilizing you," Alton said, taking the flight seat beside me, "I feel compelled to point out one more time that this plan is ludicrous."

I looked over at him. My freaking raknoth partner in crime. "If I didn't know any better, I'd say it sounds like you're afraid."

He didn't look afraid, of course. He just looked bored. And maybe a touch irritated.

"I merely recognize that our present chances of survival decrease drastically the moment our feet leave this ship," he said.

"Well," I said, pulling the slack out of my flight straps, "if the rakul are just gonna come finish the job one day anyway..."

That, if nothing else, got his goat. He didn't say anything, apparently too dignified—or maybe just too angry—to resort to petty quips. Instead, he let his flying—and my stomach—do the talking. The rapid descent did little to calm my wired nerves. But the sight of Enochia rising to meet us on the wall-wide viewing screen at least gave me something to focus on.

My planet. My divided, war-torn planet.

It looked so much more peaceful from up here, spinning innocently on, even as the spilled blood dried across its surface and tensions mounted, threatening another flood imminently. Too much tension. Too many voices clamoring to be heard above all the rest.

And here I was, flying in to add more noise to the mix.

Noise that was critically important, I believed. Maybe even the signal to the noise, if I really wanted to be audacious about it. How I felt about it probably didn't matter. It was the truth, as best as I could see it, and I needed to make it known. Simple as that.

The sun was just beginning to crest the horizon as Divinity came into view far below. It cast its first dazzling streaks across the city like a benevolent spirit reaching out to take Divinity in its palm, lighting the way to a bright new day. Lighting the White Tower up like a nice, big landing beacon.

Whether by Alton's control, or by the merit of my own focus, a section of the ship's viewing wall zoomed selectively in on the White Tower, bridging the distance in a moment of head-spinning disorientation before resolving into an impressively clear close-up of the gleaming tower. My eyes drifted to the top, where the Sanctum's expansive team of masons and other craftsmen had already nearly finished reconstructing the outer shell of the demolished Great Hall. The place where I'd lost Carlisle. And the place where, not so very long ago, I'd awaited my own hanging at the setting of the sun.

It felt oddly appropriate that I should return now at the dawn of a new day.

I opened my mouth to remind Alton of our altitude cap, then closed it again. If he couldn't remember that much, then this plan was probably already gropped anyway, and Divinity's surface-to-air defenses were the least of our concerns. I wasn't even rightly sure how high we were at the moment, given the lack of conventional meters and displays around the flight deck. Maybe, I reasoned, I could've asked the ship telepathically. But Alton leveled the ship out before I dared to test that theory, and my focus slid back to the distant gleam of the White Tower.

For a long handful of seconds, we hovered there in silence.

"For the life of me, I cannot seem to recall why I agreed to this," Alton finally said.

Snapped back to reality by the broken silence, I unbuckled my flight straps and went to collect the ballistic helmet that would complete the rest of the jumpsuit I'd already donned. "Maybe you just have half a heart buried somewhere in there, after all."

The raknoth unbuckled his straps, frowning my way all the while, then stood and walked out of the room, ignoring the jumpsuit helmet I offered him as if the very thought was too offensive or outrageous to even dignify with a response. I slipped on my own helmet and followed him off the flight deck, down the next corridor, toward the exit. The hatch peeled open as Alton approached, moving with its odd, organic fluidity. Alton stepped out to the unfurling stairs with easy confidence. I powered up my helmet display, took an unfortunate glance at the altimeter, and followed him.

To say the fall looked longer in person would've been an understatement. Then again, my opinion on the matter might've been somewhat skewed by the lack of anything but the slender boarding steps underfoot, and even more so by the fact that I knew what came next. Somehow, it had been a lot less nerve-racking, going for a standard skydive with a team of three competent Shapers when it had been too dark to even see the ground below. And now...

Alton crouched down to one knee and took hold of the boarding steps with one inhumanly strong hand. "Ready?"

... And now, it was time to set my reservations aside, make like an arcane missile, and go strike at the heart of the overwhelming forces unknowingly arrayed against the future of Enochia.

For what I sincerely hoped would be the last time, I climbed onto Alton Parker's back, tucked myself into position, and clipped us together with a single hardsteel springhook, just in case—or, in all reality, for *when*—the flight proved even more turbulent than we already expected. The thought sent a wave of dizzy apprehension through my head.

I took a few deep breaths, resisting the onset of my adrenaline-fueled tunnel vision as best I could. "Ready when you are."

Beneath me, I could've sworn I felt the raknoth ripple with something like silent laughter.

"What? What the scud are you laughing at?"

"I just thought of something," he said. "A saying from Earth that I've always found rather amusing."

I frowned at the back of his salt-and-pepper-haired head. "Yeah? What's that?"

"Geronimo," he said.

I opened my mouth to ask what the scud that meant.

Then the ship rocketed forward, and I was holding on for dear life.

3 6

PEACES

Call it a wild hunch, but I'm guessing whoever originally drew a line between so-called "low" velocity missiles and the rest of their speedy kin had probably never been sailing through the open air astride a raknoth, dangling precariously from the slender boarding steps of a speeding alien spaceship.

Or so I reasoned as I clung to Alton with a wide-eyed death grip, buffeted by a never-ending roar of wind, rocketing along at what my jump-suit helmet display warned in flashing red letters was beyond terminal velocity for your average human being. And along with that flashing red realization, came another.

"Your helmet!" I sent, the wind rushing by far too loudly to allow for speaking. *"You don't have your helmet!"*

"I am quite aware," came Alton's reply.

"But the trajectory..." I sent dumbly, eyeing the ballistic trajectory my own display had mapped out with rising panic. "Timing and velocity and... You said yourself this was ludicrous, and now you're gonna—"

His head cocked around, just far enough for me to catch the crimson fire in his eyes. *"Did they not teach you to trust your elders, Haldin?"*

Neither I nor my somersaulting stomach had anything to say to that. We were both too busy gaping down at the docks of the Red River over two miles below, and at the southern edge of Divinity rushing by with startling speed. We were in it now. High as we were, and fancy scanner stealth aside, chances were fair that someone had spotted us by now. Which meant it was now or never. And judging by how fast the gleaming lance of the White Tower was approaching, and the way Alton tensed beneath me—like a predator preparing to pounce—it was more on the *now* side.

We're going too fast, I thought to say. But it was already happening, without fuss or warning.

Alton didn't *jump*, exactly. He didn't need to. He simply let go, spinning the ship's boarding steps out from beneath us with his telepathic control. And then we were flying. Or falling.

I hadn't noticed him shedding velocity in the last seconds, but he must've, judging from the fact that we weren't immediately slapped back into our place by the Divine Handbrakes of Alpha. The solid orange letters on my display put us flying right at the edge of our terminal velocity.

Flying through dead open air, two miles above the streets of Divinity.

Flying straight for the White Tower. Or so my display trajectory claimed. I had to admit, Alton had done an eerily perfect job of matching the calculated trajectory without any digital aid of his own. But no matter what either of them said, my gut was having a hard time believing that we were on target—that we were on *anything*, in fact, aside from our last precious moments of sweet, sweet life.

We were too damned far away from the Tower, falling too fast, and it was more than a little bit terrifying. For me, at least.

Alton, on the other hand, seemed to be having the time of his life.

"You do remember we're not killing people, right?" I sent, a little perturbed at how light—and maybe even *happy*—my partner's mind felt in the midst of a two mile free fall straight toward an entire tower full of people who wanted to kill us.

"Aye, Commander," he sent, his tone the epitome of sarcasm, and his irritation flowing clearly through our mental link. *"One terminal velocity, nonlethal landing, coming right up."*

For a second, I almost felt bad for disturbing him from his creepy raknoth happy place. I wasn't even rightly sure why I cared so much that we didn't kill anyone, aside from the fact that it would play terribly in the reels. The Onyx Guard sure as scud wouldn't be showing us any similar mercy, after all. Not unless the High Cleric managed to explicitly tell them to before it was all over. But I didn't have time to think about all this again.

The Tower was rising up to meet us at an alarming rate now, leaving no doubt in my mind that we were going to hit.

A thousand feet.

There. The wide, curved window we were shooting for. I wrapped my mind around us, gathering my energy and biting down on the primal urge to scream for dear life.

Five-hundred.

Too high. Too fast. I gave us a careful nudge. Too much.

Panic spiked through my chest.

One-hundred.

Heart thundering, vision down to a pinprick, I drew the energy and launched us forward as hard as I could, forming a spearhead of telekinetic force to head our charge.

My breath caught at the speed of the approaching wall of reinforced duraglass. Too much. My eyes snapped shut. Duraglass shattered. We hit. Alton first, some part of me knew. But I couldn't have guessed it for the way the world exploded around me. We hit again, and again—a brutal whirlwind of impacts and jolting rolls, too fast to pick out any pertinent details, other than that we were moving, and fast. I sank into my extended senses, relying on them to keep me grounded through the chaos. Grounded enough that I felt the first weapons being raised, anyway.

The response time was every bit as impressive as I'd expected. Which was the only reason I had my barrier ready in time to catch the first barrage of gunfire.

The Onyx Guard weren't gropping around.

I fumbled for the springhook connecting me to Alton, floating on a hot bed of pain and light-headed nausea between the telekinesis and the crash landing. Luckily, he managed to contain himself until I yanked the hook free. The moment I did, though, Alton launched from the ground with inhuman speed and promptly put the *no killing* rule to the test. I saw him smack two Onyx Guard clear across the High Cleric's ridiculously posh lounge room before I was distracted by the feeling of three Onyx Guard closing in on me from behind. And fast.

I spun around, rolling to my feet even as I swept their legs out with telekinesis.

That didn't stop one of them from chucking a dark dagger at me, and another from trying another burst of gunfire—all perfectly aimed, even as they fell. I caught the blade and the slugs, and drove a hard kick into the third man's dark faceplate. He bounced back to his feet like getting kicked in the face was his idea of a polite handshake, and his two partners were right there with him.

They came at me with dark blades and without hesitation, apparently recognizing that their slugs wouldn't do the trick, and that I was not to be given time to collect myself. If they were dismayed to find that my barrier could stop daggers, too, they didn't show it—just kept hammering away with a kind of emotionless brutality that was somehow more terrifying than the animal ferocity of a raknoth or a hybrid.

I felt each and every blow slamming into my barrier. Felt them too much. I backpedaled, needing to buy a moment, but they followed with mechanical persistence, refusing to allow it. I diverted enough from my barrier to hit one with a blast of telekinesis even as I caught another in a crisp hip throw and reached out to shut the third down with telepathy.

His mind resisted. More than any non-telepath had business resisting.

I didn't have time to be properly surprised before he lunged forward with his dagger. I spun clear of the blade, ducked the next dark fist sailing toward my head, and leapt straight into a high aerial at the warning scream of my extended senses. Or tried to, at least.

Something slammed into my lower half as I left the ground, and then strong arms were clamping around my legs, dragging me down, and more were joining them. I'd barely hit the floor before a dark boot stomped into my diaphragm, leaving me coughing for air as they descended on me. I was reaching to blast them all off with telekinesis when something struck my head hard enough to send the world spinning, even through the helmet. My visor was cracked. My arms pinned. Then they yanked the helmet free, and kicked me hard enough to knock the entire world out of focus.

When my senses returned, I was being hauled to my knees, my hands already bound behind my back, multiple guns and daggers all pressed to my head and throat. The door to the hallway outside had been thrown open, and gold-armored Sanctum Guard were pouring into the room, weapons ready.

"Enough," called a firm, level voice from somewhere above. "That's quite enough."

The High Cleric had appeared at the ornate railing of his loft, looking down on the commotion.

"What do we have here?" he asked. Rhetorically, I had to assume. Especially with me decidedly secured in the hands of at least three cold, hard killers, and Alton collapsed in a pile of splintered darkwood furniture ahead, surrounded by five more Onyx Guard, who were still pelting him with stun bolts with the same methodical, emotionless violence they'd used on me.

To say that we were caught would've seemed a gross understatement.

And the High Cleric didn't seem particularly surprised by any part of it. Nor did he see any need to issue commands to the Sanctum Guard rushing in with chains and pulse cannons that looked more than equal to the task of ending a raknoth.

They'd been prepared. Just like we'd expected. But that was okay. An acceptable part of the plan.

Right up until I reached out to establish telepathic contact with Alton, and my head erupted in a fiery torrent of pain.

I gasped for breath, coming back to my physical senses, cold, sickly dread filling my stomach.

A scorcher.

I'd never forget that pain—the same pain that had left me helplessly incapacitated leading up to my first Sanctum execution, when Franco had managed to convince Barbara Sanders to remove the thing and save my life. And Alpha be damned, they had another one.

Only this time, there was no Barbara Sanders coming to save me.

Panic swelled in my chest, blazing up through my sinuses and leaving me choking on too-shallow breaths from my burning lungs.

We weren't just caught. We were trapped. Helpless and gropping trapped.

"I must admit, Haldin," the High Cleric called, descending the spiral stairs from his loft with one hand—the only hand he had left, after Five had gotten hold of him back at Adam and Enid's execution—on the banister. "Even for you, this is rather unexpected. Did you think to kill me as I slept? Or perhaps..."

He looked over to Alton Parker, who was currently being chained to the gills while they kept him subdued with a steady barrage of stunner bolts. They'd already fitted him with a pendant too—one of the pendants, I recognized with a sickened feeling, that I'd created myself, to help Glenbark and everyone else deal with the raknoth threat.

"... Perhaps you came to let your friend here wrest control of the Sanctum back into the hands of your unholy ilk?" the High Cleric finished.

"Honestly," I wheezed from my burning lungs, trying not to let the panic show. "I just wanted to talk."

The High Cleric looked pointedly from us to the jagged hole we'd just breached through his impressively expansive window.

"Something told me you might not take my call," I explained.

By the look on the High Cleric's face as he turned to his Onyx Guard, I knew immediately that I was playing with fire.

"I have something to show you," I added, before he could give any hasty orders. "I have proof."

He paused, and I could see the conflict in him. He wanted to kill us. Wanted to be done with it.

I caught Alton's eye, and he gave me the faintest nod.

"Proof of what, exactly?" the High Cleric finally asked.

"You're not going to like it. But it's..." I took a deliberate breath, gathering what dignity I could. It burned. "You need to understand where we came from before you condemn any more people to die in the name of Alpha. And I have proof that will show you."

"Proof," the High Cleric echoed, like the word was dirty. "We have all the proof we need, Demon. It is in Alpha's ever-present light just as clearly as it is in our written records. Perhaps you knew that once, before you abandoned the path. Perhaps not. Regardless, there is no proof that could dissuade me of the depths from whence you came."

"Then it won't hurt to see what I've brought you," I said, holding his disgusted gaze evenly.

Silence stretched. Too long. It stretched until I was sure that I'd lost him for good, and that he'd order us killed with his next breath. But then he finally roused from his internal debate, and I saw it there: the faintest spark of intractable curiosity. He wanted to know what forbidden secrets I was hiding. *Needed* to know, even, somewhere deep down. Somewhere even he might not recognize or understand.

I could've danced when I saw that spark.

Quickly as it shone, though, he covered it up and turned to his troops with his usual holy dignity fully intact.

"You may retire to the hall with your men, Captain."

Relief flooded through me.

The one who wore the golden cape of a Sanctum Guard captain, on the other hand, went perfectly rigid. "Your Holiness, I—"

"I will call if we need you," the High Cleric said, waving him away. "Go, now."

Even with his features hidden behind the golden faceplate, the captain's lingering hesitation was clear enough. But he didn't dare question His Holiness for a second time. After a moment, he turned to his squad, issued a few hand signals, and turned to march out alongside them.

"What is it, then?" the High Cleric finally asked, when the door was closed, and it was just us and his Onyx Guard. "More of your Emmútari propaganda? You truly believe the simple fact of their predating Sarentus' revelations grants them clemency from the unholy pacts they entered to channel their demonic power? The same power you now twist to your will?"

"This isn't about the Emmútari," I said, glancing at Alton. He gave me another nod. "It's about Sarentus. It's about where all of this began."

The spark returned briefly to the High Cleric's eyes. He masked it with an expression of practiced skepticism. "You think to drag our own prophet through the mud with you now, Demon?"

"Just play the vid on my palmlight," I said, finally allowing myself to drop his gaze, allowing the defeat to show on my face.

It was too much for our holy inquisitor to resist. He gestured to one of the men behind me. The Onyx Guard stepped forward and handed him my device, having apparently already stripped it from my wrist when I'd been too busy having my head kicked in to notice.

"And what will I find," the High Cleric asked, turning my palmlight over in his hands, "if I play this little game of yours?"

I glanced at Alton. This was it.

"You will find the truth, High Cleric," Alton said, speaking for the first time.

The High Cleric frowned, looking suspiciously between the two of us, then back to the palmlight.

"Check them again," he said after a moment's thought. "Deep scan for recording devices."

I had to give it to him, His Holiness was not a stupid man. I didn't have time to open my mouth before dark hands clamped it shut and hauled me up, up and over to where two of the Onyx Guard had already broken out the hand scanners and were getting started on the raknoth. My escorts tossed me to the floor like a common gear bag, and one of the men split off from Alton to begin scanning every square inch of my body. Not that he had to look far.

It only took him a few seconds to find the first of the many microcams embedded in my jumpsuit. He made a quick hand signal to one of his team-mates, who ghosted forward to confer with the High Cleric while he kept scanning.

Among the many rumors about the Onyx Guard, I'd heard it said that they were all mute. Some even went so far as to claim the Onyx Guard had their tongues cut out as part of their initiation. I knew it was all bullscud, but I was still a little mesmerized as the Onyx Guard leaned his dark face-plate close to the High Cleric's ear. I faintly thought I even heard the word, "transmitting," but maybe that was only because I knew exactly what they'd found.

The High Cleric nodded at whatever the man said, not looking surprised as he glanced our way. "Well, I think we all see where this was headed. Propaganda begets more propaganda, yes?" He turned back to his Onyx Guard. "Destroy the devices. All of them."

No sooner had he spoken the words than a series of tingling shocks began rippling through my body from the sweeping hand scanners, sending light spasms through my muscles wherever they touched. I tried to look over to see how Alton was faring beside me, but strong hands kept my head pinned the other way on the floor. Between the two of us, I knew we had a couple dozen microcams hidden away. But I also knew the Onyx Guard were more than equal to the task.

Thorough didn't even begin to describe it.

"Did you not realize my quarters are shielded to prevent unauthorized transmissions?" the High Cleric asked as they worked. He made a tut-tut sound, shaking his head as he turned his focus back to my palmlight. "And what do we have here, then, that you intended to incriminate me with? Another rousing monologue, perhaps? Or maybe a dark confession from one of my wayward Seekers?"

The Onyx Guard hauled me back to my knees beside Alton, facing me toward the High Cleric, who was looking to me for an answer. I dropped my gaze back to the floor, not trusting myself not to give anything away.

"Very well, then." He looked to his Onyx Guard, and must've gotten the all-clear sign. "Let us see this proof of which you speak."

He touched a few commands on the palmlight display, then swiped the output up onto to the wide display hanging over the elaborate darkstone fireplace. "Ahh," he said, clearly satisfied by his own predictive prowess, when Adam Drove's face appeared on the display, and the ex-Seeker known as Four began the short but rather disturbing testimony we'd recorded from him before leaving Oasis.

On the display, Adam had barely made it past "—took me from the streets and shaped me into a killer," before the High Cleric paused the vid.

"Do you truly think the people would care if they found out we'd used demons to hunt other demons?" He turned a condescending frown my way. "Sparing the lives of good men by using these fallen spirits to combat the evils roaming our planet? They would celebrate the idea, you foolish boy."

I said nothing. I didn't need to. The High Cleric was already turning back to the display to continue skipping through Adam's confession. Then

Enid's. Then Garrett's, and Siren's. He was just about to wave the display off for good when Siren's segment ended, and the vid cut to the scene of a lush clearing, well-forested on its perimeters, and oddly foreign in a way that wasn't easy to immediately identify.

I sat silently beside Alton, watching the vid we'd spent the past few hours so carefully recording straight from his memories with a combination of modern tech and the ancient Emmútari headpiece I'd borrowed from Omelius' collection.

The High Cleric watched too, a permanent scowl of disbelief resting across his brow. But that didn't matter. Because he wasn't skipping through the footage anymore. Not as the raknoth known as Nan'Sarentus boarded the now familiar raknoth ship beside his fellows. Not as the one named Zar'Faenor returned with the news that the transplant had been successful, and that he'd left two of their kin, Valen and Sarentus to oversee the humans' adaptation to their new world. The world he called Enochia.

The High Cleric didn't even blink when the vid cut to the footage of the mountain-sized dragon, Kul'Naga, descending on an army of ice-dwelling giants and bringing a savage and bloody end to their entire clan. He just stared at the display until it had gone blank, then he stared for a while longer before finally turning to us.

His expression was as blank as the display. So blank that, for a second, I actually thought that maybe we'd reached him, that maybe some part of the impossible truths contained in the vid had actually sunk through. Then his eyes narrowed, and I watched that scrap of hope go up in flames.

"*This* is your proof?" he asked quietly, glaring down at us. "*This* is what you wish to show the world? A storyvid you worked up with your underground terrorists?"

"It's not a storyvid," I said. "It's a recording. A recording from someone who was there."

He blew out a derisive snort. "You honestly expect me to believe that?"

"The raknoth have been around much longer than any of us might've thought to believe," I said, looking to Alton. "And he can prove it to you, if you'll listen."

"Gag him," the High Cleric snapped, as Alton opened his mouth to speak.

The Onyx Guard complied with brutal efficiency while, ahead, the High Cleric let out a heavy breath and pinched at the bridge of his nose, like he'd only just realized he'd been dealing with immature children this whole time.

"I know this all sounds crazy," I started slowly, "but if you look at—"

The High Cleric gave a flick of his fingers, and something slammed into the side of my head, hard enough that I was confused when I found myself sprawled across the floor in front of Alton, head throbbing with amber waves of pain. The Onyx Guard hauled me back up beside Alton before I could get my bearings. Hauled me up *against* Alton. Our sides touching. That seemed important for some reason that my thrice-rattled brain couldn't seem to pick out right then.

This isn't going so well, said the voice in the back of my head.

"My hand still aches, you know," the High Cleric was saying ahead, almost as if he were talking to himself. "Phantom pain, they call it. Keeps me awake at night."

"Funny," I groaned, trying to blink my spotty vision clear, "it's watching a planet tear itself apart over a few scuddy lies that does it for me. I sure hope your hand feels better, though."

Are you able to dismantle my bindings?

I blinked again, trying to make sense of the disjointed voice in my head.

"I do not want this war, you insolent little monster," the High Cleric was saying ahead, cold violence in each word. "Your kind leave me no choice."

"My kind..." I echoed, trying to follow it all at once. Then it clicked.

Not *my* voice. Alton's. Because we were touching. Which meant...

I focused back on the High Cleric, anger rising as my senses returned and my brain caught up. "My *kind* are human beings, just like everyone else. And this war between us, this rift between Shapers and everyone else... it's nothing but a raknoth clan war, instigated a thousand years ago by a raknoth who was afraid he'd lost control of the planet that had been left under his charge."

"I can't," I added silently to Alton, "This pendant... it's like getting stabbed in the brain every time I try to reach out. I can't free us."

"Then give me your pain," came his immediate reply.

"—even capable of hearing how insane you sound?" the High Cleric was saying. "Demons from another planet, populating Enochia like we were nothing but livestock. Never mind the flagrant blasphemy therein for a moment, and just tell me, has this creature truly twisted your mind so completely?"

"Give me your pain," Alton repeated, his mind reaching for mine in open invitation, *"and prepare to get us out of here."*

"I suppose I needn't ask," the cleric continued, with a disgusted look between the two of us. "Needn't have even stayed your execution this long,

Alpha forgive my curiosity. Clearly, you have lost your mind to the darkness inside."

"Clearly," I growled back. "And yet we have an alien invader sitting right here—"

"This creature is a demon of the nether."

"—an alien invader who flew in on a spaceship—"

"Hold your tongue, or I will—"

"—because this universe is *bigger* than Sarentus ever dared teach us in his holy scripts. Because he wanted us to stay here like good little pets. Because that was his gropping job. To keep us under control. Subservient to one all-supreme Alpha. Like a pack of gropping wolv—"

"SILENCE!" the High Cleric snapped. "I will hear no more of your foul lies, Demon! You are a pox upon this worl—"

"THEN WHY ARE YOU STILL LISTENING TO ME?!"

The ferocity in my voice surprised even me. The High Cleric, on the other hand, recoiled and stiffened like he'd been slapped and couldn't remember how he was meant to handle such an affront.

"Why are you so *angry* right now," I continued, "if you truly believe this is all just some bullscud fable?"

I saw the shock fading from his eyes, dogmatic faith creeping back in to bolster his resolve. But he was rattled. Wasn't he?

"You're angry because, deep down, you know too much of this adds up," I pushed on, needing to believe it myself. "Because deep down, you know something is rotten at the heart of your teachings."

The look solidified on his face, and he started forward, cold justice in his eyes.

"Maybe you've always known," I pressed on, heart thundering, my mind screaming that this was the end. "Maybe you don't care if it's all a lie, so long as you're the one on top. Or maybe—"

The High Cleric of the Sanctum grabbed me then—grabbed me by the throat like a common tavern brawler, sharp eyes wide, and burning with hatred.

"I would not care if you brought Sarentus himself back from the dead, Demon," he hissed through clenched teeth, hands tightening around my throat. "It does not matter. None of it matters. I have felt Alpha's light."

He paused at the name of Alpha, seeming to remember himself. His fingers loosened on my throat. Then he released me completely, and straightened up, taking a few distancing steps backward.

"I have felt it," he repeated softly. "And that is the only truth my Sanctum requires." His eyes hardened. "The only truth it will abide."

"We are out of time," Alton sent, pushing insistently at the edges of my mind. *"Give me your pain, Haldin, and get us out of here."*

There was nothing left to say.

He was right. I saw it in the High Cleric's eyes—cold murder settling over the room. It didn't matter anymore. All that mattered was surviving.

So I set the rest aside, and opened my mind to Alton's.

It was every bit as overwhelming as it had been back in the brig, this time with the added confusion of us both being in shared control, like a single mind with two parts, and two entire bodies to control. But we didn't have time to worry about that.

Because the High Cleric was gesturing Alpha's sigil in last rites.

And our collective mind was still trapped by Alton's cloaking pendant.

Neither of us needed to ask if the other was ready. There was barely any such division left. Just one mind, reaching for the cloaking pendant on our Alton throat. In the back of our mind, we thanked the Cursed Void that the pendant wasn't one of Carlisle's, which would've been designed to protect against this kind of tampering.

Lucky for us, we hadn't been nearly as thoughtful as Carlisle.

The river of fire poured into our mind the instant we began channeling, roaring in so scorchingly hot and loud that we nearly missed the High Cleric's words.

"Kill them both."

We threw our mind at the cloaking pendant's necklace cord, liquid fire exploding through our existence, melting our focus, and—

And then, just like that, the pain was a distant afterthought, and I was me, and Alton was Alton, hoarding the suffering all to himself, utterly ablaze with it. And the Onyx Guard were squeezing their triggers.

I ripped the pendant from Alton's neck and yanked a barrier around us just as the explosion of point-blank gunfire slapped into my brain. The shots hit me like a pair of red hot spear tips—so agonizing I was sure I'd been too late.

But we were alive.

No time to worry why Alton was roaring in pain beside me. I opened myself like a conduit to all the energy in our surroundings, and let loose with a radial detonation of telekinetic force.

Distantly, I was aware of the crashes of overturned furniture and shattered glass. I didn't spare the time to check the damage. I was too busy tearing open the locks of my shackles and ripping the scorcher pendant from my neck. The moment I did, I felt Alton sag beside me.

I set in on his bindings, cursing at the number of locks they'd used, then slipping from my focus against my better judgment to quickly check our surroundings. It was good that I did.

The dagger was barely five feet from my head, and sailing in fast.

I swatted it aside with telekinesis, then hurled the Onyx Guard who'd thrown it straight at his recovering teammates like a human missile. Two of them twisted clear of the attack and joined the others who'd already regained their feet in leveling their weapons.

Behind me, the hallway door burst open, and I didn't need to look to know the Sanctum Guard reinforcements had arrived.

Too many.

I reached for my barrier as the first shots rang out, desperately ripping at Alton's locks, not knowing which way to turn as death closed in from every side.

Then a sound like a roaring mountain shook the entire room, hauntingly dissonant, and so painfully loud that it sent half the troops stumbling for cover, or down to the floor, hands clasped in futility over their ears.

"Haldin!" Alton's voice snapped, beneath the violent ringing in my head.

And then I felt it—the massive looming body that hadn't been there a moment ago. The reason, I realized, that Alton had gone vacant once I'd removed the scorcher.

The ship had arrived.

And we needed to get our asses on it. Now.

I sheared the last of Alton's locks clean through, then frantically adjusted my barrier as he burst to his feet, flinging chains every which way and roaring like a mad demon. I rolled around and lunged to my own feet, moving for the long window we'd breached. I nearly fell back down on the first step, my limbs only half-responsive, beaten and drained as my body was.

But then Alton was there, red eyes fully ablaze, half-dragging me along.

We staggered to the edge together, my vision waning as I struggled to hold out against the onslaught of softsteel slugs and charging Onyx Guard slamming into my barrier just behind us. I tripped and fell under the strain, and mustered a weak mental curse as I realized that I was going to fall through the shattered window, and that I didn't see the ship I'd been so sure was there.

Then impossibly strong arms caught me, and instead of falling out, we were flying. Flying straight out into the thousand foot fall to the streets of Divinity.

There was a moment of sheer panic. Then I saw the mercifully solid stretch of the iridescent purplish hull just below.

We thudded down onto Alton's waiting ship at full speed, and he didn't waste a second in dragging me along, practically carrying me at this point.

"Incoming," he growled.

I gave up on trying to run and let him have the rest of my weight as a fresh wave of gunfire rained down on us from the shattered window above. I closed my eyes, diverting everything I had left to maintaining the barrier, refusing to quit now, even as more shooters arrived at the edge, and the incoming fire intensified.

I held on, trusting—praying even, maybe—that Alton would get us out in time.

And then we fell.

My eyes snapped open, arms reflexively flailing out for something to grab onto. Then we hit hard ground. The ship deck, I registered, catching sight of the odd corridor wall, and the open patch of ceiling wriggling shut above us.

We'd made it?

I started to look to Alton for confirmation, then jumped at the rapid-fire thuds of slugs slamming into the ship's hull outside. Alton's eyes were closed in concentration. I looked around for something useful to do, vaguely aware of the soft electronic whine building in the air. Then the whine pulsed higher, and discharged in a low rush of sound.

And then there was nothing.

No gunfire pounding the hull. No distant cacophony of alarms and city chaos. Nothing but the gentle hum of the ship, vibrating through the deck against my aching skull.

I looked over to Alton, too rattled and overloaded to even find the words. He just nodded. I'd never seen a raknoth look so exhausted. I'd never even seen one pant before.

I laid my head gingerly back down to the deck, and gladly joined him.

We'd made it.

We'd actually freaking made it.

"Did you get all that?" I groaned, tenderly prodding at ribs I was pretty sure were broken. "Please tell me you got all that."

Alton started to sit up, like he'd just remembered he was supposed to be the dignified one here. Then he thought better of it, and plopped back to the deck with a sigh. "I don't believe I will be forgetting any part of that misadventure anytime soon."

I blew out an airy chuckle. It hurt. But not enough to stop the giddy thrill of survival building through my burning lungs. "Yeah. I think I know what you m—Agh!" I flinched as the first cough seized my lungs. It hurt worse than the chuckle had. Way worse. But I was still alive when it was over, and it was hard to argue with that.

I collapsed gratefully back to the deck, gasping for air.

"Well," I managed between breaths, "you know what they say, right?"

I felt Alton's expectant gaze on the side of my face, and I couldn't help but smile, bastard of a raknoth or no.

"Geronimo," I groaned.

And for the first time I could remember, lying beaten and bloodied on the deck beside me, I heard Alton Parker laugh.

37

WATCHERS

"Is there anything else we should know?" asked Freya Glenbark from the ship's node display, seeming to notice, as she always did, that I still had something left to say. Which, in itself, was kind of impressive, given how many aggressively blasphemous directions we'd already explored since the conversation had begun.

I'd already told her everything I could about what had happened in the White Tower. It had all been slightly redundant, of course, seeing as we'd already sent her footage of the entire event, pulled directly from Alton's immaculate raknoth memory. But Glenbark was intent on hearing my full testimony as well. Or maybe it was simply that she felt so bad about the whole thing that she figured it was only decent to let me dump some of the psychological load on her plate, too.

Whatever the case, we'd been over it all by now. All of it, except that last little five-ton haga beast in the room: the minor consideration of what the scud happened from here.

I looked at Alton, which only multiplied the complexities of that question in my head, then back to the display. "For starters, I guess I'd be on the lookout for retaliation tonight."

She watched me with that level look of hers. "Why do you say that?"

I shrugged. "Call it a bad feeling. You saw how furious His Holiness was. If he suspects there's actual footage of the whole thing, and that you intend to use it, well…"

I left the rest unsaid.

Glenbark nodded, clearly not disagreeing. "We'll keep our eyes open." She hesitated. "As for where we go from here..."

"It'd be best if I could lay low, and avoid blowing anything up?" I asked.

She tilted her head, not disagreeing with that, either. There was tension in her expression, like she wanted to add something more.

"Maybe avoid the planet altogether?" I continued, trying and failing to sound casual about it.

I'm not sure if Glenbark was unusually expressive that day, or if I was simply getting better at reading her. Either way, I could see it in the set of her jaw that she wanted to tell me that I had to do no such thing—that I should come to Oasis, and that she would protect me, no matter what. I could see it just as clearly as I could see the conflicting truth that my presence moving forward was as unlikely to be helpful as it was to be safe, for anyone involved.

It wasn't a surprise, really. It had been a long time coming. Not that that made me feel any better about having become yet another of the many pernicious weights hanging from Freya Glenbark's tired shoulders. But at least that was one last thing I could take off her plate.

"I think I'll stay clear for a little while," I said, glancing around the ship. "At least up here, I only have one monster to worry about."

Across the room, Alton gave me a flat look, but said nothing.

On the display, Glenbark's expression was grim with sympathy. "Haldin..."

I waited. There was nothing else to do. But I couldn't take the look in her eyes. I didn't like where this was going, though I couldn't have said exactly why in the moment.

"Thank you," she finally said, as I stared unseeingly through the node controls. "Thank you for everything."

I looked up, suddenly overwhelmed with the weight of it all. The finality in her words. The cold, crushing darkness of space all around me, trapping me in this alien vessel, alone with a creature I didn't understand, floating above a planet that no longer felt like home.

And Glenbark, thanking me. For everything. As if there'd been a thing she'd ever actually needed to thank me for at all. As if there could ever be enough thanks in the world to change the way I felt right then, staring down on Enochia.

There hadn't been. And there couldn't be.

I wanted to tell her that. Wanted to tell her that I knew she would've done the same—and more still—had she been in my position, and that we could leave it at that. But I couldn't seem to find the words. Couldn't seem to focus on anything but the growing ache in my chest, spreading up my throat, carrying the weight of imminent tears to the back of my eyes.

So I simply swallowed against that ache and nodded, not trusting myself to do anything else.

She seemed to understand.

"Take care of yourself up there, Hal."

"Yes, Sir," I said.

She gave me a sad smile, and killed the connection.

Silence settled in, as cold and seemingly endless as the space outside, and empty too, but for the gravity of Alton Parker sitting in his corner. The raknoth was practically motionless in the corner of my eye, but I got the impression he was watching me, waiting for something.

I let him wait. For as long as I could bear it, at least. But eventually, the silence got the best of me.

"Whatever you have to say, just say it."

I turned to see what he'd say, and found him watching me with a curious expression, like I'd interrupted something.

"What makes you think I have anything to say, at all?" he asked.

I narrowed my eyes. "Have you ever not?"

By way of reply, he only quirked one dark eyebrow, then leaned contentedly back against the bulkhead, like there was nothing in the world to be done but to indulge in a nice nap. Which, now that I thought about it, might well have been true for us, floating in orbit up here, absent any coherent plan.

Except for the tiny little part where raknoth apparently didn't require sleep.

I sighed, not wanting to think about what was going to become of me if I was to be reduced to pondering over raknoth napping habits while waiting around for calls from Elise and Johnny. Nothing good. That much was obvious. But what alternative was there?

Nothing good.

I'm not sure how long I spent staring at Alton Parker's allegedly napping form, turning over my non-options. But I don't think I'll ever forget the slow, sickening spiral of realization as I closed in, pulled by the inevitable gravity of a black hole, on precisely what alternative was left to me—the only alternative my insidious companion had ever intended to leave me with, I was suddenly certain.

"What you said before the White Tower..."

I hadn't meant to speak. Not really.

I wasn't even positive I *had* until he cracked one eye open and peered at me.

"That you've been damned ever since the reels resurrected you a terrorist?"

I nodded absentmindedly, not bothering to wonder how he'd known exactly what I was talking about.

"You never answered my question."

For a long few moments, I was sure he was going to toy with me, and ask me what question I meant—as if he couldn't remember every word we'd exchanged.

"No," he replied instead.

"No?"

He sat up, abandoning his nap ruse. "No, I did not know this was going to happen all along. No, I did not know from the moment I showed you the rakul. Or even before then."

"But this was what you wanted, wasn't it? To drive me away from my own planet? Leave me no choice but to..."

I hesitated, still not really sure what choices I even had left, but positive I didn't want to speak the one that was on the edge of my tongue.

Alton arched an eyebrow in silent, critical judgment, like he was either waiting for me to continue, or silently asking if I understood just how egocentric I sounded, assuming his every action had revolved around me. It was probably both. But I wasn't going to let him slither his way out of this.

"Tell me the truth, Alton. This is exactly what you were hoping for when you turned yourself in at Haven, isn't it?"

He held my gaze for a stretch.

"The current outcome, I'll admit, is more or less in line with what I'd hoped for," he finally said. "But you presume too much. Much as I would enjoy possessing that level of insidious ingenuity, I did not engineer your downfall to this state of pariah incommunicado. Believe it was my wish and will if you must, but I think you know this has been inevitable ever since you first entered the public eye."

"Trying to stop you and your people from destroying our planet," I growled.

He only nodded. "Yes. Just as I and my kin sought to stop the rakul. And just as the masters once fought to save our species from the brink of annihilation at the hands of another. The path of blame continues, on and on, through the eons, if one wishes to trace it."

"Which is all just a handy way of saying that none of this is your fault."

He leaned forward intently. "Then let us not shy away from the heart of it. I was willing to sacrifice your people for the greater good of my own, and for that of the universe at large. I could say that it was easier, knowing that your people were all as good as dead anyway, with the inevitable threat of the rakul looming. I could even say that I have come to regret the decision. But none of that would change the fact that I was willing, agreed?"

I only stared at him, not knowing what to say, or what to make of the sudden intensity in his words.

"You wish to have the truth?" he continued. "The truth is that I came to you because both of my plans for this world have failed spectacularly, and because you seemed to be the only one left standing in the ashes. You were my last hope, Haldin. So I came to Haven. Because I had to. And everything that's transpired since then, well..." He glanced meaningfully at the view of Enochia below. "I would be lying if I said I'd expected you to move as many mountains as you have down there. I stood patiently by, waiting for you to see the futility in trying. But move them, you did."

"Not very far," I muttered reflexively, thinking about the state of things below—Sanctum and Legion factions all crouched in their corners, Children of Enochia and one rogue raknoth Seeker lurking at the fringes. And all of it ready to catch fire at the slightest provocation. "Not nearly far enough."

Alton cocked his head. "I wouldn't be so certain. An insidious genius I may not be, but I doubt even the High Cleric of the Sanctum will be able to ride out this storm you've brought to his mighty tower steps. And with that scrutiny will come questions. Innumerable questions about what to believe, and whom to trust. And along with that, opportunities for those who would think to demonstrate their good will, and their value in the face of the obstacles to come." He fixed me with a serious look. "You've done more to open the way for a safe and just Enochia than I would have imagined possible for any lone man—much less one hounded by a public spotlight of fear and ignorant hatred. You've done everything you can, Haldin. The rest is in their hands."

I looked at him, searching his face for the reassurance I so desperately needed right then. I found it, too. And then I blew out a bitter huff, realizing that that was exactly why he was telling me these things. It was just another ploy. Another head game from the creature who'd just reminded me that he'd been willing to sacrifice untold thousands of Enochian lives to get what he wanted.

"And so I should just forget about Enochia now, right?" I asked, shaking my head. "All finished here, might as well dust off our bloody hands and fly off to go fix your problems instead?"

Alton didn't shy away—didn't even bat an eye. "I need your help, Haldin. And Enochia still needs it too. More than it knows." He shook his head. "Just not here."

I stood, not really sure where I was going, only that I needed to get as far away from this conversation as our confounded ship would allow. I made it across the room and to the corridor threshold before my temper commanded my feet to a halt, thinking to tell him that I wasn't just going to forget about Enochia and move on, and that if he wanted to fly off on his wild rakul hunt, he was welcome to drop me back on my planet and get the grop out of here once and for all.

But the words caught in my throat. I couldn't have said why. So instead, I stomped off down the corridor, resolving to tell the bastard when I was good and ready.

I'd never felt more alone.

THE NEXT FEW days passed at a disconcertingly paradoxical pace. With little to do but ignore Alton Parker and look forward to the next bit of news, or the next contact with Johnny or Elise, time passed with all the swiftness of a crippled snail. And yet, somehow, before I knew it, the displays told me it had been three whole days since Alton and I had gone into the White Tower, guns decidedly *not* blazing.

Probably, I figured, it had something to do with the fact that I no longer had a reliable night-and-day cycle to keep me tethered to the passing time. Probably, Alton could have clarified the matter quite easily. But scud if I was going to break my silent streak to ask him.

For the most part, we didn't even see each other. I stayed in my bare-bones quarters, either perusing the reels or acquainting myself with the soft purplish curves of the walls. Sometimes for hours on end. I slept intermittently, and never particularly well. Occasionally—and against my better judgment—I even ate the meals Alton prepared and left at my door, stubbornly trying to convince myself with each bite that it wasn't some of the tastiest damn cuisine I'd ever experienced.

Apparently, the bastard had had enough time to practice in his 2,800 years of life.

But scud if I was going to tell him that, either.

I was too busy stalking the reels, wondering more and more with each passing minute why I had yet to see a single flicker of movement on the battle lines out there, or to witness even a scrap of what had happened in the White Tower anywhere other than in my nightmares.

That the High Cleric had remained silent on our incursion was no great mystery. I could only imagine the Sanctum would sooner set fire to its own White Tower than willingly admit that the Demon of Divinity and his raknoth pal had come within spitting distance of the High Cleric and lived to tell about it. But that only made me wonder all the more about what Glenbark was up to down there, and why she hadn't yet acted.

Elise didn't have any more insider knowledge than I did when it was finally deemed safe for her to make contact with me. Just the well-reasoned thought that, if Glenbark was holding the footage back, she probably had very precise and calculated reasons for doing so.

Johnny, on the other hand, had been oddly comm-silent since the White Tower, though he *had* told Elise on the sly that, if she heard from me, she should relay that he was happy I wasn't dead yet, and also let me know, "And I quote," Elise had said, "'Bucky's in the barracks, broto.'"

I didn't have to think overly hard to imagine what he might've been trying to tell me by that. Bucky, as I'd started to explain to Elise, had been one of the most notorious tattle-tales in all of our tyro class. But Elise had cut me off before I'd gotten even that far, no doubt figuring that, whatever was afoot, it would've been unwise for us to unravel any bit of it over the Lights, even on a call that was theoretically secure. And she was probably right.

That alone should have convinced me that events were in motion, and that it was only a matter of time. And I guess it did, in a way. But none of that quite managed to silence the part of me that had begun to indulge in naive fantasies that maybe things didn't have to explode from here. That maybe this could all just somehow blow over without the bloodshed, and that maybe I could even return back to Enochia soon, and start piecing my way toward a quiet life with Elise, far away from the Sanctum, and everything else.

It was a nice thought to coax myself to sleep with, at least. Even if it was delusional.

But then the news hit.

It started with an attack on Oasis—an attack, it seemed from early reports, that had not only been routed, but possibly even *assimilated*, as far as field reporters could gather. It was an outrage. A military coup, some were calling it, decrying Glenbark a false general, and a traitor to her planet. Others found the wrinklies to publicly point out that, if the reports *were* true, it might've in fact been more of a return to rightful power than a coup, seeing as there'd still been no satisfactory explanation for Glenbark's unprecedented removal in the first place—especially given that the lack of a unanimous vote amongst the twelve Legion generals had been officially confirmed, and foul play was now heavily suspected.

But whether it was the lawful first step in restoring order to the ranks, or a grand betrayal of rogue Legion elements against the Sanctum and the world at large, the one thing the reels all agreed upon was that the Legion was in a state of flux the likes of which hadn't been seen in all of its centuries of steady service.

Personally, I was just glad to see that Glenbark's push to quietly secure the loyalty of Auckus' more skeptical camp had apparently paid off, and that Oasis hadn't been overrun for the second time in as many seasons. Other than that, I didn't really know what to think. A part of me—the part that had been a tyro too long to forget—mourned at seeing the Legion in such disarray, no matter the what or the why. I couldn't escape the feeling that I should've felt guilty, too, if for no other reason than having not been there to help to defend Oasis. But the guilt didn't come.

Maybe I was just too tired, too emotionally drained. Or maybe I was truly starting to believe my presence would've probably done more harm than good.

The latter, it turned out, almost certainly would've been true.

Barely an hour after news of the Oasis attack hit, the footage of our hostile chat with the High Cleric joined it in the churning dumpster of the newsreels, and I watched in a kind of reverent disbelief as that dumpster caught fire, and the Mighty, Infallible Sanctum joined the Legion on the media chopping block for the first time in... ever.

To say it was unprecedented would've been a laughable understate-ment, and probably too eloquent a word to convey the chaos that followed. If even a tenth of the threats, rage, and ill-informed world views pouring into the forums had been given power, I was certain that whatever bloodshed might've been averted in the reversal at Oasis would've easily been repaid, a thousand times over. It was madness. So much so that even the WAN didn't seem completely clear as to who should be blamed for it all—only that we should all look to Alpha for guidance in these trying times.

"Look instead to the river of blood in the streets," read the top response to that particular vid. "Your Alpha is a lie."

It was more than I'd ever dared to expect. More of *what*, exactly, I couldn't even articulate. Demons to the wind if I could've even said whether I thought it was good or bad. All I really knew was that the fire was shifting. Too quickly. Morphing into something I couldn't predict or quantify. And I'd been the one who'd carried the striker to the pyre.

I felt hollow inside. But I couldn't look away.

I was still glued to the reels hours later, when the node chimed with an incoming call, and I felt the first pang of relief I'd felt all day. I jabbed the icon to accept the connection, and started blurting questions before Johnny's image could even finish resolving on the display.

"What's happening? Why'd she wait so long to—And what's...?" I faltered as the connection stabilized, and I got a better look at him. "What happened to your face?"

The entire left side of his head was a mess of mottled purple bruising that culminated with a few impressively dark streaks right along the side of his nose, and the bottom of his eye socket. He looked like he'd taken one beast of a punch, or maybe just a mild clubbing. And the grim grin on his lips told me it hadn't been for nothing, either.

"I, my good sir, may or may not have had a heroic round of the ol' fisties, with no less than a Legion general." His expression darkened. "Traitorous goat-gropper."

For a second, I could only gape, trying to process that.

"That's what she was waiting for," Johnny explained, "to answer your"—he thought about it—"second question, I guess. Hi, by the way," he added, with a pointed little wave. "Nice to see you, and all that."

"Johnny, what the—What the scud is—"

My mouth kept working soundlessly, the questions flitting by too fast for me to catch hold of.

"Eaaasy there, buddy," Johnny crooned, patting the air as if to say, *It's all gonna be okay.* "Here's the thing. Even after everything, Freya was still pretty sure there was someone on her high command here who was ready to stab her in the back when the time came. So when you sent her that vid—nice work, by the way..." He frowned. "I think. Anyway, once she had that shining demonstration of His Holiness' not-so-holiness and other assorted mind-gropping revelations, I guess she figured it was probably her last chance to really spring our encamped enemy into action. So she shared it with her advisers. One at a time."

"Smart."

He shook his head. "You have no idea, broto. She was methodical." A frown creased his brow. "I didn't even realize what she was up to until it was already over."

"So what happened?"

"Well..." He spread his hands. "General Hopper tried to stab her in the back. Literally. Bastard was apparently planning to frame the whole thing on me."

"But..." I gaped, trying to wrap my head around it.

For General Hopper, the most vocal and steadfast of Glenbark's supporters among the twelve generals, to betray her... It just didn't seem to add up. He'd been a good man, as far as I could tell. A reasonable one. He'd even been kind to me—or not disgusted by my very presence, at least, as General Auckus and half the Legion had been.

And yet, he *had* seemed troubled every time the conversation had veered toward conflict with the Sanctum, hadn't he? But then again, so had everyone else. It was a troubling topic, after all, and these were troubling times. Troubling, and apparently even more treacherous than I'd realized.

"So he was... apprehended?"

Johnny waggled his fingers on-screen. "By none other than these five beauties." He looked at his own fingers in appreciation. "Never thought I'd live to see the day I decked a general and got away with it."

"You really...?"

"What, took him down?"

I nodded dumbly, still trying to wrap my head around it all.

"Technically?" Johnny asked, scrunching his face. "Well, let's just say it was a joint effort between me and Freya." He pursed his lips thoughtfully, as if reliving the moment. "And also that I'd never wanna throw down with her in a dark alley." His fiery eyebrows rose incrementally. "You know, unless..."

"Uh, Johnny?"

He snapped back to reality with a sharp shake of his head. "Anyway, we brigged his traitorous ass, and Auckus sprung the attack on Oasis as soon as he realized he'd lost his inside man. But we were ready for that."

"Yeah, I saw. Looks like Glenbark's ally outreach paid off?"

"Enough to survive the day, at least," Johnny said, his expression sobering. "It wasn't as pretty as the reels made it sound. Hopper had been reporting to the outside, you know? Letting them know what units and officers they might wanna keep an eye on when the slugs started flying." He dropped his gaze. "A lot of good people still died today."

The heaviness returned to my gut.

"I'm sorry, Johnny."

He shot me a critical look, and I could see the pain in his eyes, lurking beneath.

"Not like that," I said quickly. "Not because I feel guilty, or anything else. I know they were fighting for something bigger. But I'm sorry anyway. They used to be my family too, remember?"

He sighed. "We'll always be your family, broto," he said, pulling himself together, though it was hard to miss the shadow that remained. "So what's the situation up there?" he asked, looking over my shoulder at the bare walls behind me. "How's Captain Red Eyes doing?"

"Probably eavesdropping every word of this," I said rather pointedly, knowing it was likely true. "Other than that, I don't know. We're alive, I guess. But seeing everything that's happening down there right now..."

"It's a lot to take in," Johnny agreed.

That pretty much summed it up. Enough so that I wasn't sure what to add.

Silence stretched for a few moments before Johnny continued.

"But, the way I figure... Well, either everything we've kicked up is true—and I think I believe it is—and this needed to happen for the sanctity of our future anyway... Or it's all bullscud, and we've fallen for it. But either way, this planet was sick. It *is* sick. I don't know how else to explain the fact that we ended up in civil war over a freaking alien invasion. That's the kind of scud that's supposed to unite a society, not rip it apart. And if this chaos is what it takes to get us back on course, then I guess all we can do is try to keep as many people safe as we can while we all work it out together."

I turned his words over, surprised.

He shrugged, apparently noticing my surprise. "I might've borrowed a line or two of that from Freya."

I smiled despite myself, and decided there was no need to point out that it wasn't *just* the raknoth that had driven Enochia to war, but also the emergence of Shapers into the public eye, too. But we hardly needed more brooding right then. I wasn't even sure that little detail really contradicted Johnny and Glenbark's underlying point anyway. Because Enochia *was* sick, wasn't it? Hunting an innocent subsection of its own people solely because it was caught up in the fever dream lie of a raknoth who was a thousand years beyond the pyre?

That sounded like a sick planet to me.

So for once, I tried not to dwell on the negative.

"I miss being down there," I said. "I miss seeing you and Elise." I shook my head, blowing out an incredulous huff of laughter. "Terrible as it sounds, I think I actually kinda miss being at war with the hybrids. At least back then we were all in Haven together, and everyone was more or less on the same page."

"Back then," Johnny muttered. "Like it wasn't just a couple cycles ago."

"It's been a long couple cycles, broto."

He tilted his head in concession. "It *was* a lot easier to tell who the bad guys were back then. I'll give you that."

"Here's hoping we can get back to that place someday, whether it's Haven or wherever else. As long as we're together."

The last words left an aching in my throat that caught me completely unprepared. And Johnny didn't miss it.

"Yeah, about that," he said. "You're not... planning on, uh, disappearing on us, are you?"

"No," I said quickly, shaking my head. "I mean"—I glanced in Alton's general direction without really meaning to—"No. I don't really know what comes next for me. But I'm not just gonna, you know..."

"Vanish into the ether without a trace?"

"Yeah. That."

"Good." Johnny looked less than convinced. "Because we'll make a place for you down here whenever we have to." He smiled a little. "Even if we have to hide you in the wilds like a two-headed mutant for a little while. We'll make it work."

"I know," I said, not wanting to argue, or to point out all the numerous ways that their helping me would only further complicate the already murky waters down there. "I'll, uh..."

"Talk it over with Captain Red Eyes?" Johnny asked, eyes narrowing a fraction.

"I'll keep an eye on the reels," I said, "and think about how to handle our good captain."

"Personally, I'd vote you give him the ol' stabby-stabby right now." His brow furrowed. "Except that Bells is doing better."

I sat up straighter, and Johnny's frown shifted to a guilty grin.

"Yeah, guess I probably should've led with that, huh? She woke up for the first time yesterday. Therese said she was pretty disoriented, which I guess makes sense. But she's hopeful she's gonna make a full recovery. Along with all the other hybrids they treated."

"Johnny, that's... That's amazing."

"Best news I've heard in years," Johnny agreed. "You know, followed closely by finding out you were still alive after the fire, of course. And after we lost you at Sanctuary." He frowned. "And the White Tower. Twice." He shrugged. "Guess the news kind of loses its kick after the first five or six times, huh?"

I smiled. "I'm not sure *I* even care all that much anymore."

The joke fell short even before the words had finished leaving my mouth. I sobered, searching for something else to fill the painful silence.

"Well, I hope you get to see Bells soon, buddy. In person, I mean."

Johnny nodded. "It's a definite possibility. Things are gonna be moving pretty fast down here from now on. Freya was serious about retaking Haven, and I think we might even do it without bloodshed, but... Well, we'll see how things go from here."

I nodded, trying my best to look optimistic. "Have fun saving Enochia."

He smiled. "I learned from the best, broto." He paused, concern creasing his brow. "Hey, be careful up there, huh? Don't make a broto have to come avenging your ass."

"Wouldn't dream of it," I said.

"Yeah," he said, still hesitant. "And, uh... No hasty decisions up there, either?"

I nodded again, showing him my empty hands in a gesture of surrender.

"Good," he said. "Right then. Duty calls. Talk soon, broto."

With Johnny gone and nothing but the churning newsreels and the faintly discernible specter of Alton Parker left to fill my spirits, the void at my center grew unpleasantly fast. After a few more minutes of mindless scrolling, I decided there was nothing more to be gained from the reels, and stood to go try my luck elsewhere.

Much as I didn't feel like talking to Alton Parker ever again, Johnny's talk about being careful up here had reminded me of one critical consideration about being trapped aboard a not-so-large ship with a bloodthirsty raknoth, and I figured I might as well address it before I thought about closing my eyes again.

I didn't need to reach out with my extended senses to guess that Alton would be on the flight deck. And there he was. Just standing there, staring off into space, as I'd realized over the past few days he seemed to be perfectly content to do for long hours at a time.

I guess after a couple thousand years of existence, you probably get pretty good at handling boredom.

"Come to give me the ol' stabby-stabby, have you?" Alton asked, not turning from the viewing wall.

So he *had* been listening.

It wasn't much of a surprise. With how sharp his ears were, I'm not sure he even would've had a choice in the matter. But it was good to know anyway, just for future reference.

"It's been a while," I said, deciding to ignore his comment. "Do you need blood, or not?"

He turned to me with a smile. "Yes, I do."

I stared at him, waiting for him to ask, or to suggest some arrangement, or to say anything at all, really. But he was content to just keep smiling, obviously enjoying my uncertainty. It made my decision easier, at least.

Let the bastard starve, I decided, if he was going to make a game of this.

I was about to turn back for my room when his smile widened further, taking on that especially punchable look he was so adept at nailing, and he withdrew something from an inside pocket of his charcoal jacket. A dark crimson something.

"I came prepared," he said, holding up the blood bag for my inspection. "Though I do appreciate your thoughtful generosity."

I hesitated, kind of wanting to walk away now out of principle more than anything.

My curiosity got the better of me.

"How much... How long are you stocked for?"

"I have enough on board to survive for at least several seasons. Possibly for years, depending."

I watched him, waiting to see if he'd elaborate.

"Our needs can change rather drastically depending on several factors," he explained, apparently done with his games for now, "not the least of which being how... active we are, physically speaking."

"Active as in shirking off gunfire and punching through permacrete walls?"

He tilted his head. "Precisely. As far as I've observed, even that changes from individual to individual, but you may rest assured, provided we are largely at rest, I do not need nearly as much blood as you might assume."

"Well color me relieved," I said, not bothering to hide my sarcasm.

I suppose I shouldn't have been surprised to find out he was prepared for a long voyage, all things considered, but it made me uncomfortable all the same. I refrained from asking how much food he had stocked aboard. I didn't want to know the answer.

"So what do you think we should do?" I asked instead. Why, I couldn't have said. I already knew what Alton Parker wanted to do, after all. I guess I was just trying to fill the silence, and maybe make a little sense of the wild fire below that I no longer had even the illusion of any control over.

"I imagine we wait, and we watch," Alton said, echoing my own fears.

I glanced over his shoulder at the viewing wall, dreading the thought of stewing away for who knew how many more days.

"That," my raknoth companion added, brandishing the sealed blood bag one last time before sliding it back into his jacket pocket, "or we set a course, and prepare for bloody times ahead."

3 8

END OF DAYS

For all the time and breath I'd wasted bad-mouthing civilians—wondering how they could possibly be so vocal about their myriad of worldly complaints when they weren't even willing to stand up to serve and protect the freedoms they so readily spat upon—I quickly realized something in the days that followed.

It wasn't easy, watching the world tick by as a powerless observer.

I'd thought I'd understood that well enough during my years as a Legion tyro, toeing regulation lines and snapping to orders day in and day out. But that was unmistakably different. Because even at the most degrading, helpless moments of Legion service—even as I'd scrubbed scud from the nooks and crannies, with Docere Mathis barking at me that we didn't have all day, Silver Spoon... Even then, I'd known that it was supposed to stand for something. That it was all in service to something bigger than any one of us.

But now, adrift in space with no one but Alton Parker for company, I felt like less than a civilian. I practically felt like an alien to my own damn planet, watching events below unfolding like a storyvid drama. And unfold, they did.

It started with the news that the High Cleric had been asked by both his Sanctum advisers and the praetors of Divinity to abdicate his position and make way for a less controversial successor.

It was probably a smart move on the Sanctum's part, judging by the unparalleled crisis of faith that had been blazing across Enochia ever since the world had gotten a good behind-the-scenes look at their High Cleric strangling the kid who'd come to tell him that his religion was in fact a raknoth construct, birthed as a vessel to keep the planet's inhabitants under control.

Not that the truth about Sarentus and the rakul had been widely accepted.

For the most part, it seemed like almost everyone thought it was all wild bullscud, and those who actually believed any part of it were almost guaranteed to be laughed straight out of any so-called *serious* debate about the future of the Sanctum. But the fact that no one actually *believed* our wild claims didn't seem to have done anything to prevent half of Alpha's loyal children from looking up for the first time in their lives to question whether the Sanctum was to be so blindly trusted as they'd once thought.

I admit, I didn't really understand the rationale, there. But maybe I was too biased by what I'd seen in Alton's head, or just too far removed from it all up there on my alien spaceship.

Whatever the case, when it came to the High Cleric, it wasn't hard to understand why the Sanctum's decision rankled the man. Because that was the point, really. He *was* a man—just another prideful man like the rest of us, no matter what the Sanctum had wanted to believe. And I doubted any amount of mental gymnastics would ever allow him to escape the fact that his so-called *less controversial* successor could only also be thought of as his *more worthy* better.

And so the High Cleric rebelled against his advisers, clerics and praetors alike.

That, at least, I understood—even if I'd never thought to expect it. Then again, I probably shouldn't have been surprised. It wasn't like the world was making much sense these days.

And so I watched, with a disbelief that was quickly becoming so routine as to be mind-numbing, as the Sanctum followed the Legion's example and splintered into warring factions, with the disgraced High Cleric fleeing—somewhat ironically, I thought—to Humility, where his support remained the strongest. Meanwhile, a new High Cleric took the dais in the White Tower, and promptly proceeded to pretend as if nothing were truly amiss, and that this was all nothing but a fleeting test of the loyalty of Alpha's faithful.

It was the first time I'd ever witnessed a High Cleric booed on the dais. And so the War of the Four began, according to the growing inferno of reel commentary.

It wasn't pretty. And it didn't exactly set me at ease, either, knowing that the crux of the Sanctum's in-fighting had just landed itself directly over Elise's head in Humility. But given how long the Emmútari remnants had apparently been hiding down there, I trusted she and the Children of Enochia would be safe enough until they decided to make their move and maybe just bump it up to the War of the Five.

What that move might be, I hadn't a clue. I wasn't privy to that sort of intel as a demon-loving blue-blue-red—a status Elise still hadn't seen fit to shine satisfactory illumination upon in our few hurried conversations over the Lights.

"They're frightened because you're powerful," she finally snapped, on the day I refused to drop it. "Can we just leave it at that?"

"Is that what the red means?" I asked immediately, pathologically incapable at that point of simply leaving it at that.

"No." She shook her head, sighing. "No. That's the blue. Raw power, and emotional empathy, and..." She bit her lip, looking more flustered than I was used to seeing. "... And they don't actually know what the red means, so can we please just stop talking about it? It's just gonna drive you crazy."

I didn't know how to take that. It was the most tight-lipped Elise had been about anything since we'd met. And it kind of scared the crap out of me.

Luckily, I had nothing but free time and a constant stream of dark tidings with which to drive myself slowly insane.

Disgraced High Clerics and worldwide crises aside, I found myself worrying more and more every day that our parting act hadn't been enough —that, no matter what might happen to the Sanctum, we hadn't changed a thing for the Shapers of Enochia. Because as tumultuous as things were down there, if there was any one thing the people of Enochia could still collectively agree on, it was that the Demon of Divinity and his raknoth pal needed to be found and put to the noose, right along with the rest of our demonic brethren.

If anything, the words, "raknoth" and "demon," seemed to be becoming more interchangeable.

Rumors of where we'd gone had been rampant since the attack on the White Tower—many of them more accurate than their perpetrators probably knew. Then again, maybe the conclusion that Alton and I had fled into space wasn't such an impressive one to reach, given that we'd done so in an Alpha-damned spaceship, but Alton assured me that no scanner or scope on

Enochia would be capable of spotting us without a hefty dose of sheer, dumb luck.

I might've taken more comfort in that, if it hadn't been so clear that even the knowledge of my continued existence was still a source of trouble below. Some days, I wondered if I shouldn't just say demons to the wind with it, and head back down to rejoin the fight. Others, I wondered if maybe Alton and I shouldn't have had the decency to at least fake our deaths on the way out. But it was too late now.

Slowly, though, my name began to fade from the reels, and the conversations turned more and more away from the reactionary mudslinging and toward the serious question of how many threats remained lurking unseen on Enochia, and how the good people were ever to repair the widening rifts within and between the Sanctum and Legion after everything that had happened.

Glenbark, at least, had a resounding answer for the latter query.

Day after day, her campaign to cast out Auckus and reclaim her rightful seat as High General had proceeded at a seemingly unstoppable charge. It was the only decidedly good news I could seem to rely on in all of the chaos. Every time I spoke with Johnny, they were gaining more support, winning control of another outpost, another legion. It was only a matter of time, he told me.

Even so, I could scarcely believe it the day he called me from Annabelle's bedside in Haven to let me say hi, and to tell me that General Auckus had been marched to the Haven brig in shackles just an hour earlier.

Glenbark had done it. They all had. Together. And as much good as it did my heart to smile and laugh with Johnny and Annabelle just like old times, it only made me feel that much more alone when the call ended, and I was left staring down at Enochia.

They'd all done it, together. And here I was, floating in orbit. The world's most useless spectator. Losing my mind a little more each day. Losing my will, my sense of purpose.

I telekinetically crushed a lightsteel shipping container I found in storage that day, just to prove to myself that I could.

All that power, crackling through my fingertips, and here I was, powerless to help anyone.

"I can't stay here," I whispered, rather unexpectedly, like some deeper part of my brain had stepped forward to take control of my mouth and give me a piece of my own mind. I wasn't even sure what I meant by it. That I couldn't stay here on the ship? That I needed to return planetside, and take my chances hiding out?

I told myself that's what I'd meant. Just like I told myself I hadn't noticed that Alton had appeared quietly at the storage room hatchway moments before I'd said the words. Because I wouldn't have knowingly said those words in front of the raknoth. Couldn't have.

Could I?

I turned to the raknoth, fully expecting him to launch into a timely pitch on the many logical reasons to leave Enochia behind and begin the hunt elsewhere, and fully ready to tell him to shove it all up his scaly ass. But he didn't say a word. Just studied me for another long moment, then turned and headed back for the flight deck to go stare at his damned wall.

I stood there for a long while, paralyzed by the kind of full body malaise I hadn't experienced since I'd lost Carlisle. I thought of him then, and of my mom and dad. I didn't bother trying to imagine what they would've done in my boots. For the first time, I didn't need to. Instead, I just thought of their faces, and of how much I missed them. Then I cleaned up my mess and went back to check on the reels. Again.

Days passed by. More days than I cared to count. But I counted anyway.

Day after day, I felt more disconnected from the world below. I thought of it more and more *as* the world below. Like it was something separate. Something other. Some days, it began to feel like I was genuinely looking down on an alien planet. Others, I just browsed the reels, feeling utterly psychopathic, like I'd knowingly lit the house on fire and had come out here to the shadows to watch it burn, marveling at the ineffable beauty of the thing, even as the voice in the back of my head pointed out that there'd still been a living, breathing family inside.

It was a little scary, how much I felt like I was losing touch.

"So I see you're a beard guy now, eh?" Johnny asked one day, during one of our check-ins.

We were into the Harvest season then. Over two full cycles aboard that damned ship with Alton Parker—thirty three days, according to the tally I couldn't for the life of me explain why I was still keeping, other than an apparent knack for self-loathing masochism.

I pulled up a full-display view of myself through the node camera to see what he meant. There were no mirrors aboard the ship, as far as I knew. And when I got a good look at myself, I was kind of glad for that.

I looked like a wreck. And I felt like one, too.

"I can't stay here," I whispered softly, staring at my wild, ragged appearance, and trying to remember the feeling of Elise's skin on mine, and the joy of soft, woodland dirt beneath my boots.

"What was that, broto?" Johnny's voice crackled through the amps on the still-running call, nearly making me jump. "Ah scud, I think we might be losing you."

FINALLY, the day came.

I couldn't have said how I knew. I couldn't have even said what it was I'd been waiting for. But on that day, I woke with the visceral certainty that something had changed, and that now there was truly nothing left for me to do on Enochia. Nothing that wouldn't be done better and more peacefully by hands other than mine.

It wasn't a good feeling. But it wasn't necessarily a bad one, either. Bittersweet might've been the word, if there'd actually been anything sweet about it. Instead, it was only a placid sense of inevitability that I felt. Something like peace and calm, but unmistakably marred by the bitter certainty that, whatever lasting peace might arise out of all of this chaos, I was never again to exist anywhere but on its fringes. And maybe not even there, I couldn't help but think, as I trudged onto the flight deck and found Alton staring down at Enochia.

"They killed Nan'Alar," he said, not turning.

I didn't need to ask who Nan'Alar was. There was only one possible answer.

The last of the raknoth Seekers. The one who'd escaped back at Adam and Enid's public execution outside the White Tower.

"I think I felt it, somehow," I said, thinking about the way I'd awoken.

If Alton was surprised by that, he didn't see fit to say it. Didn't see fit to say much of anything, apparently.

I hesitated in the corridor, wondering if I should leave him be, and give him the privacy to mourn his fallen kin.

Did raknoth even mourn? I couldn't help but wonder. It was a strange concept to think about, and yet another question to which I wasn't sure I wanted to know the answer. But the longer I stood there, the more I felt like I should say something.

"Were you... close?"

I felt foolish about the words as soon as they left my mouth. Alton, though, didn't seem especially bothered as he turned to regard me.

"He was of my clan," he said, as if that should be answer enough. Then, as if remembering who he was talking to, he added, "I did not harbor any particular affection for him, if that's what you mean. Friendships—what humans would call friendships, at least—are not so common among my people. We are too... pragmatic for such relationships."

I took a few hesitant steps onto the flight deck, not really sure this was a conversation I wanted to be having.

"Why didn't you recruit Nan'Alar and his companion for your rakul hunting party before, then, if you're so pragmatic?"

If I wasn't so sure he was a heartless reptile, I might've felt bad about the question. As it was, he didn't seem to mind. So I continued on.

"Frosty, too. They were all stronger than I ever could be. Seems like it would've been the pragmatic thing to do."

"Does it?" He studied me for a long while. "Why are you alive, Haldin?"

I frowned, not really sure what he meant by that.

"They were all stronger than you, in a purely physical sense," he continued. "Yes?"

I searched his inscrutable expression, looking for the shape of this new game. "You know they were."

He tilted his head in admission. "Yes." A flat smile stretched his lips. "And did you ever allow that to stop you, even for a moment?"

I said nothing, understanding immediately what he was getting at, and not liking it one bit. I couldn't have even said why, aside from that it felt like he was preparing to deliberately stroke my ego.

His smile widened at my hesitation, perfectly reptilian in his empty eyes. "That is why, Haldin. Simply for the reason that you have out-survived all other challengers, whether you may take direct credit or not." He shrugged, and turned back to the viewing wall. "Perhaps your human naivety has finally began rubbing off on me after all this time."

I watched his turned back, wondering for the thousandth time if I could trust a single word he'd ever said. The worst part—the most troubling part —was that, ever since I'd sprung him from the Haven brig over a season ago, he'd never once lied to me. Not that I could prove. Even before Haven, I couldn't cite a single direct lie he'd ever told me. Not for sure.

Then again, that hardly made him trustworthy.

Alton Parker had lied to Enochia. He'd committed crimes against this planet that even now were beyond my ability to fully grasp. Not just crimes. Atrocities. Bloody, unforgivable atrocities. That much was all beyond question. And while he might not have directly lied to me at any point, he'd certainly mislead on multiple occasions—sometimes toying with me seemingly for little more than the fun of it.

And yet despite all that, for the life of me, I was starting to wonder if—or, rather, to worry that—in some sick way, Alton Parker might actually be less likely to lie to my face than pretty much anyone else on the planet.

And that alone told me I'd been on this ship for far too long.

"And that's it?" I finally asked. "You really expect me to believe that that's all this has ever been about? My unwillingness to die?"

He glanced back at me over his shoulder. "Do you see any other reason? What else would I possibly be playing at at this point?" He smirked. "Unless you wish to believe I simply desired to procure the most stubborn human blood source on the planet for my travels?"

I held his gaze, searching in futility for the lie. Pulling at frayed threads of the wildest conspiracy theories I could dream up, seeking the catch, the ulterior motive. Nothing caught. Nothing but the secondhand memories of the unstoppable monsters that would one day find their way to Enochia, and the notion that this lone raknoth, for reasons of his own, wanted the bastards dead.

"What harm could possibly befall your world for your absence, Haldin," Alton asked, "which hasn't already befallen it a thousand times over by now?"

With that, he returned his attention to the viewing wall, leaving me to stare at his turned back in mute horror.

Because he was right. I'd known it since I awoke that morning, adrift in that soft but certain tide of inevitability. Scud, maybe I'd known it ever since I'd made the decision to spring the raknoth from Haven. I'd only been hanging onto a dream, holding at the fraying lines of idealistic hope. But there was no more hanging on. Because he was right. Forty-four days watching the chaos below unfolding through the reels, watching my friends extinguishing fires and building futures more effectively than I could ever again hope to. And he was right.

"What do I do?"

The words escaped my mouth in a hollow whisper, unintended, least of all for Alton Parker. Because I knew what he would say—knew that this was the very moment he'd been waiting for for nigh two seasons now.

Only he didn't say it.

For a long while, he didn't say anything. Only stared out at the vast, star-dotted blackness of space.

"Would you believe me," he finally asked, "if I told you that I, too, am afraid of what lies ahead?"

I wasn't sure what I believed in that moment, other than the two most fundamental pillars that rose up in my mind like a pair of darksteel mountains.

On the one was the flame-carved reminder that the creature in front of me had been unflinchingly willing to sacrifice an entire planet for this mission of his, and that I must *never* forget that. And on the other, burning just as clearly now, was the harsh certainty that my time of service on Enochia was done.

I'd done everything I could do on the planet.

But not everything I could do *for* the planet.

No. Not even close.

And so it was that I found myself marching slowly over to the viewing wall, moving like I was dragging softsteel boots, and yet somehow feeling perversely lighter for each step. I kept walking until I stood beside Alton Parker, staring out into the dark expanse.

"So this plan of yours..." I said, feeling like the softsteel had spread to my lungs, yet unable to deny the thrill of perverse excitement that accompanied it at the thought of taking action. Taking control. Doing something— anything—other than sitting here in this damned ship for one more impotent, helpless moment. "What did you have in mind, exactly?"

3 9

LEGACIES

I was going to die.

Outside of literal life-and-death situations, I'd always thought phrases like that were nothing but overly dramatic embellishments, used either thoughtlessly, or in a desperate play for attention. But nonetheless, there it was, as the ship veered lower, and the lush green canopy of the southern forests of Divinity rose closer into view.

I'd never felt such dread in my life—so thick and heavy and all-consuming that my brain didn't seem equipped to interpret it, other than that I was going to die.

I couldn't do this.

Desperately, I looked to Alton. I'm not sure what manner of mercy I was hoping to find from the sociopathic raknoth, but he was occupied with the ship's descent anyway, his eyes vacant with telepathic focus.

For a second, I considered trying to wrest control of the ship from him. Scud, for a second, I almost wished the rakul would actually show up right then and there, and that we could have it out with those intergalactic tyrants right on our home soil, for better or for worse, even if it *did* mean the end of the world. Because in that moment, I couldn't believe that anything else in the universe could ever be worse than this. Worse than the thought of what I was about to do.

I couldn't leave her.

I just couldn't. That was all there was to it.

But I had to. It had already been decided. Decided by *me*, no less, back when we'd still been far enough away from this conversation that I'd actually been able to think rationally. Back when I'd still had the objectivity to properly weigh the threat of everything Alton had shown me against the promise of the dark chasm that was already beginning to tear open in my heart.

But Elise would survive this. That was all that mattered. And I would too. Enough to fight on, at least. Because fight on, we must. Her here, where she could help the Children of Enochia to build on the momentum of their first major victory and, fates willing, usher in some meaningful peace between Enochia and its Shapers. And me out there, where Alton Parker and I might—just *might*—have a shot at turning the rakul away before they could ever reach Earth or Enochia and prematurely render any such peace irrelevant in the wake of their cataclysmic fury.

I still ached inside at having found out that it had been the Children of Enochia who'd taken down the last reeker, Nan'Alar. It was good news, to be sure. The best news we could've hoped for, really, and a solid foothold for the Children's entry into the public eye. But knowing that I'd been idly sitting by while Elise and Garrett and the rest of the Children's finest fighters had been fighting to white-knuckled, bloody death against the last of the living raknoth on Enochia...

It had been for the greater good, I'd told myself. Elise had told me the same, when we'd finally had a chance to speak, afterward. The victory had needed to belong to them, and to them only. My involvement only would've tarnished the deed in the eyes of Enochia. Which is why I hadn't learned about it until the deed was done. Smart move on their part, I'd had to admit, as I'd sat shaking with helpless rage, listening to Elise's recounting of what they'd been through, and seeing the scrapes and bruises on her face, and the flinches she tried to hide every time she shifted.

At least no one had died.

And honestly, after everything Alton had shown me in the past few days, a small part of me had to admit that it would've been doing them no kindness to deprive them of the chance to slay a reeker on their own. At least now they knew they could. Because if Alton and I were to fail out there, and if even one of the rakul actually reached Enochia someday...

After some of the memories Alton had shared with me, I almost would've rather faced an entire company of reekers than a single Kul.

But hopefully it wouldn't come to that. There were still avenues to explore—the remaining raknoth clans of Earth, and the tentative hope we might yet find the daughter of the Earthborn Shaper who'd originally created the raknoth blood curse chief among them. Not that any of that really made me feel any better—about the mission itself, or about my leaving everything behind on Enochia. It should have, some part of my would-be rational mind insisted. I was stepping right up to the martyr block, after all, wasn't I? I was practically being a hero. Or so that voice told me on the outside. But on the inside...

Inside, I just felt vile. I felt like a lesser being than even the dumpster fire reels were giving me credit for—like the joke was on them for having been so focused on what I was and what I'd done when there was such a ripe trove of cowardice and other shameful truths lingering just beyond their expert scrutiny. The thought made me want to laugh. And cry.

Why had I chosen this place? I couldn't stop wondering, as the forest rose to meet us. Why here, of all the places on Enochia?

In my head, the old Emmútari outpost that had once served as hideout and home for me and Carlisle had seemed as good a place as any for this last discreet meeting. It might not have been perfect, given that the location had technically been compromised when Johnny had once dispatched a Legion skimmer out there to collect me when I'd lost my scud after the original White Tower massacre. But to my surprise, neither he nor Elise had argued when I'd made the suggestion.

Maybe they'd already figured out it wouldn't matter anymore after today. I hadn't told them why I needed to meet in person. Not explicitly. But I would've been surprised if they hadn't at least guessed what was coming.

Maybe that's why coming here of all places to say my goodbyes suddenly felt so macabre—like some part of me just wanted to see to it that my every precious relationship on Enochia was consolidated here in this final resting place. Here, where I'd mourned the loss of my parents under the protection of the man who'd quickly become a father of a different kind. Here, where I'd returned to mourn *his* loss, once he'd sacrificed his life for mine. And now here again, for this.

We gather here today to mourn the loss of Haldin Raish, and all that he held dear.

I quelled the bitter thoughts and looked to the trees below, seeking some peace of mind among the tranquil greenery. Thinking of my parents again, I lamented the fact that I hadn't had the chance to visit them one last time in Sanctuary. Or maybe it was the fact that I hadn't even tried that truly bothered me. Somehow, though, risking our entire rakul insurance voyage just to see their ashes one more time hadn't seemed reasonable.

That realization hadn't exactly helped my current feelings of self-worth, but it didn't matter anyway. I didn't need to touch a pyre stone to feel them there with me.

The dread in my stomach tightened as I began to catch familiar landmarks and spotted the pair of mighty oak trees on my old hillside lookout. I pointed the way wordlessly to Alton before remembering that he was busy flying. It didn't seem to matter anyway. He was already bringing the ship down as if he knew exactly where he was headed. Maybe he—or the ship— could sense it.

When we cleared the bountiful forest canopy, and the old ruins themselves came into partial view at the edge below, what I expected to see was a lone skimmer—maybe two—and a small gathering of the most beloved family I had left on Enochia.

What I saw instead, looked like the better part of a full-blown Legion parade.

For a long moment, all I could do was stare as the ship descended to join the veritable landing field of transports and skimmers and dozens upon dozens of waiting figures that populated the once quiet clearing in front of the ruins. A jolt of panic splashed in over the high wall of my shock, spurred in on the sudden fear that this must be some kind of trap—that our communications must have been compromised, and that some vengeful faction of the Legion or the Sanctum or just the good old Enochian people had scraped together the ships and guns to come see to it that I never set foot on their planet or anywhere else ever again.

But then I spotted Elise and Johnny at the head of the reception committee, standing right alongside Freya Glenbark, who was dressed in her finest High General ceremonial garb, and standing at respectful attention.

"What did you do?" I whispered, only vaguely registering that the question was most likely intended for Alton.

The raknoth said nothing, only finished setting the ship down to an easy landing opposite the waiting parade.

For what felt like an eternity, no one moved.

I wanted to. Tried to, even. Most of me wanted nothing more than to run from that damned ship, grab hold of Elise, and never let go again. But the rest of me was frozen, trying to process what was happening, and arriving with growing dread at an unacceptable conclusion.

Finally, I found my voice.

"What have you done?" I hissed, rounding on Alton, feeling my control of the situation slipping away. Scud, it was going up in damned flames.

At the edge of my vision, I noticed the first movement from outside. Elise, I confirmed at a glance, stepping forward from the unwelcome welcoming committee to cross the short space between us and them. I looked back to Alton, anger flaring hotter for reasons I couldn't even begin to process right then.

He just held my glare with even certainty and raised a hand toward the exit corridor. "Go. Speak with your people."

I stood rooted in place, refusing to move at first simply out of principle, and then because I was too busy wondering whether or not it was possible to hurl the treacherous bastard into the sprawling translucent viewing wall hard enough to break through—or at least to break a few bones and give him something to think about.

The sight of Elise steadily approaching outside, though, jarred me back to reality faster than I was ready to be jarred.

I didn't know what to do. By default, I turned for the corridor without a word, deciding that I could test the durability of Alton Parker's cursed raknoth bones later, after I'd dealt with... whatever the scud this was.

Elise was already waiting when I reached the open exit hatch, standing there at the base of the boarding steps with all the calm certainty of a mighty dark boulder patiently weathering the incessant forces of a rushing river. Her staff was strapped across her back, and she had a bulging knapsack thrown over one shoulder. The look on her face was one I'd never seen before.

My eyes settled on that knapsack for a long, breathless moment before I finally found the willpower to meet her eyes. The answer I saw there was unmistakable. The same answer I'd felt in my bones the moment I'd seen our waiting reception, even if I couldn't have said why.

She thought she was coming with me.

I found myself marching down the ship's boarding steps before I'd thought about it, my wriggling insides hardening into something determined, and resolute, and downright ugly.

I couldn't let this happen.

I marched down the steps, preparing to say whatever it was going to take to make this right. Only, when I drew up to Elise at the bottom of the ramp and felt the warmth and unflinching resolve of her presence, I couldn't seem to find any words at all.

"You shaved," she finally said, eyeing my jawline with the faintest hint of a tentative smile.

"You can't do this," I replied, hands curling themselves into fists.

I waited for my words to sink in—for her expression to darken, and for her biting comeback about which one of us had any right to say what she could or couldn't do. But she only gave me a slow, sad nod.

"I understand, Hal."

I shook my head, refusing to be taken aback by whatever she was getting at. "I'm serious, Lise. You can't. This is... This can't happen. This world is..."

I tore my eyes from her and looked toward the waiting assembly, trying to gather my racing thoughts and find the right words. All I found, though, were the watching eyes of Glenbark and Johnny. Of Franco, James, and Phineas. Therese and Barbara. Adam and Enid. Dillard and Edwards and the rest of the Hounds.

Alpha be damned, it seemed like everyone on Enochia I'd fought beside at one point or another was gathered there, watching us. But in that moment, all I could think about was Elise, and the knapsack on her back, and the galaxy's-worth of reasons that I couldn't just let her drop everything and fly away with me.

"They need you, Lise. And you—You deserve..."

I couldn't say it.

Why couldn't I say it?

I hung my head, unable to meet her eyes. But she was already there, her arms encircling me, drawing me closer.

"You deserve better," I whispered. "A real life. Here, on Enochia. You can't do this. I won't let you."

A part of me cringed at the words, both at how domineering they sought to be, and at how miserably flat they sounded leaving my mouth. Another part screamed at me to go further—to tell her that it was over, and that I didn't want her with me. To shove her away, and bolt back into the ship for an emergency takeoff. Anything to keep her from throwing it all away.

But all I could seem to do was stand there, waiting for her to react.

She just squeezed me tighter, stroking my hair almost roughly.

"I feel the same way, my love," she said softly, her gentle tone at odds with the strength of her grip. I tried to draw back—tried to find the strength to tell her to stop this—but she held tighter still, and spoke before I could. "Which is why I'm coming with you."

"No," I said, shaking my head even as I felt some part of my weak inner self perking up in desperation, offering the first tremulous foothold to the fluttering hope that sought to enter. But I couldn't let it. "No, you can't."

"Give me one reason."

"I just did," I said, forcefully drawing back until I had her by the shoulders at arm's length. "This world needs you here."

She held my gaze evenly. "They don't. You do."

"The Children of Enochia—"

"Will be just fine in the hands of their new champions," she said, tilting her head toward our crowd of unwelcome spectators.

I followed her gesture and spotted Garrett and Alexia there with Adam and Enid. The ex-Seekers averted their eyes like they hadn't been staring—as did pretty much everyone else in the uncomfortably large crowd of spectators. Everyone but Garrett, who winked and threw me a sarcastic salute. The bastard.

I turned back to Elise, wishing we could move the conversation into the privacy of the ship, but adamantly refusing to allow even the illusion that this conversation ended anywhere but with her feet firmly on the ground.

"Lise, you can't..."

She showed me a sad smile, and cupped my cheek in her hand. "I think you said that one already, my love."

"Please." I shook my head, tears welling. "Please, don't make me—"

She swept my arms aside and pulled me in with an abruptness that bordered on violence.

"Don't," she practically growled in my ear. "Don't even try it."

"Lise..."

"Where you go, I go," she whispered. "That was the deal. Did you really think a little revolution was going to change that?"

I felt the first hot tears spill over, felt the trembling building at my center. Felt the entire damn thing threatening to come apart completely.

"But... Franco. The others. You can't just..."

Can't just leave them, I tried to say. But the look on her face said everything there was to say about that. And that's when I noticed the knapsack slung over Johnny's shoulder, and the multiple skimmer sleds of metallic packing crates piled up behind James and Phineas.

It's also when I lost my scud completely.

If anyone had come there that day thinking that I was a brave soldier, or some dark demon to be feared—or anything more than a sniveling child with a few tricks up his sleeve, really—I'm pretty sure I set the record straight right then and there.

I wasn't really sure how long it lasted. I only know that what was left of my pathetic walls came crashing down then—crashing down so hard that I couldn't help but wonder if I'd ever even truly intended for them to hold up at all. I didn't know. But Elise held me through every wet tear and shaking sob of it. More of both than I cared to admit. At some point, Johnny joined us in a group hug long enough to deliver some comment about how I needed to get my scud together before I embarrassed him on his big day. I'm pretty sure I only cried harder at that. And again when Franco and James both took a turn at squeezing my shoulder before moving on to help Phineas load the considerable supplies they'd hauled along.

It was all too much. A tiny voice in the back of my mind pointed out that I should probably call a stop to their incessant loading, seeing as I was going to be doing this thing alone. But that voice grew quieter with each second spent in Elise's embrace. Weaker and weaker, until there was no escaping it.

I couldn't let them do this. And I couldn't stop them, either.

I cursed myself for my weakness. I wished I would've had the courage to simply say goodbye over the Lights from a safe distance, and simply have had done with it there. Told myself I should've known all along that they wouldn't be willing to let me fly off on my own, and that I should've known I never could've found the strength to stop them from stopping me.

But I hadn't done any of those things. I'd failed to protect my family. And now they were here to protect me, for better or worse.

And merciful Alpha, was I relieved.

Bitterly, guiltily, utterly self-loathingly relieved.

I felt sick with it. So sick and relieved that I cried some more. I couldn't even bring myself to speak. By the time Elise and I finally parted, I could barely bring myself to turn toward the crowd for the shame of it all. I was sure they'd be pointing and laughing and muttering behind raised hands, or just packing up to leave, disappointed at the sad sight.

The last thing I expected was a crisp parade salute from a few hundred legionnaires, led by the High General herself. But it's what we got.

"She was tempted to say demons to the wind with all of it, and have this send-off right in the heart of Haven," Johnny said quietly beside me. I'd been too stunned to even notice him approaching. "If she hadn't kept this thing quiet, we would've been overflowing out here."

I glanced pointedly toward the veritable parade of saluting soldiers and assembled ships. "You call this quiet?"

They were the first words I'd managed in I don't know how many minutes. They came out with a croak, and they felt horribly inadequate in the moment, but Johnny didn't seem to mind.

"I call this a heroes' sendoff," he said with a smile that looked only a little pained. "Obviously."

He turned at something, and when I tracked the focus of his pained smile, I saw Glenbark approaching, her stride so regal and perfectly disciplined that no legionnaire on her flank would've ever thought to guess that she could be smiling. But smile, she did. More warmly and freely than I was used to seeing from her. It was radiant. So radiant that I'm pretty sure I heard Johnny bubbling down into a warm puddle beside me.

"On behalf of the Enochian Legion, and of the people we have sworn to defend," Glenbark said as she drew up to us, "I hereby thank and commend each and every one of you for your service to the planet."

I followed her scanning eyes over my shoulder and saw that Franco and the others had joined us. I almost could've shed more tears at the sight of our brave little family, fully assembled and ready to fly off into Alpha—or, rather, *Alton Parker*—knew what, but then I noticed Glenbark's gaze had tracked with a slight frown to the ship, and to Alton himself, who'd appeared in the open hatchway, and was frowning right back.

"Reticent as many among us are to say goodbye to such fine servants of Enochia"—she glanced Alton's way again—"not to mention to release a potentially hostile alien ship into the wild, as it were, I for one will be glad to know you are out there, protecting the future of Enochia. I wish you nothing but good fortune." Her brow arched, and in a voice that seemed intended for Alton, she added, "And fortunately, I'm told by our technicians that we already harvested sufficient samples from the ship to get to work on adequate countermeasures anyway, in the event that any such threat were to return to our planet in the future."

"I noticed," Alton grumbled, just loudly enough that we could hear. He disappeared back into the ship, apparently in no mood to be on display.

Glenbark turned back to us, relaxing ever so slightly for the raknoth's absence. "Alien threats aside, I also thought you might be relieved to learn that I recently opened official communications with our new High Cleric, and that, in light of our numerous recent discoveries, he seems much more prepared to keep an open mind than his predecessor was." She focused on me. "Though he did specifically ask if *you* would be continuing to serve at my side." Her lips twitched at the memory. "With notable apprehension, I might add."

"You take down two High Clerics," Johnny muttered, "and suddenly everyone starts getting all superstitious."

I looked over at my friend. He was unusually downcast, eyes to the ground, like he was afraid to even look at Glenbark. It broke my heart all over again, thinking about everything they were all planning to give up here to join me.

I wanted to tell him then that he didn't have to. That he *shouldn't*. But now probably wasn't the time. Not in front of the others like this.

"So what did you say to him?" I asked, turning back to Glenbark.

"I told him that, to the best of my knowledge, you were considering stepping back from your short but bright jaunt into Enochian politics."

"Guess that's one way of putting it," Elise said with a faint grin.

Part of me wanted to smile at that too. The rest was too mired down in the guilt.

"Suffice it to say, I expect news of your departure will be... eagerly received by the White Tower." Glenbark frowned slightly at her own words before adding, "For whatever comfort that thought is worth."

It was something. Not nearly enough to quell the guilt. But something.

"I know I don't have to tell you all to be careful out there," she continued, looking around at our gathered party. "So I won't." She stepped forward and placed a hand each on my shoulder, and on Elise's. "I will only say that I have faith in you. In all of you. Please, take care of one another, and never forget that your home is waiting for you when the time comes." She focused on me. "I won't stop here until that rings true for all of you. I promise you that much."

I let go of Elise's hand to lay my own over Glenbark's. "Thank you, Sir."

"Please..." she said, tilting her head expectantly.

"Thank you, Freya," Elise said.

Glenbark showed her a warm smile, then stepped back from us, composing herself. "You are welcome. Always. And now," she added, with a backward glance at the waiting crowd, "I do believe I had better stop keeping you all to myself."

THE NEXT HOUR was a whirlwind of friendly faces, shaken hands, and heartily patted backs—or in the case of Edwards, *painfully* patted ones. More than that, it was an endless string of goodbyes that I had to admit I'd been utterly unprepared to make, no matter what I'd told myself from the safe distance of orbit. Difficult as it was, though, realizing just a little bit more with each hug and handshake everything that we would be leaving behind, I was glad for the opportunity.

Somewhere between promising my most helpful medic, Melanie Mills, that I'd do my best to keep myself in one piece, and between sharing a good laugh—and several apologies—with Ordo Dillard and the 51st Hounds about what an unholy pain in the ass I'd been for them on more occasions than we could all easily count, I had to admit something else.

I'd been wrong to think that Johnny and Elise were all I had left on Enochia.

I had Melanie and Dillard. I had Edwards, and Therese, and Barbara Sanders, who I realized with a jolt of unease was there with her camera crew, quietly documenting the entire procession. She gave me a warm hug, and told me that she was going to show Enochia the man I truly was, even if it took the rest of her life.

I had Annabelle and the Wingards, who pulled me into a hug beside Johnny and told us to take care of each other so vehemently that I almost lost control all over again.

Scud, I even had Docere Mathis.

"Silver Spoon," he said, in that perpetually disgusted tone of his, "I just want you to know, you have to be the most stubborn, steel-headed, sad excuse for a legionnaire I've ever had the displeasure of instructing." He grinned then—something I'm positive I'd never had the uncomfortable pleasure of witnessing. It looked more like the man had accidentally swallowed a bag of hardsteel bolts than an expression of joy, but that hardly mattered when he took my hand and spoke his next words. "Just like your father."

Coming from Mathis, I think it was the highest compliment I ever could've received.

The feeling culminated when Edwards pushed his hulking way through the crowd to come see us again, this time escorting a lean, limping soldier with eyes like hardsteel.

Mara.

I felt a pang of guilt at the sight of the injured specter sniper, and it only deepened when I took in the sight of the prosthetic leg she was obviously still acclimating to—the one she'd been forced to swap for the real thing after she'd gone at Frosty with a knife to keep the reeker away from Glenbark. The one I'd failed to save, after having dragged her and the Hounds into that canyon ambush to start with.

But Evangeline Mara didn't look like she blamed me.

On the contrary, she gave me the closest thing to a friendly smile I'd ever seen from her.

"I was wrong about you, Raish," she said, to which Edwards immediately cleared his throat and stooped down to show her an over-dramatized expression of wide-eyed shock.

Mara rolled her eyes, and gave him a rather firm elbow to the gut. "Maybe I'm kinda glad this big idiot has a soft spot for hopeless cases and broken things with sharp edges," she admitted.

I couldn't help but smile at that as she followed her elbow strike up with a tender hand to Edwards' cheek, in keeping with their oddly physical—and sometimes borderline frightening—relationship. I was pretty certain I wasn't the only broken thing to which she was referring. "I'll take that as a compliment, I guess."

She shrugged, matching my grin. "Whatever you gotta do, Raish. All I'm saying is, maybe once I've gotten the hang of this damn thing"—she patted her prosthetic leg—"someone'll see fit to build a nice shiny spaceship and let us Hounds come cover your ass out there. Alpha knows you could use it."

I looked from her to Edwards, not really disagreeing with the sentiment, even if I was skeptical about the timeliness of its execution. I smiled as best I could, reassuring myself with the not-so-comforting thought that, if we did find ourselves in need of that much backup out there, it would probably mean we were already gropped anyway.

"I'll try to keep out of trouble until you get there," I promised.

For some reason, they both laughed at that.

As the goodbyes waned and the time drew inexorably near, I looked around for Johnny, thinking to try one last time to dissuade him from all of this, or at least to offer him a genuine out. After a minute of looking, I spotted him behind one of the transports, lunging in to catch a rather startled Glenbark in an abrupt and slightly awkward hug. And maybe it was the bad angle or just my imagination, but after recovering from her moment of wide-eyed surprise, I could've sworn she repaid him with a regal kiss on the cheek.

Judging by the way he floated back over to us afterward, flushed cheeks out-burning his flaming red hair, I might not even have imagined it.

"What did she tell you?" Elise asked him.

He looked at us dazedly, touching at the cheek in question. "That I'll never love like that again."

Elise and I traded a look.

"She said that?" I asked.

"Well... I mean, I guess her words were actually more like, 'You were a better servitor than I ever would have thought to ask for,' but..." He shook his head and blinked at us. "Sorry, what was the question?"

Elise gave him a hug. "It's all gonna be okay, you know?"

"Yeah..." Johnny bobbed his head numbly, still too frazzled to return Elise's hug. "Yeah, you're probably right."

"Johnny..." I started, sure that this was the time, but unsure what exactly to say.

He jabbed a finger in my face before I could say more anyway, then swept it over into Elise's personal space preemptively when she pulled back from their hug. Back and forth, the finger went, daring either of us to say a thing, until Elise raised her hands in surrender. Satisfied, Johnny nodded to himself and stalked off, mumbling something about *a hero's sendoff, Alpha-dammit.*

I could only watch, silently marveling at my friend's strength, suddenly certain that it wasn't my place to stop Johnny or Elise or anyone else from choosing to join this expedition of ours, and that it never had been.

I glanced at the ship, wondering whether any of us really had any appreciable idea of what we were getting ourselves into, and realized that Alton had reappeared in the open hatchway, watching the procession below with an inscrutable expression. His eyes turned to meet mine as soon as I spotted him.

"This was all your doing," I sent, not really sure whether I meant the words as thanks, or as an accusation. Probably a bit of both.

"Speaking from a point of pure self-interest," he sent back evenly, *"I need you at your best for what lies ahead. And they are your best,"* he added, nodding down to where Elise was checking in with the others. *"Your true clan, as it were."*

I looked back up at the raknoth, too many conflicting emotions running through me to even begin to narrow down the predominant consensus. *"I don't know whether to thank you for this, or to burn your eyes out."*

Alton grinned, and turned to stride back into the quiet of the ship. *"Fortunately,"* his voice came in my mind, *"you'll have plenty of time to decide that on the way. Provided we ever actually manage to depart, that is."*

If I hadn't known any better, I might've thought he actually sounded a bit bitter about our farewell parade.

I pushed the thought aside and looked around at the crowd, wondering who I'd missed even as I realized there was no number of goodbyes I could say that would actually leave me feeling like it was time. I was thinking maybe I should just find Glenbark and the others and get on with the inevitable when I noticed Garrett and Alexia watching me from over in the ruins, decidedly separate from the crowd. Adam and Enid lurked behind them, looking even less excited about the prospect of mingling with anyone.

They watched me approach, looking like they weren't quite sure whether to smile and wave, or to brace themselves for tense final words. I wasn't really sure myself. All I knew was that the four of them were probably some of the strongest Shapers left on Enochia, and that, judging by the intricate silver sigils they all wore over their left breasts—identical to the one I'd noticed Elise wearing—they'd all apparently decided to pick up the fight in a way I no longer could.

"I take it I'm looking at four Children of Enochia?" I asked when I reached them.

"Afraid so," Alexia said.

"Out of one cult..." Garrett added.

"And into a revolution," Adam finished, looking only slightly less dubious than Garrett about his own words.

"Praise Valen," Alexia added, patting at her shiny little sigil, and drawing a disapproving frown from Enid.

It would've been hard to pretend like Enochia couldn't have asked for more qualified champions to fight for the freedom of Shaper kind. But I suppose we could've done worse, too.

"So you all passed the test, then?" I asked before I could stop myself, looking around the group.

It was a little eerie, how quickly they all went from friendly-ish smiles to avoiding my gaze completely. Like someone had put the fear of Alpha into them. Or the fear of Elise, I realized, when I turned to find her approaching, and staring them all down.

"Ah, who's counting?" Alexia asked.

"Bullscud test, anyway," Garrett agreed.

Adam nodded his absent-minded agreement, seemingly lost in thought behind his dark frown.

"That's what I've been trying to tell him all this time," Elise said, with a pointed look at me. "For all we know, that thing could've miscalculated for any number of reasons. And it doesn't matter anyway, because no one actually has a good explanation for what that red dot even means."

"Thing was probably just confused by how freakishly strong you are," Alexia said.

I frowned, positive she was only stroking my ego. At least until Garrett turned his own indignant frown on her, and she shrugged and added, "What? You try melding with him in battle and see how you like it."

Garrett looked back and forth between us multiple times, brow deeply furrowed, until he finally shrugged it off and muttered, "Yeah, well I killed two of those things with my bare hands."

"Yes, you did, my big, strong man," Alexia crooned, running her hands up Garrett's chest. I might've thought she was only teasing him if I hadn't already been intimately acquainted with the preternatural boldness and frequency of their swiving habits. As it was, I wouldn't have been all that surprised if they just went for it then and there.

"I'm not really sure I see how a dagger counts as your bare hands," Adam chimed in. But Garrett was obviously too distracted at that point thinking about all the other things he'd like to do with those hands of his.

I think we're all ready, came Elise's voice in my mind, to the overture of Alexia's lascivious giggling. It was an odd contrast, and the growing unease in my gut only doubled when I looked over to Elise and saw my apprehension reflected on her face. I nodded, and took her hand, trying to push the lingering doubts and questions out of my mind.

It wasn't like it would really matter out there in the depths of space, what some magic helmet thought about my validity to be a representative of the Emmútari legacy. Out there, we had our own job to do.

It was enough. More than enough, after everything I'd seen of the rakul.

We said our goodbyes to the ex-Seekers, exchanging a few handshakes and awkward half-hugs, with wishes of safety and good luck. Only Alexia seemed fully at ease with the situation. It was almost like she'd never tried to kill me at all, as she took Elise and I both in a warm, sensuous group hug, and told us to be careful out there, and not to have too much fun without her. I might have blushed when her hand traced down to my backside for one last firm squeeze, but when I felt Elise stiffen beside me as if she'd had her own surprise, and saw Alexia's beaming smile for both of us, it was all I could do not to simply laugh at the woman's utter lack of personal boundaries.

At least it gave the two of us a fleeting iota of distraction as we turned and started back for the ship, silently clutching hands as tightly as if we didn't know what else to do. Because we didn't.

The first tendrils of fear crept through my insides, more potent and visceral than the edgy nerves I'd been sporting all day long. Fear at the great unknown we were about to fly off into. Fear that I'd somehow read it all wrong, and that now I was leading the people I loved most into fates only knew what manner of trap. Fear at too many things to count.

A voice in my mind interrupted me from trying.

"It's some kind of danger rating." After a confused second, I recognized the voice as Garrett's. *"The last color, I mean. Your red. Magic helmet speak for 'walking time bomb,' apparently."*

I stopped at the base of the steps, waited as Elise parted to go check on the others, then turned and stared back at Garrett, trying to process what he was saying, and why he was even telling me this at all.

"I don't want that scud festering in your head out there," he explained, apparently picking up on my confusion. *"Just move on, kid. It's a bullscud test. It has to be, if us cutthroats all skirted by in the yellow. We both know you're too much of a scud-nosed boot shiner to ever break bad anyway, so just gropping forget it, you hear me? Move on, and go see to it we don't end up with any more aliens raining down on our heads before we're ready, yeah?"*

Across the way, in the ruins, Alexia was frowning up at Garrett from her place on his chest, clearly sensing that something was amiss. She looked over at me, then back to him. My head was too busy spinning with implications to care all that much who else might notice.

Move on. Move on from the fact that an Emmútari relic thought I was more of a walking time bomb than a bunch of professional murderers? Because that was the more reasonable explanation, wasn't it? The one no one seemed to want to point out.

Either the test *was* flawed, enough so to let a bunch of Shaper-killing cutthroats skirt by when I'd failed... or it *wasn't*, and that arcane brain scanner had seen something in my mind that was even more troubling than a cutthroat's capacity to kill innocents in order to survive.

And that thought, right there, was probably exactly why no one wanted me stewing over this.

An impact on my shoulder jolted me nearly into the atmosphere, then back down to heart-thundering reality, where Johnny had just clapped a hand on me.

"You okay, broto?" he asked.

"Fine," I said, too quickly.

I looked back to Garrett, who gave me a grave nod. I returned it. Beside him, Alexia waved goodbye, actually looking concerned about me.

Demons to the wind, if I stayed here any longer I was going to start thinking even they were my friends.

"What's that about?" Johnny asked, giving a half-hearted wave to the new Children of Enochia.

"Just keeping good relations with the cutthroats," I said. "You know how it goes."

"Very wise," Johnny said, nodding sagely. He turned to me. "You ready to go kill a space dragon, broto?"

I frowned at him, burying my dark thoughts for later. "That's not really the intended goal of this mission. You do realize that, right?"

Johnny just shrugged. "Not the intended goal of *your* mission, maybe. I need me a worthwhile mantle to haul back here when we're all done saving the universe."

It made me smile, how confident he sounded that we *would* be returning at all. I hoped to Alpha—and to any other deity, real or fabricated—that he was right. Especially when I noticed Franco and Phineas sharing their last quiet moments with Barbara Sanders and Therese Brown beside the ship.

For the thousandth time, I felt a wave of nauseating guilt that any of them should leave their lives behind like this, even if it was for something we all believed in. It just didn't seem right. But I guess not much did when you went around wishing that life could be fair.

"I think it's time," Elise said softly behind us.

I traded a look with Johnny.

"For ours is not to ask..." he said softly.

I opened my mouth to finish the mantra, then thought better of it and, on a whim, called a small stone from the ground to the palm of my hand with telekinesis instead.

"Souvenir," I explained weakly, thinking back to the days I'd spent with Carlisle, straining hard enough to risk a brain bleed just to budge a little pebble.

We all turned to the ship with an unspoken agreement that it was for real this time. Franco, James, and Phineas mounted the steps ahead of us, seeming to feel the same. Elise fell in behind them, Johnny behind her. I was halfway up the steps, fighting the urge to take a last look back, when Barbara Sanders' voice called out from behind.

"Is there anything you'd like to say to Enochia before you go, Haldin?"

I stopped and turned, mind racing for the magical combination of words that might somehow make a difference for the world we were leaving behind.

I didn't find it. Mostly, I just stared dumbly at the camera instead.

"Be good to each other," I finally said.

I started to think about saying more—about telling the world what we were off to do, and about the safety and prosperity I wished for them here, even after everything. There was a lot to be said, after all. Volumes and volumes. But when I glanced back to meet Elise's gaze, seeking her guidance, and saw her soft, loving smile, that's when I knew. That was enough.

So I turned and walked into the ship, leaving Enochia with those five words. And I didn't look back.

"You're sure about this?" I asked the others, once the hatch was sealed behind us, and we were all alone in the cold, alien walls of the ship corridor. "You're all sure?"

I looked to Johnny, expecting a witty remark, but he had nothing. Nor did the others. Nothing but heavy silence until, almost as one, we all started to nod.

"Right. Let's strap in, then."

Fifteen minutes and a few sickly pale faces later, we were back in space, outside of orbit this time, the gentle grey-blue sphere of Enochia receding behind us on the viewing wall, swallowed by the darkness of space on all sides at an alarming rate.

"Are we all ready for the first jump, then?"

Alton looked slightly irritated to even be asking the question.

"Scud nuggets," Johnny murmured from the other side of Elise, two seats down. "We're really doing this, aren't we?"

I didn't know what to say. I wanted to tell him that there was still time, that we could go back. That he didn't have to sign away what might well be the rest of his life just to prove that he was a brave soldier and a loyal friend. But then Elise found my hand and squeezed, and when I looked over, I saw she had Johnny's hand too. Across from us, Franco and James were similarly braced.

Even Phineas begrudgingly allowed James to lay a hand on his shoulder.

"We're really doing this," Elise confirmed. Then, cracking the hint of a sly grin, she added, "Just think how impressed Freya's gonna be when you get back."

Johnny blew out a ragged laugh. "Hey, what the scud else do you think I'm doing up here with you people?"

We all shared a shaky smile, holding hands there at the edge of the infinite unknown, and taking silent solace in the fact that, whatever awaited us out there, we would face it together. It was a profoundly touching moment, right up until Alton Parker pointedly cleared his throat.

"I'll take that for a yes, then," the raknoth said flatly. "And you don't need to be strapped in for this part, by the way," he added, looking around at us like we were all being a little bit ridiculous. "The jump is perfectly safe."

For some odd reason, none of us seemed to be in any hurry to go unbuckling our restraints and testing that claim.

Alton shrugged, and looked to me as if for final confirmation. I gripped Elise's hand tighter, thanking all the fates above and below that she and the others were here with me. Then I nodded. "Let's go."

"Very well," Alton said, closing his eyes in concentration. The ship began to thrum. "First jump commencing."

"Next stop, Earth?" Johnny asked.

Alton cracked open one eye. "Were you not paying attention when I explained that the journey would be—"

"On the order of several hundred jumps, at the very least," Johnny interjected, in a passable imitation of Alton's voice. "Yeah, I remember, Captain Downerpants. Now can we please just say 'next stop, Earth,' for the love of wrinklies, before I scud this nice fancy flight seat of yours?"

Alton arched one strong, dark eyebrow at him.

I just smiled. "Next stop, Earth?"

"Next stop, Earth," Elise agreed.

James took up the mantra, followed by Franco. Alton turned to Phineas, looking, more than anything, curious as to whether the decidedly human display would conclude with or fall short of the quiet, pragmatic bear of a man.

"Next stop, Earth," Phineas grumbled with a shrug.

Alton let out a soft sigh, shaking his head. "Very well, then."

The thrumming built throughout the ship, until I could feel the vibrations in my teeth. I clutched Elise's hand tighter—painfully tight—and felt her clutching right back, both of us transfixed on the all-consuming void of dark space around us, the thrumming building stronger and stronger by the moment.

"Next stop, Earth," Alton said.

And then we jumped.

THE END

A LETTER FROM THE AUTHOR

Sweet Alpha, we did it.

And so ends the Enochian War trilogy—the second series I've ever published. (*Though, funnily enough, the FIRST series I ever started writing.*)

I sure hope you've enjoyed it, Dear Reader.

As I'm finding out (with my oh-so-impressive sample size of *two*), it's not the easiest thing in the world, drawing a beloved series to a satisfying end.

For one thing, if I've done my job right, by this point in the stage, I love my characters every bit as much as the next Book Fan. (And who wants to say goodbye to the people they love—fictional or otherwise?)

For another, it's a fair bit of pressure, trying to flush out that tenuous path where all the major story decisions feel "right," and all of the heart-strings properly caressed, just so.

I won't lie. When I first attempted to finish this book, I was worried I'd missed the mark. So worried that I stepped back and went to write another entire book before coming back to try to get this thing right. And I THINK I'm even pretty happy with how it turned out.

But this isn't really about me. I've had my time with the story.

It belongs to you now.

(*You know, in like a TOTALLY more heartfelt way than for the simple fact that it is currently in your hands.*)

ahem

Point is, I just wanna take a moment to say *thank you*.

Thank you, Dear Reader, for coming on this adventure with me. I truly do appreciate it. So much so that I'd love to give you a free book and keep you around for more. (*And that's not even the GOOD news!*)

The good news, my friend, is that, if you're still licking your lips for more Enochian adventures, the story isn't actually over yet.

Which brings us right back to that FIRST series I ever published...

Wanna know what happens when Hal and crew reach Earth? Well damn skippy, do I have a rip-roaring answer for you. It's called the Harvesters Series. And more importantly, you can grab the first book, *Red Gambit*, for free!

Just go to *lukermitchell.com/children-of-enochia-signup*

There, you'll be able to join my mailing list, where, in addition to your first foray into the Harvesters Series, you'll also receive free copies of the bonus Enochian War stories, *Fallen* and *Eye of the Storm*, as well as behind-the-scenes updates, additional free books from the rest of my fictional worlds, and some sweet discounts and short stories you won't find anywhere else. (Carlisle's *Eye of the Storm* story, for instance, is only available in the Enochian box set or to my mailing list readers.)

All you have to do is visit the link above to join the party and grab your free books today!

And if newsletters and email shenanigans aren't your bag, no worries. You can always visit *lukermitchell.com/books* to check out my published works and grab *Red Gambit* the old-fashioned way! If you're fully on board and would like to save some money, I recommend you grab the Complete 8-story Harvesters Collection, which delivers the entire saga in one neat eBook package, complete with a handy reading roadmap.

Whichever way you go, I sure do hope you enjoy your next adventure!

Thanks so much for reading.

We'll see you on the other side.

Cheers,
Luke Mitchell

ABOUT THE AUTHOR

Not a llama. Mostly human.

Luke is a storyteller whose dreams include learning the ways of the Force, becoming a sentient robot, and maybe even one day growing up. Also, lots of zombies… Don't ask.

Oh, and that "growing up" bit? That was a lie.

After studying engineering science at Penn State and neuroengineering at Drexel, Luke finally decided to throw in the towel on building a working Iron Man suit and opted instead to simply make things up and write them down. Boy, is he having more fun now.

When he's not holed up in his writing cave trying to string words together, he can often be found powerlifting, video-gaming, reading, and/or drinking the darkest, most roasty beers he can get his mitts on. Sometimes all at once.

But you know what? That's enough about Luke. He's really not that interesting. Still, if you'd like to say hi to him for whatever reason, he'd probably be glad to hear from you!

Go to **lukermitchell.com/children-of-enochia-signup** to join the mailing list and grab your free copies of *Fallen* and the list-exclusive, *Eye of the Storm*, today!

Additionally (as you wish)…

Follow me on BookBub for new release alerts
bookbub.com/authors/luke-r-mitchell

Browse the rest of my published titles
lukermitchell.com/books

Join the Patreon team for digital copies of ALL of my work (past, present, and future) — and much more!
patreon.com/lukermitchell

Thank you for reading!